The Reckoning

S. L. SCOTT

The Reckoning
First Edition

Copyright © S. L. Scott 2015

The right of S.L. Scott to be identified as the author of this work has been asserted by her under the *Copyright Amendment (Moral Rights) Act 2000*

This work is copyright. Apart from any use as permitted under the Copyright Act 1968, no part may be reproduced, copied, scanned, stored in a retrieval system, recorded or transmitted, in any form or by any means, without the prior written permission of the publisher.

This book is a work of fiction. Names, characters, places and incidents are either a product of the author's imagination or are used fictitiously. Any resemblance to actual people living or dead, events or locales is entirely coincidental.

paperback: 978-1-940071-30-5

Cover design: Sarah Hansen of Okay Creations
http://www.okaycreations.com/

Interior Design: Angela McLaurin, Fictional Formats
https://www.facebook.com/FictionalFormats

Photo credit: Yuri Arcurs

All My Love to My Husband and Kids

A Personal Note

There's something magical about you finding 'your people', those you connect with on a different, deeper level. Whether it by happenstance, kismet, or destiny, people are brought into your life for a reason. The true blessings I have the honor of calling friends—Amy, Cara, Danielle, Flavia, Heather, Irene, Kandace, Kellie, Kerri, Lisa, Lynsey, Marla, Mary, Ruth—deserve a HUGE Thank You for all of their kindness, hard work, support, encouragement, fun times, and big smiles. You make the journey that much more exciting.

My family is everything. Truly the best. Thank you for not only putting up with the crazy hours, but also for the endless support you give me. I love you.

I wanted to say Thank You to Sarah of Okay Creations for the magnificent covers you've made me over the years. And to Angela for the beautiful formatting of my books. You both make things pretty pretty and make me proud to show them off. To Melissa, Thank You for the wonderful, artful teasers. They are always a huge hit.

To the Readers, you are Gold in my eyes. I adore your support, your enthusiasm, and your sweet messages. I am grateful to have found it onto your bookshelves—virtual and real shelves.

Now, *rubs hands together* are we ready?

Prologue

The paper falls from my hands. I stand there in the middle of the street staring at it as it lands at my feet. A small ache that started days earlier has become a pulsing pain, tearing my heart apart.

This isn't how things were supposed to go. This isn't how *we* were supposed to end. This isn't how our melody goes. This isn't how we were supposed to play out.

I want my life back.

I want my wife back.

"Hey buddy, you gotta pay for that."

I look at the guy from the newsstand and pull out my wallet. I give him a ten and walk away, hoping to walk back into the life I'll recognize because this one doesn't feel like mine at all. But the weather sucks and it's cold out. The rain has picked up and that pain inside me is getting worse.

The pedestrian crossing beeps while I remain standing there still in shock. I never saw this coming. People bump me on both sides as they hurry past, but I've become numb to everything that's not Holliday... and that fucking pain.

Despite the crushing pain, I'm not giving her up—not easily.
Not to him.
Not ever.

1

Holliday Hughes

"Loneliness is the other side of Love. You can't feel one without having experienced the other." ~ Johnny Outlaw

The color of Dalton's eyes are electric, a color I've become familiar with. It's the color that sets in before each show, part of the transformation into Johnny Outlaw.

Backstage, in the largest dressing room, I watch my husband strum on his acoustic guitar while lounging on the burgundy leather sofa that has seen more than its fair share of musical legends. He's another one to add to the list. Propped up against the makeup mirror, I bring my knees to my chest. I'm usually quiet before a show, not wanting to disturb the band's preshow mental prep, but since it's just the two of us, I ask, "Do you want to go out after or back to the hotel?"

Dalton glances up at me before returning his gaze down to the guitar in his lap. "I want to go to the hotel. Just the two of us."

I smile. "Do you need anything?"

"I need some caffeine and a bottle of water."

I slip off the counter and get a bottle of water from the tray of requested tour rider items. Holding it out for him, his hand wraps around mine. He looks up again and smiles. "I'm glad you're here."

Leaning down, I kiss him on the top of the head. "Me too."

The door opens and the band's manager, Tommy, walks in with Dex, the drummer. Tommy's face is contorted, irritated by analyzing the lines running across his forehead. "Where the fuck are Kaz and Derrick? They were supposed to be here by now."

Dex grabs a bottle of water and plops down in a reclining chair just as I sit down next to Dalton. He says, "Traffic sucked getting here. We should have made them ride with us."

Tommy leans against the wall near the door. "You fuckers are gonna put me in an early grave." He seems to catch himself right after the words leave his mouth. I jump as he swings so fast the air gushes past me, followed by a loud thump when he hits the wall with his fist. "Fuck!"

Dalton sits up and I worry the subject will disturb his calm. It does. A bitterness seeps in when he says, "We all miss Cory, man. You can still be frustrated and shit. It's not going to change the outcome."

I gulp heavily, my heart hurting from the topic. I didn't know Cory Dean as well as the band, but I miss him. I'm reminded of his crash every time I get on a plane or look at his kids. I know Dalton does too. He's talked to me about it, but he's still trying to work through life without his best friend, and the other guitarist of The Resistance. It's been a struggle for the band to move forward. Dex and Tommy have had their own ghosts to deal with regarding the loss. Kaz and Derrick will probably always feel they're playing in Cory's shadow considering they only have their guitar gig with the band because of his death. There's so much to work through emotionally for everyone and they will each try to come to terms in their own way. But my heart hurts the most for Rochelle, the woman he left behind, who's become one of my closest friends. I reach for Dalton's hand. Our fingers entwine as my thoughts go back to Rochelle and her two young boys who will never really know their father.

Dex drops his head into his hands, and groans, "Can we talk about something else?"

The room is silent for at least a minute, before we're startled. The door slams open. "What's up?" Derrick says coming inside the dressing room. He stops when he sees everyone's expressions. The vibe of the room clueing him in, his voice drops and he sounds solemn this time when he asks, "What's wrong?"

Tommy flicks him on the head. "Nothing, Fucker! You're late."

Melodramatic, he grabs his head. "Ow! Fuck you, dude."

Kaz comes in after him, ducking out of Tommy's reach before he gets flicked. Tommy announces, "Ten minutes until show time. Piss or..." He looks at us. "Fuck or do whatever you're gonna do, but be ready in ten minutes." He turns and disappears out the door, closing it behind him.

Rolling my eyes, I ask, "Does he have to be so offensive?"

"Yes, that's why we pay him the big bucks. He makes sure things go off without a hitch. But he should know that there's no ten minute fucks when it comes to us."

I laugh. "He shouldn't know that actually, but I know you guys talk sometimes, so I'll let that comment slide."

Dalton chuckles. "Yeah, probably best."

A few minutes later, Dalton finishes his water and asks, "Can you get me a soda or Red Bull? I need to tell Rochelle to add it to our rider so we have them at the next show."

I start for the door. "I think I saw a machine down the hall. I'll go check."

"Thanks, Baby."

I leave the room and close the door. It's best that they have a few minutes to themselves while I search for that caffeine. A table with snacks and cans of sodas is near the stairs to the stage. I grab a Coke and head back. I slowly open the door, but stop when I overhear them talking. I don't want to eavesdrop, but Dex's voice is not low, wanting to be heard by everyone. "I'm not the same person. You're not. These two punks are still learning the songs. But this is it, Johnny. This is the band. You're either with us or you're not."

I have no idea what spurred Dex to say that, but it worries me. Cory's death destroyed Dalton and almost destroyed us in the process. It was a black abyss that left him lost for a long time. But together we found the light and I intend to keep us there. "I found one," I say loud enough for that conversation to end just in case they didn't want me to hear.

When Dalton sees me, he puts on a smile that I can tell is only for show. My stomach tenses, concerned about what's going on with him. I don't dare ask before a performance though. He gets up, sets his guitar down, and takes the can, popping the top. "Thanks."

"You're welcome." Pointing over my shoulder, I say, "I'm going out to find my spot." I give him a quick kiss, and add, "Break a leg."

Dalton nods and returns to the couch as I make my way out again. As I walk out from backstage, I find an usher to help me figure out where my seat is. My breath momentarily catches in my throat as I look out over almost twenty-thousand people all screaming for The Resistance. More than half seem to be women screaming for Johnny Outlaw alone. I'm reminded of the life the lead singer of a band lives.

I push down the anxious thoughts that these women all want what I have, and find my seat.

TR

Magnetic.

Johnny Outlaw is magnetic. Captivating is an understatement. Like every other woman in this arena and most of the men, I haven't been able to take my eyes off of him since he walked out on stage. I'm drawn to him as he sings, his words arouse like thrusts to my heart.

In the beginning of us, nothing seemed to matter beyond the deep attraction I had for that man. Standing here today in the VIP section and watching him, I realize I also get the glory—the romantic side of this complicated man. The dark strides alongside as well, but every dark day is worth the hundred light ones he gives in return. Jack Dalton was born to be a star, and as I watch his legacy play out before me, I'm pushed hard from behind, my hands slamming against the railing. "What the hell?" I move quickly to get to safety. But my quick is not fast enough as some woman claws at me from over the shoulder of the guy between us. Standing on a chair, she catches my hair just as I try to duck. She still manages to swipe a little of it, causing me to scream. I try to escape my spot, but get trapped by the audience closing in around me.

The crowd starts to ebb and flow like a large lung needing air. The crazy woman pushes forward with the audience as The Resistance plays one of their most popular hits. I brace myself against the barricade and look for a way out. I'm yanked back by my shirt, which rips, sinewy fingers and fake red nails gripping tightly. I scream for her to let me go and the guy between us finally blocks her. She's yelling how Johnny is hers forever and belongs to only her. "I wish you would die," she yells.

Struck with fear gripping me, my heart is pounding, my head telling me to flee, but I can't find a way out. The guy hits her arm until she releases me. Pushing away from her, I'm smashed against the barricade. About to jump on it, I step up and come face-to-face with Dalton. He grabs me and lifts me to safety on the other side of the barrier. As I slide down the front of his body, he asks, "You okay, Angel?"

Security is flanking him, two guys suddenly behind me, protecting us from the groping crowd. The band continues playing on stage, but the rest seems to disappear, leaving us in our own world. I rub where I had my hair pulled. "I'm okay."

He looks at me, cups my face, and kisses me. My eyes close and I'm transported, the universe once again revolving around us. When our lips separate, it's not hurried, but slow as if we have all the time in the world. His hands slide from my face down over my shoulders and arms until he's holding my hands. "Come with me," he mouths as we come crashing back into reality.

I follow him. Like an agile cat, he hops back up on stage easily. Leaning down, he offers me a hand. One of the roadies lifts me up and I take Dalton's hand so he can bring me into his arms again. Together, we walk to the microphone. I don't want to look out, hating attention on me, but I can't resist this opportunity, this once in a lifetime chance.

Dex does a drum roll as Dalton talks to the crowd, "Hello San Diegoooo!" He holds the mic out to the audience, listening for their response. They do not disappointment. The arena is loud and excited, hellos and whistles heard in return. Dalton suddenly looks a bit bashful, nothing like the Johnny Outlaw from minutes before. He sends a sideways glance to me before turning forward and smiling. "I'm not always lucky enough to have this beautiful woman at my shows, but tonight is different and I wanted to introduce you to my wife, Holliday."

My face turns red while I laugh from the exhilaration. "I can't believe you did that," I say, hitting him playfully on the chest. He grabs me as my name is chanted throughout the arena. The name Holliday is quickly replaced by the request for us to kiss.

He grabs me and does a slight dip. With the smile that could get me to do anything, he says, "We don't want to disappoint the fans, Love."

"No, we wouldn't want to do th—" The lips I adore take ownership of mine right there in the middle of the stage during a live concert in San Diego.

And I savor every second.

We're both laughing too hard, having too much fun, to keep it going. He hugs me and swings me around. "Love you. Now get back to your concert," I say.

When he sets me down, he winks at me. I blow him a kiss and run off stage. I hear him through the speakers ask, "How about some more music?" The audience reacts loudly and the band starts playing again.

My smile is huge, my heart racing fast from the excitement. That's the first time we ever made a public statement about our relationship and we did it in front of that many people... Wow. I can't seem to wrap my head around it. I'm just giddy and so happy.

"You're a lucky woman." Standing nearby with a clipboard, a woman I don't recognize eyes me. She has her dark hair woven into an intricate braid that hangs over one shoulder. Her glasses conceal her eyes a bit, but not enough to hide her beauty. She's thin and wears a fitted Resistance T-shirt that fits over her large breasts rather snuggly.

I take notice because there was no true friendliness in her comment, reminding me that millions of women are infatuated with my husband no matter what kind of public displays of dedication we put on. "Thanks," I reply, looking at her before walking away.

Tommy comes to me and says, "Well that just made the crowd go crazy."

"Yeah, unexpected. Sorry for throwing the show off."

"No, no," he says, "I think it was great. I know it wasn't a stunt but I think it was great to help with rumors and…" He holds his phone up. "The video is already online."

"No way."

"Yep." My face must show my anxiety because he puts his arm around me and laughs. "Don't stress. It's great. It's great for the band. It's great for the tabloids. They eat this shit up."

Rolling my eyes, I give my best fake excited, not amused at all look. "Yay!"

"I know how much you love the press," he says sarcastically. "Can I buy you a drink to ease the pain?"

"I think I need one."

"If it makes a difference, look at Johnny out there." He leads me to a spot where I can see Dalton on stage. "A year ago I didn't think I'd ever see him perform this song again, but look at him."

We stand there and listen while watching him bleed his heart out through lyrics and riffs he used to play alongside his best friend. I say, "He's where he was always meant to be."

Tommy adds, "He sounds better than ever. That's because of you. You gave him what he needed to heal."

"I don't know if he's healed, but he's in a better place." The woman with the clipboard catches my attention again. She's still waiting at the bottom stairs. Her glasses are tucked into her shirt now. "Hey Tommy, who's that?"

"Ashley? She's new on this tour."

I watch as she speaks into a walkie-talkie before clipping it back onto her belt again. "What does she do?"

"She's part of the crew that changes out the mics and instruments."

The Reckoning

"Like when Dalton changes to his acoustic guitar?"

"Yeah, and Dex goes through three sets of drumsticks on average per show. She makes sure the guys get what they need when they need it."

"That's a new position?"

"Other bands have Equipment Managers for it, we never needed it before. We have a great stage crew, but we agreed to try it out on this tour. She's working out well. She's the daughter of a roadie who worked for Metallica for years, so she knows her way around a backstage."

"Interesting." I eye her, but I feel a heat starting to burn me on the inside.

"How about that drink now?"

"Sounds good."

The bourbon and cola touches my lips just as I see the band coming toward us. Dalton is leading, Dex next, Kaz and Derrick after. I think this is Dalton and Dex's version of hazing the new kids. Or Kaz and Derrick just know to give them the respect they deserve. Either way, it's amusing to watch.

When Dalton passes me, he grits his teeth and says, "You're getting security."

I'm left standing there with my drink to my lips as the guys pass by one-by-one and follow him inside the dressing room. To avoid a heated discussion, I'm thinking I might stay out here, maybe find the women's restroom and touch up my lipstick when Dalton comes out and commands, "Come in here."

Releasing a hard breath, I turn and walk inside. The door is shut behind me, making me feel like I'm walking into the principal's office. I stand near the door and take a long gulp from my glass. Dalton watches me, seemingly fascinated by my every move. He cocks an eyebrow up and asks, "What happened down there?"

Shrugging, I reply, "I'm not sure. Just some crazy woman."

Everybody's watching me as if I'm supposed to be doing something other than what I'm doing. I shift uncomfortably. Dalton sits down on the recliner and says, "I know you like your freedom, but this life comes with a price." The guys lose interest and scatter around the room with their phones in hand as Dalton continues, "I can't risk your safety. So you can watch the show from backstage or take two guards with you back to the floor."

"Maybe the insane lady who says that you're hers forever should be escorted out. I'm not worried about me—"

"I am!" The leather takes a pounding from his fist. "Some people take their obsessions too far. I'm not willing to take the chance."

His concern for me is heartfelt, but I worry about him just as much. "Then you need security too."

"I have four guys. I'll be fine. And don't turn this around on me. If you're going out there, you're going with bodyguards."

"Security makes me feel self-conscious." I try a softer angle on him. "I'm not arguing with you about tonight, Babe. I just want us to make the right decisions for the right reason. I'm not having guards back home if that's what you're getting at."

He drinks from a bottle of water. Eyeing me, I can see him trying to figure a way into my head, my thoughts, analyzing me to maneuver his next play. I look away. Reaching for me, he grabs my hand, his tone calmer. "We're not arguing. I just can't be worrying about your safety when I'm out there."

"You don't have to worry about me. It was being handled, so we can let this go."

"You were being crushed by the crowd. I've seen it happen and *you* just want me to let it go." Frustrated, he runs his fingers through his hair. "This is not the battle to fight, Holliday. It's in your best interest to have protection."

"I don't want to fight with you or affect your performance." I feel the fight drain from my shoulders. "It's fine. You win."

A small smile creases his cheeks. "It's not about winning." He loves to win. Who doesn't? Standing up, he kisses me. His eyes flicker with animation when he asks, "How'd you like being on stage?"

Damn him and his sexiness. I smile. "It was incredible."

"Is it bad that I liked telling the whole fucking world you're mine?"

Raising my eyebrows, I say, "Apparently it's already on YouTube."

"I don't care... I did that for us. It's what I've wanted to do forever and it felt good."

"We've never hidden our relationship. We just didn't talk to the press about it. But for some reason, tonight, it felt so freeing, like the secret was out. Now the crazies know we're together and they've got no hope." I stroke some of his hair back. "But I'm not sure I want to go in front of that many people again. It was exhilarating and equally terrifying."

He breaks out laughing. "Okay, I won't torture you now... but no promises for later."

With that settled I kiss his chest and take his arm. When we walk out of the dressing room, I see Ashley lingering around nearby, watching us. Casually, I ask, "Do you know Ashley?"

"Who?" Dalton responds.

Happy, I kiss his cheek. "Never mind." I take another sip of my cocktail, then say, "I want to see you perform, so get the bodyguards."

He eyes me with that winning grin that made him famous as we all walk out. Dalton says to Tommy, "Get her detail—two guys." Tommy nods. Dalton kisses me quickly. "I'll see you after."

"Play my favorite song."

He walks backwards, keeping his eyes on me and smiling. "I'll play it just for you."

I hear Tommy calling some guys and he points to me. When they come over, I say, "Sorry you're stuck with me."

A light blond, burly man says, "It gets dangerous out there. I would do the same for my wife in this kind of situation."

Together with the bodyguards, I watch the rest of the concert. The band is incredible, like Tommy said earlier, better than ever. And when Dalton plays the song that he wrote for me, the one he started writing on our first trip to Texas together, he finds me in the audience and melts my heart all over again.

2

"Every breath you take makes my heart beat. I am, only because of you." ~ *Johnny Outlaw*

Dalton whispers, "One night. That's all I get?"

"I have to leave in the morning."

"Let's not waste time then. I want to spend every minute with you in bed."

I nod, his sweetness making me smile. We enter the two-story suite. Just inside, he drops his keys and wallet on the table, and we head for the stairs. "I was hoping for the bathroom."

The playfulness is heard in his voice. "You love to watch."

"Don't make it sound like I'm the only one," I say, laughing. "You love to watch, too."

"Oh I like to watch. I'm just wondering when you're going to let me install mirrors above our bed."

"Never. Too obvious."

"Too obvious for whom?" he asks.

"I may like to watch, but I don't want to sleep on the set of a porno."

I laugh right when we reach the top of the stairs, but he doesn't. He pulls me to the side, pressing me against the wall. His lips are on my neck, his talented hands squeezing my breasts. "I want you," he murmurs. We've been married a year and a half and he's been touring on and off the last four months. His mouth feels so good on me. He adds, "This is our last chance to make the most of our time together and I intend to... several times."

With my head tilted back, I don't bother whispering, "You have me. I'm yours all night. However you want me."

His hands slide under my shirt as he presses his hips against me. Dalton is passionate about everything he does, but he's especially passionate for me. I feel the same, so I take his hands in mine. When he opens his eyes, I whisper, "Come with me." Pulling him toward the bedroom, I walk backward, keeping my eyes on him.

When we enter the room, love is replaced with a lust that's seen in his eyes—deep emerald with flecks of danger in them.

I stop in front of the bathroom door and discard my shirt. "Eyes down here," I say, making sure he's watching as I strip for him. I slowly turn around, sliding my jeans down over my hips. Peeking over my shoulder, I challenge with eye contact. "What are you waiting for? Get naked for me."

His thumb runs over his bottom lip and then licks it. "So damn demanding."

"You love it."

"I might. I might also need to punish you for it."

My eyebrows go up. "Is it still a punishment if I enjoy it?" I bend all the way down and step out of my jeans. Curving my back up, I stand and unfasten my bra while he works on his belt. "Leave the wristband on."

"Get your ass in there, woman."

Letting my bra fall from my finger, I move quickly into the bathroom and lean against the counter.

When he enters, he's only wearing black boxer briefs. The muscles of his stomach are ripped, his biceps defined without effort, and his legs built by the perfect mix of strength and agility. His eyes narrow as he skims over my body. Through his gaze, he stakes claim before he even touches me. "No underwear, Mrs. Dalton?"

"I wanted to be ready for you. Don't leave me waiting."

His tongue drags over his lower lip, his hunger for me evident by the large bulge in his briefs. "I'm appreciating the view."

I slip backwards onto the cold marble counter and lean back against the mirrored glass. "I want you to appreciate it up close and personal... with your mouth."

"Fuck me," he says, his voice slipping between desire and disbelief, a reminder of what we have together hitting us both. He says, "I fucking love your dirty mouth, Holliday."

"You love my dirty mouth or you love to fuck my dirty mouth?"

"Both."

"Then come closer."

He drops his drawers and comes right up to me. "Your choice—fuck me or fuck my mouth first?

"I want to fuck your dirty mouth, but I want to fuck you more. Get off the counter and turn around."

I continue to stare into his eyes for a few more seconds before moving quickly into place. His phone is set down on the counter next to me. "Pick a song."

Sliding the phone in front of me, I start scrolling his playlists wanting a new soundtrack. I find the song quickly—"Stay" by Thirty Seconds to Mars.

His hands warm my backside as he presses his erection against me. Leaning forward, he takes the phone back just as the song begins to play. "I'm not gonna listen to fucking Jared Leto when I'm fucking you." Turning to the side, I see him scrolling on the screen. The song begins and I smile, making sure to look down so he doesn't see me laughing at him. The Resistance's remake of the song starts playing. They were asked to perform it for an awards show, so it's the live version and so hauntingly sexy.

Looking into the mirror, I wait for his eyes to reflect mine. When they do, I say, "For the record, I don't fantasize about anyone but you, Dalton."

The feel of him ignites my body, flames beginning to flick on the inside. I wiggle, unable to wait any longer. Kisses are placed on my shoulders, and he whispers, "Be patient, Baby."

"I want you."

"I want you too."

My heart begins racing, a pressure poised at my entrance. His eyes stay on mine until he thrusts forward, inside me, causing me to drop my head and hold on tight. Our connection is intense and my mouth drops open as he moves even deeper—solid and steady, filling me and reminding my body who it belongs to.

My hands are flat and I look up, wanting to watch as he takes me, owns me, conquering me entirely. Uncontrolled thoughts escape into words. "I love being married to a rock star!"

Dalton stops moving and a laugh breaks free. The right side of his mouth slides up and I realize what I just said. But right when I gain the nerve to look up, he thrusts again. Flat palms anchor me while I wish I could dig my nails into the bed to hold on. His hands cover the tops of mine to ease the power of his body's thrusting against me. My breath is shorted and I drop my head down, wanting to appreciate every sensation.

He stops and I catch my breath. "Open your eyes, Angel."

Pushing up when I open my eyes, I lock my elbows to hold

myself steady. His hands slide slowly up my arms, traveling the length until he takes hold of my shoulders. "Are you ready?"

With my hazels still locked on his greens, I analyze his mood. He's calculated and sexy and I want him to devour me whole. "I'm ready. Are you?"

In one fast move, my head hits the mirror as he pounds into me.

Holding tight to my shoulders he fucks me hard. "Dalton!" I cry out, needing all of it, all of him, taking it all and loving the feel of him more. My knees weaken and deep inside I begin to uncoil.

I watch him as I push myself closer to that edge where reality meets ecstasy. His jaw tightens, highlighting the rigid angles that wrap around his chin. There's a vein that I only see in two settings—on stage singing and when we're fucking. He drives me to want more, so I move against him. His fingers dig into my hips, one hand directly over the tattoo he loves to trace when we're sleepy.

One hand moves between us and two fingers find the spot he knows will send me over again and he rubs. My world bends, perpetuating the gratification. "Oh God! Dalton!" I collapse onto the counter, too tired to hold myself up. My hips are grabbed and he hits my soul in places I forget exist until he touches them, bringing me to life again.

He shudders, moaning my name as he comes. With his body molded to the back of mine, he licks a spot on my shoulder at the back of my neck. Desire getting the best of me again, through breathy whispers, I say, "I want you to mark me."

"You're too beautiful to damage."

I open my eyes and lift up to find his on mine in the mirror again. "I'll heal, but I want a piece of you while you're gone." He smiles, and I add, "Guess that makes me a groupie after all."

"A groupie is a one-sided infatuation." Bringing me upright with his arms around me, he lifts me up and carries me into the bedroom. He sets me down on the bed and lies down next to me. I maneuver over him, wanting to have him beneath me. I rest my head on his shoulder, my bare body on top of his. Rubbing my back, he says, "There's nothing one-sided about us, Angel. We fuck hard, but we love harder." I hear the sincerity in his voice, feeding my soul. I close my eyes, enjoying this time together.

I wake up before the alarm goes off. His dark brown hair is messy from sex. Just the way I like it most. Seeing him now and having a nap were enough to renew me. A room service order is placed before I start the shower. Once under the warm water, I close my eyes. It feels good to be drenched by the spray. As my body relaxes, so does my mind.

Over the course of our relationship, I've learned that taking a shower is like a beacon, calling Dalton to me. He steps into the shower behind me and kisses my shoulder. "Hi," he says as the water hits him.

"Hi."

"So what did you have to promise Tracy to let you skip out of work?"

I turn in his arms, sharing the warm water. "I have to leave tomorrow morning and work through the weekend."

"Is it worth it?"

Lifting up on my toes, I kiss his chin. "More than worth it."

The grin on his face is small and completely charming. "I'm glad you're here."

"Me too." I trade places with him and shampoo my hair as he soaks his. "You ready for tonight? You have to leave in forty-five minutes."

He nods with his eyes closed. The water rains down on him and I see his body relax under the heat. "You coming?"

"I just did. Twice. Thank you for that." I poke him in the abs, which are rock hard, and laugh as I change places with him and start rinsing my hair.

He tries to hide it, but I see his smile. "You're welcome. I still owe you for way more."

"After what we just did, I say we're even." His voice is low, calm, and deep. His lips are pressed behind my ear while his hands roam over my breasts. My head falls back on his shoulder and my eyes close, enjoying the intimacy.

When his fingers slide smooth like water between my legs, I whisper, "I can't. I think I need a little recovery time." I turn around and his hand graces my cheek, tilting my head up. His hair is flat down, drenched, water droplets running over his face and down his body. "I only need a short reprieve."

With a sly grin, out of nowhere he asks, "Why do you love being married to a rock star?"

"What?" I reply, not understanding where this is coming from.

"You said you love being married to a rock star... you said that earlier."

"I remember now," I say, giggling. "I love it because everything people hear about rock stars is true—the passion, the highs, the lows, and the fantastic sex. And despite living in the eye of a hurricane, we've managed to weather more than our fair share of obstacles in our way."

"We're stronger than the will of the universe trying to keep us apart."

He's right. "We're bonded by more than a marriage license." Our hearts are connected on a level that can never be put into words.

Like the song we both sing in our hearts, he says, "Among the hardness of the world is the softness of home. Our bodies make a melody that's become our anthem." He moves closer and runs his nose down the length of my jaw, then comes back and kisses my lips. Our kisses are love and gentleness, packed with intentions for more.

"I'll always love you," I whisper relaxing in his arms, somewhere between euphoria and lucidity. I'm tired, but I never tire of his hands on me. Dalton caresses my body much like he caresses his guitar, sensual, and careful, playing by heart.

"Why do you love me?" he asks, his voice a whisper in my ear as I close my eyes.

"Because you gave me the fairytale when I didn't believe in them."

His lips find that softest spot behind my ear and he lingers before gently placing a kiss. "Don't ever leave me."

I turn in his arms so I'm facing him. Stroking the backs of my fingers against the rough scruff of his cheek, I reply "I could never leave you. You're a part of my soul. Besides, it's you who's leaving me."

The water is shut off and towels are grabbed. He says, "Not by choice. Duty calls, but I'd change it all if you asked."

How can I not be madly in love with this man? "The life of a musician doesn't quit just because his wife gets lonely."

Taking my hand, he leads me back to bed. Despite the dark hour, I feel the light, the hope, in his words. He holds me tighter. "I'd change everything for you."

"I love who you are. I don't want you to change."

"We're everlasting," he says, closing his eyes.

Everlasting—we have that one word engraved inside our wedding bands. I don't say anything else, letting him rest before his flight in the morning. This time tomorrow I'll be alone, something I've come to dread about his band, The Resistance, touring. Johnny Outlaw, the lead singer of the band and my husband Jack Dalton's alter ego, will be thrown to his adoring fans and I'll be here stuck watching his life play out online over the next few months. I'll live life, run my business, and count the days until his return. Not only

The Reckoning

for him so he doesn't worry, but to hold onto who I am without him, to stay sane.

"I love you," I whisper to his shoulder as he holds me tight.

When our breathing evens, I gently move to the side where I find my favorite spot anywhere—pressed against his body with his arm around me. He kisses the top of my head and sighs as if all the world's burdens have escaped him. We find solace together.

I just hope we can keep this peace when we're not.

3

"All men covet something that doesn't belong to them. Some men just have more honor than others" ~ Johnny Outlaw

I wake up alone in bed. Dalton was kind enough to let me sleep in, but I would have preferred a kiss, even if it is a goodbye kiss. Rolling to his side of the bed, I rest my head on the pillow he slept on. It's not enough to satisfy, so I turn my face and inhale deeply. I miss him already. When I fall to my back again, I stare up at the ceiling realizing we've shared more goodbyes than hellos lately.

Grumpy, I throw the covers off and sit up. I'm supposed to be grateful. The band touring brings in a lot of money.

I'd rather have my husband back.

Over the last five years my company, Limelight, has boomed and I've made more money than I could have imagined. With that said, I wouldn't be living in the mansion I do in Los Angeles on my salary. My money pales in comparison to Dalton's, but I'm thrilled with the success my Bite Me Lime meme has given me. I have a career I never dreamed possible.

My phone starts vibrating on the nightstand. It must be seven. I swipe my finger over the screen shutting the alarm off, then stand up and take a shower.

I arrive home a few hours later. The house is stale, his absence filling the space, making me sluggish. I carry the pillow I stole from the hotel, the one he used, up to the bedroom. His scent is still strong and I'll need it over the next few weeks.

Last night when I should have been laying there in his arms satisfied from our time together, I was restless. I wish I could have enjoyed the time we did have instead of worrying about a conversation we had a few nights earlier...

"Are you okay?"

"Yeah, I'm okay."

"Are we okay?"

The pause between us grows as I wait for him to answer. My patience has gone just like he usually is. A heavy breath is heard, then he speaks from the heart. "We're more than okay. I know I'm not supposed to say this stuff because we've had this conversation and it puts pressure on you, but I'm gonna say it anyway."

"Okay," I reply, bracing myself.

"I'm tired of leaving you, Holliday. I know you have a life and your business, but it's hard on the road without you."

"It's hard being here without you, Dalton. I love you and I love you for telling me how you're feeling, but we've been over this."

"So it's a no-go?" His question deviates to an obvious frustration I know I can't ease.

"I have that photoshoot in New York next Monday, Babe. I'll see you then but my schedule is full of meetings and work until the

minute I leave. If I could, I would be with you."

I hear a turn signal from inside his car. "I'll be home soon. Wait up for me."

"Of course."

When we hang up, sadness and guilt come over me. I have so much to do in the next week, but for him I wish I could chuck it all, blow it off, or reschedule. This campaign is too important and I can't afford to lose my investment by rescheduling this late.

Closing my eyes, I try to push my worries aside and get some rest to make up for last night.

TR

When Dalton's not home, I tend to work away from the house. Luckily, I kept my old townhome. I head over because I tend to get more work done when there, it's a break from the monotony and the change of scenery is nice. The beach is nearby and offers a nice distraction from the emptiness of the house. Maybe I'm just not ready to let go of this place entirely and it works great as my office.

I carry my laptop outside to the patio. I stop and smile when I see Danny working out—shirtless. I say, "Hey there, stranger."

He looks over and smiles. "Hi, it's been a while."

"Yeah." I agree but don't add anything.

"You working here today?"

I set a bottle of water down next to the chaise, and sit. "I'll be here all week. I have a lot to get done."

Up to his old tricks, he hops the two short walls and lands on my patio. He's sweaty and snags my water, opening it as he takes a seat facing me. "Come on, Holli, admit it. You miss me." He downs half my water, then smirks.

Danny has always been easy on the eyes—an underwear model, body built beyond amazing, tan, handsome face, and dark hair.

Totally my type, if I had a type other than Dalton.

He drags the back of his wrist across his forehead, wiping away some sweat while I admire his physique. Seeing him reminds me of the photoshoot. "Yeah. Yeah. Don't flatter yourself too much," I joke. "So hey, I have a shoot next week."

"Oh yeah? Your own campaign?"

"Yes, there's no way I want to make modeling a career though. I'm already dreading it."

"What do you need to do to get ready for it?"

"I need to exercise." I make a wonky face. "I'm going to be in my underwear."

His eyebrows quirk up. "Sounds like my kind of photoshoot."

I throw him a hard glare. "Don't tease. I'm nervous."

"Oh I'm not teasing," he says, laughing. He finishes the bottle of water and holds it up. "Thanks by the way." He stands and looks down at me. "If you want any pointers, I'm happy to help."

"Really? You'll give me some inside tips?"

He shrugs. "Sure, but you've done some shoots before. Why are you so nervous this time?"

"Because I'm gonna be half-naked with another man in these pics."

Dramatically feigning offense, his hands go to his heart. "I'll try not to be offended that I was overlooked for the job."

Laughing, I say, "If it makes you feel better, you came to mind, but there's no way. Dalton would lose it."

"What are you talking about? We're friends now."

"Yes... kind of, but only when you're fully dressed and not touching me intimately."

"Whoa! There's intimate touching involved? Nice!" He sits back down looking totally intrigued, and asks, "Who's the model?"

"Sebastian Lassiter." Danny is shaking his head before the name is fully out of my mouth. "What? What is it? You know him?"

"I know him. I've met him on a shoot in Paris and at New York Fashion Week."

"And?"

"Look, Holli, he's young and a hot commodity right now. He'll do a great job at the shoot. But he'll also try to do you as well."

Feeling smug, I pop my chin up. "I can handle him on that front. He was fine when we met him last month."

"Be careful. He's got a bad temper, but I guess you're used to that already," he says, taking a dig at Dalton. "He also has an appetite for the forbidden."

"Stop speaking in metaphors. Are you saying he goes after married women?"

"He goes after women who seem unattainable." He rests forward, raises an eyebrow, and lowers his voice when he says, "I'd say you're pretty unattainable, Mrs. Outlaw."

I shrug nonchalantly. "Like I said, I can handle him. But if you think he's not a good fit for the campaign, tell me now."

"I think you two will be very convincing together." He stands again. "Offer still stands, if you want some tips or to work out before the shoot, you know where I live."

Dropping my sunglasses over my eyes, I lean back on the chair and look up at the blue skies. "Thanks."

Within seconds, I'm alone, the door to his balcony patio closing behind him. I search Sebastian online and look at him again. His face is sculpted, the Italian from his mother's side showing through his olive skin and brown hair. His eyes are a vibrant blue tipped with green, matching the Mediterranean Ocean. We approved him initially for the campaign based on his defined features and strong presence in black and white photos. That was before I knew about his reputation. Image after image appears onscreen and I scroll down, eyeing them. He's very attractive, his looks giving him a good reason to be cocky. Regardless, I know I can handle Sebastian Lassiter.

My email dings. I close the search window and click over to my inbox. There's an email from Danny. *What is he up to?* I glance over my shoulder at his house. His door is still closed, so I laugh and open the email.

Holli, this is a detox I use three days before a shoot when I know I'm going to be shirtless. You don't need it, but if you're feeling nervous, it gets rid of bloat and water weight.

I burst out laughing that I'm getting an email with advice on getting rid of water retention and bloat from a guy. But really, he's probably the most qualified person I know since he's made a career by looking good shirtless. So I pay close attention to the recipe as I read further.

Drink three glasses a day for three days and only lean protein and vegetables. No alcohol or sugar. And get a spray tan. A little color goes a long way.

Danny

Most of the summer I was holed up inside because of my heavy workload. I look down at my arms. I'm not exactly pale, but maybe a little more color would be good.

When I return to my work emails, I click through slowly, but here I am not focused. My mind keeps drifting back to last night and how Dalton's lips felt against mine, how he made me come twice, and how even if he's had a crazy day, he smiles when he sees me.

Dalton was in Vancouver by lunch and guilt has taken up residence in my gut for not going with him.

"There you are."

I slam my laptop closed, startled because I'm busted by Tracy, my office manager, for not working. "Hi," I say, my voice all pitchy and definitely guilty sounding. I clear my throat. "I didn't know you were coming today."

"I come here almost every day. You know that. Anyway, what

are you doing out here? Getting fresh air?" Tracy sits down on the lounger previously occupied by Danny.

"It's nice out today, so I was trying to get some work done while enjoying the sunshine. Dalton left this morning and I wanted a change of scenery from the home office."

"Well I know this week is busy and you're nervous about next week, but it's all gonna be great. Everything is organized and ready to go. So you don't need to stress too much."

"What if I was to throw a wrench in that perfectly organized schedule?"

Her smile disappears. "Depends. Throw a wrench or mess it up all together?"

"Maybe mess it up all together."

"Holli..." she says, my name voiced in an irritated way while her hands are positioned on her hips. "Tell me what you're doing?"

"I rarely miss work, deadlines, or meetings, Tracy. Don't treat me like this is a pattern of mine."

Her judgy stance is dropped and she says, "I didn't mean to. I'm sorry. I know you work hard. It's just—"

"It's just that I can't concentrate. I hate to disappoint you and any clients, but I miss my husband. I got him for forty-eight hours and out of those forty-eight, I saw him less than fifteen. That includes sleeping. I went to my meetings. He went to his. Last night I was lying next to him wondering when I'm going to see him next, when I'm going to get to touch him and not just see him on a screen."

"That's *his* lifestyle. *Your* life, your business is here. I can see how difficult this is for you. I want to help you, but I just don't know how."

A sense of urgency builds inside and my mind starts turning to come up with any viable reason that will justify it to her *and* me. Tucking the hair that has fallen forward behind my ear, I say, "I understand why we don't want to reschedule the meetings, but I need a few days off. I can't go into this trip feeling like this."

"Are you asking me or telling me?"

I sigh. "I'm asking... kindly with all the pleases and thank yous and hot guys on top."

After a momentary debate, she relents. "Fine. I'll make it happen, especially because there are hot guys on top. You've got today. Twenty-four hours. I need you back here by then to prepare for the campaign."

We have a tough week ahead, so I accept the deal without argument. "I'll take it. Thank you."

She stands and asks, "You need a flight booked?"

I nod.

"Where?"

"Vancouver."

"Go home and pack. I'll book you on the next available flight and text you the details."

With my laptop tucked to my side, I give her a one-armed hug. "Thank you so much, Trace."

"You realize you could have just told me you were going and I'd have to deal with the consequences. You own the company and make all the final decisions."

Leaning back, I say, "I don't want to run my company like that. What we do matters and I don't ever want to leave you in a lurch."

"I appreciate that," she says. "Now go!"

I take off with a smile on my face, knowing I get to see my love again later today. Vancouver, here I come.

4

"My life is more chaotic in some ways and less in other ways. It's not just about me anymore" ~ Johnny Outlaw

I didn't know my heart wasn't beating until I saw Dalton again, and it's now triple-timing. Standing center stage at the microphone, he isn't singing, but he's humming a melody I recognize from many nights in bed. Without any instrumental accompaniment, he starts singing the song we played the night before when we were together. It's not a part of the concert playlist, but I think it should be. A sliver of his stomach is revealed as he takes hold of the mic, his T-shirt riding up while his jeans hang low despite the belt.

His voice is strong, the emotions raw, so real as he sings the first chorus. Then he stops, looking out into the empty arena. There are no fans screaming his name, no photographers recording or taking photos. Just the road crew setting up on stage, the technician at the soundboard on the floor... and me, sitting in a row too far back for Dalton to really notice. But he stares out anyway as if he can sense me.

The technician tells him to sing one of their faster hits and on command, he does without reservation. His voice is unique and intimidating in talent, and has a sexual undercurrent that drives me wild. But considering how many hits they have, his voice drives a lot of women wild.

I stand up and start walking toward the stage. The tech cuts him off, requesting Dex, the drummer, on stage for his check. Dalton walks away from the mic, but stops. I'm close enough for him to see me if he looks in my direction, but a war seems to be waging in his head and he shakes it. When I reach the barrier on the floor, I yell, "Hey rock star?"

He turns with a wry grin sliding into place. It's the one that can get me naked anywhere. Slowly, he walks closer until he's at the edge of the stage. "What are you doing here?"

"I had an unexpected wanderlust."

"I like you lusting."

I laugh and step up on the barrier, leaning closer. "What does a groupie have to do to get her idol alone?"

"Idol, huh?" He squats, his arms resting on his knees as he watches me. "I could get used to that."

"Go ahead. There's no point in hiding the truth."

Hopping down to the floor, he lands, then moves in front of me. My lips reunite with his. When we part, he says, "You have never understood the depth of my love for you. I could never be your idol, when I happily bow at your feet."

"I don't want you bowing. I want you face-to-face, your lips on mine, and your arms around me."

He does just that and we kiss again. With the barricade still between us, I lean my head on his chest and say, "I missed you too much to stay away."

"I miss you always."

We order room service and have an early dinner since he has the show tonight. Sitting across from each other at the table by the window, I say, "Watching the sun set always makes me reflective."

"I don't need reflection. I've done enough of that for five lifetimes."

He has too. From his childhood to Cory's death, he's been to the darkest recesses of those dreaded places in his head. Pulling him back was not easy, but I love him too much to let him dwell in the despair that impaired him. He's such a beautiful man—inside and out—he deserves to live this beautiful life to its fullest. Changing the subject, I say, "The colors of the sky are amazing."

"The way the orange bleeds from yellow to red—"

"And the purples and blues. It's stunning."

He looks at me, and asks, "If you could have anything, only one thing, what would it be?"

Slumping down, I lift my leg up onto the chair under me and get comfortable. "Hmmm... that's hard. Let me think about it. How about you?"

"I think I would have played some small gigs before hitting the road on this big tour." His expression isn't somber. He's resolved.

"Why?" I ask.

"I feel lost on stage sometimes without Cory. I think playing some smaller shows would have prepared me for the stage without him there."

"Your shows are sold out. Fans are loving the tour. Tommy says your voice is stronger than ever. I agree with him. The time off in Ojai helped you, so how would playing small shows better your performance?"

He pauses, his discomfort obvious as he turns his drink around in his hand. When he sets it down on the table between us, he looks me in the eyes, and says, "In most bands, the drummer sets the pace, the beat of each song, pacing us. But not with us. Cory did. He was an amazing fucking guitarist. So much talent. Did you know he wanted to be a drummer in high school?"

I watch him as he tells the story. "He met Rochelle and that was it. He would have learned any instrument she was interested in just to spend time with her."

"Wow. He's a guitar legend because of her," I say, reflecting on the memories of Cory and Rochelle together.

"She's a natural. She didn't have formal lessons. Just picked it up and started playing. Did you know she hasn't played since we finished the album?"

"I know it's not easy for her," I say, referring to her getting over Cory's death. "But she's a strong woman and she'll remain strong for the boys."

He nods as he looks out the window. When his eyes meet mine again, he asks, "What about kids?"

"What about them?"

"We haven't talked about kids in a while. Where's your head at?"

Looking down, I take my drink and down two big gulps. "Not while you're on the road."

"The tour won't last forever, but there will probably always be some traveling."

"I want you home longer than two days at a time when we have kids. I want you there for the birth. I don't want to be hoping you make it to the hospital in time."

The passion he feels about this comes through in his determined tone. "I'll be there."

"I'm not asking you to stop forever. I'm just asking around the time I would be due."

The Reckoning

Hope rises in his face. "So what you're saying is we can start tonight?"

"No," I say, laughing. "I want to share all the moments with you. That includes peeing on the stick."

The left side of his mouth lifts up as he looks me in the eyes. "I'll even hold it if you want."

"This train has officially jumped the rails," I joke, shaking my head. "I think I can handle that part." My smile falls as the reality of the conversation takes hold. "Are you really ready to have kids and settle down?"

"I'm a music man, so I don't know if I'll ever truly be able to settle down. I know this isn't my last tour—"

"I'm not asking you to give this up. I'm just asking you to be present when you are home."

"Lying in bed all day isn't enough?"

"I love lying in bed with you all day. But we can't do that with a baby."

He leans forward, resting his arms on the table. After a long pause, he says, "I'm not saying now. I'm just saying one day. I'm almost thirty and although I had no idea what my life would be like once I left Texas, I know that I want it to be with you, so let's just say 'one day' and take the pressure off."

I can't seem to take my eyes off him—his handsome face mixed with his sweet words and vulnerable side. It's enough to make my ovaries give in right here on the spot. "I can do one day with you."

TR

Dalton's fingers dance down my skin and I exhale, the air pushed from my lungs when two enter me. I open my legs and he reaches, obliterating everything but this moment.

He watches as my back arches, his teeth scraping across his

bottom lip as his eyes devour me. Leaving me bare, empty without his touch, he kneels at the end of the bed. Adrenaline from the show earlier courses through him and he grabs my ankles, pulling me down the mattress until his mouth is on me. I gasp from the intensity of the union as he alternates between sucking and his tongue greedily taking all my willpower, making me come. Dalton is above me, stretching my arms high above my head. Holding my wrists in one of his hands, he lifts my leg with the other, making me bend at the knee. With my other leg hanging off the bed, he's quick, ridding any thoughts I might have had of gentler sex. I take his pounding, relishing his need for me.

Caught up in the act, I free my hands and push off. I'm lithe, fast as I roll over and look over my shoulder. Wiggling my ass, I try to lure him over. "Don't leave me waiting," I whisper my own demand.

I see the spark in his eyes. He's a man who can't resist a challenge or luckily, he can't resist me. Facing forward while he tries to get control of the situation, he comes to me, crawling up the bed until his cock is touching my backside. "You want me, Angel? You want this?" he asks, rubbing one hand over my ass and using his other to stroke himself several times. He's riled up after the show, high on the adrenaline and I've got a contact high.

My breathing picks up from the anticipation and I wait... and wait.

"Answer me."

Our eyes meet over my shoulder while I hold steady on all fours. "I want you. I want you so much."

Rubbing the tip of his cock against my pussy several times, I clench wanting to keep him there. He's at my entrance and I wait while the pressure of his hands slide up my back. Gripping me by the shoulders, he pushes in achingly slow. But I know how to get what I want, so I beg, "Johnny?"

A mumbled "Fuck" is heard from behind me.

"Fuck me."

Slam!

"Ahhh," I react loudly, the sounds of his own pleasure weighing equally with mine.

Clawing at the sheets beneath me, I hold on and meet each conjoining with my own thrusts back. He stands tall on his knees, his hands gripping my hips, leveraging my body to his will. "So good," I moan.

"So good, but..." He thrusts hard a few more times, then pulls out suddenly.

"What's wrong?" I ask, disappointed he stopped when I was getting so close again.

"I want to see your face. I want to memorize it and remember it when you're gone."

My mouth drops open. Managing to close it, I swallow hard. "Okay," I reply, my voice soft, my heart blanketed in his sweet words. I move to my back and he positions himself and pushes in. This time he's gentle in his touches, his body moving with calculation, taking his time to illicit a deeper desire.

Stroking along his hairline, I reply, "It's not been long, but I've missed you, missed this so much."

All at once, we come together, our bodies moving with desire. No holding back, I moan again and he drops down all the way, burying his head against my neck. His warm breath and the weight of him on top of me brings me to the edge again. When he kisses me, our tongues uniting, I concentrate on my orgasm and pulling it forth. All the stimulation teasing my mind and I let go.

His loss of control will be visible later, but I don't care. As my body relaxes, his teeth sink into my skin. The weight of him covers me as we attempt to recover from our passion.

My breathing is staggered. "I need to get up," I whisper. When he moves, I slip out of bed and use the restroom. After freshening up, I go back into the bedroom to find Dalton asleep. I quickly check the time before setting the alarm for one hour and climb back into bed. Snuggling against his back, I wrap my arm around his middle. This is Heaven on Earth, our own paradise found.

In the darkest hours of night, the bed dips and I wake. Dalton's back is to me as he sits hunched over. "Are you okay?"

Without turning around, he says, "Before you go off and defend why it's okay and tit for tat and all that shit, I know I don't have a right to be jealous or say shit about this photoshoot you're gonna do. I know I make videos that probably don't sit well with you. It's art. I get it, but it sucks and I don't like the thought of some guy touching you." His tone is jaded, deep with emotion—aggression, frustration, concern, sadness.

I remain motionless, taking in his words. He adds, "So when you're doing the shoot, don't lose yourself and don't do anything that you aren't comfortable doing. Photographers like to push boundaries, to get 'the shot' at the expense of the model. They think in terms of them, not you. There's an agenda. Don't get caught up in it, Holliday. Trust me, the photos will always surface."

Wanting to be offended that he thinks I can't handle myself, I'm too tired to get that upset. He's on my side and only wants the best for me. I finally gulp, then say, "I've done other photoshoots."

"Not like this. You're taking Limelight in a new direction and changing the image of the company. Represent it how you want the public to perceive it."

He's had photos surface that he's not fond of, ones that were taken of him when he was high or drunk. They aren't flattering, but he dealt with it. Maybe it's easier for those types of images to be dismissed because he's a musician. Me, not so much. I learned in that first year of marriage that we're a brand in and of itself. What we do individually affects the other whether it's business related or personal. We are a reflection of each other. What we do matters to the other. "I'll keep that in mind."

"Please keep us in mind," he says. His voice is low and I barely hear him, but the gist is caught without a threat or any harsh words as he lies back down.

"I expect the same."

He closes his eyes and says, "I know."

We lie in the breaking hours of day... or I do, listening to him breathe as it steadies with his sleep—my newest favorite pastime. I don't remember falling asleep, but my eyes burn when he turns allowing more light to shine across the room. Dalton is standing at the window staring out. He's not moving, but he is dressed. "Morning," I say and lightly clear my throat to rid the roughness.

"We'll be in New York at the same time."

"We'll make sure to see each other." I sit up, leaning on my arm. "Why are you dressed?"

"I have to leave. Our jet takes off in an hour."

"Were you going to sneak out on me?"

He scrubs his face with his hands, obviously tired. "I hate goodbyes."

"I hate when you sneak out."

"I hate sneaking out, but I hate that look in your eyes more—the one that makes me feel like I'm letting you down."

I get up and go to him. Holding him from behind, we both stare out the window now. "You're not letting me down. I just hate seeing you go."

"It's a vicious cycle."

"It sure is."

He turns around and we kiss. The eagerness of my arrival is gone this time; a sadness embraces us just as our tongues embrace each other.

When we part, he runs his hands up the sides of my neck until he's cupping my face. "Don't forget me when I'm gone."

"You're hard to forget and I enjoy remembering you too much to try." Making sure to look him in the eyes, I add, "I love you more than you will ever know."

"I love you deeper than you thought possible." With a small smile on my face, I climb back into bed. He takes hold of the suitcase handle and says, "Wanderlust is a magical thing."

"I hope it strikes soon." I roll, turning away from the door, not wanting to watch him leave and close my eyes. He walks out leaving the goodbye in silence, both of us hating saying it more than hearing it.

5

"Absence is sometimes just absence without any ulterior motives." ~ *Johnny Outlaw*

I thought it would get easier, that I would get used to the silence that fills our home. But I miss the little things. I miss Dalton strumming on his guitar. I miss the way he hogs the bed and covers me with his heat at night. I miss his playful side and the way he watches me as if he can't take his eyes off of me. I miss his jeans and T-shirts lying on the bedroom floor where he dumped them. I miss those stupid little hairs in the sink that remain after he shaves. I miss the fucking toilet lid being left up.

I miss him.

Dwelling on issues was never a good skill of mine. Usually, I'm more of a tackle and confront kind of person. So I push all my sad emotions away that Dalton's absence has created and focus on my work, something that I'm better at. Fortunately with the new deals in place, I have plenty to do before the photoshoot.

On Sunday, Tracy and I board a plane for New York. I have no idea what to expect from this shoot and doubts have been creeping in regarding the new brand imaging. Maybe a little guilt as well, though I wasn't sure what I was guilty of, yet.

Due to scheduling conflicts at the last minute Sebastian, the model had to push our shoot until Tuesday. Tracy was not thrilled since everything else had to be rescheduled but by the time we were on the plane, she was calm and collected again. What I wasn't thrilled about was this 'cleanse' diet Danny suggested. Pushing the shoot one more day meant one more day of me living off herbal waters and lettuce.

I wasn't good with lettuce. I liked lettuce, sure, but living off lettuce and water wasn't helping my mood. The flight attendant asked what we'd like for our dinner and I started to drool over airplane food. That was a first. Tracy ordered her pasta with cream sauce with an extra buttery roll and the cheesecake for dessert. I practically growled, "Nothing for me."

"Holli, you're thin enough. You always look good. You should eat."

"These ads are going to be in magazines, including Elle and Cosmo."

"I know all this, but you still don't have to starve yourself."

Her dinner is placed in front of her, the smell wafting in front of my nose as it's passed over me to Tracy's tray. "Do you think Giselle eats pasta with cream sauce when she has a photoshoot to prepare for?" I snap, crossing my arms and now totally annoyed.

"You're not Giselle. You're Holli. You own a business that you built from the ground up from your mind and creativity, not your looks, so slow the rage and have a roll." She sets a roll down on a napkin on the tray in front of me, then turns and puts her headphones on and starts eating as her movie on the screen in front of her lights up.

She's right. Shockingly, I'm not a supermodel. I roll my eyes at my ridiculousness and order, "I'll have what she's having." I can always start back on the water and lettuce tomorrow.

I devour the noodles. Best dinner ever... at least when you're hungry. But soon after, I get sleepy. My arm slips off the armrest waking me up. I look around to gather my senses and realize we're still on the plane. Tracy says, "We're landing soon. Did you get some rest?"

I laugh. "I wasn't even tired. I think the carb overload made me pass out."

Just as she begins laughing, the pilot comes on and announces our impending arrival and we prepare for landing.

We get our stuff from baggage claim and head to the long taxi line. "Where are we staying?" I ask after we settle into the cab at the airport.

"I rented an apartment in SoHo. On the last trip, you said you were tired of hotel living and I thought it would be fun to be in the neighborhood since we're here for a few days."

"We're having the Nordie's buyers over to the apartment?"

"It's no ordinary apartment."

And it isn't.

The apartment is stunning. Wood and marble play together in a modern and clean, but classic way. The wood gives the floors warmth and the marble compass insert is striking. We stand in the grand entrance with our mouths hanging open. She steps forward and says, "The best part. We're having the shoot here too. Our other space was booked for Tuesday so we're shooting in the master bedroom and in the living room. Come on. Let's check it out."

I follow her through the grand entryway to the living room. A wall of windows greets us with a large white sofa in the middle of the floor. The tones of the room are neutral—white and beige—with a pop of black here and there. "This room is gorgeous."

"Can't you just see using the couch with that view?"

The buildings are lit up against the dark background. Even though it's night, I bet the view is just as great in the day time. "I can," I reply in awe. We retrieve our luggage from the foyer. "So if we're using the master bedroom, where are we sleeping?"

She smiles and does a giddy clap and little jump. "You can sleep in the master. The look is messy for the campaign, just waking up and sexy. It will be perfect. Just keep your clothes out of sight."

"You mean, don't be a slob?"

"Precisely."

We laugh, and my phone buzzes. I walk to the window. *"Hello,"* I answer feeling the love for my love.

"Are you in New York?"

"We just got to the apartment. Dalton, you better hold onto your bank account. I might be in love with this place."

Hearing him laugh makes me happy and I smile. "Spend it. We can't take it with us."

"You say that now... before you've seen the price tag."

"Good point." I hear him exhale as if he's tired, but he says, "I could be there in less than two hours."

"Do it."

"Don't tempt me."

"I would do anything to tempt you right now."

His laugh is lower, more relaxed. "I like the offer, but I have a show tomorrow night."

Though I knew he couldn't visit, I'm still disappointed. Looking at my watch I see the time. "It's after one in the morning. Why are you still up?"

"I was worried about you. I wanted to make sure you made it safely."

"I made it safely," I repeat, finding a spot in a chair and staring out the window. "What do you have planned for tomorrow?"

"I'll check in with Tommy in the morning. I know we have to do some press, but I'm not sure after that."

Standing up, I confess, "I ate really amazing pasta on the plane tonight."

"Wow, I didn't see that coming."

"I've been on this diet for models—"

"Alcohol and cigarettes?"

"Bah da bum!" I chime in. "Actually no. It's a cleanse. A water diet."

"Why do I already not like the sound of this?"

"It's just one more day since the shoot got pushed until Tuesday—"

"Holliday, what are you doing?"

Confused, I ask, "What do you mean?"

"I mean, what are you doing? This isn't you. You don't do Hollywood diets. You don't do half-naked photoshoots. You work out. You live life. You don't care what others think. You're the most you person I know."

"What does that mean?"

"It means that you've always been exactly who you are. You've always known who you are, but right now." He sighs, frustration clearly heard. "I'm not sure I do."

My own frustration sets in from trying to explain my side. "The camera adds weight. The tabloids are watching for your baby to start showing anytime, even though I'm not even pregnant. I deal with shit all the time regarding my weight. I just want to feel *and* look good, and most of all to *feel* like I look good."

"That's very LA of you." His disdain is obvious.

"Fu—" I stop myself and take a deep breath. "Are you calling me shallow?"

He starts raising his voice. "I don't want you to change for *them*. Fuck, you can gain weight if you want, but you sure as hell don't need to lose any. I'm telling you this as someone who loves you. Don't let them win."

Furious, my hands start to shake. "This has gotten blown way out of proportion. I'm gonna let you go before it gets worse. I'll talk to you later. If I don't, have a great show tonight."

"Don't be mad."

"I'm tired, Dalton," I snap. "I don't want to be lectured. The world is not our enemy."

"But the paps are. You're beautiful the way you are."

"I'm not changing. I just did this for a few days to be in top shape. That's all."

His exhale is heavy into the receiver and I can tell he wants to say so much more than he does. But he doesn't for some reason. "I should go. I love you."

I don't want to hang up mad, but I'm still a little irritated. "I love you, too," I reply before hanging up because even though I don't like the conversation we just had, I do love him. Grabbing my suitcase, I yell goodnight to Tracy who's in her room already and go into the large bedroom.

I'm tired from traveling and emotionally exhausted after having to defend myself. But to get to sleep, I still have to unpack a few things. The rest can wait until tomorrow. After closing the door, I get ready for bed and climb under the covers. My body sinks into the pillow-top mattress and I lie there with my arms spread wide. There's a wall of windows in here as well, giving me a killer view of the city at night. But it's beyond this city and across the border where my heart hovers.

Taking the remote from the bedside table, I click the button for the curtains and they start to close, shutting off the rest of the world in the process. Once it's pitch black, I close my eyes and fall asleep.

The Reckoning

Knocking wakes me. I roll over and look toward the bedroom door. I sigh and flop back down. "Come in."

The light is bright as if day has stolen the dark away. Tracy whispers, "You gonna sleep all day?"

"Yes," I reply, grumpy with my eyes closed hoping to find sleep again.

The bed dips and she rubs my shoulder. "Hey, what's wrong?"

"I'm hungry and tired."

"This isn't like you. You've slept over ten hours. How much more sleep do you need?"

"I want to sleep until my husband comes home."

"But we're in New York."

I open my eyes. "Oh yeah, that's right." Rolling to my back, I rub my eyes. "Wanna go shopping?"

"Thought you'd never ask," she says, standing and going to the door. "Get up and let's go."

An hour and a half later, we arrive at a street filled with high-end fashion. We blow through some money and the afternoon—filling our time with laughter and great clothes. By seven, the granola bar I had a few hours ago has burned off and I'm starved. "I can't buy another thing unless I eat."

"Then eat we shall."

We head back toward our apartment and right into a trendy restaurant in SoHo. We're seated right away in an area that's open to the exposed kitchen. It's fascinating to watch the behind the scenes play out for entertainment purposes.

"I like the wine," I say, and take another sip.

"I like the view," Tracy says.

"Yeah, it's a really cool setup."

"I'm not talking about the setup or scenery." She nods toward one of the chefs that happens to be looking in our direction.

With my eyes wide, I whisper, "Stop. He can see you."

She laughs loudly, so I ask, "Are you drunk off half a glass of wine?"

"No silly. I just don't go out much these days. It's nice to get the attention."

Leaning forward I rest my chin on my hand. "What's going on with you and Adam?"

She starts waving her hand around. "Oh nothing. He's great. We've been talking about having kids. It's just been too long since I've had a girl's night."

"We have the next few days too."

A spark of excitement sets in her eyes. "I know. It also feels good to get out of LA. Manhattan is always so different. It's a nice change of pace."

The waiter brings a plate of poutine to our table and says, "Compliments of the Chef."

We both look in his direction and he sends us a small smile and a wave. I say, "Tell him thank you."

As soon as we're alone again, I drop my head into my hands. "I can't resist French fries. You know this. I'm weak. Don't they smell amazing?"

"They do," she replies, stabbing her fork into them. With her mouth full, she says, "And taste heavenly."

I roll my eyes and laugh. "You're really terrible, you know that? Mean and terrible."

"Eat one. Just one."

They do look so damn good. I pick up my fork and stab a small bite. I inhale the deliciousness first then savor the bite as I chew. "Heaven. This is Heaven."

The plate is empty, just a sad reminder that something amazing was once there and now is in my belly. I set my fork down and rub my stomach. "So good."

She takes another drink of her wine, and asks, "So good. So

The Reckoning

earlier, PP—pre-poutine—I was going to ask about you and Johnny."

"What about us?"

"How are you guys doing?"

Looking around the restaurant, I hesitate. "He's touring. End of story really." I suspect she can pick up on the change in my tone and body language.

"How much longer?"

"Two more months."

"You can visit him. I'll arrange your schedule so you can."

"Thanks. I think that will help my blues." I smile just as our food is served... or should I say my water with mint and lime squeezed in. I already cheated with the wine. I'll try to balance the bad with the water. Her salad sure does look divine though. "You gonna eat that tomato?"

She bursts out laughing and shakes her head. "Nope. Go right ahead."

Two women in their early twenties are drinking next to us and getting louder and more raucous as the night rolls on. I hear one saying, "See? Told you it wouldn't last."

I peek over and see her holding her phone in front of the other girl's face. Her friend replies, "But I liked them together. She made me feel like we had a real chance with Johnny Outlaw."

"Apparently, we do now," the first girl laughs.

My heart sinks to the pit of my stomach. I want to run away from this conversation and forget I ever heard that, but like a train wreck, I'm glued to it, waiting to hear the gossip.

His name being spoken draws Tracy's attention to the girls and she points to the phone. "Is that a picture of him?"

"Yes, he was seen out on a date tonight..." She smiles and her hot pink lip-glossed lips sneer. "And not with his wife."

Leaning forward, I ask, "Where were they?"

The second girls answers, "Toronto. They played a show. He was at an after party with some other woman." She eyes me and maybe it's the booze speaking or maybe she's just always that rude, but she adds, "I think you might be a little old for him." Flashing the phone at me with the photo on display, her condescending tone makes me want to punch her in the silicone-injected lips. "As you can clearly see, he prefers younger women."

"Like you?" I ask, sardonically.

"Yes, exactly like us."

"Since I'm so old, how about I take my walker and shove it right up your a—"

"Check!" Tracy announces, cutting me off. Her eyes lock on mine. "Time to go."

I stand, tossing my napkin. Needing to say one last thing to these plastic Barbies, I add, "I'm apparently not that hideously old since the chef sent over a dish just—"

A waiter arrives at their side with the same dish and says, "Compliments of the Chef."

Totally defeated, I grumble, "For fuck's sake." I grab my purse and go. "I'll meet you outside."

When she joins me outside, she says, "How are you?"

"Shitty."

She nods. "Hey, don't jump to conclusions. Okay?"

"Sure. Right. Okay," I say, my mind reeling in a haze of messed up emotions. "But I don't understand." My head is pounding, so I rub my temples.

"Who's the woman?" Tracy asks.

One word. "Ashley."

She sighs, "Did you know the most common name for crazy girls is Ashley. Go figure. I thought they were always so innocent years ago when I was into Laura Ashley dresses." Throwing her arm up, she hails a cab.

Feeling sick to my stomach, I say, "They're not."

"Clearly."

Three glasses of wine is not good when you've only had a few fries and a tomato to eat. With my head against the car window on our way back to the apartment, I close my eyes, but my mind whirls making the world spin. I reopen them quickly while spreading my arms out to anchor me to the car.

"We're almost there. Can you make it, Holli?" Tracy asks.

The driver says, "She better not throw up in my car."

"She won't," Tracy barks back. When she turns to me, she looks at me like she doesn't believe her own response.

"I won't," I reassure her and the driver. "I just need to get back."

"We're not far, thank goodness."

I nod, focusing my energy on feeling better. The car pulls over and Tracy drops some bills to him as I climb out. Once we're on the sidewalk, she takes my arm and leads me into the lobby.

Before we even make it onto the elevator, my eyes are filled with tears. She says, "Aww, don't. Please, Holli. It's okay. I promise you. This is just a misunderstanding. He would never hurt you like that."

One tear, then another slips out and down my cheek. She pulls me into a hug as the elevator dings each passing floor. "Hols, honey. It looked bad, but it's a tabloid. It's their job to make their photos more scandalous."

My body is numb as my insides hurricane out of control. A sob breaks free just as the door opens. "Come on," she says, taking my hand. Once we're in the apartment again, I try to say goodnight and make for a quick getaway, but she's not having it. "Call him. Talk to him." She sets the stuff down and digs into my purse. She hands me my phone and sits on the couch. "Call him."

With it in my hand, I stare down at the phone. "What if it's true?"

"It's not. You know in your gut it's not."

I nod automatically, then take the plunge and dial without any debate. Each ring makes me more anxious while I stand there. My foot starts tapping and I find myself muttering, "Answer. Answer. Come on, Dalton. Answer." When my call is directed to voicemail, I turn my back to Tracy and leave a message to call me right away.

When I turn back, I whisper, "I'm going to bed."

She stands suddenly. "Are you sure?"

"I am. I need some rest before tomorrow and I can't just stand here waiting for who knows how long for him to call me back."

"I think sleep is good." She comes over and hugs me. "It will all be explained when you talk to him. I promise you. I know he loves you more than anything."

"Thanks." I give her a big hug, release, and go into the bedroom.

Immediately, I open my laptop and search for the photo to see what the story says. When I find it, I read:

Johnny Outlaw was spotted out with a mysterious woman after playing a live show in Toronto. His wife, Holliday Hughes, was spotted out with friends in New York City. Could this mean it's over already? We'll be updating this story as it unfolds.

I stare at the photo, analyzing every possible reason she would be with him, leaving anywhere, *with* him, and why he would be reaching for her hand and be that close. None of this makes sense. He wouldn't cheat on me. I know he wouldn't, I repeat silently closing my eyes and praying on every star in the sky.

Tracy knocks lightly, then peeks in. "Hey, I wanted to check on you one more time. You okay?"

"I'm fine," I say, looking up from the computer and flat-out lying to her.

The Reckoning

"That's good. You know how the tabs blow the most innocent thing out of proportion, twisting it to fit their storyline."

"Yeah, I know."

"I'm gonna go to bed. You should get some sleep, but if you need me, just come in."

"Thank you, Trace," I say, trying to keep my voice from trembling. "Goodnight."

"Goodnight." She leaves me with a sympathetic smile before closing the door.

Picking up my phone, I call, again. My call goes to voicemail, again. This time, I say, "I'm going to bed. I'll call you in the morning."

Trying to keep my better sensibilities intact, I take two deep breaths and exhale slowly before going into the bathroom to brush my teeth. I set the phone down on a towel and stare at it, willing it to light up with Dalton's name. But it doesn't.

I spit and rinse my mouth, exhaustion getting the best of me. I turn out the light and climb back into bed. I've developed a terrible headache and my head is spinning. I close my eyes needing to deal with this mess in the morning. I hope to have a better perspective on the situation by then.

6

Jack Dalton

"Fame is what happens when you lose sight of your priorities." ~ Holliday Hughes

I stare at my phone as I listen to the message play out over the speaker. "Call me, Dalton." Holliday sounds pissed, but I have no idea why. I thought she was okay when we hung up the last time. I listen to the second message—"I'm going to bed. Call me in the morning when you get up."

Fuck that! I call her, but my call goes to voicemail.

Fuck! Fuck. Fuck. She doesn't answer. Why the fuck is she not answering? Shit! What day was her shoot—today or tomorrow? Is she with that douchebag model?

Tommy opens the door and asks, "You ready to go?"

"Yes," I say, standing up. I walk past him, our shoulders colliding. "Get me out of here."

"What's up?" He catches up, then passes me and opens the door to the outside where a white limo is waiting.

I stop and glare at him. "Nothing shouts douche more than a white limo."

"If the shoe fits..."

"Whatever." I get into the car and he slides in after. "Can you pack my shit? I want to take the jet to New York."

Tommy leans back as the car takes off. "What are you talking about? We're flying out in the morning. You can't wait eight hours?"

"No, I can't."

"Tough shit."

"I can get a plane or a flight on my own."

"Yes, you can and you're welcome to do that, but the band's not picking up the tab for you to go tonight. Why are you in such a hurry to get to New York anyway?"

"Holliday."

"Figures." Tommy sits up and looks at me—annoyed and thoughtful—an interesting expression. "What's going on?"

"I can't get a hold of her."

"She's probably sleeping."

Scratching the back of my neck, I say, "Maybe, but it's not like her to not answer. She left a message and sounded upset."

"Can't you call the hotel and have them ring her room."

"She's staying at some apartment in the city. I don't have an address or number for it."

Sitting up, he says, "Let me get this straight. She has email after email with all your shit and schedule right there handy and you never bothered to find out where she's staying? Yikes, man. Not the best way to show you care."

"Shut the fuck up." I go through all the other options to reach

The Reckoning

her and get an idea. Grabbing my phone from my pocket, I call Tracy. "I'll call her friend." Scrolling through my numbers, I realize I don't have any Tracy's. "Fuck!" I shake my head and lean my elbow on the door, totally fucking annoyed at myself.

"Look, Johnny, I don't know what's going on, but I'm sure she'll call you. In the meantime, sit back and relax."

The stress of not knowing what's wrong is eating me up, but Tommy's right and I have no other choice anyway. I fist my hands on the seat beside me, pounding it lightly. "Fine."

Once I'm back in my suite, I call Holliday again, but go to voicemail again. I've lost all patience. "Call me back."

Why the fuck is she not answering?

Glancing at the clock, it's past midnight. I'm still too wired to sleep, so I take a shower and slip on a pair of boxer briefs when I get out. Turning on my laptop in bed, I decide to check emails. Scrolling down the list, it's all the usual crap, including an email from Rory, our Publicist. I click on it.

Shit!

Seeing the photo of me with that new equipment manager—*Shit, this looks bad.* Paparazzi have a talent for making something look like something it's not. I'd get in a car and drive right now if it wouldn't take all night and half the morning. I shut my laptop and lie back, exhaustion from the show finally setting in. Holliday's not one to hide her emotions. She's straight-forward with me as I am with her, but the fact that I can't reach her makes me feel this time things are different. That something is seriously wrong.

TR

I wake up to the light on and my laptop on the bed next to me. Grabbing my phone, I look at the time. 4:30. I reach over and turn off the lamp and go back to sleep.

When my alarm sounds, I get up, still irritated over last night. It's fate that's landing us in the same city on the same day. My phone rings while we're in the air. Taking the call at the back of the plane for privacy, I answer, "Hey."

"Hey," she says. "Where are you?"

"On the plane. We're landing in an hour or so. Where are you?"

"At the apartment where the photoshoot is taking place. Everybody is running around to get ready so I don't have long, but I wanted to see if you can meet after?"

"I can come by today." Without bringing up the photo specifically, I test the waters, "So other than the shoot, is everything all right?"

"You know I saw the photo. You know I'm not happy—"

"You know I didn't do anything wrong."

"I'm not saying you did." She releases a frustrated sigh. "I feel like something's off with us. I feel it in my gut."

I sigh. "Nothing is going on. I swear to you."

"She's after you."

"Who?"

Her voice dips into a sadness I'm not used to hearing. "The one in the picture. She wants you. I can tell."

Spontaneously, I laugh.

"It's not funny, Dalton!"

"What? You're being serious right now?"

"Yes, dead serious."

"I don't even know her," I say, feeling defensive.

"Then why does it look like you're about to hold hands with her?"

Remembering the photo, I reply, "I thought Tommy was behind me. He got our room keys earlier when he checked us in. I got it in the car since all the paps were surrounding us."

I listen to every sound she makes, analyzing the heavy breath she releases as if it will indicate where her heads at. She says, "This whole conversation bothers me, Dalton. This isn't what we do. All of the sudden I'm the jealous wife. I hate it. I hate feeling this way."

"I'm not going anywhere."

"Promise me you will always be faithful to me."

"I did, when I said I do."

She huffs into the phone. "Good point. You got me there." I hear her swallow hard. "I'm sorry for jumping to conclusions. Just know that in my heart, I didn't believe it. My eyes were telling me something else though."

"I know. It sucks, but I don't want anyone but you."

I hear Tracy in the background, and Holliday says, "Unfortunately, I have to go."

"I'll want to come by the shoot."

"I'll text you the address."

Still wondering how we got to this point and hoping to get past it, I say, "I'll see you soon."

Looking around, the street is fairly empty as I walk toward the glass and metal high rise building. A doorman opens the door and welcomes me inside. A security desk greets visitors. "Good afternoon, Sir. How may I help you?"

Dropping my stage name gets me every time, so I say, "I'm Johnny Outlaw. Limelight is shooting here today."

"Yes, Sir. You're on the list. You may go to the nineteenth floor. And Sir?"

"Yes?"

"Rock on, dude."

"Thanks. I will," I reply, saluting a peace sign as I walk past him. The elevator arrives and I ride up to the right floor. When the door opens, there are only two doors on the floor. I go with my gut and go right. My heartbeat picks up as I get closer. I knock once, but there's no answer. I can hear music on the other side so I'm guessing this is it. I open the door and walk in. I'm careful to be quiet just in case they're shooting.

I'm greeted by racks of hanging Limelight shirts with the logo, a table of accessories and another with underwear on top of it. I quietly walk around the corner where I hear the photographer giving direction. The apartment is modern in design and I catch a glimpse of the incredible view before I walk to the bedroom where the commotion is coming from. Beyond the equipment, there's a bed covered in a rumpled white blanket with Holliday wearing practically nothing on her knees facing the camera as some guy kisses her neck.

Everything goes red—my vision, my body—my anger flairs. Somehow through the anger, I keep my voice controlled. "Holliday!"

She turns abruptly, her hands against the guy's chest, pushing him away. Her hair makes her look freshly-fucked and falls over her shoulders as she quickly gets to her feet. Her arms wrap around herself as she tries to cover the bra and string bikini bottoms she's dressed in. *Is she covering her body from me?* Salt in the wound.

My eyes go back to him, the motherfucker molesting my wife. No shirt, messed up fucking hair, white boxers with the Bite Me Lime on them, and a punkass grin that might get his face punched in. When I see the boner he had pressed against my wife, I want to break him in fucking two.

"Dalton," Holliday says, reaching me. Her arms wrap around my neck, but I can't seem to return the welcoming. She leans back with concern on her face. "What's wrong?"

"You tell me."

"Is this about last night?"

"No," I snarl, my hands solid at my sides. "It's about what I fucking walked in on."

Her head jerks back in surprise, then she smiles as if I'm being ludicrous. "The photoshoot?"

"Why didn't you tell me it was going to be like this?"

"What do you mean? I told you it was for my clothing line," she placates.

I turn and walk around the corner, hating the prying eyes on us. I hear her footsteps against the wood floors as she follows behind. When we're alone, I fist my hands in front of me and keep my voice low, growling, "That guy has his mouth on you and his dick on your body."

"No he did not."

"He fucking did."

"I didn't notice."

Incredulously, I ask, "You didn't notice his dick against you?"

"Whatever. I'm nervous and not paying attention to him in that way. The camera is on us with people watching every move and angle, so I failed to notice his *dick*. He's modeling, pretending. Being paid to be here. Trust me, it's nothing more."

"I understand what models do, Holliday, but I don't like it and I don't like him. What I saw—"

"Well I don't like the videos you make," she bites back. "You have a different girl playing your 'girlfriend' when you're married. How do you think that makes me feel? How is that different?"

"You know it's different. You know how I feel about you."

"So you don't know how I feel about you?"

"I guess not if you don't mind some guy's dick on your body."

"You're out of line, Dalton."

"*You're* out of line! Why didn't you answer your phone last night? Were you with him? And where's your God damn wedding ring?"

The glare she sends me as she crosses her arms tells me how

this is going to play out. "How dare you!"

"How dare you!"

She pushes my chest. "Stop repeating what I'm saying." I grab her wrists, holding her close. She's strong, but doesn't move when she asks, "What do you think I'm doing here? Do you think I'm going to have sex with Sebastian while a photographer takes our picture? Is that what you're worried about? Cuz I'm kind of lost right now."

"Don't twist my intentions. I came over here to see you. I didn't expect *Sebastian* to have his hands all over you." The prick catches my eye over her shoulder. "Speaking of—"

"Holli, you all right?" Sebastian stands at a distance, smart enough not to come near. His stance solidifies to the spot as if he's staking some claim to be a part of this.

"You can fuck off. She's fine," I reply, dropping her wrists and staring at him.

"I'd like to hear it from her," he says, ballsy enough to stare me in the eyes.

I step forward, but Holliday stops me, her hands pressed hard to my chest. "Dalton, no! I'm fine, Sebastian," she calls over her shoulder.

Being the asshole he is, he laughs and says, "You should try a leash, Holli."

I push forward but she grabs my arm, hanging onto me. "Ignore him." I glare at the back of his head as he walks around the corner.

When I turn back, I ask, "Why didn't you answer? You almost always answer."

Her gaze drops to the ground, her hands fidgeting. She's lying when she says, "I was tired and left it in the bathroom without thinking."

I lift her chin to look me in the eyes. "Tell me the truth. Please."

We hold each other's gaze a moment before she says, "I was

The Reckoning

mad and hurt last night seeing that photo of you and *her*, but I didn't leave it there on purpose. I waited for you to call me back. When you didn't, I went to bed."

"So is this," I lift my arms up and out, and ask, "revenge?"

Shaking her head, she denies it. "No. this is not revenge. This is a photoshoot. I was just following direction. They want playful and sexy. That's the campaign. Just like when you film videos, I trust you and now I need you to trust me. This," she says, signaling around us, "is not real." The feel of her hands as soon as they touch my face calm the fury brewing inside me. "It's business. *Only* business."

She moves against me and places her head on my chest. We're so close I can feel her heartbeat and my breath extends, my agitation throbbing. I try to remember back to all the photoshoots and videos I've done. Not once did I hook up with the models after the director yelled cut. Not once, though I could have easily, time and time again. "I get how important this is to you. I understand this is 'business,' but because it's business doesn't mean I have to like it." Wrapping my arms around her, holding her tightly in my arms, I say, "I want to nutpunch him so hard that he'll never come near you again. I don't trust him, Holliday."

"You don't have to, but you should trust me."

I kiss her on the head, and whisper, "How is this fair that he gets to touch you like that and I don't."

Her arms come around me. "Your touch is real, it means something to me. He means nothing."

"I fucking miss you all the time."

"I miss you, too. More than you know."

I release her and step back. "I should go. I don't want to watch this. Call me when you're done."

Her hesitation is felt before she looks up at me. "Dalton, please."

I shake my head. "It's fine. You go do your job. I have stuff to do anyway. You go and call me later."

She knows when to push and when not to. She takes a step back and says, "I will."

I can't believe I'm doing this, but for her, I need to leave. It's business, I remind myself. "I want to see you tonight."

Looking down, she smiles before lifting her lashes up toward me. There's the woman I know. "Of course."

There's an unsettling distance still between us. But tonight, I have tonight to get us back on the same wavelength.

TR

When I close my eyes, I get lost in the melody of the song I'm singing. The world drifts away and I go back to that day, the day I lost my best friend, the day I lost the man I called my brother—not my brother by birth, but by choice. Cory Dean was my family and this song was my anthem to him.

My thoughts switch to Holliday. Most days, touring has lost its luster. When I'm away from her, fear blackens my insides, mimicking Cory's loss. My hands start shaking, wondering if I'm going to lose her too.

The large New York crowd screams when the drums and bass kick in, bringing me back to the present. It's a privilege to play Madison Square Garden and when I open my eyes, I'm reminded why. The crowd is loud and enthusiastic. New Yorkers have always supported us even when we were a small band that few knew. Releasing the microphone, I take my guitar in hand and join in at the chorus.

Johnny Outlaw is chanted like a river that runs through the audience toward the stage. I inhale the glory, letting it race through my veins, giving me life, giving me the jolt to give them what they want.

It's harder to get high from the adoration these days with so many ties bracing me to the lows. Letting my gaze drift to the first few rows, I see it, the want in their eyes, the way they crave me. They'd rip me apart if I let them... I've thought about it.

The song ends and I leave the stage as fast as I got on, needing to get away. No one should be loved that much. No one deserves that kind of attention, it feeds an insatiable ego that will never be satisfied.

"Short break. Three minutes. We're running behind," Tommy shouts.

There's a message waiting when I leave the stage during our break. "Hey," Holliday says on the voicemail. "We wrapped up and the gang is grabbing dinner. Call me when you're done. I want to go out and celebrate."

I grab a water and text her: *Going out for encore now. I'll call after.*

She texts me immediately back: *Love you.*

I hand my phone to Tommy as I wait to go back on stage. Dex is out doing a solo while Kaz and Derrick stand behind me. Reaching down for my guitar, I stop. "Where's my guitar?" I ask Tommy.

Before he can answer that new roadie girl is there with it in her hands. "You broke a string. We fixed it."

Perplexed, I look down at it not remembering breaking a string. "Thanks," I reply, taking it from her.

I put the strap over my head and start strumming, testing it.

"I'm Ashley."

Looking up, I see she's talking to me, though I'm not sure why. Tommy knows I don't make chitchat during a show. "Okay." Closing my eyes, I take a deep breath and exhale, wanting to take it all in, wanting to own the world in these last few songs. Dex hits the beat that cues our entrance and the three of us dash up the stairs. The crowd screams and I soak it in, not sure how much longer I have left living in the spotlight.

7

Holliday Hughes

*"It wouldn't be called reasonable doubt
if it was irrational. But somehow we always
find a way to ease our own conscience."*
~ Johnny Outlaw

"I love champagne," I say, holding up my glass.

"Apparently." Tracy's sarcastic addition earns her a glare and then a giggle.

I bring my glass to my lips to sip, then realize it's empty, understanding her sarcasm now.

Sebastian announces, "Another bottle."

"No, no," I say, stopping him. "We'll be leaving soon."

The pupils of his blue eyes are large, the alcohol affecting him.

His light brown hair is flopping down over his eyes. The gel that worked hours ago has given up. When he looks at me, I can almost see his inner thoughts exposed. He's suave with the ladies, but I remember what Danny warned me about him. Pointing an unsteady, slightly tipsy... maybe drunk finger at him, I squint and say, "I'm not falling for your act."

The devil himself creates the smile that appears on his face. He leans forward and whispers, "Oh really?"

"Really," I say, completely self-assured.

"Guess we'll see."

Shaking my head, I correct him, "There will be no seeing, no seeing at all. I'm a happily married woman."

"I find the women who say that are saying it as a reminder to themselves than a warning for me."

I stand up, taking offense, but my mind isn't in this argument. It's not worth the trouble. "I'm ready to go."

"Where are we going?" he asks, paying the large tab without hesitation.

Dropping my guard, I reply, "Somewhere fabulous I'm sure. Somewhere cool and trendy where I won't fit in at all." I laugh at my joke.

Tracy laughs too, but says, "Holli's one of those drop dead gorgeous looking women who has no true concept of how beautiful she is. It's quite annoying actually." Still laughing, she grabs my hand. "These photos are going to prove to you once and for all how gorgeous you really are."

With his little cheek dimples on display, Sebastian adds, "I have a hard time believing you have low self-esteem."

Tracy responds quickly, correcting him, "She doesn't have low self-esteem. She's just too damn down to earth to realize how attractive she really is."

The photographer, Gracie, now joins in a hardy laugh. "I think it's refreshing. She's a confident and beautiful woman who's not caught up on her looks. I see the appeal."

"Guys, you're making me blush. Let's not talk about me. Today was hard enough being in front of the camera. Those two shots of whiskey were needed." My phone buzzes and I check my messages. It's a message with a location from Dalton: *Blackout. I'll be there in twenty.*

Gracie says, "The photos are stunning. I think you're going to be pleased once I get them out of editing. I'll be in LA next week, I can have them ready and we can go over them."

"That'll be great," Tracy says.

Then Gracie asks, "Sebastian, what's your schedule next week?"

"I'm not sure," he says before finishing off his glass of champagne. "I'll message you tomorrow, but I can probably swing LA into the mix. We can have a party and go over the photos."

"Fun!" Tracy adds.

Leaning just slightly to the left, I grab a roll from the basket on the table and start eating. "I might need more food." Sebastian grabs another for me as we walk out. The heat of his stare warms me and I look over. His eyes lock with mine. Feeling embarrassed under his gaze, I look away after a few seconds, and say, "Let's go."

𝒯𝑅

Blackout is located in an industrial and grey converted warehouse. Lights flicker overhead as I walk through the large, open space. The music is loud and the DJ is on a stage in the middle of the dance floor. I have no idea where Dalton is in here, so I stop and tell Tracy. "I don't know where to go."

She lifts up on her toes, using my shoulders as leverage, and scans the place. "I think I see a VIP area in the far right corner. Follow me." She takes my hand and starts leading me in the direction she mentioned. Sebastian and Gracie right behind me.

Tracy's pace picks up and she says, "Over there." Swinging me in front of her, I see Kaz, then Tommy. A huge smile takes over because seeing Kaz and Tommy means I'll see my man.

I hurry through the crowded club and land right in front of a huge bouncer. I point. "I'm with them."

"Sure you are, sweetheart. Keep moving and take your friends with you."

"I'm married to Dalt... to Johnny Outlaw."

"Keep moving," he says sternly, crossing his arms.

As I'm pulling my phone out to text Dalton, Sebastian squeezes through and says, "Kace, what's up, man."

"Sebastian Lassiter, How's it going, man?"

"It's going. Chin deep in models."

"Tough life."

"Yeah, but someone's gotta do them... I mean do it."

The bouncer laughs and says, "Last time I saw you was with that model—"

"Not a model. She was Miss International."

"She was hot. You hit that?"

"Of course I did," he says, laughing, "disqualifying her from future pageants technically, but I promised to keep that a secret. Oops."

The bouncer laughs and they fistbump, then he lifts the red rope. "Come on in."

Once we're past security, I walk up two steps and past a louvered wall to the band's private area. Dalton is sitting in the middle of a U-shaped grey leather couch. He's pouring himself a drink from the bottle in front of him. Dex and Derrick are on one side of him talking to each other. Ashley, some other girl, and a guy I don't recognize are on the other side of him. I stand there staring, in shock.

When Dalton sits back, raising the glass to his mouth, he stops when his eyes land on mine. A smile that holds many secrets shows up and he stands. "Hey Baby." Then his gaze drifts, the lines of his mouth hardening.

Sebastian. Dalton spots him.

The people on the couch sit back as he steps over them, Ashley whining, "I want a drink."

"Why is *he* here?" Dalton asks, his lips touching mine right after.

"Why is *she* here?" I ask, tossing the jealousy back in his court.

He shrugs. "She understands band life, life on the road."

She understands him…

Taking a deep breath, I block her out reminding him that I know the real him, not just the persona he puts on. I wrap my arms around his neck and kiss him again, this time longer and harder. Tingles reach my toes and I sigh, content in the moment. The span of his hands cover my sides and I forget about everyone else. "How'd the show go?"

With a knees-weakening wry grin, he says, "The show was great. Great crowd and no screw-ups."

"That's good."

"What are you drinking?"

"Champagne. Too much I think, but I'm in the mood to celebrate."

"The photoshoot went well?"

"I think so. Tracy wouldn't let me see the pics. She said I'd get all self-conscious and bossy and that would ruin the vibe."

He chuckles. "Sounds about right."

His arm is smacked before he even finishes his comment. "Very funny. Now where's my drink?"

"Coming right up."

"I like you coming," I state.

He turns back to me amused. "How much did you have to drink already?"

Tapping my chin, I say, "A few... bottles, but who's counting."

"You sure you want more?"

"I'm sure."

He signals the waitress over and orders three bottles of champagne.

Leaning in again so he can hear me over the loud music, I say, "I want to introduce you to the photographer."

He nods and with his hand in mine, I guide him to the area close to Kaz and Derrick where she's hanging out with Tracy. "Gracie, this is my husband Johnny Outlaw," I introduce him by his public persona. Dalton's just for me.

They shake hands and Gracie says, "You have a beautiful wife. Very intelligent and she was great to work with."

"Did she take direction well?"

Giving him a hip bump, I say, "Ignore that. He's being pervy."

She laughs. "It's good to see a couple so sexually inspired."

"I'm actually feeling inspired by her right now," he adds.

My cheeks heat and I shake my head. "I think it's time for a change of subject."

Gracie leans in and says, "She was uptight at the shoot at first too. We had to loosen her up with some shots of whiskey." She laughs because she doesn't understand how touchy that subject is between Dalton and I.

His arm comes around my shoulder and I'm held to him. I wrap mine around his middle. He's in good spirits, so the conversation stays light even when his eyes land on Sebastian. "Yeah, we may all need some shots."

The waitress hands me a glass of champagne and I quickly start to drink.

The Reckoning

Dalton takes a gulp of his drink while eyeing him. "How was dinner?"

Tracy joins in, sensing we need to tread carefully. "We ate at this great bistro by The Park."

Leaning my head against his shoulder, I say, "The food was amazing. I was so hungry after being so careful for days. Did you eat?"

"I ate some pasta before the show and had a piece of pizza after."

Gracie starts telling Dalton how she'd like to take his photo or even do a shoot with the two of us when I'm tapped on the shoulder. I glance to my side to find Sebastian. "Hey, you gonna formally introduce us?"

I nod. "Yeah, sure." When Gracie finishes, I move so everyone is included in the group and say, "Hey Babe, I want you to meet Sebastian."

"Why?" Dalton chuckles.

"Easy now." That earns him an elbow nudge. "Johnny Outlaw. Sebastian Lassiter."

Sebastian reaches forward and they shake hands. Although I can feel how tight Dalton's body has gotten, by outer appearances, nothing has changed at all. Not impressed, Sebastian says, "The great Johnny Outlaw."

"We can save the pissing contest for another day. Tonight I want to celebrate."

"I think I've seen you before," Dalton says, starting to ease.

"My ex-girlfriend was in your last video. Blonde Sports Illustrated model named Yayla."

"Right," he replies. "I remember you broke up with her while we were filming."

"My girlfriend was making out with a rock star. Some men's egos can't handle that kind of competition. If I'd only known then that I'd be making out with your wife... Guess we can call it even."

He holds his glass up for a bonding toast and maybe a laugh, but Dalton doesn't move. His stare hardens, so I try to break the building tension. "How long do you want to stay?"

Ignoring me altogether, his focus remains on Sebastian. "It's funny how many people are threatened by a persona." His arm tightens around my shoulders and Dalton says, "As you can see we're happily married, so you broke up with her for nothing."

"Nah, she was fucking a guy from Europe's Next Top Model on the side. And between us, she wasn't a great lay, so it was no big deal. Now your wife on the other hand—"

It happens so fast—one moment I'm tucked under the loving arm of my husband, the next my glass flies from my hand and I land on the grey couch falling against Dex. Sebastian is pinned to the ground by Dalton, his hand firmly on his chest, the other about to pummel him. "Don't you ever disrespect my wife nor me or I will fucking end you."

Dex and Tommy are off the couch in an instant, grabbing Dalton off of Sebastian. "Let it go, Johnny," Tommy yells. "He's half your size."

"And a fucking punk ass," Dex adds.

All three men are standing while Sebastian begins to sit up. Gracie helps him to his feet and I jump to mine. When I reach Dalton, I plead, "Don't do this. Calm down."

With his shoulders back, his arrogance is seen in his smartass smile. His eyes are narrowed on me when he says, "See, I have self-control." He smirks and a laugh follows as his body relaxes again.

That is until Sebastian says, "When you're fucking her tonight, remember it was me who got her wet and ready."

A blur of fists flying and bodies rushing together sends me to protectively duck out of the way, turning my back. I'm grabbed by somebody and pulled back out of the way. Dalton descends on

The Reckoning

Sebastian as the band tries to stop the fight.

In the middle of it all, the prick of a thousand knives being stabbed into my back alert me and I turn around to find Ashley standing too close for my comfort. Tracking Dalton like prey, she says, "He could be the most powerful man in music." She's loud enough for me to hear over the commotion, but quiet enough to only be heard by me.

"He is now."

"I'm not talking about *one* of the most powerful. I'm talking about *the* most powerful. Without distractions, he could be king."

Is she referring to me? "And by distractions, you mean what?"

Her head turns, slowly and her eyes pierce me. As if she catches herself, a fake smile appears and she shrugs, then says, "If the shoe fits," and walks away.

Her words fill my body with anxiety. I can't lose him. *I won't.* The scuffle draws my attention back as the bouncer pulls Sebastian from the fight, taking him toward the front door. Dalton drags his arm across his mouth, leaving a bloody streak across his skin. I rush to him, but Tommy grabs my arm as Dex, Derrick, and Kaz barricade Dalton. "We're leaving." Tommy takes the tail, holding me to his side for safety as we head for the back exit.

Dalton climbs into a cab and the guys let me through to get in next to him. Tommy hops in the front seat and we take off down the alley. I look back and see the other guys getting in the cab behind us. When I turn back around, I place my hand on Dalton's arm, but he jerks away from me, and says, "Don't." The word harsh and pained.

Hurt bubbles up inside as I stare at him in disbelief. "Dalton—"

"Not now, Holliday!" he roars, filling the car.

Tommy turns back from the front and says, "Calm down, Johnny."

Stunned into silence, I scoot toward the door and look out the window. I'm not sure where we're going. Tommy gave the driver directions. Dalton lowers his voice and says to me, "We're not doing this in the cab."

My hands are now shaking and my heart is racing for all the wrong reasons. A tear slips down my cheek as the lights from outside flash by like sirens across my face. I'm sick to my stomach and wounded by how he's treating me, but I'll wait like he commanded for what seems to be building into the worst fight we've ever had.

Tommy exits the elevator at the hotel on floor seventeen. I remain quiet across the vestibule from Dalton, glancing at the button for our floor still lit up. The doors close and we ride in a torturous silence to the twenty-fifth floor. I wonder if he feels as sick as I do right now. It's hard to tell when he has huge walls barricading his emotions inside.

He waits for me to get off before coming up behind me and leading me down the hall to his room. The heavy door is opened and he keeps his foot and hand on it until after I've entered. Walking to the window, I look. The view is okay, but tension lays heavy, not only on my head but also on my heart, obstructing the view. I want to say his name and break the stifled emotions between us. I want to scream his name in fury for making me feel as though I've betrayed him. I want to slap him for implanting dread into the base of my belly. I want to hug him and make it all better. I want to kiss him and remind him who we are to each other. I want to whisper his name in caresses and show him what he means to me.

But I can't.

My feet are planted, my body exhausted, and my more stubborn side wants him to speak first. When he does, I instantly regret it.

"Holliday..." His tone is somber as he sits down in a chair across from a cream-colored couch. The pea green throw draped across it bothers me, briefly distracting me from his body language, which is breaking my heart. "What he said... Look at me. Please." When I build enough strength to look up, he says, "I need you to tell me what he meant."

"Dalton," I start, hating the plea in my own tone. "Do you really think I did something with him, that I would do that not only against our vows, but in front of a crowd and a camera?" His brow is furrowed as he seems to stare right through me. "Are you listening? I would never hurt you."

"You were drinking. Things happen."

"I had two shots. That's it. I didn't do anything." Having to defend myself like this twists my emotions, putting me on the defensive. "I can't believe you're saying this. After what we talked about this afternoon, after being married and making a lifelong commitment to you. I'm not one of your ex-girlfriends who fucks around behind your back. I'm your wife, the one who has been to hell and back with you, Dalton."

He stands abruptly and the motion makes me flinch. "I don't like what's happening with us."

"I don't either. You haven't just lost trust. You've lost faith in me. Why?"

He grabs a bottle of water from the silver tray on the TV console and opens it. Before he takes a drink, he says, "Things have changed between us and I don't like it. I'm fighting with you because I'm fighting *for* us."

"You don't have to fight for us. We're fine. We're together. We're all that matters."

"No, we're not anymore. I see the stories about you. I watch your interviews. Your company has grown a lot in the last two years. It's only natural you grow... or change with it. I don't want to be forgotten."

I sigh, relieved that he can confess such fears. I walk across the room and touch his chest. "You are unforgettable. You are everything to me. I will always love you, but just as important, I will always be faithful to you."

He leans down to kiss me, but Ashley's words echo in my ear—*without distractions, he could be king.*

8

"The world unravels like time—second by second, slipping like sand through your fingers." *~ Johnny Outlaw*

His mind is messing with him.

Dalton's tentativeness with me is felt in his light touch. I want him. I want him to touch me like he always does, like he can't get enough of me. I kiss his neck, my bare chest against his as we try to overcome earlier events. "Come back to me," I whisper.

"I'm here." His voice is distant, his eyes hold emptiness. I avoid the heavy and try to recover and reconnect. The fabric of his jeans is rough as I straddle him on the chair. Whiskey is tasted as our tongues mingle and the coarseness from the shadow of his beard pricks under my fingertips as I hold him close. Looking him in the eyes, I close mine and lean in to kiss him again. "Don't just touch me. *Feel* me, Dalton. I'm right here. I need you to touch me like you mean it."

"I do mean it."

Sex isn't going to solve our problems. We need to talk. Leaning back just a hint, I kiss the side of his mouth where it was split during the fight. "Does it hurt?"

"No."

"Was he hurt?"

"I fucking hope so."

When heaviness conspires to ruin our time, I smile while tilting my head. "Rest assured, he does nothing for me."

"He's a model. He's designed to do something to you."

"He's not you."

There's a flicker of life in his eyes, bringing him back to me. Our mouths come together quickly as he lifts me up and carries me to the large canopy bed. He sets me down carefully and pops the snap of my jeans. As the zipper is dragged down, his gaze travels over my body, taking me in. I slide my hands down over my hips when my jeans are removed, then up his to unbutton his jeans. With the fly open, he drops them and steps out. In only our underwear, we move up the bed and start kissing.

Kissing Dalton is sensual and always laced with more behind its innocence. His hand slinks between us and touches me over the lace of my underwear. Back and forth he rubs lightly. "Harder," I whisper, my resolve to take this slow abandoned along with my bra.

The pressure intensifies and I dip my head back to enjoy the sensation. My neck is met by his tongue as it drags up the length before his lips meet under my jaw and he sucks. If he wants to leave a mark, I'll let him, needing it as much as he does. Dalton sits up just as I'm about to give in entirely and lose myself. He's left me wet and wanton and that makes me snarky. "What the fuck?"

A God forsaken roguish grin slides into place as he takes the sides of my panties and asks, "Do you want to keep these?"

I know better than to pause when we play these games, but I do anyway just to prove a point. "Last chance," he warns, no smile to be seen.

"I'll take my chan—" My thong is ripped from my body before I finish speaking, the burn on my sides, stinging with desire.

Dalton is direct in his wants and when his head goes between my legs, I know he wants to please me. He's always been amazing about more than satisfying my needs first. A light pressure spreads my legs further apart as his hands warm the insides of my knees. The heat of his breath hits my sensitivity and I squirm while gripping his hair between my fingers. "Babe…"

His hand goes flat over my stomach, holding me in place while his mouth makes love to me. I want to scream, wanting him deeper than he can go… "Fuck me, Dalton."

He continues for a second, then looks up. "I want to finish."

"I can't take it. I need you inside me!" Boxers are discarded and he's above me positioning himself within seconds. When he sinks inside, my eyes close and my mouth opens. "I missed you. I missed this."

Kissing my neck, he sighs as the sensation strikes him causing him to exhale heavily. "I miss you, all of you. All the fucking time."

"Soon," I say, "we'll be together again, soon." Our bodies move slower than before as we begin to make love. Each kiss caresses my lips and my heart equally. His love flows through my veins giving me life as our bodies slide against each other's until he's panting against my collarbone, begging for release. It hits him hard before hitting me and we fall together.

We lie there a minute or two, maybe three before I whisper, "Dalton?"

"Yeah?"

"Even when we're falling apart emotionally, we find our way

back physically. But I want you to know that we're more than sex."

"We're infinite."

"Yes," I repeat, "infinite." With my arm over his chest and my leg across his, I realize we really are infinite. Our love has no boundaries. "There is no beginning to us—"

"And no end. We're infinite. Always." Our fingers entangle together and I close my eyes.

But then I sit up suddenly. "Hey," I say getting his attention. His eyes are tired, his expression matching as he yawns.

"What?"

"I have a flight in the morning."

"Stay."

"I can't. I have to pack and I have a dinner meeting with a greeting card company tomorrow night."

He tugs my arm and I give in, falling down next to him. His body maneuvers over mine and he says, "But I want you to."

"I wish I could. I want to..." I close my eyes, feeling guilty denying him the only thing he asks of me. "I can't," I whisper, a slight plea heard and I open my eyes. "I rescheduled once already when the shoot got pushed."

"It's almost three in the morning." There's a resolve in his tone that I've gotten used to lately. He doesn't try as hard anymore, knowing I can't drop everything for his schedule. I hate it. It makes me feel terrible. He asks, "You want to go back to where you're staying?"

Resting my chin on his chest, I say, "I have to. We're leaving for the airport at eight."

He moves over and sits, then drops his feet to the ground and stands. Shaking his head, he mumbles, "One day our lives will sync."

"One day." When I get out of bed, I add, "You stay and get some rest."

"I'm not sending you across town in a cab at three in the

The Reckoning

morning by yourself. I'm coming with you."

"Is the time of day the only reason?"

His eyes, the green seemingly darker than usual, land on me. I stop and sit on the end of the bed, waiting to hear what he has to say. He looks down mulling his answer before he speaks. "You think I wouldn't leave this life for you, as if you're second to a life that feels greater than it should be. But I would. I would for you. So the time of day really has nothing to do with it."

He doesn't have to say anything more and knowing him, he probably won't. He's made his feelings known so he won't drag it out for the sake of it. I watch as he gets dressed, in awe of his ability to not just say what I need to hear, but to make my soul feel his love. "I love you."

"I know."

I scoff through a wide smile and stand up to get dressed. "Leave your ego behind, Han Solo."

"You're very good with the trivia."

"That line from Star Wars is very memorable."

"How about me?" he says, twisting my hips back and forth.

I touch his nose. "I couldn't forget you even if I wanted to," I tease. "But luckily for you, I don't want to."

A sweet kiss is given before he says, "We should get going."

We walk into the apartment thirty minutes later. I lead him to the bedroom and we go about getting settled in. I'm about to get undressed, but before I have time to put on pjs, I'm distracted by Dalton. He's standing in front of the wall of windows staring out. His voice is calm and deep, fitting for the early morning hour. "I've been working on a song."

"What's it about?" I whisper not wanting to disturb the tranquility.

I climb onto the bed and under the covers, sitting and bringing my knees up to my chest. "We're surrounded by people all the time, but some days, I feel isolated, alone."

"Touring can be a lonely endeavor. You're with your friends, the band and crew, but you're away from the ones you love."

His head goes lightly to the window when he leans against it. "I have everything everyone wants in life."

"What about you?"

"What about me?" he asks, peeking back at me.

"Do you have everything you want in life?"

Standing upright, his shoulders full of pride as he looks back out the large window. "I have an amazing life."

"Are you telling me or reminding yourself?"

"Both." He sighs, the weight of the world suddenly burdening him. "I've been thinking about taking a break..."

"A break from music or from the band?" I ask, hating that I only seem to have questions instead of reassurances for him.

He looks over his shoulder and I can see the conviction in his eyes. "I can't live without music."

I suck in a quiet breath, my heart stilling until I finally exhale. "Do what makes your heart happy, Dalton."

"I know one person who makes my heart happy." The weight of our words seem to have disappeared. His hair is messy, his shoulders relaxed, and a grin that few people ever get the chance to see turns up the corners of his mouth. This is Jack Dalton. No pretenses or personas. JD from Elgin, Texas. "We could leave all this behind and disappear for a while." His eyes are lit up as if that's a real possibility.

But running away from a company I love doesn't sound appealing. "I like what I do. I'm good at what I do. I can't just run off and leave it."

He looks away. "I was just kidding around anyway." I can tell he's hurt, but I don't know how to fix his pain. I want to see that small town, all-star smile again. Leaning back against the

The Reckoning

headboard, I watch, enjoying his many different sides. He's the most complicated man I've ever known. I guess my expression gives me away because he asks, "What? What are you looking at?"

"You."

He cocks his head to the side and grins. "You want me to do it, don't you?"

I do so badly. "Yes." I bat my eyelashes.

Pretending to be put out, he rolls his eyes and then fastens his jeans. "It's only because you're naked under those covers and so fucking hot that I'll do this for you. You know that, right?"

"I know," I reply easily, putting on an act of my own like this isn't the best ever. He starts to get into position, but I interrupt and request, "Without the shirt please." His low chuckle makes me giggle as I sit up for a better view.

"Without the shirt it is."

The T-shirt goes flying, hitting me in the face. I pull it down over my nose and inhale, then cough. "Ew, this one is dirty."

"No shit. I haven't had my laundry cleaned this week," he says, laughing.

"Fine. Message received loud and clear. I'll send some clean shirts."

He winks at me. "Thanks."

"You know... if I didn't though, that might help keep the groupies away."

"Believe me. A dirty shirt won't deter a determined groupie."

My sagging shoulders kind of say it all. But he touches my chin, tilting my head up to look at him again. "We're infinite. Remember that."

With his tattoos on display, my eyes trace over the hard lines of his chest, his defined arms, and land on that V made of muscle and hours of working out. Following it down, I land on the top of his jeans, then look back up at his eyes. "You ready?" he asks.

I nod.

His hands go to the floor, his body in push-up position. His feet slowly start to come up off the ground. Stopping at just about a thirty degree angle, I exhale louder than I like. "Amazing," I say, admiring him. His body is perfection, his tattoos cradling muscles that beg to be touched.

His feet drop suddenly and he pops up. Clapping his hands together, he says, "Was it good for you?"

"Orgasmic." Standing up to stroke his ego... and his hard muscles, I slide my hands over his shoulders and around his neck. With a kiss to the skin under his jaw, I whisper, "I've never wanted anyone as much as I want you."

"What makes me so special?"

Moving my hand downward, I take his in mine and place it on the curve of my naked waist. "Everything," I breathe.

I'm swept up in his arms as we move across the room. The light is low in the room, the blinds wide open, the floor-to-ceiling window our destination. Leaning against a small wall that juts out about a foot, I angle my hips forward until I'm pressed to him and we're kissing.

Sex in the window is daring, but I'm not worried. We can't be more than figures, silhouettes to any onlookers. Sliding his hand from the side of my face down my body, he grips my hip and says, "Turn around."

9

"Charm and a bad sense of humor only get you so far. After that, you have to give them something real." ~ *Johnny Outlaw*

I should sneak out. I really, really, really should. But when I look at him all wrapped in the covers instead of me, my heart starts to ache and I go back. Climbing back in bed with him, I kiss him lightly on the cheek, then whisper, "Dalton?" His arm comes around me, pulling me close. "I've gotta go, Babe."

"I'll see you," he says, still mostly asleep.

"Soon," I reply and place another kiss on his cheek, this time lingering a moment longer.

When I stand up, I walk out without looking back. If I look back, I'll stay and I have to go.

Tracy and I are standing at the airport counter. While we wait in the security line, she asks, "No coffee this morning?"

"I didn't have time to make any before I left."

"We can get one before we board. How did last night turn out?"

"Like all my nights with him."

"You always speak so vaguely when it comes to you guys."

"No I don't," I reply. "I only tend to do that when he's touring and things are… strained."

"So you admit you do it?" She moves her suitcase up as the line goes forward and I follow with mine. When we stop again, she says, "I'm sorry things are strained. Do you want to talk about it?"

We scoot our luggage forward again. "When Dalton tours, he changes. He's divided, having to play two roles. It takes him longer to come back to me, to be who he is when he's home. You'd think I'd be used to it by now." I laugh without humor.

"I imagine it's difficult for him to play a role for the public and slip back into who he really is. Last night at the club was intense."

"Sebastian crossed a line, with him and with me. What he said was inappropriate and to say that to my husband, even more so."

"Guess he learned his lesson."

"Dalton's jealous streak is well documented, but he still shouldn't have hit him."

"Sebastian got a hit in too, but I agree with you. This might not be good for our campaign."

A security agent calls her and the other one calls me. Once we're through, we're sitting on a bench putting our shoes back on when I say, "I'll make sure the campaign is a success." We grab our bags and head for our gate.

"You have the details for the dinner tonight?"

"Yes. Spago at seven."

"Look at you, fancy pants. All Spago-ing like the power players."

Laughing, I say, "Oh yeah. I'm a real power player all right."

"I think you're more powerful than you think. If you're not, we're doing it wrong."

"I'd like you to come, Trace."

"Can't. I have dinner with Adam and two of his bosses tonight. They don't call it an interrogation, but they're basically trying to figure out who to promote into the Jr. VP's role."

We stop in line at the coffee stand on the way to our gate. My phone buzzes with a text. When I pull it from my purse, it reads: *Infinite.*

Smiling, I type: *Infinite,* and push send.

"What is it?" Tracy asks.

"Mr. Complicated himself. He just texted me." Looking at my watch, I see it's just gone nine. "Guess he just got up."

"Where do they play next?"

"I don't even know. I'd have to look it up. But they're staying until tomorrow because he has meetings today." Thinking about what he told me last night about giving it all up, I start to wonder how it will affect the meetings he has with the label, a new producer, and his interview this evening. Worrying about him is part of caring about him, but he might just have to work this one out on his own, figure out his own direction.

We order our coffee and step to the side after paying. I dump two packets of sugar into mine and three creamers. While stirring her own coffee, Tracy says, "If I'm being honest and I always want to be with you, I can see the change in you when he's not around." I look up briefly, but avoid her eyes, wanting to hide from the truth a little longer. "I know it's hard, but you need to remember who you are, Holli, and hold tight to that."

"Maybe I like who I am better when I'm with him."

"I know you do. I don't live in your shoes so I'm not going to claim I fully understand the situation." We start walking to the gate. "I can't even imagine life without Adam or how you survive for weeks on end without Johnny home with you. But you need to. I didn't want to say anything, but you can't be all things all the time. You need to get your head in the game. You need to be present."

"I am. I'm here when I'd rather be back in bed with him."

"But that's what I mean. You need to *want* to be here."

"Like you said, you don't understand what it's like," I snap, feeling defensive. We reach the gate and I find two chairs and sit down. And I do what I hate doing—I sulk. I do it because it's early and I'm tired, but also because I know she's right.

She nudges my arm. "I still love ya."

"I love ya too." And like that, all's okay again.

TR

Spago is busy, but it's Wednesday, no surprise—prime wheelin' and dealin' night of the week. I see at least four A-list celebrities, two C-list, and several recognizable movie directors as I'm lead to the table. Cliff Sorden and Jason Halstrom from the card company stand when I arrive. I greet them both by shaking their hands, saving the Hollywood cheek kiss for the movie industry types.

I sit down and Cliff holds up his glass. "We ordered champagne."

"Great." I pick up the glass in front of me. "Are we celebrating?"

"We hope we are. We want your lime."

"If you said that over tequila, you might get slapped," I joke.

Jason says, "That's what we want. We want your humor and that lime. Together, this line of cards is going to be huge." He taps his glass against mine as does Cliff.

The Reckoning

I sip, then say, "I've got a small line of cards already. How will this be different?"

"You get free reign," Cliff says, "the brand is ready to go in a new, contemporary direction."

Jason adds, "No curse words, of course."

"Of course," I say.

"But from there, we're ready to give you a wide berth on creativity..." While Jason is talking my eyes drift behind him. A man with shoulder length brown hair, six-three, broad chest and an outfit that's appears professionally styled is walking toward our table. I know who he is before I even make eye contact. Kiefer Keys—my ex-boyfriend.

My knee starts bouncing as anxiety strikes. I didn't date anyone for months after I caught him in bed with my hairdresser. For months, I lost trust in men and faith in humanity.

"Holliday Hughes... or is it Outlaw now?" he asks with an arrogant gleam in his eyes. His voice rises at the end like he's suddenly British.

"Mrs. Outlaw will do," I say straight-faced, not as happy to see him as he seems to be to see me.

Laughing as he works his way around to my side, he ignores Cliff and Jason and leans down to kiss my cheek. I don't return the greeting. "I've missed your spunk."

"I can't say the same. This is a business meeting, Todd."

"It's Kiefer, remember?"

"Ahh, right." I struggle to call him Kiefer. I knew him back when he was Todd from Missouri. He changed his name to land commercials. It worked for a while, then he formed a band that's had some success. Since he remains standing here, I feel obligated to introduce him. "Cliff Sorden and Jason Halstrom, this is Kiefer Keys."

Cliff shakes his hand excitedly. "I'm a big fan. I saw The

Mattresses two years ago in Cincinnati."

Kiefer nods his head and I roll my eyes. Kiefer says, "Thanks. We're rolling out a tour in a few months. Make sure to come out."

"I will. Thanks." Cliff looks at me and asks, "So how do you know each other?"

"College," I respond just as Kiefer says, "We used to date."

Instantly annoyed, I shift uncomfortable in my chair. I don't want to do this with business associates. Kiefer says, "I inspired her lemon."

"Lime," I correct.

"Right. Lime."

Jason says, "Oh really?"

"Long story." I stand up. "Please excuse me for a minute." They both nod as I speak to Kiefer in a hushed tone, "C'mon."

"Gladly."

I head for the exit, weaving my way through the restaurant and out the main door. After putting some distance between us and the entrance, I cross my arms and ask, "What do you want?"

"You're so hostile."

"Yes, call me bitter, but the last time I saw you, you were fucking a friend of mine."

"She was your hairdresser, not a friend."

"We were roommates."

"Okay, fine. You were friends. I didn't think you were that close. Anyway, I'm not here to discuss her."

"Why are you here?"

"I was having dinner with some guys from the label. I heard your boy is talking to producers. You know I do that?"

"I don't know anything about you, Todd."

That makes him laugh sardonically. "For the record, if I could change what I did, I would."

"For the record, it doesn't matter what you would do if you

could because you can't, so what's done is done."

"I loved you."

My arms fall to my sides and I sigh. Looking down, I bring my bottom lip in and scrape my teeth across and releasing while I think about what I want to say and how. "Look, I cared about you. A lot. That's what hurt so much."

"I apologized back then. I'll apologize now. I'm sorry. I screwed up. You were the best thing I had in my life and I fucked it up. I'm sorry."

Seeing the sincerity in his eyes, I say, "Thank you." He hands me a business card. "What is this?" I look down and read it. "Since when do musicians start carrying business cards?"

"Since the band announced the next tour is their last. We're breaking up. I'm producing now. I'd like to work with The Resistance."

I hand the card back to him, offended this was all a ploy to get to my husband. "Then you need to talk to them. I can't get you an in."

"You can. You just don't want to."

Shrugging, I say, "Maybe that's it too, but I don't make band decisions or even have a say, and I'm not going to start now."

I walk around him, but he takes my arm, stopping me. "I bought you a ring." My mouth opens and he says, "I was going to ask you to marry me, but I had a breakdown. I freaked out inside. We were twenty-one. Way too young."

Freeing my arm, I look down as old hurt comes back like the boyfriend who once stabbed me in the back. I shrug, shaking my head. "It doesn't matter now."

"It matters to me that you know the truth."

"The truth doesn't matter anymore."

"Does knowing I still have the ring?"

"Knowing you still have the ring just makes me sad for some

reason." I glance to the door and back to him. "I need to go. That really is a business meeting, an important one, that I need to return to."

"Okay."

I start to leave again, but this time I stop and turn back. "Thank you for telling me the truth. I lied before. The truth does matter."

He nods and I turn back around and go inside.

When I sit back down at the table, I see Kiefer join his party in the corner. While I make my apologies to Cliff and Jason, I watch him down his drink, pretending that what just happened didn't affect him like it did. I still know him well enough to see past the pretenses.

The waitress arrives and I order the special. From time to time, I can sense Kiefer watching me, but I keep my eyes on my dinner companions. We talk about the extensive line they want to carry from Limelight and wanting me to endorse it with an ad campaign. I drink the one glass of champagne but no more. I like to be alert when discussing business. By the end of our meal, I say, "No numbers have been mentioned. Do you want to talk about it or would you prefer to send something over this week?"

"Let's enjoy dessert and we'll send the numbers over this week," Cliff suggests. "How did your photoshoot go?"

"It went well. The delay was hard to work around and we lost some key elements, but I think we more than made up for it."

Jason asks, "Have you modeled before?"

"Not professionally. I've done some stuff with the company as the face of Limelight, but this was different being a model in the campaign, playing a role, and taking direction."

"Does your husband play an active role in the company?" Cliff asks.

"No. I started it years before I met him. I'm living my passion and he's living his. We're both fortunate to be able to do that."

The Reckoning

"Any plans for kids?" he asks, making me uncomfortable.

"One day," I answer. My tone is clipped, though I didn't mean it to be. "I should probably get going." I look around for the waitress, but I don't see her.

Jason says, "Dinner's on us."

"Thank you. It's been a really nice evening." I stand with my purse in hand. "I look forward to working with you. Hopefully we'll get the finances in order so we can make that happen."

Jason stands and takes my hand. "It was a very nice night."

While waiting on the sidewalk for the valet to pull my car around, Kiefer comes out with an unlit cigarette hanging from his mouth. He smiles and pulls the cigarette from between his lips. "Meeting went well?"

"Yes. It went well. Did you have a nice dinner?"

"I did." He lights the cigarette and inhales deeply. "I always knew you'd do well."

Smoke circles above his head and by the kind smile, I'm almost convinced he might not be that bad. "Thank you."

"Not only a successful businesswoman, but married to a superstar. Impressive. How'd you two meet?"

"We had a one-night stand in Vegas." I smirk, cocking an eyebrow up. "That led to two nights and phone calls, trips to see each other and lots of great sex."

"Apparently," he says, taking my bluntness in stride. "You were always beautiful, Holli."

That wipes the smile from my face, making me suddenly feel shy under his attention. "That's very nice of you to say."

"Yeah, I wasn't all bad then, but I'm different now."

Stepping closer, I lower my voice so only he hears instead of all the valet drivers. "You weren't that bad. But when you were... that was hard to get past."

"Well I'm single if you ever want to hang out," he throws the offer out so casually.

"That's not gonna happen, but I appreciate the offer."

"Understandable." He tosses his half-smoked cigarette to the ground as my car is parked in front of me. "Maybe our paths will cross again."

I don't try to reassure of him or make niceties over a future get together. I'm glad tonight happened though. It's good to put your demons to rest. I say, "Take care of yourself, okay?"

He doesn't say anything. Instead, he nods and watches as I tip the valet and climb into the driver's seat. In my rearview mirror, he stays where I left him, watching as I drive away.

I'm exhausted from the whirlwind week and it's only half over. I want to climb into bed when I get home and sleep for days. It won't be the same without Dalton, but I'm hoping to find sleep fast anyway. I need to call Tracy and update her, so I do it while I'm driving. The Bluetooth connects and she answers, "Hey Hols, how'd it go?"

"We have a deal if we want one," I reply.

Her voice goes up an octave. "That's fantastic! Great job. I knew you could do it."

"I don't know if I did anything. Seems they already had made up their mind before I got there."

"The brands' success sold them on the product. You sealed the deal."

Leaning my head back, I smile as I drive. "Do you remember Kiefer?"

There's a long pause, then she asks, "Your *Ex* Kiefer?"

"The one and only. He came over to the table. We went outside and talked."

"About?"

"About our breakup. And he wants me to hook him up with the band. The Mattresses are breaking up after the next tour.

He's producing now."

"What the hell?"

"It was all weird and brought up those old angry feelings I used to have, but then it was... I don't know, okay. *I* was okay."

"You're in a better place. That's why."

Dalton pops into my head and I smile. "It's funny how seeing an Ex can remind you how good you have it now."

"Sometimes we have to go through the bad stuff to get to the good stuff."

"I guess so." I turn down a street and slow for a stop sign ahead. "Anyway, I called because I wanted to share the good news about the deal. Let me know if you see anything come through. I'll see you tomorrow."

"We have a busy day, so be ready."

"I'm ready. I'm going home and going straight to bed."

She laughs. "Yes, get some rest. It's been a crazy few days. I'll see you tomorrow."

"Bye."

"Night."

10

"Your mind will play tricks on you even when your heart tells you otherwise." *~ Johnny Outlaw*

My eyes slowly open. Five forty-five in the morning and I'm awake. Seven hours sleep must be my max. I look toward the patio door. It's dark outside, but a slip of moonlight is streaming in. Lying there motionless for a few minutes I let the fog clear from my brain and reach for my phone on the nightstand.

I don't have the energy to tackle my emails yet. My inbox gets flooded overnight by overseas emails, but I do check my texts. I have two—one from Dalton and another from Rochelle.

I read Daltons first. *I fucked up.*

My heart sinks. I flip back to the main messages and then to his again hoping to find out what he means, but there's nothing else. No other texts. *What the fuck? How can he send me that and nothing else?* I feel sick to my stomach. I know he won't pick up his phone this early, so I pop out of bed and run down the stairs to the kitchen and grab my laptop. I open it at the bar and start searching, typing *'Johnny Outlaw'* into the search bar.

Pages of results show up, but the top three are from yesterday and three hours ago. I click the first titled, "Johnny Outlaw on Going Solo and Being Single."

I brace myself, trying to block the bile filling my mouth. My hands start shaking and the article pops up—the interview he had yesterday. "Shit, what did you do, Dalton?" I quietly ask myself. I start rapidly reading the article looking for his responses. I come across this, *'Being married has changed my perspective on life. My priorities have changed.'*

Interviewer—*You've never talked openly about your marriage. Last week you brought Holliday Hughes onstage with you. So you're changing your stance on this? She's changed you?*

'She has made me realize my true priorities.'

Interviewer—*What does that mean for the band?*

'It means I'm considering all my options.'

Interviewer—*You might go solo or quit?*

'Music isn't a hobby for me. It's more than a career. Music saved me. Music is a part of me, like an organ that pumps and thrives, keeping me alive.'

I continue reading the article.

Outlaw downs his fourth shot, so I down my third having trouble keeping up with the brooding musician. Casey James' "Let's Don't Call It A Night" comes on the jukebox. The small country-themed bar is buried in the middle of Manhattan and over the course of the last hour has a few more customers. This dark corner offers protection from Outlaw's enormous fan base and he seems to appreciate that fact.

He speaks in riddles and often doesn't answer at all. For

The Reckoning

someone that the world seems to know everything about, I get the distinctive feeling that we actually know very little about him. I've danced around his personal life though it's a topic that endlessly fascinates the media and the world. Maybe that's because we don't know anything about it.

Interviewer—You're a different man from the last time we met. Yet I don't feel like I know you any better than back then.

'When was that?'

Interviewer—Three years ago before the Grammy's.

He looks around. When he turns back, he says, 'That was before the band change-up.'

It was back when Cory Dean, the lead guitarist and much beloved member of The Resistance died in a plane crash, leaving two young sons and a fiancée behind. Outlaw has been very vocal about how much this tragedy affected him. By his body language, it is still a source of discord for him.

Interviewer—Do you get along with the new members?

'Yeah.'

Switching tactics, I return back to the man himself.

Interviewer—How do you really feel about fame, Johnny?

'Fame has no substance. It's a word, something people use to categorize you. There's this misperception that fame equals happiness. It doesn't. It doesn't hold that kind of power. It can give you glimpses of happiness, but there's no solid foundation in it.' The lead singer leans forward and I can tell how passionate he is about the topic. I've touched a nerve. 'Your family, your friends, your art—those have substance. Those hold value and weight over your soul. Losing fame isn't a loss. Losing a friend is.'

Interviewer—You're referring to Cory Dean?

'I'm referring to people and things that matter.'

Interviewer—Your fans may take your reaction as ungrateful.

'My fans know where I stand and how much I care about my

music and them. I won't be drawn in to defend my stance on something that glorifies failure. That's what fame does. As soon as you start to lose fame, you're considered a failure. I've got a history I hope one day becomes a legacy. There's no failure in my accomplishments.'

Interviewer—No, there's not. You're legacy already exists.

Two of the newer members of The Resistance walk in with a woman I don't recognize. She calls Johnny and the guys signal for him to leave. Johnny stands and thanks me. He pays for our drinks and says maybe we'll catch up in LA later this year.

Interviewer—I'd like to. I'll set something up.

'Thanks. Have a good night.'

I watch as the group disappears out onto the streets of New York wondering how far this, using a term he seems to despise, famous man will get without being recognized. Although this interview, like the last one is shorter than I'd like, I've learned that he has changed in many way from three years ago, but the mystery still remains.

Not sure what to make of this, I stare at the screen. Getting up quickly, I hurry back upstairs and grab my phone. I see Rochelle's text still waiting to be read and open it. *Call me after you read the interview. I'm worried about Johnny.*

I doubt she's up. Looking at the time, it's just gone six, but I text her anyway. *I just read it. I haven't talked to him yet. I'll call you after I do.*

Next, I call Dalton. I don't care what time it is. Closing my eyes, I stand next to the bed holding the phone to my ear. Groggily, he answers, "Hello?"

"Dalton, it's me."

"What's wrong?"

"You tell me."

"What do you mean?"

The Reckoning

"You sent me a text that says you fucked up." I can't contain the strain in my voice, my nerves getting the best of me. "What happened? How did you fuck up?"

A female voice in the background, sounding tired, way too relaxed, says, "Hang up, Johnny."

My heart stops, my fingers losing hold of the phone as my soul loses grasp of my world. The phone falls from my hand as I run to the bathroom. Flipping the seat up, I'm hunched over heaving until my body rids itself of the poison of my former life. I roll back and lie down on the cold marble. My thoughts are spinning too fast to keep up and my stomach is churning from the pain that my husband has fucked up and fucked our life.

Standing up, my knees go weak and my hands need something solid to hold onto. I lean on the counter and grab a washcloth, wet it, and dab it to my face. The cool water feels good despite how numb the rest of my body feels. I brush my teeth and go back into the bedroom. My phone has several missed calls from Dalton on the screen even though I never hung up. Guess he did and called back.

But I can't. I can't talk to him right now. Just as I set the phone down on the nightstand, it buzzes with a text from him—*call me back.*

Fuck you!

Then it buzzes again. This time with a text from Rochelle—*call me when you can.*

I call her back because I'd rather talk to her than sit here for the next few hours letting the fact that my husband is fucking another woman run rampant through my mind.

"Hello?" she answers.

"Rochelle..." the name doesn't even fully leave my mouth before I burst into tears.

"Holli, honey, what's wrong?"

"He's cheating on me."

105

"What?" The word spikes in her throat. "What do you mean? How do you know?"

"I just," I start to say and sniffle, "called him and I heard a woman in the background."

"Uh!" She gasps as if she can't comprehend what I'm saying. "Holli..."

After she pauses, I pick up the conversation with, "I know."

"I feel sick."

"I was sick. I just threw up."

"Holli, I'm in shock right now. I know the band had a meeting in his room last night. Tommy called me to say I needed to get Rory on an interview he'd just done because he seemed different, drunk and sad. I know you left yesterday. Did you leave on a bad note?"

"No, we were good. More than good. I, uh..." I start to cry again.

"I'm coming over."

"You don't hav—"

"I'm coming. Okay."

"Okay."

"Holli?" Rochelle calls from downstairs.

I roll away from the door and don't answer. I'm sick of crying and emotionally exhausted.

"I have good news." I feel her cozy up behind me and hug me. "The whole band was there, Holli. He wasn't alone with any woman. It was their equipment manager Ash—"

Facing her, I say, "Ashley. I'm very familiar with her."

"See? It's nothing. They were just meeting and partying all night."

We both sit up and lean against the headboard. My eyes burn from the tears. "In New York, she told me without distractions, he could be king, Ro."

"What does that mean?"

"She insinuated that I'm distracting him from his potential."

Rochelle's eyes are fixed on me in disbelief. "That's bullshit. She actually said that?" Scoffing, she adds, "He's at the top of his game and owes a lot to you being by his side, so don't let her give you doubts."

"Since when does the crew hang out with the band?"

She understands why I'm asking, but still doesn't sugarcoat the facts. "They don't normally."

"Normally," I repeat in disgust. "I read the article. She was the one with Kaz and Derrick who got him out of the rest of the interview. He didn't really know who she was when I was there and suddenly it's like they're old friends."

"I... I'm not quite sure what to say. But I talked to Tommy on the way over and Johnny was never alone with her. Derrick was still there when he checked on him. He said Johnny was flipping out because he couldn't get a hold of you." She grabs my phone from the other side of me and says, "I think you should call him."

"I don't want to. I can't..." I turn away from her and wipe at my eyes.

"You owe him that much. Just like he owes you his side of things."

"Everybody owes everybody something," I remark disgruntled. With a huff I take the phone from her and call him.

He answers on the first ring. My name rushes from his mouth panicked, "Holliday? What's going on? Are you okay? I almost called the police."

"Dalton..." I say between quiet sobs that have risen at the sound of his voice. "Is *she* still there with you?"

"Who's *she*?"

"Ashley?"

He sighs. "Fuck. Is that what earlier was about?"

"I don't like her, Dalton. I don't want her around you anymore."

"She was here to discuss Derrick's acoustic."

"She got you from the bar. I read that. I read the interview. You sent me a text that you fucked up, then I hear her calling your name at three in the morning from your suite," I say.

"This has been twisted. Nothing happened. I swear to you."

"Then why did you text me that?"

"Because I fucked up the interview, I said things I shouldn't have. I drank too much. He kept asking about us. It was setting me off."

"You scared the shit out of me and broke my heart at the same time. I've been puking I was so sick over the thought of you cheating on me and worse, leaving me."

"I'm sorry." With the phone to my ear, I look back at Rochelle. She gives a faint smile, but I drop my gaze to the duvet and start crying again. He says, "Talk to me, Baby."

"I feel so stupid."

"We're in a tough situation. You got jealous just like I got jealous of that model. It puts a strain on our relationship, but I don't want that. I don't want you upset or jealous. You can trust me. I promise you."

"Dalton?"

"Yeah?"

"I can't tell you to fire her, but I don't want you near her. I don't want you hanging out with her. She's trying to come between us."

"You're thinking too much into this. She's the Equipments Manager. That's it."

"Please. For us."

"She's nothing to me, Holliday."

"You're not going to fire her, are you?"

My eyes meet Rochelle and she shakes her head and whispers,

"He can't. It's not that easy."

With a heavy sigh, he repeats, "She's nothing to me."

He's not frivolous with his emotions. He doesn't love easily. The text... I think he was searching for reassurance that he didn't fuck everything up. For him, *for us*, I need to push down my feelings regarding her and deal with the fact that she's not going anywhere anytime soon. I take a deep breath and exhale. "The interview is fine. It's not what the band wants to hear, but you didn't disrespect them. If they bring it up, talk to them like you're talking to me. Be honest with them."

"Dex is gonna be angry. Tommy is going to be furious with me."

"Let them. Hear them out, but let them. Just don't make any rash decisions. All right?"

"All right."

I hear him yawn on the other end of the line. Thinking of his schedule today, I glance at the hour again and say, "Get some sleep. You need it for the show tonight and I need it."

"I'll call you later." We hang up without goodbyes, sick of that word anyway. Our business may be left unfinished, but we're both too tired to continue the fight.

When I fall back on the pillow, I peek over at Rochelle. She has the I-told-you-so expression all over her face, but she doesn't say it. But I don't mind if she does. "Go ahead," I say.

Snuggling down next to me, she says, "I don't need to. I'm just glad you guys were able to talk."

"Me too."

11

"My whole life has consisted of me taking chances. Why change now?" ~ *Johnny Outlaw*

I find my solace at the beach. Sitting down in the sand, I kick off my flip flops and dig my toes in, covering them. The waves crash gently along the shoreline, the tide low. Wrapping my arms around my knees I rest my chin on top of one of them and stare out into the distance. My dark sunglasses hide my puffy eyes. This morning was a shitstorm waiting to happen.

My jealousy.

Dalton's jealousy.

It's explosive and I'm surprised it hasn't collided before. Distance creates insecurities that didn't exist before.

I hate that.

"I thought I'd find you here."

It's the voice that feeds my soul. The voice that sings my life's melody. The man that makes everyday worth living. I turn around and find Dalton standing there in all his handsome glory. There is nothing ordinary about this man. Nothing that blends in. No one that compares. He makes my heart race and my blood flow. He's my everything.

"Wanderlust?" I ask, my heart fluttering.

"Nope." He smiles and it's one of my favorites—the one that I go to bed with when his mind is quiet and his heart is full. It's also the one I wake up to—content, peaceful, full of love.

"In the neighborhood?"

"Nowhere near." He squats down next to me, looking ahead.

I smile because how can I not? He's here. For me. "Just a coincidence?"

"Completely on purpose." He takes my hand and helps me to my feet. With his arms wrapped around my waist, he says, "Hate to be a dick..."

I burst out laughing and drop my head to his chest. "I'm sorry for assum—"

"No sorries, remember?" He holds me tightly to him.

"I don't want us to be jealous. I don't want us to lose trust."

Stroking my cheek, he says, "We're better than that."

Leaning back, I look into his eyes. "Are you gonna just stand here all day or are you gonna kiss me?"

"I'm thinking kiss."

I lift up and close my eyes, waiting for the moment my lips get to touch his again... and wait... and wait. When I open my eyes, he's grinning. "Well kiss me all right already," I say with a slight pout.

He cups my face and comes in really close. With his lips just about touching mine, he whispers, "I'm not gonna rush it. I'm going to savor the taste of you."

My lids drop closed in an instant, my anticipation built, but this time I don't have to wait. This time, the fullness of his lips press pillow soft at first, then with pressure intensifies as our lips part and our tongues meet again. This time, the world swirls around us, the waves beating heavy in the background to the song our connection creates. When we part, I suck in a staggered breath of air and slowly open my eyes in awe that he can still sweep me off my feet so easily.

"Fuck!" I wince from his curse. Dalton grabs my hand and starts pulling me to the sidewalk. "Walk faster. We've been spotted."

"Where?" I ask, looking around.

"Two lenses near the ice cream cart and one on the beach to the right. Don't give them anything."

I look down while fighting the urge to seek them out, to spy on them like they're spying on us. Once we reach the sidewalk, we walk twice as fast. "Are we going to my place?"

"No. We're getting in the car and going home." His voice is as tight as his hand's grip.

"What if we didn't?"

He glances over at me. "What do you mean?"

"What if we didn't run? What if we went about our day? What if we lived our lives?"

"I don't want to see my life play out in the media."

"I don't want to always hide."

Stopping suddenly, I halt abruptly at his side. My eyes go up to meet his. That line between his eyebrows is present as he looks at me perplexed. "So you want them to take photos of us, put captions under them that have no basis in reality, and watch as they rake in money from selling their stories to the public?"

"No. That's not what I'm saying. I," I say, then let out a heavy sigh. "I just want to live our life and not always be on the run from the paparazzi."

He rubs over his jaw. As if too exasperated to argue, he says, "Fine. What do you want to do?"

"I want to walk down the beach with you."

The intensity disappears from his face and a small, fractured smile appears, and we start walking. "I guess when it comes to stalkers my instinct is get out of danger. But we can do that. We should. It's beautiful out."

"It is, even more so with you here. How are you even here?"

He chuckles. "Travel day. Show's tomorrow." Stopping at the edge of the water, he peeks over at me and says, "I wish I could give you what you deserve."

Stepping closer just to be near him, I ask, "What do I deserve that I don't have already?"

"A life full of walks on the beach."

Leaning my head on his shoulder, his arm comes around my back holding me close. "You've given me more. You've given me you."

TR

"Do you want to come to dinner with us?" I call from the closet.

"Nah, you should go," Dalton replies.

I peek out at him lying on the bed. "I'd like you there. You can leave for your flight straight from the restaurant."

Relenting, he says, "Let's go be seen."

Laughing, I clarify, "It's not about being seen. It's about not having to hide all the time."

"I get it. I don't think it will end the way you want, but for you, I'll do this. I'll give it a fair shake."

"Thank you," I reply, going back into the closet.

His warm body cradles around mine and I smile.

He asks, "How long 'til we leave?"

"Thirty."

"I should really go shower, but being in here kind of makes me wanna fuck."

"Is it the shoes or the clothes that turn you on so much?"

"It's you, Baby. No doubt. Always you."

Giggling I say, "I thought I did a pretty thorough job earlier."

"It's the last time we're together for a week."

Turning around, I start to push him back into the bedroom. "You're insatiable! Now go shower so I can show off my hot husband tonight."

"I don't need to shower for you to do that."

"No, you don't. But it would be nice since this is a business dinner."

He walks into the bathroom, but yells, "Do you always have so many business dinners?"

"I have a lot when we're launching new campaigns and products. Most of the time it's lunches or meetings at offices."

I hear the shower start. "What's tonight's meeting about?"

"A video game based on the Limelight fruit."

"Cool."

Thirty minutes later, he loads his duffle bag into the trunk and we leave for the meeting.

We park the car once we arrive and walk into the darkly lit Italian restaurant. "Hughes, party of four," I tell the hostess when she asks to check us in.

"Right this way," she says, and leads us through the main dining room to a smaller one with only four tables in it. We're seated in the corner and given menus while we wait for the other two guests.

We're not left waiting long. The marketing manager for the video game company, Laurie, introduces me to the Director of Programming, Nelson. I introduce Dalton and he says, "I'm just Mr. Hughes tonight."

That garners a good laugh and makes me feel good to have his support. Over dinner they present their ideas and Nelson explains how it will work with the game play and the visuals. Enthusiastically, I say, "It sounds amazing. I've had the app for almost a year now and it's sold incredibly. What do you project for sales based on your current marketing plan?"

Laurie says, "I think we can hit eight million copies in the first year with the right pricing, retail backing, smart marketing, and a great game plan in place."

"From here, if I decide to move forward, the next step is ironing out the contract details."

"Yes," she says.

"You have both put a lot of work into this and brought it to life, making it easy to imagine. I think I'd like to move forward. It sounds fun, and fun fits the brand."

She exclaims, "Fantastic!"

Dalton touches my leg.

"I'm excited," I say, looking at him.

"I need to leave," he says. Standing up, he adds, "My apologies for ducking out, but I have a flight to catch."

After the goodbyes, I walk outside with him. I lean against the car as he grabs his bag out. "Don't look like that," he says.

"Like what?"

"Like the sun won't shine again."

"It doesn't shine the same when you're gone."

"It's all clouds and rain in my world too, but it doesn't change the facts."

"Let me just pout a minute more. Okay?"

Chuckling, he leans against the car, trapping me between his arms. "You look so damn cute like that, I'm inclined to let you."

Toying with his jacket, I bat my eyelashes. "You know what would make me smile?"

He looks up from his watch. "We don't have enough time for me to go down on you right now."

I hit his arm. "Noooo! I didn't mean that, though yes, that would make me smile. I meant a kiss on my lips... on my upper lips."

"I like that you have to clarify."

"I only have to clarify because of your gutter-mind."

"Eh, why bother hiding it."

"Yeah, don't ever hide those thoughts. Maybe we can Skype and act out those thoughts."

"Now that sounds like a plan."

I grab him by the jacket and pull him as close as I can get him. I kiss him, then say, "You need to go or you'll miss your flight. We'll finish this later."

He kisses me again. When our bodies part, I leave my eyes closed a moment longer not wanting to watch him walk away from me again. When I reopen them, I think he feels the same. His eyes slowly open and a small wicked grin sneaks onto his lips. I ask, "What?"

"I haven't told you how proud I am of you."

I squeeze his hand, in awe of his sweetness. "For what?"

Eyeing me then looking down shyly, he says, "For everything. I think you're a brilliant woman and you don't take my shit."

"You mean I keep you in line."

"I wouldn't go that far, but I want you to know I respect you. You hold us together while running this growing empire. It's impressive. *You're* amazing."

I tear up. "Really?"

"Look, I know I get all the glory, but you're damn fantastic all on your own."

Smiling ear-to-ear, I reply, "Thank you. That means a lot to me." Dalton doesn't do sappy long when he does do it, so to end his torture, he turns his back to me and walks over to the waiting cab he arranged before dinner.

Still leaning against the car, I continue watching until the car turns out of the lot and I'm left alone again. As I walk inside, my heart hurts and I wonder how many more goodbyes I'm going to have to survive over the next year. My heart is breaking little by little with each one and I worry that one day there will be nothing left of it.

I return to finish the dinner meeting before going home and falling asleep on his side of the bed.

Dalton was right.

The iPad was set down on the desk in front of me with the headline "Holliday Hughes and Johnny Outlaw on the Rocks."

I sigh, hating that his point was proven and so fast.

Tracy says from behind me, "We can spin this into a positive for the underwear campaign."

Spinning around in my chair, my face contorts in horror. "What? No. I don't want people to think my marriage is on the rocks."

"Business aside, why do you care what people think?"

Her question makes me stumble over the thoughts rambling through my mind. "I, uh… I don't care, but I care if it's wrong."

"Look Holli, as your friend, I know this is hard to deal with. I feel bad. I know you and Dalton are great together, but you know what they say, 'No press is bad press.' So maybe you can use this in some way."

"I don't want to use my marriage like that. I don't want to see my relationship as trashy fodder at the checkout stand."

With her hands up in the surrender, she says, "Take a breath.

The Reckoning

You don't have to. I was just playing devil's advocate. That's all."

"I didn't even want to be in this campaign and now it seems that's all everyone is focused on. Don't forget I'm an actual person, not just an underwear salesman."

She picks the iPad back up and starts to leave the office. I shouldn't have griped at her. "I'm sorry. I'm snippy. I don't mean to be. I appreciate you looking at the situation from all angles. Thank you."

"You're welcome. And I'm here if you need to talk. Oh, and Gracie called. Can you meet tomorrow at six to go over the photos? She suggested The Polo Lounge."

I nod before getting back to work.

Lying in bed later that night, I scroll the sites looking for tidbits on Dalton. I'm not sure what I'm looking for exactly—incriminating evidence, support of his love for me, or just to see what my husband is up to in life since I don't know firsthand. But no matter what, I feel dirty doing this, stalkerish, and shut the laptop down.

I'm going to have to go back to what I used to do and ignore the media when it comes to him, the band, and myself. I have to trust in us and trusting in us means, I wait for him to tell me directly.

When I wake up in the morning, I feel refreshed for the first time in ages. Calmness has come over me. That feeling that always bonded me and Dalton has returned. I've shut off the world and all the rumors. The jealousy seems to have gone once I relied on my faith in us instead. I missed this feeling.

Sitting up, I reach for my phone and text Dalton: *Good Morning.*

I don't hear from him for another hour. I've been working at the kitchen table when I read: *Morning.*

Me: *Morning. Where are you?*

Dalton: *I have no idea.*

Chuckling, I type: *Where you headed?*

Dalton: *Clueless.*

I look at his schedule on my phone, then type: *Atlanta tonight. Orlando tomorrow.*

He doesn't respond right away, but when he does, I feel all the need in his words because I'm counting the days too. *Twelve days 'til home.*

"Twelve days 'til home," I repeat as I type: *Sounds like a song.*

My phone rings. "Hi," I answer. "Just so you know, it's only home when you're here."

"I've been thinking about us a lot lately. We're caught in this cycle and we need to break it. I don't want to fight with you anymore and I don't want you sad."

"I'm losing myself to this life."

"Don't let it control you."

"How do you control it, Dalton? Tell me. How do you do it?"

"Take each day as it comes. I mean, you asked me where I was and I still don't have a fucking clue though you just told me. I'm lying in a room in the middle of a city. By the H on the pillow I'm thinking at a Hilton or Hyatt. But I'm okay with not knowing. It just doesn't matter because we played an amazing show last night to a sold out crowd. So I'm doing my job."

"I bury myself in work."

"Bury yourself in what makes you happy cuz you never know if you'll get this chance again."

"Chocolate makes me happy. I could bury myself in chocolate."

That makes him laugh. "I'd like to see that... and taste you." Changing the subject, he asks, "Working today?"

This time I laugh. "Do you really want to know about this boring stuff?"

"It's not boring to me."

My heart skips a beat from his sweetness. "I have to go over the contracts with the greeting card line and tonight I'm seeing the photos from the campaign we shot in New York. I can only imagine the touch-ups required."

"You fuck amazing... I mean you look amazing to me."

"Ha ha, Romeo. There are rumors of a billboard. I might be twenty feet tall, so yeah, I hope I look good."

"Billboard or no billboard, you'll always be hot to me."

"Awww thanks, Babe."

A low groan is heard from his end of the call and he says, "I should get going. It's a travel day."

"Hit the road and call me if you get bored."

"I will. Now get your ass out of bed and don't forget about me."

I laugh in response. "Love you."

"Love you."

I like waking up this way a lot better.

12

"Fame is a double-edged sword. You think you want it until you have it." ~ *Johnny Outlaw*

Traci and I walk into The Polo Lounge exactly on time though typical LA traffic tried to make us late. Gracie is seated and waiting for us.

After our greeting, we sit and order a bottle of wine. We're one bottle in when Sebastian saunters to the table. "My apologies, ladies."

I keep my eyes down while turning the stem of my glass nervously around between my fingertips. I'm not sure how to feel about him or what he thinks of me since the fight in New York.

He sits next to me and says, "How are you Holli?"

When I look up, I go with polite, "I'm good. And you?"

His light blue eyes pierce mine. His voice is raspy with all the insinuation of the world backing him. "Sorry, I'm late. I was tied up." He coughs. "You know how that can be."

"I have no idea what you're talking about."

One side of his mouth slithers into place as he watches me stir in my chair, uncomfortable with this conversation. He whispers, "Sexual experimentation, Holliday."

My full name slipping from his lips feels wrong. I feel the heat rising over my cheeks. Changing the topic, I ask, "Are we ready to order?"

The intensity of his stare hits me like a Mac truck. "I know what I want."

Looking away, I rub the back of my neck, feeling self-conscious. I'm saved by the waiter arriving to take our order. "I think I'll have the apple and fennel salad and the tortilla soup please," I say.

Gracie and Tracy order before Sebastian. Letting my eyes drift in his direction again, I watch him as he peruses the menu. He looks up, busting me. "I've got quite the appetite tonight." Glancing to the waiter, he says, "I'll have the burger and we'll need another bottle of the wine."

Once it's the four of us again, Gracie says, "Let's look at the photos. I think you're gonna love them."

"Why am I nervous?" I ask excitedly.

Sebastian smiles. "Nothing to be nervous about. You were great. Very sexy. Better than most models I work with."

"Thanks," I reply shyly.

The photos are laid on the table and we each take one. I stare at the one in my hands, almost unable to recognize myself in it. Not because it doesn't look like me, but because I look so good. "Gracie... this is amazing."

Traci says, "Look at this one. This one has definitely made the short list and I haven't even seen the others."

We trade photos and my mouth drops open. My head is back,

The Reckoning

my eyes closed. Sebastian's mouth is on my neck and his hand on my waist lifting the Bite Me tank top ever so slightly. I see what I couldn't see in the moment. This is pure sex and Dalton saw this live and in person. No wonder he got upset. I would flip if it was him. I can't even watch some of his videos because of how he has to act with the girls in them.

I feel terrible and look away. Setting the photo back down, I finish my wine.

"What's wrong," asks Gracie.

My eyes meet Tracy's briefly. She knows me too well and offers, "Bathroom break?"

Nodding, I set my napkin down and walk with her. Once the door is closed, I try to contain the panic building inside. My voice is harsh, the words commanded, feeling like I will lose everything if I don't nix these photos. "We need to talk about this, Trace. Those pics, they look real."

"They are real, but that doesn't mean what the camera caught was real."

"If Dalton sees those—"

"Deep breaths, Holli. They're photos. Everyone knows that ads and movies are fake. No one is gonna think you're cheating on your husband. So don't freak out over this. They are exactly what we wanted and you two together—Wow, so hot."

They *were* hot. *Too hot.*

Shrugging, she says, "It's acting. Everyone knows it's acting."

"Exactly." Wanting to reaffirm it to myself, I say, "Everyone knows that."

"Don't stress. It's a good thing. Okay?"

Words are lost in my crazed thoughts, so I nod again. She leaves, but I stay a moment longer to collect myself. While applying lipstick, I look in the mirror, remembering how great I looked in those photos. Despite how sexy the photos appear, it's a much needed self-esteem boost. Stretching my arms out, I take a deep breath and slowly exhale while lowering my arms again. We created exactly what we were trying to accomplish. Now I have to get my head back in the game. This ad campaign is going to kickass. Walking out, I run into Sebastian.

"Hey," he says, gently taking hold of my arm.

"Hey." I look into his eyes that seem to be filled with more intent than concern for my well being. Not wanting to go any deeper with him, I nod and say, "I'll see you at the table."

His grip tightens just enough to keep me there, but not enough to make me nervous. He says, "I'm here for a few days. Maybe we can spend some time together."

"Why?"

He shrugs. "Why not?"

"I'm married, Sebastian."

"I didn't ask to have sex with you," he says with a wink. "Unless that's still an option, then I'm asking."

My back hits the wall as I back away. Stunned by his crudeness, I say, "There's no option whatsoever."

"He sure does have a lot of control over you. Does he make your business decisions as well?"

I glare at him, then turn to leave.

With a loud laugh, he says, "I'm teasing you... I only meant two associates discussing business over lunch or a drink."

I look back toward the tables and reply, "I can't."

"Why?"

"Because we won't be working together anymore," I state flatly.

"He's really possessive of you." He releases my arm.

When my eyes meet his again, I say, "He has that right. Just like he had the right to be upset over your inappropriate comments in New York."

"I don't blame him, but don't blame me for trying."

The Reckoning

"What were you trying to gain by saying that?"

He looks around and the way he shifts appears to be more of a swagger, his arrogance coming out. "He's smothering you and you don't even see it."

"Actually it might be the reverse. It's me who can't seem to live without him."

Sebastian seems to ponder this before speaking. "You're an amazing woman, Holli. I hope you don't forget that."

"I won't. Neither will my husband." I walk back to the table.

When I sit down, Tracy says, "You're flushed. Are you feeling all right?"

"No, actually. I'm not. I think I should leave."

"The waiter's coming with the food though." My bowl of soup is set down in front of me. Tracy adds, "Maybe you need to eat something. I know you get cranky when you're hungry."

"Maybe that's it," I reply absently.

I must look worse than I think because her hand touches mine and she whispers, "Are you okay?"

"Does Sebastian have a girlfriend?" I ask.

Gracie is quick to answer with an amused grin, "Sebastian has many girlfriends."

"I hear my name," Sebastian says, coming from behind me and sitting down.

Tracy says, "We were talking about your photos—"

"And your girlfriends," interrupts Gracie.

His eyes flash to mine. "Interesting, but for the record, I don't have a girlfriend."

I pick up my spoon and start eating, needing this awkward tension to be gone. Tracy chimes in, "So, Holli, we were thinking out of the twelve here that three of these are top contenders for billboard, print ad, and packaging. What are your thoughts?"

I kick into business mode, and reply, "I think they're stunning.

They're sexy and intense. Gracie did an incredible job."

Gracie muses, "I had great models. I'm glad we captured everything you were going for the first time."

Keeping my eyes on her and away from the man burning holes in me, I say, "Me too."

A lot of dinner is spent with Sebastian's words rolling through my head on repeat. I glance over several times, but look away just as fast. I don't get him. I don't understand his need to pursue something he'll never have. But it goes back once again to what Danny said about him. It's not about me. It's about acquiring something unattainable. *The chase.*

When dinner is done, the ladies talk about ordering dessert and more drinks, but I'm done. I've had enough discomfort for one night. "I think I'm gonna head out. Two glasses of wine is enough for me."

Tracy leans back. "I'm gonna hang out a bit longer. Adam said he would come get me if I wanted him to."

I stand and hug Gracie, then Tracy. "Be safe and don't party too hard."

"I won't," she says. By how she's giggling she might already be past that point.

Appearing to be the perfect gentleman, Sebastian stands and says, "I'll walk you out."

"That's okay. My car's with valet."

He walks around quickly to pull my chair the rest of the way out. His tone is straight, but polite. He's driving me crazy with his different moods. "No worries. It's my pleasure."

He's persistent. "Okay," I reply, not wanting to make a big deal out of it.

On the way out, he asks, "I really do hope we get the chance to work together again, Holli?"

"We have no reason to work together again."

Conspiratorially, he leans close to my ear and whispers, "Then we'll have to come up with one."

"Like I said before, Sebast—"

I'm grabbed and he leans in to kiss me, but I turn just in time for his lips to land on my cheek. Pushing off of him, my hand goes flying toward his face. "Sebastian, don't!"

But he blocks me just before I land the slap. Taking my arm, he moves it down and with a smirk on his face, he says, "Sorry. I just find you so damn irresistible."

Irritation bubbles over and I jerk my arm away, then snap, "Is it me or the fact that I'm married that you find so irresistible?"

"*You*, Holli. All you."

I close my eyes and shake my head. When I reopen them, I demand, "You can't do this. This flirting or whatever it is. It won't work on me, so just stop. Okay?"

With his arrogance on full display in his grin, he says, "Okay." Backing up toward the door, he adds, "But man, we would have been great together."

I give my ticket stub to the valet guy while Sebastian disappears into the restaurant. My stomach feels unsettled and I lean against the wall to wait for my car. Danny was right about him. Sebastian Lassiter can't take a hint or a flat out rejection.

As soon as I get in the car, my phone connects to the Bluetooth and I notice I missed a call from Dalton. Looking at the time, I think he might be done with his show, so I call. After four rings my call goes to voicemail. Disappointment replaces my earlier discomfort as I drive home.

Walking into the house, I drop my keys on the table and my purse on the floor. I slip off my shoes and walk to the back doors and slide them open. It's a beautiful night. The moon is big and bright reflecting off the pool. Flickers of light dance across the surface as I sit on the edge and dangle my feet in the warm water.

When I lie back I can see forever tonight. Every star seems to have escaped the clouds, smog, and the city lights to show me the world outside my thoughts.

A ringing disrupts the tranquility. I hope it's Dalton, so I run back inside to answer it. "Hey," I answer out of breath after I see his name on the screen.

Dalton's voice is scratchy moving into hoarse. "Hey."

"How was the show?"

"Good." He sounded like he was going to say more, but instead there's an uncomfortable pause. I hear him breathing, shuffling around, but not saying anything. The butterflies in my stomach stall with concern. Just when I'm about to speak he says, "Hey Holliday?"

"Yes?" I whisper, feeling the need to match his more serious tone.

"If anything bad ever happens—"

"Don't talk like that, Dalton."

"Just hear me out. If anything bad... just know, you were the best thing that ever happened to me."

Gulping heavily, I keep my reply in the present, trying to keep him here with me. "You are the best thing to ever happen to me." Trying to soothe my emotional state, I ask, "What happened tonight? Do you want to talk about it?"

"Life is too fucking short for our own good."

I move back outside and resume my spot under a blanket of stars to calm my trembling heart. "You're scaring me."

"No need to be scared. Just thoughts I've been having." I hear him blow, sounding like he's exhaling cigarette smoke.

"Are you smoking again?"

"I am." It should comfort me that he doesn't even bother to lie, but it doesn't when it comes to this.

"Why?"

"Because I'm weak."

"No, you're strong. So much stronger than you know."

"I'm weak without you."

"You need to remember I'm always with you just like you said you're always with me." I hear him blow out again before what sounds like a squeaky chair being pushed to it's limits. I ask, "Where are you right now?"

"My hotel balcony."

"Is the night as clear as it is here?"

"No, but I can see some stars."

"I wonder if they're the same ones I see."

"Our bodies are stardust in the air. I left you when you should have been the one to dare. Your beauty haunts me for the stars can't compare. The morning light gave us a new reason to care."

I close my eyes and inhale his words, letting them engulf me wholly. Dalton sounds tired as if that took all the effort he could afford to give. "That's beautiful. Lyrics?"

"It's a song I've been working on."

"I'd love to hear the melody."

"It's not fleshed out."

"I don't mind."

There's another light screeching noise and then I hear his door slide open. "I'll play it for you."

Going inside while he retrieves his guitar, I head upstairs and lie in the middle of our bed, and get comfortable. When the first notes plays, I silently lie in the dark, the notes drifting through me. His voice is rough, but caressing as he blends with the melody. I find security in this, the deepest of emotions bleed through his guitar for only my ears across three-thousand miles.

I'm cold, so I shuffle under and snuggle the blanket around me. This is peace and comfort. With my eyes closed and my mind still heavy from sleep, I lie there listening. He asks, "Want me to sing you to sleep?"

In my mind, I can see the way he tilts his head when he smiles at me, the spark in his eyes when he looks at me, and hear him over the phone, his voice calming our storm.

This is the man I fell madly in love with.

"I'd like that." And even though he'll never see it, I smile as his melody becomes the blood in my veins and the lyrics the beat to my heart.

13

"Humility is admirable, but rarely achievable when living in the public eye." ~ *Johnny Outlaw*

I wake up in the morning with a huge grin on my face. My heart is happy and life is good. The only thing that could make it better is if Dalton was home. I've got to see him soon—one way or the other.

But the twenty texts I have waiting on my phone wipes that happy delirium away in an instant. My world comes crashing down and I find myself struggling for breath. Dalton, Rory, Rochelle, Tracy, Sebastian, Tommy, my mother. Multiple texts from each, all with the same headline and photo…

Holli Hughes Leaves Johnny Outlaw for Hot Model.

Dalton's text is first. My heart clenches when I read it: *Call me.*

His second: *What the fuck, Holliday! Call me now!*

His third: *Why is your phone off? Are you with him?*

His fourth: *I love you. I loved you so fucking much.*

His fifth: *Call me.*

I call him not caring about the other texts or what they have to say. Holding the phone to my ear with a shaky hand, I pace across our bedroom. I don't give him a chance to speak when he answers, "I would never cheat on you. You believed *them*?" My anger replaces my nerves.

"I believed what I saw."

"Well that's perfectly convenient for you, but what you saw was a photo taken at a perfectly misconstruing angle, Dalton. How dare you! After all the pictures I've seen of you over the years. How dare you believe what you've always told me not to! You just assumed the worst... the worst of me, your wife, the person you committed your soul to—"

"I was sent that photo when it went live at four in the morning. Imagine how I felt when I saw it."

With my hand on my hip, I stop, now even more annoyed. "And what were you doing up at four in the morning anyway?"

"I wasn't. I was sleeping. But people love to share bad news. So maybe I wasn't thinking clearly when I first saw it, but what the fuck were you doing with him? Why were you at dinner with him after what he said to me, after what he did to you? That fucker has some nerve."

"It was a business dinner. Nothing more."

"Your business needs to stop including men that want to fuck you."

I gasp, shocked that he has the nerve to turn this around on me. "I did nothing wrong, Dalton, and I won't apologize. You told me that you woke up to that photo, but I woke up to your texts. How do you think those made me feel?" Exhaling my exhaustion, I say, "I can't deal with this right now. I need to go."

He's firm, his voice threatening, "Don't hang up."

"I don't want to talk about this anymore."

"Don't do this, Holliday."

"I don't want us to say anything we'll regret and I'm close, so I'll call you when I've calmed down."

"I'm sorry." His words are hurried. His tone is suddenly regretful, the defensiveness gone.

"I'm sorry too." Delivered with a flatter tone, my apology comes for a whole other reason than his. I'm sorry this happened. I'm sorry he lost faith. I'm sorry that I can't stay and talk this through with him.

He could be king.

The words haunt me and I'm afraid they will eventually tear us apart. My beating heart pounds, aching in my chest, but I hang up anyway.

Standing at the patio door, I open it and step outside. With the phone still in my hand, I start to wonder if he'll call me back or let this settle before attempting to talk again. Smog is covering the tops of downtown LA in the distance, ruining the view. I should be used to it, but it feels ominous in the moment and stands out.

Hours pass and the phone never rings. By two o'clock I almost expect to see him walking in the front door, but that can't happen with him on tour. But Rochelle does come over.

I answer the door, sluggish and defeated. "I'm fine. You didn't need to come over."

Walking past me, she says, "Obviously I did since you never responded to my texts."

I follow her to the kitchen table where she sets her bag down. She turns to me and asks, "What's going on, Holli?" Her tone is calm and understanding, in complete opposite of Dalton's this morning.

"It was a kiss to my cheek."

"I knew you didn't kiss him. But it looks really bad."

"I can't control how it looks." With my arms crossed, I lean against the archway to the breakfast room.

"Have you talked to Johnny?"

"First thing this morning—"

"How'd that go?"

"How do you think that went?" I move to sit in a chair at the table, feeling too weak to keep my defenses up.

"I think he freaked out."

"Ding. Ding. Ding. You win the prize."

She sits in a chair across from me. "Are you okay?"

"Not really. He always told me not to believe what the tabloids post, to talk to him before jumping to conclusions. But he did exactly what he told me not to. He basically accused me of fucking Sebastian Lassiter."

Reaching across the table, her hand covers mine. "Being on the road is difficult for musicians. They're gone for long periods of time and have the world thrown at their feet, including women. Add in their own insecurities with the loved ones they leave behind and it can be downright ugly. But, being the one left behind while they live out their dream is even harder. I know. I've been on both sides and it sucks. Musicians don't win. Significant others don't win. The fans win. It's the trade-off that's given for living that dream."

"It sucks."

"Yep, it plain sucks, but you guys have worked through press stuff before. I believe you can again if you both give each other the support you need to share your fears and concerns. You have to stick together through this kind of stuff. You have to keep on loving each other, but more importantly, you have to continue to trust each other. Johnny wouldn't cheat on you. He's never been the type, but with you, I know he never would. I know in my heart. As for you, I know you well enough to know that you aren't that type of person either."

The Reckoning

"I told him I needed to calm down before we spoke again."

"Are you calm?"

I nod.

"Don't wait then."

I bite the inside of my cheek, then agree. "I don't want him hurting."

She stands and takes her bag in hand. "Then tell him."

Taking a deep breath, I exhale slowly. "I will."

"I have to go. I need to pick the boys up from school shortly." She walks to the door, but stops and says, "Holli?" I turn toward her and she adds, "Love each other as much as you can. Time is fleeting." Rochelle walks out, shutting the front door behind her.

Her words are like a slap of reality. Time is precious and I don't want to waste another second. I run upstairs and grab my phone from the dresser and call him.

"Hi," he says tentatively.

"I love you. I would never cheat on you."

"I know."

"You forgot."

"I wasn't thinking about you," he says. "I was thinking about him and knowing what he wanted to do."

Sighing, something I feel I do too much of lately, I gather my thoughts. "Babe?"

"Yeah?"

"It doesn't matter what he wanted to do, I'd never let him or any other man for that matter do anything that would break my vow to you."

"These magazines and gossip columns, they're in the business of selling sex to get people to buy their stories. That's the bottom line. I get it. But that doesn't mean that every so often there isn't a grain of truth to be found. I've watched marriages break up after tabloids exposed their issues. The truth of the matter is that I don't want any fuckers touching you. Sorry, if that feels like a double standard. That's how I feel. Period."

"Okay, that's like all ego and pride. The real bottom line is you are going to have to trust me."

"I trust you."

"But? I know there's a but coming."

"But I don't trust those assholes and I never will."

I smile. "Fine. Don't trust them, but don't take it out on me then."

"Deal."

Slowly, we find our way back to each other despite the miles separating us. "If you must know," I say, "You're my dream come true."

"Good thing you're mine since we're stuck together for better or worse."

"For richer or poorer."

"In sickness and health."

I emphasize the next part, "And forsaking all others."

His tone turns, the lightheartedness gone. "For as long as we both shall live."

Even though he can't see me, I nod, but don't repeat it. Wanting to hear the smile in his voice, I ask, "So we're good?"

"More than good. Thanks for calling me back."

"Did you think I wouldn't?"

He chuckles lightly. "I wasn't sure. All I wanted to do this morning was hop on that plane and come back, but I couldn't. I didn't want to fuck things up more than I already had."

"I love your surprise visits, but I don't think Tommy and the band would've been too happy since you have a show tonight."

"No, probably not. Not to forget the fans."

"Yeah, they wouldn't be happy at all." I sigh. "They would definitely blame me."

"You can't let that stuff bother you. It's not gonna change. They know what an asshole I am, so it's easy to blame you for everything. It's bullshit and everyone who knows you knows that."

Not wanting to feel like the woman who is destroying the great Johnny Outlaw, I roll onto my side and close my eyes, hearing Ashley silently taunting me. Whispering, I say, "Today has sucked to say the least, but you don't need to worry about me, Dalton. I'm going to take a nap and work tonight. It will all be fine."

"Okay. So I'll talk to later?"

"Yes, I'll call you."

"Love you, Baby."

"Love you, too."

I set the phone next to me and lie there staring up at the ceiling. I don't want to hold him back if he can be even greater than he is. My lids drop down as the heaviness of the day sends me drifting away into sleep.

TR

"When did things get so complicated?"

Tracy eyes me. "Are you kidding me? You and Johnny have always been complicated."

"I guess," I reply absently, staring out the large window in my office.

"You are crazy in love with each other." When I peek over at her, she sits up from the couch, and adds, "You have a love to be envious of…"

I follow her out onto the patio. The sun is shining and almost distracts me from my mission. She leans against the wall that faces the ocean. I join her, but keep my eyes on the distance so she doesn't feel under the microscope. "How are things at home?"

She smiles and it's genuine, taking away some of my worry.

"Good. Your love may be envious, but mine makes me happy. We've never been the over the top kind of passionate love, but we're steady and that is all I need."

"Steady sounds good." I confess, "Sometimes it feels like the world is conspiring against us."

"When it comes to you guys and the love you share, you two are the most qualified for the job."

I smile this time, turning back to face into the wind. "Applicants need not apply, the job is taken."

She giggles. "Exactly. It may get bumpy, but try to enjoy the ride."

"I love that man so much. I hope no matter what crap comes our way, he can remember that."

"Are you referring to the tabloid stuff? This was inevitable even without the photos. Interest in you has grown as fast as the company. I've been getting calls about you and Sebastian."

"The ad campaign comes out in three weeks. Dalton's going to be tested once more when those photos come out."

"He'll handle it. He loves you. It's a set of ads selling a product. That's all. You can send them over to break it to him gently if you like."

"It's a set of ads selling me and Sebastian as a couple to sell underwear." Turning my back to the wall, I say, "I'll make Dalton forget all about it. I'll remind him of how good we are together."

"Maybe you two need to be in the next campaign together."

"Tracy, you just might be onto something there."

"That's why I'm paid the big bucks."

"You're paid the big bucks to work." Nodding toward the door, I say, "Let's get back to it."

"The fun is over. A smartass lime is calling."

The Reckoning

TR

Dalton promised I wouldn't be lonely and he was right. If I wasn't chatting with him, I was receiving deliveries from each destination he visited. Barbeque sauce from Kansas City. Peaches from Atlanta. Fresh crab cakes flown in from Maryland. These gifts arrived every two days or so and I couldn't wait to find out what was in them. His love felt packed in with the thoughtful gifts and started to fill in the lonely spaces that he left behind.

For New Orleans, he sent a chef to make dinner for me, Tracy, and Rochelle. Jambalaya, red beans and rice, blackened fish, buttery biscuits, bananas foster, and beignets. We wore beads and had our own Mardi Gras right here in the house while drinking Hurricanes. "I'm gonna have a raging headache from these drinks in the morning," I speak loudly before turning the jazz CD down so we can talk.

Rochelle rubs her stomach. "I'm never eating again. Did we really need three main courses, bread, and two desserts?"

Tracy laughs. "Yes, we needed it all. What's sad is that we ate almost all of it too."

I add, "It was too good not to."

Rochelle plops down on the couch next to Tracy. "The dancing burned some of it off, right?"

Tracy and I shake our heads and I say, "If it didn't, I don't want to know. I just want to enjoy."

Tracy says, "This has got to be the best gift ever." Sitting up, she leans in scheming. "Where does the band play next?"

Rochelle's much quicker than I am, but it is her job to know these things so I'll let her have the glory. "Houston." She looks at me as I sit in a chair and kick my feet up. "Aren't you from Houston?"

I nod. "I sure am. My mom still lives there."

Rochelle asks, "It's funny, but you never really talk about your life before you came out to Cali."

Dropping my head back and closing my eyes, I reply, "My past is exactly where I want it to be—in the past. It's boring. I could totally fall asleep right now I'm so stuffed."

"Maybe we should meet the guys in Houston," Rochelle suggests way too innocent for her own good.

Tracy sits up abruptly. "A getaway would be fun."

"You could bring Adam," I suggest.

"He would love to hang out with the band and see the show," she adds enthusiastically.

Leaning back on my elbows, I roll my neck to the side and look at Rochelle. "So you're in?"

"I'm in."

Clapping her hands together, Tracy says, "It's settled. We're off to Houston in the morning."

And just like that, I was heading back to Texas...

14

"Home will be redefined throughout life. Only your heart knows its true place." ~ Johnny Outlaw

I love a good surprise and Dalton has absolutely no clue we're coming. I've been beyond giddy the whole flight. The two coffees this morning are not helping to calm me down. When we arrive at the hotel, I dump my stuff in Rochelle's room and we start getting ready. A bottle of wine is ordered before we even leave the front desk, and arrives shortly after we do. With our glasses in hand, I toast, "To spur of the moment trips, great friendships, and wanderlust."

After we take a drink, she asks, "We're supposed to meet Tracy and Adam in an hour. Will you be ready?"

I sit on the edge of the bed. "I'll be ready."

"You excited?"

"Beside myself. I can't wait to see him."

She smiles. "I bet. In the meantime, we have a concert to get ready for."

TR

On the drive over, I hold out hope that Dalton doesn't know we're coming. The press caught us at LAX, so I'm sure people were tweeting already, but it would be awesome if we actually pulled off this surprise.

Tracy says, "I'm glad we did this."

Her happiness makes me happy. "So am I." I rub Rochelle's hand, then whisper, "It's gonna be great."

She continues staring out the window, deep in thought, but nods. After going through security, Tommy meets us to take us backstage. "Johnny and Dex have their own dressing rooms. Kaz and Derrick are testing the strings on their guitars. We have thirty minutes until show time. That gives you twenty," he says, eyeing me as we walk steadily. "Third door on the right is Johnny. Dex is the second door."

"Thanks," I reply as I walk to the door he pointed out. Excitement has officially bubbled up in my stomach and is running over as I knock.

"Come in," I hear him shout from the other side of the door.

Slowly, I open it. His back is to me, but he glances over his shoulder. I see the second it registers, that he recognizes me in his double take. The right side of his mouth works up and he turns around. "I need better security to keep the groupies out," he says, struggling to keep a straight face.

I tilt my head, my hair falling to the side. "This groupie is here to stay," I say, putting my hand on my hip.

He sets his guitar down on a chair and comes to me as I shut the door. His hands are on my waist, pressing my back to the black wood door. "What are you doing here, Pretty Girl?"

"I was feeling reckless."

"It's contagious," he says, then kisses me. His hands are on my breasts, his erection pressed to my middle as his lips kiss down my neck.

Closing my eyes, I moan from the pleasure, but it's cut short when I'm picked up. As he carries me across the room, he whispers in my ear, "I want you."

Matching his volume, I ask, "You sure, before the show?"

"Posi-fucking-tively." Our mouths crash with enough pressure to let me know this is gonna be quick and probably hard. I squirm with my legs wrapped around his middle just from the anticipation. I'm set down on a table against a wall. "Take your pants off."

I slip off the table. Bending over, I slide the zippers down on my boots and quickly remove my jeans.

After unzipping his jeans, he watches me and asks, "*Fuuuuck.* No panties?"

"I wanted to save time."

"It's gonna be fast."

"Then make it count."

"Turn around, Holliday." I turn and press my hands against the wall like I'm about to be frisked—*hoping actually*. He chuckles behind me, but the lightness leaves the moment his fingertips side down my back and over my ass. "You are perfection," Dalton adds as his fingers slide between my legs. "And so wet for me."

Teeth sink into the skin over my shoulder, not enough to break the skin, but enough to leave a print long after the concert starts. His fingers rub as his tongue soothes the mark. I struggle to keep my eyes open and my head up. "I can't take the teasing, Babe."

"I just got started—"

"We don't have much time."

"I want you to come on my hand. I want you all over me. I want to play your pussy, then I want to play my guitar." His words are sultry and naughty, a secret that will be ours in spite of the thousands surrounding us.

"Faster," I say, my breath coming out harsher as he brings me closer to making his wish come true. "Oh God, Dalton. Harder!" The pressure mounts and my body tremors as I lose focus and my hold loosens against the wall.

His hand is swiftly replaced with his cock. I drop my hands to the table in front of me as he thrusts in deep, causing my head to drop back and my mouth to open. He holds me tight as his pace picks up. "Fucking hell, you feel amazing, Baby."

I drop my head forward, keeping my eyes closed and enjoying the feel of him filling me. His hands glide up my body and under my shirt and bra. He grabs my breasts again, squeezing them while fucking me from behind. Angling back, I tilt my neck for a kiss, but my body goes stiff and I gasp loudly.

"What?" Dalton asks, stopping.

"Sorry," Ashley says, standing at the door, not sounding sorry at all. "The door was open."

His head whips around. "Get the *fuck* out!"

"I was sent to tell you—"

"Get out!" he shouts louder than I've ever heard him before, making me jump.

She hurries out, slamming the door as she leaves. His hands move down and his arms tighten around me, covering me from behind. "You okay?"

I can't say anything, all words escaping me as the shock of what just happened solidifies in my veins. My vision blurs as I reach for the stability of the hard surface in front of me. My heart picks up, beating faster, and the world spins around.

Dalton's voice is bogged down underwater as his words fade off,

"Holliday? Holliday? Are you okay? Baby?" The distance grows... until the room goes black.

TR

"She'll be okay..."

"...no doctors."

"...only a ten minute delay..."

Rochelle's voice breaks through my foggy brain, "Holli?"

I slowly open my eyes and see her first, then Dalton just behind her. "Hi," he says, stepping around her. His tone is friendly, too friendly, opposite of the expression on his face.

Rochelle smiles. "I think you're gonna be okay. Can you sit up?"

Nodding, I move to the side and drop my feet to the ground. "What happened?"

Dalton sits next to me. "You passed out. How are you feeling? Do you need a doctor?"

I lean my head on his shoulder. He rubs my bare leg and I jump remembering I was naked from the waist down. When I look down, I see I'm in boxer shorts. Finding relief in that, I ask, "Do I even want to know?"

Dalton smiles. "Probably not."

Tommy stands across the room near the door. "If you're feeling well enough to skip a hospital visit, we need to start the show."

Shocked they held the show up, I start apologizing profusely, "Go. Don't keep the crowd waiting because of me. I'm sorry."

Dalton says, "I wasn't going to leave you."

Taking his hand in mine, I kiss it and say, "I'll be fine. Go on. I want to watch you play."

Kissing me on the cheek, his hand tightens around mine. "Only if you're sure."

"I'm sure. I'll go out after I drink some water."

Rochelle adds, "I'll get her something to eat too. We haven't eaten much. I'm sure it's just that and the travel."

He stands and grabs his guitar from the chair where he set it down earlier. "Don't come out unless you're feeling better. You know how it gets out there."

"Don't worry about me. You go and kick ass on stage."

He walks out and Tommy shuts the door, following him out.

Rochelle puts her hand to my forehead. "You don't feel warm. That's good. What happened? You scared us."

"I got dizzy, I guess."

"I think you've been working too much and been dealing with a lot of stress, but you're gonna be okay." She stands and hands me my jeans. "Or maybe Johnny Outlaw is just so fucking good that you passed out from the shear ecstasy of it all."

That makes me giggle. "Yeah, that's it for sure."

Standing up, I go to the bathroom. A few minutes later, I'm cleaned up, have color back in my cheeks, and my jeans are in place. When I walk out, she asks, "Seriously, do you know what happened?"

Flashes of *that* girl come to mind and I grip the door frame. I take a deep breath, trying to act as normal as possible, and then head for the main door. "I want to support Dalton. He's worried. I need to be out there, so he can see I'm all right."

"Good point. Let's get a sandwich on the way out. I think you should have a soda to get some sugar in you as well."

Fifteen minutes later, we're led to our seats. Everyone is standing, so we find our spot in front of our chairs. It doesn't take long for Dalton to find me. I see a small smile quirk as he sings into the microphone while strumming hard on his guitar.

I watch him, captive to his energy and passion, drawn to the darkness in his voice as he sings about broken pieces of ourselves often lost, seldom found again. The muscles in his arms flex, his power visible. There's an edge to his tone that speaks of desperation and desire, sexual prowess, and hunger. In the large arena, I'm not unique in my desire for him. I'm unique because he only desires me.

The next song is fast and hard, the tempo reminding me of our dressing room escapades before the interruption. I let my gaze move to where *she* stands. Her hair is up, messy, her shirt tight around her chest, her eyes fixed on Dalton. Leaning over, I can't keep the distaste out of my mouth when I tell Rochelle, "The new equipment manager walked in on us."

Her eyes go wide. "In the middle of sex?"

I nod.

"You didn't lock the door?"

"I thought *he* did."

She laughs, but stops. "That's what caused you to pass out?"

"I don't know what caused it." Reminded, I take another gulp of the cold soda. "I'm feeling better though. I think it was the lack of food and drink."

"That or you're preg..." Her hand touches my back and she leans in. "Could you be pregnant, Holli?"

My head is shaking before I even answer. "No. No. No way. I'm on the pill." Our eyes hold steady on each others. I know what she's thinking because I'm now thinking the same thing. She's just nice enough not to say it. "I've never had a problem with the pill. I don't see why it would fail now."

"You're probably right. The pill is super safe."

She starts laughing, so I ask, "What's so funny?"

"Dex said he wants his boxers back after the show."

I start wiggling. "Ewwwww. Why am I wearing his underwear?"

She's still laughing, now holding her stomach. "Because your husband wasn't wearing any."

I shake my head. "I'll be showering all night now."

She makes a frowny face. "Aww, Dex isn't so bad."

I glance over surprised by her response. "Well, you're not wearing his dirty underwear."

Laughing, she says, "True."

Tracy and Adam are dancing next to me and she hip bumps me. I smile and start dancing too. Rochelle rubs my back once more before her hand drops away.

I look back up at the stage, wanting to savor every minute of the show, wanting to be as present as I can for him. Dalton sings as if the flames burn too hot to keep the fire inside. Holding his finger in front of his mouth, he sucks in and slowly drags it back out. The crowd goes crazy over the blatant sexual act. My knees weaken and I whimper knowing exactly what he tastes.

15

"Sometimes you're fucked before you even know it." *~ Johnny Outlaw*

We went backstage as soon as the show was over. The band and Tommy were already in the dressing room by the time we got there. Dalton stands and comes over. He appears tired, maybe from the performance, maybe from something else, but he puts me first, always. "You okay?" he asks.

"I'm fine, better than fine. I'm good. I ate a sandwich and had a soda. I think Rochelle was right—too much stress, not enough eating, dehydrated, and then traveling." I force my tongue to slow down, so I don't worry him more. "I think life just caught up with me. I feel fine now."

"Good," he says as if he doesn't quite believe me. Pushing some strands of hair away from my face, he grins. "So maybe later we can finish what we started."

I play with his shirt, lightly twisting it with my fingers. When I look up, I say, "I'd be disappointed if we didn't." I'm not sure that I want to bring *her* up, but I do want to verify. "Why didn't you lock the door earlier? It was really embarrassing to be walked in on and who knows how long she was standing there or would have if I hadn't notice her."

"I did lock it. I have no idea how she got in. Maybe the lock is broken."

"Yeah. Maybe." My suspicions tell me otherwise, but I'm not looking to start a war after the issues we've dealt with lately.

After glancing at his watch, he says, "We need to go out for the encore. Why don't you head back to the hotel and get some rest."

"I want to stay and watch."

Strong fingers weave into the back of my hair and he pulls me close until his lips are on my forehead. "Okay, but be careful."

"I will."

His body leaves mine and the band follows him out the door, walking around me. The rest of the concert is spot on. The band has really gelled over the first half of the tour and it's showing on the second leg.

An hour and a half later we're sitting at the hotel bar on some couches in a dimly lit corner. Three sips into my wine, I feel ill. My head feels heated and I get a rushing sensation. I hurry to the bathroom and vomit into the toilet. With my arms out, holding onto the stall walls, I try to take a deep breath to clear my head and focus on feeling better, but my stomach churns again, sending me down. When I have nothing left, I wipe my mouth and walk out of the stall to find Rochelle walking in. "Hey, are you all right?" she asks.

Shaking my head, I say, "I was just sick. I think I've caught a bug."

Her eyes go wide. "Holli, I think you've caught a baby."

As I wash my hands, I send her a hard stare in the mirror. "I'm not pregnant. I've been on the pill forever and it's never failed." Leaning down, I splash some water in my mouth and rinse.

"Take a pregnancy test to be on the safe side."

"Not now," I snap. "Not here and keep your voice down. I just need to focus on Dalton and our marriage."

She leans against the wall and eyes me. "What's going on? Do you need to talk about it?"

"No." I calm myself, but I'm firm, "We're fine. We just finished getting over those tabloid pics of me and Sebastian, but we're fine now and I just want us to be normal again. I need us to be how we were before I return."

"I understand. Just promise me you'll take one as soon as you get back."

"I promise."

"I'm gonna hold you to that." But right now she holds the door open for me and a piece of gum instead. "Let's go."

When I reach the VIP corner, Dalton stands and says his goodbyes. He turns to me and says, "You ready?"

"Yeah."

Rochelle sits down next to Dex and I sing song, "Have a good night."

A look of worry covers her expression, but she says, "Have a good night guys."

"Night, Trace. Night, everybody."

I take Dalton's hand and we walk through the lobby to the elevators. The doors open and we step inside. Just before the doors close again, Ashley hops in. "Caught it just in time," she says, laughing as if she has no concerns in the world. Maybe she doesn't... Maybe this is all a game to her.

Neither of us responds. When she pushes the button to her floor, the anger I feel toward her is hard to restrain. My hand tightens just as his does on mine. She leans her back against the mirrored wall and with her eyes on Dalton, she asks, "So you're done for the night? I was hoping to get a group to go out."

"Holliday's here," is his only response. "She's not feeling well."

She looks at me as if just noticing me standing here for the first time."Oh, yeah..." Her tone dips as if I've ruined the fun.

"Excuse me?" I reply.

Her eyebrows shoot up, innocence trying to overtake the conniving that's imprinted in the lines of her face. "Huh?"

"What did you mean by 'Oh yeah?' "

She shrugs and turns away from me. "Nothing."

"You meant something."

"Fine. I just meant he's not as fun when you're around. He always seems like he's in a bad mood. You could always let her sleep it off and come out with us, Johnny?"

Just when I'm about to start firing away at her, he says, "My wife is everything to me. You should show her the respect she deserves or you can find another tour to work on."

The elevator doors open on her floor, but she stays, staring at him. The shock on her face disappears and she laughs, waving her hands in the air. "I get it. I can play along, no problem." Backing out, she smiles at him and says, "Goodnight, Johnny."

I'm left shell-shocked by her onslaught. The brass doors close stopping me from lunging at her. "I want her gone, Dalton."

Five floors up, the doors open for us. I state again, "I want her gone!" and walk down the hall ahead of him.

"Don't worry about her. I rarely see her."

Turning around in the middle of the hall, I ask, "Don't you see what she's doing? Can't you tell she wants you? She's flat-out rude to me and flirting with you."

"Yeah, just like Sebastian."

"I didn't punch her though?"

He quirks an eyebrow. "I thought you might."

"She's lucky I didn't."

"Look, I didn't let it slide. I handled both situations." When he walks past me, while rubbing his temples, he lets out a heavy sigh. "I'm tired, Holliday. Can we just go to bed?"

And there it is...

I'm suddenly the one who is the problem. Not her with her indiscreet flirting. Not her with her obvious disrespect to me as his wife and as a person. Not her with her too tight T-shirts. Not her...

Me.

The door is unlocked and I walk inside. Then I realize my suitcase is still in Rochelle's room. I'm standing in the middle of the room caught up in a major dilemma—do I stay or do I go?

I head back to the door.

Dalton had just sat down on the bed when he looks up and asks, "Where are you going?"

Dropping my head down, I squeeze my eyes tight, hoping to find the strength to do what I need to do. When I turn around, I don't see concern on his face, just an innocent curiosity. He's about to be blindsided with a harsh truth and it's gonna be heartbreaking to not only do it, but to watch it play out. I can't hold him back, the weight of the guilt bogs me down and I say, "I'm leaving."

He stands. "Why?"

Whispering, I say, "Because I need to."

"Why?" He starts to come closer, but I back up with each step he takes until he stops. "Holliday?"

With my hand on the door and tears in my eyes, I drop my head down, my vision becoming blurry. "I'll see you in LA."

I open the door, but it's slammed shut before I have a chance to escape. "You're not leaving. Is this about that girl?"

"This is about us."

"What's wrong with us?"

"Lately?" I ask. I can't look him in the eyes when I finish. "Almost everything." My stomach turns and I think I'm going to be sick again, this time for entirely different reasons.

He hovers over me, his hands planted on the door above my shoulders. The intensity of his eyes is felt through the thick skin I thought I had. When I dare look up, he asks again, "What is this about? Talk to me."

I'm weak when I need to be strong. I should be strong for him, for me, for us. But I can't when I love him so much. "You could have everything, Dalton."

"You *are* everything to me."

Remembering how he defended me to not only Sebastian but also to Ashley mixed in with his sweet words now, the tears overlap my bottom lids and slide down my cheeks. The emotions of the day are getting the better of me. Instead of denying myself the one thing I want most in the world, I give in and wrap my arms around him. Leaning my head on his chest, my sobs break through and I cry. And he lets me, but comforts me by warming me with his arms around my body, his head leaning against the top of mine. "I'm not letting you leave, not tonight, not ever."

And I believe him. I nod, my tears soaking spots on his shirt.

His hand cradles my head and there is no more denying what we have together, what we are together.

He says, "Tommy will handle Ashley."

I sniffle, hating that I've put him in this position. "I hate playing the jealous wife role, but she makes me."

Taking a step back, he brings me with him and we walk to the bed. "You have nothing to be jealous over." His hand caresses my cheek, his thumb gliding back and forth softly. "If you only knew how I saw you... how I feel about you, you'd never have a doubt." His lips brush against mine and then with a light pressure he says, "I'm in love with you—madly, deeply, soul-achingly in love with only you." His thumbs wipe away my tears and he kisses me with all the intention in the world to show me his love.

Leaning back, he comes with me, my back to the bed, his chest to mine.

In the silence, I start thinking about how I might be holding him back now, much less if I am pregnant. Despite what he says, is he really ready to settle down that much? *Are we?*

I don't want him to ever blame me for keeping him from achieving his dreams or worse, resenting me in the future. I cradle my arm around my stomach, mad that I've let my head... and my heart get wrapped up in the possibility of a little baby.

Shifting in his arms, I lean my cheek against his chest and concentrate on the calm of his heartbeat and fall asleep.

Out of the corner of my eye, I see Rochelle put her sunglasses on and look down to avoid the flashes. I flip my sunglasses over my eyes and lower my gaze to the floor of LAX. Tracy and Adam with a security guard lead us to the waiting SUV and we quickly climb in. "I'll call you later," she yells louder than the paparazzi, then shuts the door.

The SUV drives off quickly and I take what feels like my first breath in minutes. Once we hit the highway, Rochelle tells the driver to stop at a CVS before we get to my house. I stare at her. "I'm tired and want to get some sleep. It can wait an hour or two."

"No, it can't. You promised me you would do this as soon as we got back."

"I thought you meant once we got home, not literally right after we land."

"You're lucky I didn't make you take one at the airport. If you're pregnant, you need to see your doctor and care for that baby in there. So we're stopping and picking up the pregnancy test or three. I did four each time, but whatever, I'm weird like that. You only need one. They're like 99.9% accurate."

"Geez, like the pill I've been taking."

"You stopped that yesterday. You didn't take one today, right?"

"Nosy much."

"Just caring..."

I let my guard down and look over at her. "I know you are. I'm sorry I'm so grumpy. I'm nervous and stressed over this."

"That's why you should take it now."

As soon as we walk into my house, we leave our luggage by the door and I take the package and head upstairs to my bedroom. She comes with me, but waits while I go into the bathroom.

Gulping heavily, I rip the foil package and pull the stick out. After reading the directions, I follow them to a T, then set the stick on the edge of the bathtub. I open the door and bemoan, "The deed is done. My whole world is balanced on the tip of a pregnancy stick."

"Either way, it's going to be okay. I promise you. Dalton will be thrilled if you are and supportive if you're not. I'm also here for you no matter what."

We both sit on the counter, leaning against the mirror and staring at the stick across from us on the tub. "How long has it been?" I ask.

"Two minutes. That one said wait three."

"Should I look now?"

"Let's wait for the three minutes." I don't think either of us breathes over the next sixty seconds. She says, "It's time."

Slipping off the counter, she waits as I walk forward. Standing over it, peering down, I ask, "Two pink lines. What do two pink lines mean?"

16

"Sometimes the smallest things can have the biggest impact." ~ Johnny Outlaw

Rochelle's sniffle draws my attention. Her eyes are glassy, tears filling them and my own tears fall from the emotional overload. "I'm pregnant," I say, though clearly she already knows.

Her arms open as she walks to me. "You're pregnant," she repeats, hugging me tight. "Congratulations."

"Thanks," I reply, my mind a bit numb. The embrace of my true friend calms my mind. "How am I going to tell Dalton?"

As we part, she says, "Call him. He'll be so excited, Holli."

My voice wavers as more tears prick my eyes. Grabbing a tissue from the counter, I dab my eyes. "He has a show tonight. He'll want to fly home and he can't." When I start to get the feeling of this life-altering change under control, I smile. I can't wait to tell him, my excitement growing as I picture his sweetest smile when he finds out. "He wants this baby, Rochelle."

She dabs the corner of her own eyes. "Now I'm a mess. He's gonna be so happy, but I think you're right. He's impulsive and needs to do the show tonight, so you can't tell him beforehand."

My eyes flash up, a plan coming together. "I'm gonna surprise him. I can do something special to tell him the news."

"Ooooh, I like this idea."

"I see him in two weeks. If I can hold off and not tell him, and that's a big if, then I'll get to see his reaction. Selfishly, I want that."

"Understandable. You can celebrate together. What do you have in mind?"

I smile. "I'm not sure. I'll have to give it some thought." I rub my stomach. "I just can't believe I'm pregnant. I wasn't even sure if I was ready before and now I feel this baby is right on time."

"It's wonderful." She hugs me again. "Congratulations."

"Thank you." We walk back into the bedroom and out the door. "Do you want to stay for tea?"

"I need to get back for the boys and catch up on some work."

When the car service arrives, I walk her to the door and give her another hug. "Thank you for going on the adventure and for being here for me."

"You're welcome. Before I go," she says, "I want you to know that I think you and Johnny will be amazing parents."

"Thank you. That really means a lot to me."

She walks down the steps dragging her suitcase to the waiting car. "Call ya soon."

I shut the door and lean against it. Taking in a long deep breath, I hold it and then release slowly. "I'm pregnant." A huge smile covers my face as my hand covers my stomach. "I'm pregnant!" I squeal in excitement.

The Reckoning

But the jumping makes my stomach curl and I run to the restroom.

TR

"So the agency thinks we should do a video."

I stare at the phone as if it's alien technology and the language Tracy is speaking is foreign to me. "What?"

"They loved the photos from the shoot and want to do a video that backs the campaign. Department stores will play it on monitors in the lingerie section, commercials will be made, film style videos produced. I think this is brilliant. It changes the brand completely. This can take it from gag gifts and funny cards to a brand that reaches a bigger mainstream audience, which could lead to even more opportunities."

"Slow down. You're making my head spin. What would filming a video entail?" Rubbing my stomach, I think of Dalton, knowing he won't be happy with a video of me and Sebastian.

"Big city backdrop. We were thinking the same apartment we stayed in with that amazing view. Shooting in the morning, late day, and then night. The couple never leaves the apartment. They lounge in their Limelight skivvies all day. The agency suggested domestic scenes—cooking breakfast, watching movies, lounging on the couch—mixed with sexy parts."

"Sexy parts?"

"We'll keep them tasteful. I know you don't want to hear it, but you and Sebastian have chemistry in front of the lens. I agree with the ad agency. You two will spark on video."

"I don't want to spark with Sebastian."

"Holli, this is the next level we've been working to reach. We have something solid to work with that people are flipping out over in the best way possible. Let's grow this company in the direction we've worked so hard to grow it in."

"So you're wanting me to say yes?"

"I'm advising you to say yes. Ultimately, the final decision is yours."

Reminded of growing, I rub my stomach again. "If we do this, we have to do it soon."

"How's next week?"

TR

Gracie has done high-end fashion videos for designers, and after the photos she produced, she was hired to film our video. Tracy knew I needed to trust whoever was going to be working on this set as much as possible to loosen up. What she didn't know was that I couldn't do shots this time to get to that state.

Sebastian is in town attending LA Fashion Week, so the four of us meet for lunch to discuss the job. Gracie lays her plans out on the table and runs her fingers over the sketch of the bedroom with that spectacular view. "We'll start with the sunrise. You'll be in bed, eyes opening as the sun starts to peek in. You said it's an Eastern view from the bedroom?"

Tracy answers, "Yes, barely since it's on the corner, but there will be enough light to get the message across. The living room gets the sunset."

Starting in about the team she's bringing in for the filming, she turns to Tracy to finalize wardrobe so she knows what she's working with and how far she can go. Sebastian leans closer and whispers, "How have you been?"

"Good."

"Look Holliday, I'm sorry. I really am. I crossed a line. My head was full of... I don't know. I just feel, *felt* a connection with you. But I'm sorry. It won't happen again."

The Reckoning

I could rake him over the coals for trying to kiss me or pushing every one of Dalton's buttons to anger him, but I have to work with him, so I'll keep things as light as possible until the job is done. "Thank you. I appreciate that."

"From before sunrise to past sunset," he notes. "It's gonna be a long day."

"Yeah, I'm gonna have to rest up for it. I'm not used to working in this way. I kind of work like a nomad, when and where I want." I laugh. "And a lot late at night."

"All the travel fucks with my sleep habits. I take a lot of sleeping pills."

Gracie says, "Your body is insanely perfect, Holli. Sebastian, I saw you walked the runway yesterday shirtless and looked phenomenal. Whatever you guys did to prepare for our last shoot, do it again. We want the photos to be an extension of that photoshoot."

The baby is always on my mind, but especially since I'm going to have my stomach exposed. My hand covers my stomach as it drops, knowing I can't do Danny's crazy diet this time. It wouldn't be healthy for the baby. I'm gonna have to kick in some extra yoga this time.

I inwardly roll my eyes at myself over my ridiculousness. I haven't even confirmed the pregnancy from the doctor yet. But from what I read online, those pee sticks are pretty damn accurate, so I've treated my body like I'm pregnant already.

While we're waiting on the check, Tracy gets a call and excuses herself from the table. I pick up the tab and pay when it arrives, then ask, "So this coming Tuesday or Wednesday in New York?"

"I'll have everything confirmed by tonight," Gracie says. "I'll let Tracy know for sure before you book your tickets. Sebastian, you do or don't also have availability on Wednesday?"

"Tuesday is my only free day. Wednesday I have to fly to Barcelona."

"That settles it then," she adds. "We will make this happen on Tuesday."

Leaning my arms on the table, I smile. "It's more exciting flying by the seat of our pants anyway."

"Which you do way too much," Tracy says rejoining us. She grabs her purse and touches my shoulder. "I can't give you a ride home, but I'll have the valet get you a cab. Adam has a client dinner in Malibu in two hours. I'll never make it if I drive you home. Is that okay?"

"I actually have a doctor's appointment, but I can get a cab or Uber."

Gracie asks with concern, "Is everything all right?"

"Yes. No worries. It's just a checkup. It's that time of year." I look away, realizing I've said more than she needs to know.

"I can give you a ride." The three of us look at Sebastian as he sits up. "I don't have to be anywhere until seven, so I have a few hours to kill."

"That's very kind of you, but I can just cab it over."

"Really, it's no trouble."

"Actually I have Uber on speed dial. I'll call them."

Gracie is watching us like a tennis match. She steps into the conversation and says, "It's just a ride, Holli. What's the big deal?"

I want to give her an evil glare. Whose side is she on anyways? Apparently no one's since she's been Switzerland since the incident in New York. The awkwardness grows as everyone sits in silence. I glance to Tracy who's biting her lip nervously as if she's the one put on the spot. Ugh! Dalton is gonna kill me, but I'm out of excuses and just feel rude if I don't accept at this point. It's just a ride there. No big deal in the scheme of things. "Okay, thank you."

We leave the table and this time, I follow Sebastian, not

The Reckoning

wanting his eyes burning up my backside. He's a perfect gentleman while we wait for the car. Thank goodness. I burst out laughing when his car is pulled around. "The car is very subtle," I say, laughing at him for being so pretentious. "No one will ever guess a celebrity isn't driving the neon yellow Maserati."

"I'm a model, Holli. I don't mind being seen." He floors the accelerator and we speed down the highway.

"I do mind dying. Slow down a bit. Okay?"

He laughs. "Sure."

I'm seeing a new side to him, one I can appreciate. Once 'the chase' is taken out of our relationship, I'm discovering he can be quite funny and he has a great laugh—lighthearted like only someone who loves life can manage.

We talk about the shoot and wardrobe or lack thereof. He keeps everything professional with no innuendoes at all, which is appreciated. As we get closer to the doctor's office, I start to get nervous, suddenly attached to the thought of having this baby more than I should before it's conception is confirmed. Sadness creeps into my thoughts if I'm not pregnant, but I take a deep breath and pray that I am while holding my stomach.

Pulling up to the front of the building, he says, "Here we are." I watch as his eyes go to the gold lettering on the building—OBGYN. "Would you like me to drive you home after?"

"No. Thank you. I can call a car service. They're usually very fast in Beverly Hills." He rolls the window down once I get out. Leaning in once the door is closed again, I say, "Thank you again. I really appreciate it."

"You're welcome. So I'll see you next Tuesday?"

My mind goes to ridiculous places when he says that. So I repeat, "Yes. See you next Tuesday."

One of his eyebrows arches, surprised I followed through with the crude joke. "I'm impressed. I didn't think you'd catch that."

While we laugh, I pretend to pop my collar. "See? I'm not always so lame."

His smile softens and he leans over the console and peers up. "I don't think you're lame at all, Holli. But I do think you're quite fascinating."

In the moment, it's easy to see the appeal. I stand up straight and back away on the sidewalk. "I should go. I hate being late."

"Hey Holli?"

I stop and look back. He's leaning closer to the open window so I can hear. His eyes go down and he says, "I'm sorry for coming on so strong and for… all that's happened."

I smile. "Thanks, Sebastian."

"See ya around."

"See you around."

I'm a few minutes late for the appointment, but they're used to it with LA traffic. I only have to wait ten minutes before I'm taken back and given a cup to pee in. Then, I'm left alone with my anxiety to wait in an exam room for the results. With my phone in hand, I call Dalton to help sway the nerves to settle down. The static is bad when he answers, "Hey, we're going through a tunnel right now."

"That's okay. I can hear you. Where are you going?"

"To dinner. We're meeting with a producer to talk about the new album. I thought we were working with the last guy but he can't start ours for five months because of other projects."

"Maybe this is the guy you were meant to work with all along. You know how that goes."

"Yeah, we'll see. How are you?"

"I'm good. I just had lunch with Gracie, Sebastian, and Tracy." I pause, giving him a second to let the Sebastian stuff pass. "We're moving forward with a video. Isn't that great? Gracie has so many cool ideas—"

The static is gone and the connection is crystal clear when he

The Reckoning

asks, "A video for what?"

"The ad agency liked the photos so much they developed a bigger campaign around them, which includes doing a video. Commercials will be made and a longer director's cut will be put out." Going in for the hard sell, I add, "It will play where the line is sold, in department stores and such."

His voice is brusque when he asks, "Why didn't you tell me?"

"I wasn't 100% on board."

"Now you are?" He sounds surprised.

"After I heard the ideas, yes. Are you mad?"

"Why would I be mad, Holliday?" He's resorted to answering my questions with questions.

He's definitely mad.

I hear the clipboard rattle just outside the door. "Dalton, I'll call you later. I have to go." I hate that I have to hang up, but I don't want to ruin this surprise after the bomb I just laid on him. He calls right back, but I don't answer, and now I feel terrible.

"Mrs. Dalton, how are you?"

"I'm good. Nervous. Anxious. Excited. Scared."

"Well, that's totally normal," Dr. Cambert reassures. He flips the paper over the clipboard and scans the page. When he looks up, he smiles. "Congratulations. You're pregnant, Mrs. Dalton."

Tears flood my eyes as fast as the words left his mouth. Overwhelmed, I lean down covering my face with my hands. "Take a tissue," he adds, handing me the box.

Taking it, I dab the corners of my eyes. "I'm sorry. I'm just so happy. I didn't even know I was ready until I peed on that stick. I was waiting and realized it would have been devastating if I wasn't."

"Happy tears are always welcome. Do you have any questions for me?"

My mind is blank except for the fact that I'm going to be a mother, someone's mom. I can't wait to share the news with Dalton.

"Nothing right now. I'm sure as soon as I leave I'll have a million."

He heads for the door. "That's fine. You have the office number. Call us whenever you need. The nurse will give you some paperwork, including information on prenatal vitamins and a follow-up appointment. While you're here today, we'd like to draw blood for some tests. Other than that, go home and celebrate the happy news and if you have any questions, just call the office. Congratulations again."

"Thank you."

I go through the requested test in a haze of happiness and thoughts of Dalton. Will we have a girl or boy? Will they have my artistic skills or his musical talent? My creativity or his baseball ability? My hazel or his green eyes? I can't believe I'm going to have a baby. I can't believe that Dalton and I will have children. I can't process the magnitude of this moment while having my blood drawn. I also can't stop smiling.

Once the tests are done, I tuck my paperwork into my purse and head out the front doors. Sebastian is leaning against the Maserati sipping an iced coffee. To a single woman, the sight of him would surely make their heart do flip flops and swoon. Though I'm married, I can still appreciate the gesture. "What are you still doing here?"

"Waiting," he says, reminding me of Jake Ryan in Sixteen Candles—a little cocky. A lot thoughtful.

"You didn't have to."

"I know," he says, opening the door for me. "I wanted to. Your chariot awaits."

Before I get in, I stop grateful for his thoughtfulness. "Thank you."

Ducking inside the car, I put my seatbelt in place and wait for him. He buckles in, then he glances over at my arm that still has a cotton ball and tape stuck to it. "Everything good?"

Leaning back with a huge secret and even bigger smile, I say, "Everything's great."

17

"Sometimes we make the right decision. Sometimes a bad choice. At the end of the day it's how you handle it that makes the difference." ~ *Johnny Outlaw*

"Why did you hang up on me?" Dalton asks, his voice sounding as tense as I'm assuming his body must be.

I search for a reasonable lie, one that won't spoil the surprise, but I suck at lying. "I had a call I had to take."

"Why didn't you say that?"

"I don't know. I was flustered."

"You sound flustered now. What's going on?"

"Nothing. I'm just tired and need to eat something." There's that awful silence lingering between us. It shows up when he's thinking too deep for this to turn out any good.

"Can we talk about the video?" I'd be hesitant to bring it up again if the role was reversed, but he asks, his words steady.

It's something we need to talk about, so I reply, "We can talk about it."

"Things are changing for you and for Limelight. I'm just wondering if you know what you're getting yourself into."

"We're growing. I see it as a positive, my hard work paying off."

"But when celebrity gets involved, it shifts the intent."

"I'm not doing this to become famous," I say, remembering how much I'm hounded already. "Hell, I already get more attention than I like."

"Then why put yourself in that position, Holliday? You know the outcome. The writing's on the wall. You picked a guy that already has his own set of media baggage, then throw our relationship into the mix. What result did you think you'd get?"

"I don't understand why me growing my business has suddenly become a negative thing."

He sighs, clearly misunderstood. I can picture him running his hand through his hair, frustrated. "It's not. That's not what I mean."

I don't want to fight with him and I know he wants the best for me and Limelight, so I back down the defenses and ask, "What do you mean then?"

"I'm not saying don't do the video. Just be careful and remember that the road to hell was paved with good intentions."

I could tease him for using such a cliché, but his point is taken, hitting me hard. What I do affects more than just me and even my best efforts could backfire in ways that I can't predict. "Point taken," I say. "I'll keep that mind."

The silence creeps in between us again, and he asks, "What's wrong. Talk to me."

"Just thinking about what you said. That's all."

A charm works its way in, and he says, "I support your

decisions, Holliday. And I have no doubt the video will be amazing."

He's struggling with giving me the freedom for the world to perceive me in a whole new way, the most gracious way he can because he loves me. "Thank you. That means more to me than you know." A yawn slips out just as my stomach growls. "I'm starving and tired. I'm gonna go to bed early."

This time he talks to me with love and concern. "Do you want me to order you something?"

And my heart goes mushy for this man. "You'd order me food when you're out of town?"

"Sure. I know what you like. I have the restaurants programmed into my phone. You're tired and you sound like you need rest. Go do that and I'll order one of your favorites."

"You spoil me," I say, lying back on the couch.

His voice gets quieter. "I wish I could do it more." A smile is heard through his tone when he says, "Go relax. Dinner will be there in less than thirty."

"It always takes an hour."

"Don't worry," he says, laughing. "I'm gonna offer them a big tip to rush it."

Grinning from ear to ear, I plop down on the couch. "Have I told you how much I love you?"

"All the time, but I can always hear it again."

"I love you."

"I love you, too."

We leave for Manhattan the next evening and arrive late that night. Tracy and I are tired and after grabbing a snack, we go straight to bed.

Gasping, I sit up when the alarm goes off. "Damn it!" I turn it off, pissed from the annoying intrusion, my hands still shaking.

Tracy cracks the door open, and sounding way too chipper sings, "Good morning."

"Morning." My stomach rolls and I hurry to the bathroom...

After the usual bout of morning sickness, I brush my teeth and take a shower, and then brush my teeth again in the shower just to be on the clean side.

I slip on my robe and walk into the living room. A few production people have arrived. Some are moving the furniture. Two others rush past me into the bedroom and start working on that room. The set designer is talking to Tracy who waves me over. "There's decaf over on the island for you."

"Thank you."

On the kitchen island the caterers are setting up trays of pastries, fruit, and juices. Coffee is brewing and a warm mug is waiting for me.

Getting the final touches by makeup and hair, I sit in a chair by the window when Sebastian walks into the apartment. He greets everyone with self-assuredness and sends a wink my way. All the thoughtfulness from the other day is gone and The Model is back.

Gracie gets me from the living room and talks to me about positioning on the bed and what angles she's going for. Sebastian is in the bathroom with hair and makeup while we wait. When the door opens, he fastens his eyes on me and walks to the end of the bed. His clothes are dropped in the middle of the bedroom, in front of me and the crew. Wardrobe hands him the white Bite Me boxers, but before he puts them on, he says, "Good morning, Holli." Then he bends down to put the boxers on. *Whoa!* Not only is he not shy, but he has reason to not be shy. I send my gaze to the window before he catches me looking.

He climbs under the covers and leans forward, trying to kiss me on the cheek. Even with my head moved back, away from him, he still smiles. "Good to see you again."

"I can't say it's that good of a morning at this hour."

"Well, you look beautiful no matter what the time."

"Thank you," I reply, suddenly feeling my cheeks heat from the compliment. His good mood is actually a nice change on him.

After being directed, we lie there, his chest to my back, his arm over me holding me. He kisses my neck as I stare out the window. I try to block out the fact that this isn't my husband. I'm going for content, not sad right now.

With the sun barely sneaking in through the tall buildings, I'm pressed against the glass forty minutes later, Sebastian's hand under the hem of my lace tank top. His hand caresses my side and the back of my head goes to the window. We're told to freeze as wardrobe rushes in to lower his boxers enough to expose the side of the deep V of muscles pressing against me. Dalton's words come back about Sebastian's dick on me and I shift, trying to shake away the thought. *It* isn't against me now, so that's good. I roll my head to the side as instructed and he kisses my neck. I don't fall under any spell, the kisses feeling all wrong. I stare into the camera, keeping this centered on business, then close my eyes again, needing to block this out.

As soon as cut is yelled, I grab the robe from the bed and walk into the kitchen for a bottle of water. Tracy whispers, "You okay?"

"No," I whisper between gritted teeth. "I'm not okay. You guys have me practically making out with him. He's not my husband. I feel like I'm cheating. It makes me feel like shit."

"It's business. Remember that. Johnny's done the same and worse in videos."

"I don't need you to justify it," I snap, feeling exposed though I'm completely covered by the velour robe. I tighten the belt around me. "I need you to understand I'm not okay. This is not what I do."

"I'll check on the next scene and see if I can cool the heat so to speak." She leaves me there to cool down. Returning a few minutes later, she hands me my phone. "Call him. I think that will make you feel better. I'll tell them we need a ten minute break."

She's right. I do need to talk to him. I call despite the early morning hour. When he answers, I say, "I'm sorry. I know it's early. I needed to hear your voice though."

"I like hearing yours too. How's it going?"

"I'm sorry, Dalton. I'm sorry for doing this video," I say, sniffling, my emotions getting the best of me.

"Hey," he says, his voice becoming intimate, speaking directly to my heart. "Why are you sad? What's wrong?"

"He's not you." My confession comes out, traveling the distance between us and making my heart ache.

The phone cracks, the pause longer than I want. He whispers though he sounds like he wants to yell. "That makes me want to kick his ass for touching you like I do—"

"He doesn't. No one can touch me like you do. Doing this makes me feel guilty."

It's instant and unexpected. The man whose jealousy sometimes drives me wild and sometimes drives me mad knows exactly how to make me feel better. "Just imagine me, Baby. That's what I do. I picture you. It makes it easier to get through."

It's not easy for him to do this kind of thing either. Somehow hearing this makes me feel better. My body calms and I hold the phone a little tighter, and whisper, "I wish you were here."

"I can be. I'm close. I'm in Jersey."

"You are? I thought you would have left already."

"Tommy's still trying to get a meeting moved. We leave tonight to fly to Phoenix, but if I can get there. I need to see you too."

Wanting to see him more than anything, I ask, "You do?"

"I had a shit night."

"What happened?"

He stalls. "Nothing to worry about."

"I worry about you anyway, so please tell me."

His gulp is heard. Silently, he whispers, "I don't know what I'm doing anymore. I'm going through the motions, pretending I want this. I don't think I do."

Worry is now an understatement. "Babe, it's going to be okay. You can do this and then you take all the time off you want."

"He's not here. You're not here. They want us to sign another three record deal. They want us to play Super Bowl next year. I look in the mirror and I don't recognize me anymore."

My problems seem to pale under the weight of his world as it crashes down around him. He needs to come first. "Dalton, you left Texas on your own. You worked hard, practiced, and wrote songs on your own. I know you believe Cory and Rochelle made you who you are, but they didn't. They just brought out the best of who you were already."

"With Cory gone, what's left of me then?"

I gasp, but it's quiet. Until now, I hadn't realized how bad off he really was. I thought we were past the darker days, but touring seems to have stolen the light right out from under him. "Come see me. Please. Take a later flight if you have to, but come see me before you leave."

His pause is too long, but I exhale when he says, "I will. I promise."

Gracie calls me, "Holli, we're ready for you."

"I've got to go," I whisper into the phone. "But keep your promise."

"I will." Before I hang up, he adds, "I Love you. And, Angel, don't let him pull any shit with you."

I want to giggle, but the tension lessens the response. Instead I smile and reply, "Don't worry. I won't. I love you."

I hesitantly hang up and return to the set, counting the

minutes until he arrives.

I'm exhausted by three. I've been up for twelve hours and I'm feeling it. Sebastian and I are jumping on the bed having a pillow fight when I hear Tracy raise her voice, "Please stop, Johnny. Don't go in there. Please."

Johnny?

I stop jumping, but Sebastian doesn't and a pillow smacks me in the face. When it drops, he says, "Yikes, sorry, Holli."

But I barely hear him.

Dalton stands in the doorway, his chest heaving as harsh as his breath. Devastation lies heavy as his eyes pierce my middle. I'm held captive to the spot where I stand, seconds feeling like exaggerated minutes as he seems to be processing something I'm not privy to.

When his eyes meet mine, his face has drained of color, his eyes are cold and heartless, causing me to flinch. Dalton has only ever given me love. He would never look at me as if I'm his mortal enemy.

But he is...

He knows. He knows I'm pregnant. But where's the smile? Where's his joy? His striking features have been replaced by the wreckage of something tragic.

I've only seen this expression once before. *When Cory died.*

My heart starts to race, panging to reach him, but for the first time in our lives, I'm scared and hesitate to go to him. A heavy blink blocks out the pain on his face I'm witnessing, but only momentarily. Anger gets the best of him and he points at Sebastian. "Motherfucker." The room is dead silent, and he says, "We're gonna have a talk, but first I need to speak with my wife."

As soon as his gaze hits me, a look of disgust blindsides me. My hands drop down and cover my belly as if I can protect the baby. Thoughts run through my mind to why he's looking at me as if I've

The Reckoning

hurt him. Why he's looking at me like I'm guilty of something unforgivable. Although my fears are wrapped around my neck, strangling me, I step off the bed anyway and go to him. For someone that seems to have a million emotions pent up inside by the look on his face, his tone is even... too even, when he says, "In the other room. Now." He turns his back to me and walks across the living room into the other bedroom.

I gulp heavily, knowing something is wrong and hoping his devastation isn't because of our baby. I quietly shut the door after I enter. He stands at the window with his back to me and I feel sick, but for a different reason than this morning. "What's wrong?" I ask, afraid of his answer.

When he turns to confront me, his eyes narrow and he holds up a magazine I failed to notice. "This! This is what's wrong!" He struggles to get the next words out. "You, you're pregnant!"

Storming closer, he shakes the paper in my face, the rattling sound making me nauseous. "Dalton, calm down."

"I can't fucking calm down!" I reach out to touch his hand, but it drops away and he throws the paper. As he speaks, "This story is everywhere," I glance down to see the magazine cover of Sebastian and me in front of my doctor's office. The headline is in bold white— **Holliday and Sebastian Having a Love Child.** I look up at Dalton when he says, "I can't live like this. Not knowing." When he turns, his green eyes penetrate mine. "I need to know, Holliday."

"You need to know what?" I ask confused to what's really going on.

His face is flawed, contorted in pain that makes him unrecognizable when he snarls, "You know."

This is not the man I married. This is not my life, but the anger over the allegation is overtaking every other emotion I might have had, ones that would have me cling to him, to comfort him like he needs. Those emotions are lost to darker ones that have eaten him up and now he feels this need to spew at me. I cover my stomach, protecting the baby from his rage. "Dalton..."

"Tell me, Holliday."

Then I realize, the picture becoming clear. I see the hope in his eyes—hope that I will say what he wants to hear. But the hurt he's instilled inside me wins out. "If you're asking me what I think you are, I want you to leave."

"I'm not leaving until I have answers. Did you fuck him?"

My heart has never been so wrecked, so betrayed. I walk to the door and hold it wide open. "Get out!" I scream, my anguish morphing into rage.

"Shut the damn door!"

"No! Not if you're gonna come in here with insinuations or accusations." I don't recognize the man before me, the one who has decided to destroy our lives while his crumbles. "Get out, Dalton. I want you gone before this gets worse."

His sarcasm is dripping. "Be careful what you wish for, sweetheart. I don't take threats lightly."

How have we come to this? How did we get here? Sadness shrouds my clearer thoughts. "It's not a threat." My anguish comes in tears that slip down my cheek. I wipe them away, hating the weakness. "If you have to ask me who the father of my baby is, there's nothing more for us to say."

Flipping from one emotion to the next, he grits his teeth. "Say it's not true. Deny it!"

My insides are black, set on fire by the man I love, burned by the man I thought would always be on my side. I refuse to be part of this downward spiral and placate on the back end of his insults. "I shouldn't have to!"

"Do you know how humiliated I am? A roadie was reading this trash." His head drops down, his own anguish eating away at him until he's left with the ugliness of this, what lies between us. Trust is

The Reckoning

gone, shattered by our pride. I can't give him what he needs when he sucker-punched me with this accusation. And he knows I won't, too stubborn to admit fault sometimes. In this case, there is none so I won't win anyway. But he won't walk out of here a winner either. I know him too well. Regret will take hold soon enough, but I won't take the brunt in the meantime. "Leave," I say, a slight plea has set in, making my throat ache with rawness. Another tear falls and then another. I let them.

"If I walk out that door, I'm not coming back." His threat appears idle on the surface, but even if regret sets in later, he has his ego to deal with. When he looks up, his eyes are a bright green, shining through his own tears. "I need you to tell me. I need to hear that this is all made up, that they faked the photos."

I can't deny those photos. "They're real, but the story is—"

In one fast motion, he swings and punches a hole in the wall. I jump, flinching from the action as the plaster falls in bits and pieces to the floor at my feet. His hand is bloody and I gasp from shock and fear as he barrels over in pain. I cry, "Babe, what are you doing?"

Dalton stands, knocking my hands off of him and walks right past me and straight out the apartment door. I follow him. "Dalton. Don't go!"

He doesn't bother stopping or looking back. He doesn't even bother with the elevator though I'm twenty-one floors up. He kicks the stairwell door open and disappears, leaving me with the tears of heartache, the worry of my marriage, and the obliterated plaster on the floor.

In the middle of Manhattan, my husband leaves me and I think it might be for good.

18

Jack Dalton

"Not all fairytales have a happy ending."
~ Holliday Hughes

The stairwell is too bright and my legs feel weak. I stop one flight down from Holliday... one flight down from my soul... one flight down from my destruction. Leaning over the railing, I might be sick, so I sit on a step and put my head between my legs.

Closing my eyes, I breathe in slowly and exhale slower. None of it helps. It doesn't make this nightmare go away. I stand up, debating if I should go back, if I should ask her one more time and hope for an answer. But the fact remains that Holliday can't, or won't, deny those headlines. I gave her a chance, several chances, and she chose not to deny the rumors.

As I run down the stairs, the photos of them together at her doctor's office, of them talking with their mouths practically kissing, of her getting into his car flash through my head like a movie reel. Shoving the door to the lobby open, I head for the street. "A taxi," I say to the doorman.

I'm sweating and he's eyeing me as if something's wrong with me. There is. So much wrong. A cab pulls to the curb and I get in. "Will you go to Jersey?"

"For the right price."

I open my wallet and look inside. "Three hundred dollars?"

"You got it, buddy."

I pull my phone from my jacket and stare at the screen, so fucking tempted to call her. But I can't. Not like this.

I'm so fucking stupid. I take a deep breath trying to erase the embarrassment I felt, still feel, when I saw one of my roadies reading that magazine in the hotel lobby. I handed her my guitar to pack up and she hands me that. It was a shitty tradeoff, but the truth hurts and this cuts deep...

"Do you think it's true?" Ashley asks, turning the cover to face me. Her expression is one of concern, but I'm confused because I'm not sure who she's concerned for.

"What are you talking about?" I look down at the magazine in her hands. I blink. Then blink hard again, knowing I didn't read that right. But when I read the headline again and match it to the photo, it reads the same. "No fucking way. No."

"Are you sure?"

Setting my guitar case down, I grab the magazine from her and leave in a blaze of fury, headed to Manhattan. It's the longest fucking hour of my life. I stare at the photo, not able to read the article. It's got to be bullshit, but nothing makes sense. Why would that motherfucker be at the doctor with her? Why are they kissing... almost kissing? What the fuck ever. Why are they *together at all? I'm fucking touring two countries and she's back in LA fucking a motherfucking model.*

The driver stops. I roll the magazine up, pay him, and get out. The doorman recognizes me and lets me pass without a word. The elevator door closes and I start to sweat as I ascend.

My stomach tightens, and I brace myself for the confrontation. I've got to hear her side, got to give her a chance. This could be lies, all tabloid made up shit.

... Or it could be true.

Please God, don't let it be true.

I walk into the apartment and hear laughter—hers and his—coming from the bedroom. My heart is racing, but my feet slow, dread taking over. When I look through the door, there they are—on the bed together, flirting like lovers. Feathers fly through the air and she laughs without care. I look at him and see the way he looks at her, recognizing it immediately. It's how I look at her. He's in love with her.

She's been fucking that douche and lying to me. I turn off my phone and pack it away. My chest fucking hurts. I lean my head against the window, thankful for the odd hour of travel. Less traffic means I can get the fuck out of this city.

Tommy is waiting in the suite when I get back to the hotel. "Get out," I say, slamming the door closed behind me.

"Fuck off. What's wrong with you?"

"I'm not in the mood to talk, Tommy. I'm warning you."

He stands and walks around the coffee table. "You're warning me?"

"Yeah, I'm fucking warning you to fuck off."

"Or what?"

"God damn it! Can't I just be alone?"

"I'm not sure if that's wise. What the fuck happened?" I walk into the bedroom, ignoring him. But the asshole follows me in. I say,

"I don't want to talk. I just want to leave this shithole."

"Then you're about to be even more pissed off because the plane is having mechanical issues."

"Fine. I'll fly commercial."

"No flights. I already looked. The best we could do is a flight out of La Guardia tomorrow at noon. Works out though because I need to stop by the record label to drop off the first song demo and hear some cover ideas they have."

"I'm leaving tonight."

He walks back out into the living and says, "Then leave. Be in Seattle at five sharp."

I hear the door close when he leaves. "Asshole," I call just in case he can still hear me. I strip my clothes from my body, feeling their taint seeping under my skin. I get into the shower wanting to drench myself, wanting to drown my thoughts. Dropping against the cold marble wall, I sink down to the bottom as the water rains down on me. The water runs over my head and streaks across my face, falling like tears. My own tears replacing the blood that used to flow through my heart, Holliday the only person to ever make it beat, is now gone.

She was everything.

Every. Fucking. Thing. To me, and she betrayed me just like the others.

I want to hit something but I don't stand a chance against the marble in this bathroom. I've got to get out of here. I've got to leave, go as far away as I can get tonight.

TR

I land in Seattle just after midnight. I kept my head down and to myself on the flight. I had my headphones on and nobody disturbed me. The sky was black as I flew across the country chasing daylight.

The Reckoning

I never caught it, but then again, I never expected to.

My bag comes around on the carousel and I grab it, ignoring the few weary travelers who recognize me. I'm in no mood for autographs or pictures. I exit fast, finding a cab quickly at this hour.

Sucking up my pride, I had called Tommy on the way to the airport and he agreed to set up the hotel for the night. I didn't even know where we were staying. But I had to apologize to get back in his good graces.

Collapsing on the bed, I stare up at the ceiling. My body hurts. My mind has been torturing me by replaying the look on her face, the hurt she displayed. She's a good fucking actress. Seeing her in that skimpy fucking top and even smaller bottoms. Seeing her having a pillow fight with that fuck. Hearing her silence as I begged her to lie to me. That's the last fucking time I will ever beg. That's the last fucking time I will ever let a woman ruin me.

The mini bar is stocked, but I call room service for full sized bottles. While waiting, I finish off the mini Jack Daniels and Crown Royal. When the bottles arrive, I take the Jack and stand at the window. I'm on fucking top of the world with Seattle laid at my feet, but it's meaningless. Nothing matters anymore.

Every time I think of Holliday, I drink. I drink until the bottle is half empty. I drink until I can't balance. I drink until I can't remember the sound of her voice as she called after me. I drink until my head goes black and my body falls.

Red.

Orange.

Yellow.

My eyes are closed but the bright yellow wakes me, hurting my eyes. I try to open one of my eyes, but the sun is blaring into the room, the curtains wide open. *Damn it.*

I get up and take a piss, then search for the remote to shut the curtains. When I can't find it, I yank them closed and go back to bed. Once the room is dark, I lie there. But it's useless when someone starts banging on my door.

Rolling out of bed, I go to answer it. Tommy looks tired and his patience is apparently wearing. "You look like shit," he says, barging in.

Annoyed, I flip him off. "Thanks."

"And you have a show in three hours," Tommy says. "I need answers."

"I need my wife! But we don't always get what we want. Now do we?"

He shakes his head. "Fuck." Shaking his head, he looks down and I can see it—the first sympathetic glance my way. "Go take a shower, then meet me downstairs and we'll talk."

"I don't want to talk."

"Tough shit. Go."

I glare at him. "I'm getting really fucking tired of you treating me like this."

"Like what, man?" He sounds exasperated.

That pisses me off even more. "Like I'm not Johnny Fucking Outlaw."

"Save the ego trip for your fans. It doesn't work on me. Now go shower and clear your fucking head."

We both face each other in a stand-off. But he's not worth the aggravation, so I walk around him and slam the bedroom shut behind me.

My head is killing me, so I find the pills I need and down them in the shower. The water covers me. It won't wash away what's happened, but I feel less dirty than before.

On the elevator down, I spin the ring on my finger, not sure if I want to wear it or not or even if I should. I leave it on, for now.

Nobody's in the lobby when I get down there, so I go outside. It's cold and I pull my jacket tighter to block the wind. There's no

The Reckoning

vehicle and none of the guys are out here. I see a newsstand a few feet away. All the tabloids covers are on display. The pregnancy story is featured on three of them front and centered. I pick one up and stare, my stomach spinning—not sure if it's from the booze this morning or the photos of my wife with that asshole.

I rip one from the stand and look at it, reading the headline over and over. The anger doesn't last. It alters into something that feels closer to heartbreak. The magazine falls from my hands. I stand there in the middle of the street staring at it as it lands at my feet. A small ache that started days earlier has become a pulsing pain, tearing my heart apart.

This isn't how things were supposed to go. This isn't how we were supposed to end. This isn't how our melody goes, how we were supposed to play out.

I want my life back.

I want my wife back.

"Hey buddy, you gotta pay for that."

I look at the guy from the newsstand and pull out my wallet. I give him a ten and walk away, hoping to walk back into the life I'll recognize because this one doesn't feel like mine at all. But the weather sucks and it's cold out. The rain has picked up and that pain inside me is getting worse.

The pedestrian crossing beeps while I remain standing there still in shock. I never saw this coming. People bump me on both sides as they hurry past, but I've become numb to everything that's not Holliday... and that fucking pain.

Despite the crushing pain, I'm not giving her up—not easily.

Not to him.

Not ever.

My knees hit the ground and my palms go flat against the pavement. The sound of traffic surrounds me but distances itself. Voices fill my ears, a faint echoing of *Outlaw... Outlaw... Outlaw.*

My breaths are shallow, coming in quick bursts, despite me trying to deepen it. I inhale, then again, focusing on each one as if it's my last until I'm grabbed and hauled backwards.

When I wake up, I have fading memories of being put in the car and checked into the hospital. Dex is at the end of my bed eyeing me. "Look fucker, don't pull that shit again," he says, pissed off. "I've lost Cory and even though you and me don't get along all the time, I'm not ready to lose you too."

I scowl and look away, unfortunately coming face to face with Tommy. His demeanor is completely different from Dex and it worries me. "What?"

"How are you feel—"

A nurse barges in looking down at her clipboard. When she looks up, she smiles and it's a nice reprieve from the guys. "How are you feeling, Mr. Dalton?"

"Outlaw," I correct.

She tilts her head to the side. "Do you prefer for me to call you Mr. Outlaw? I was going off of your chart."

"I prefer Outlaw." But I'm not sure why. I haven't felt much like Johnny Outlaw in a while. Maybe it's just that it feels too foreign for her to call me by my given name.

"Certainly. How are you feeling?"

"Confused."

"That's natural."

"Not to me. Why am I here?"

She touches the clipboard down on the bed, tapping it twice. "We're thinking you experienced a psychogenic blackout." Looking at me, she smiles. "In your case, I don't think there's reason for alarm at this time. It's actually more common than people realize and usually associated with high stress jobs." She picks the clipboard back up and studies it again. "After reviewing your chart, your doctor feels certain this is what happened in your case since you don't have the history related to other factors. Fortunately, the only real side effect is temporary memory loss." When she looks back up, she asks, "Do you remember what might have brought this on? How you got here? Meeting me yesterday?"

"Yesterday?" I ask, surprised. Memories of Holliday—her on the bed with *him*, her tears as she told me to leave, the covers of the magazines—play like a slideshow.

"Yes, you were admitted yesterday evening. I know your manager here says you are in the middle of a tour. Are you under a lot of stress?"

"Where's my wife?"

Tommy steps to the side of my bed. "She's flying in. She got on the first flight she could get this morning. We had so much going on with cancelling the show last night, I forgot to call her until close to ten. She should be landing in the next hour or so."

I nod and turn away. "How long do I have to stay here?"

"We want to run a 12-lead EKG on you. That will check your heart rhythm for any potential irregularities so we can rule out epilepsy. You have no history of epilepsy, so we feel fairly confident that this is a onetime occurrence. The doctor will be in shortly to answer any questions you may have and then we'll take you to get that EKG."

"You didn't answer my question."

"I can't answer your question, Mr. Outlaw. Not until the doctor reads the results from the test." She walks to the door and says, "Just buzz us if you need anything. The doctor should be in shortly."

I turn to Tommy. "I want out of here."

"You need to stay. Do the test. We can't tour if something's wrong. I think you'll be released today or at the latest in the morning, but part of your contract says you must follow doctors orders if medical attention is required." He rubs his eyes. "You're looking good, Johnny. Don't stress and you'll get out of here sooner.

I'm gonna go back to the hotel and get some sleep. Call me if you need me. I'll leave the ringer on."

Before he leaves, I say, "Thanks... for everything."

"It's my job."

He makes it sound so casual, but I know it's really his big heart that kept him here overnight.

Dex comes to the side of the bed and we slap our hands together doing the same handshake we've done for years. It used to be done between the three of us, but since Cory's gone... Dex says, "Get better. Okay?"

"Okay. Thanks."

"I meant what I said earlier. It's not your time, so stop trying to force it."

I chuckle lightly. "Deal."

He follows Tommy out of the room and I close my eyes. My body feels heavy, exhausted from the trauma it's been through. I can feel the sluggishness in my veins, a sleeping pill of some sort still running through them. I let go before I have a chance to grasp onto the memory of what happened between me and Holliday.

Sensing her, the smell of her, I can feel her next to me. She's my angel who saved me from my own living hell. She pulled me from the ashes of self-destruction and let me dirty her soul all in the name of love. Her fingertips rub my arm and reality comes rushing in, bringing me back to consciousness. I open my eyes and the back of my head presses heavy into the pillow, surprised. *This is not my angel.* "What are you doing here?"

Ashley's tone is soft, too soft like we're actually friends, like she has real concern for me. "I was worried. I know the band went back to the hotel to get some rest so I thought I should stay with you just in case you needed anything."

"I don't," I start, but stop to clear my throat. "Need anything."

She rushes around the bed and pours me a cup of water. "Here. Drink this."

I feel my brows buckle together, still perplexed to why she's here. "I'm okay."

"Maybe I can bring you some food from someplace nearby?"

I see a blanket on the couch and her shoes on the floor in front of it. "Were you sleeping here?"

"I rested while you did. I didn't want you to wake up alone."

"I'm fine," I say, "you can go."

"I promised Tommy I would stay with you and take care of you until they return."

"What are you talking about? I don't need you to take care of me."

Her fingers reach forward and she pushes my hair back. "I'm here for you. I would never hurt you or cheat on you."

I try to shift away, but I can't. I'm hooked up to a machine with an IV in me that tugs when I move. "I think you should go."

Her voice lowers, too intimate. "My dreams are your dreams." Her hand slides down my face and stops on my chest. "I can support you the way you deserve." She leans in and whispers in my ear, "I'll treat you like the man you are." She leaves a kiss on my cheek, but stays, her breath heavy against my skin.

I turn away to tell her to leave, but when I see the door, Holliday is standing there. *"Angel?"*

She's blinking as if she can't believe her eyes. "I got here as fast as I could."

Ashley stands next to me, her hand still on my body, her voice cool. "You didn't need to rush. I was here for him since you weren't."

Holliday's eyes fill with heavy tears as she looks at her. "My mistake."

"Baby?" I say, shaking my head. "It's not—"

"Guess I was right all along. I thought I was special, Johnny. But being with you didn't make me special. It made me a groupie."

Johnny? I sit up, determined to get to her. "No!"

I can feel our connection shattering between us, my words come tripping out, making no sense. "I thought we were broken back in New York."

"We weren't, but we are now." She turns and disappears from the doorway too fast for me to rip this fucking IV out and get to her.

"Holliday?" I yell, not caring that I'm in a hospital.

There's no response from her, but two nurses come rushing in. "Sir, please lie back down." The sound of the beeping increases and they each grab one of my arms. I struggle to get out, but my body fails me. I see one of the nurses pushing a button and then close my eyes.

19

Holliday Hughes

"Dreams aren't for the masses to share. My dreams can't be televised, but achieving my goals can." ~ Johnny Outlaw

I can't get out of that hospital fast enough, taking the stairs, running past the nurse's station and straight out the wide sliding glass doors. Looking both ways, there are no cabs in sight, so I keep running. As soon as I round the corner, I fall back against the side of the building and bend over—out of breath, cramping, heart missing entirely. With my arm wrapped around my stomach, I let the sobs take over. There's no stopping them anyway.

Brown loafers stop in front of me. "Do you need help, Miss?"

When I look up, the grey clouds frame the elderly man's grey hair. "I'm," I have trouble speaking while trying to reign in the tears, but continue, "I'll be fine."

"Are you sure? I can call someone for you."

Standing upright, I say, "I need a taxi. Can you please help me find one?"

"Yes, there's a pickup at the hotel right around the corner. Can I assist you over there?"

"No, I'm okay. Thank you." I walk away, noticing no one ever came after me, which if I still had my heart, would break it even more, as if that could be possible.

Standing in the cab line at the hotel, I realize, I have nowhere to go. My luggage flew home with Tracy straight from New York since I thought I'd be taking Dalton out of here today. I have a toothbrush in my purse and that's about it. And since Ashley's now taking care of my husband, there's no reason for me to stay. As soon as I get in the cab, I say, "The airport please."

Nine hours later I walk into my house, drop my purse on the floor, and go upstairs to the bedroom. I crawl into bed. My eyes, still burning from all the tears I've cried, can't stay open any longer.

TR

My eyes flash open just after two in the morning. The room is dark, but there's enough light to see the vast bedroom. My heart has returned... or been returned by Dalton, because it starts to immediately ache.

I hate being here alone. My heartbreak is magnified when surrounded by the superficial stuff that fills our lives. The silver framed photo from our vacation to the Maldives last summer shines in the moonlight. I get up and turn it face down, not allowing myself to look at him in the photo.

I still can't believe he did this to me. I still can't believe she

The Reckoning

worked her way into his life. Like a knife slicing through a whole heart, she cut us apart and I'm left here trying to figure out what remains, if anything.

The last thirty-six hours replay in my mind, drawing out the tears again. We never finished the video. I couldn't walk back onto that set. Tracy said they got enough footage, but I couldn't be moved to care... I still don't.

I wanted to run after Dalton when he walked out of that apartment, but I couldn't in the underwear I was wearing. I stood there for ten minutes thinking he would return. But he didn't. The filming had stopped and everyone packed up and left. Tracy dragged me into the bedroom where my husband left me to end the fascination from the crew. I sat on the end of the bed with plaster under my feet from the broken wall.

My phone was in my hand, but he didn't call. I wanted to call him, but I stared at the hole before me, remembering his face when he accused me of cheating on him. My pride got in the way. Later that night, my rattled brain cleared and I called...

I push send and close my eyes while listening to his phone ringing. After four rings, my call transfers to voicemail leaving me empty. I call again. And again. Still no answer.

Hunching over the toilet I try to expel the nightmare that plagues my thoughts. This didn't happen. Not to us. It makes no sense, but I can't escape the reality that it did happen. That he did accuse me of cheating. That he thinks his baby is someone else's. This happened and now I'm left to live in the pain of it playing on repeat in my head.

I call again in the dark of the bedroom where I'm expected to sleep, but Tracy knows as well as I do that sleep won't be a part of my night. No answer. Again.

Lying down on top of the covers, I stare up at a feather that floats toward me without a care in the world. I reach up and catch it between two fingers. It's delicate, but strong, so much like my relationship with Dalton, until tonight.

My phone rings and I quickly answer it. "Hello?"

"Holli?" The voice sounds familiar, but the male voice is panicked, disguising the caller. "It's Tommy."

My gut tightens and I sit upright. "Tommy? What's wrong?"

"It's Johnny."

No!

He says, "He's in the hospit—"

"Where?" My feet land hard on the wood floor and I run to my suitcase.

"Seattle."

"What happened?" I ask, grabbing jeans and a shirt.

"We don't know yet, but I thought I should call you."

"Yes. Thank you. I'm catching the next flight I can get on."

"The media doesn't know yet. I've got a call in to add security without alerting the paps. I'll let them know to expect you so you can get in to see him."

I stop with a death grip on the phone as I hold it to my ear. "Tell me the truth, Tommy. Is he okay?"

"He passed out on the street. He's sleeping, but a nurse told me his vitals are steady. They don't foresee anything bad right now, but they'll be doing some tests when he wakes up."

"I'm coming as fast as I can. Please call me if anything changes."

"I will."

Within minutes of hanging up, I receive the text with the hospital address and I'm running out the door to catch a flight. After hours of trying to negotiate a way on to two different flights, they book me on one that leaves early in the morning.

Now lying in the treachery of New York and Seattle, visions of Ashley appear. Maybe I should have answered him in New York, but now... Fuck him for thinking I could ever cheat on him. My anger surges and I roll over, burying my face into the pillow and cry as if my supply has been renewed while I slept. I pray for mercy. I pray to wake up from this nightmare. I pray to go back to sleep and avoid thinking at all. But my head and heart have other plans that don't include rest.

As my thoughts run wild, remembering everything he accused me of and then seeing her at his bedside, her hand on him as if it belonged there, I have no words, just emotions that border on exploding from my chest. I grab the TV remote, needing to stop everything, needing to not think about the pain of losing the man I love.

The noise is nice, even if it is an infomercial. I go to the bathroom, then brush my teeth and change into pajamas before getting back in bed and spending the next two hours being sold on four different products...

"She was in his hospital room," I say, crying on the phone to customer service. "What am I supposed to do with that?"

"Ma'am, I just need the code on the back of the card and we'll get the Amazing Can Opener out to you priority mail."

Sighing, I say, "Forty-three."

"I'm so sorry about your husband. I wish you the best of luck. I need to take the next customer's order."

"Thank you," I sniffle and hang up.

I fall back asleep just before five.

TR

There's no hiding my heartbreak. My swollen lids, the dark circles under my eyes, and my blotchy skin are dead giveaways. I debate not going to work, but I slather on some eye serum and head over to the townhouse.

Tracy comes downstairs when she hears me come in. "What are you doing? How is Johnny?" I burst into tears, my only true skill today. "Oh honey," she says, grabbing me into a tight hug. "What happened?"

"*She* was there."

"Who was there? Who is *she*?"

"Ashley."

She leans back and looks at me. Totally confused, and asks, "Who's Ashley?" We sit on the couch and I tell her the story from the first time I ever saw Ashley to seeing her at his bedside at the hospital. Tracy looks as stunned as I still feel. There's nothing she can say to make this better, but I appreciate her efforts. "I'm so sorry, Hols." She hugs me and I close my eyes and cry again.

After a few moments, she says, "Just because she grew up on the road doesn't make her better for Johnny. You know that right?"

"I did. I don't anymore. I'm not supporting his caree—"

"Bullshit, Holli! You support him and that's the same thing. Don't let her get in your head. Just because you have a life of your own, have your own business, doesn't mean you're not supportive of him." Standing up, she takes my hands and tugs. I stay seated so she says, "You shouldn't be here."

Looking down, I shake my head. "I can't be at home."

"What can I do?" she asks, sitting down again. "How can I help?"

"There's nothing anyone can do. I don't even know what I can do."

"Are you going to stay here?"

"Why does staying here make me feel like a failure?"

"A failure at what?"

Looking down at my wedding ring, I spin it around, and reply, "My marriage. I stayed here before because I was lonely. Staying here now feels like I'm running away." I glance at her. "Why couldn't I just suck up my pride, push my hurt feelings aside and tell him what he wanted to hear?"

"Because you shouldn't have to. He should've trusted you."

I lie back and close my eyes. "When did this become my life? When did we become this chaos of lies and betrayal?"

"When you started believing everyone else and not each other."

My eyelids pop open, slapped by the truth. "I want to believe him. I do so much, but she was there as if she had a right to be."

"Maybe there's more to the story than you know. Don't you think you should ask him?"

"After what happened in New York and seeing him all cozy with her in Seattle, I can't. I just can't." I put my arms over my stomach. "If he wants to talk, he needs to come to me. He needs to apologize."

"As long as you realize that being right may come at the cost of being alone." Tracy stands up and walks back upstairs, leaving me there to drown in the after effect of her words.

Curling up on the couch, I rest my head and close my eyes. I didn't mean to fall asleep, but when a door closes, I wake up. I open my eyes and find Danny sitting on the coffee table in front of me. He whispers, "Hi."

"Hi." I don't bother sitting up, too depressed to move.

With a sympathetic smile that just feels all wrong on him, he asks, "How are you doing?"

I roll onto my back and rest my arm above my head. "I've been better."

"Are you pregnant?"

Glancing at him, I ask, "Where'd you hear that?"

"It's everywhere online and breaking news on CNN."

Just when I think I'm out of sighs, I conjure enough energy for one more heavy one. "I am."

"What's this bullshit about Sebastian being the father?"

"He's not."

He grins. "I know he's not."

My eyebrows go up and my gaze flashes to him. "You do?"

"Sure, I do."

"How?"

"Because I know you."

I want to cry that he can see the truth so easily. "I wish Dalton did."

"These situations are tricky when they play out in the media. The truth gets twisted. You know that."

"Dalton's forgotten."

"Has he forgotten or he just doesn't like the reminders?"

"What's the difference?" I ask and look away, my melancholy getting the better of me as tears build in the corners of my eyes.

"Maybe none right now." His fingers touch my chin and he turns me toward him. "Hey, he knows." His hand goes back to his lap and he says, "He knows in his heart, so give him time."

"In the meantime, I'm here carrying his baby and going through this alone. This is not how I pictured it going."

Danny stands up. "That's the problem with expectations. Sometimes they don't live up to our dreams." He walks to the door, but says, "I have to go. I have a hot date waiting. I'm even taking her to dinner."

I roll my eyes. "Wow, dinner before the sex. Such a novel idea."

"Eh, even the bad boys can be good sometimes."

Silly woman falling for his charms, but I've got my own bad boy issues to worry about, so before he leaves, I sit up and ask, "Hey, Danny? Why do women fall for the bad boy?"

He laughs and steps outside. Looking back at me with a big grin on his face, he says, "There's no fun in playing it safe."

I throw one of the couch's pillows as hard as I can at him, but the door shuts and it hits the back of it and drops. Flopping back again, I huff. He's so ridiculous that I actually smile. He didn't come here for my pity party. He was just a friend when I needed one and that means a lot to me.

TR

Over the next week, neither of us calls the other, our anger, pride, whatever we want to call it getting in the way of our hearts. I know Dalton well enough to know that's what is holding him back as well. I want to though. It makes me wonder if he does too. The Resistance resumed their tour only missing the one show in Seattle, which they played the next night after he left the hospital.

With my mouth full of a turkey and provolone sandwich, I swivel back and forth in my chair, staring at my monitor, but not taking any of it in.

Her voice is lilt, ending on a hopeful high when Tracy says, "I got an update if you want one."

I had forbidden her to talk about him a few days ago. She's held true to that until now. My heart aches again reminding me that it still exists, it still beats, it's still shattered in my chest. I had briefly wondered if I'd lost it forever. Maybe it's just Dalton I lost forever... "Tell me." I grip the arms of my chair and spin around to face her across the office.

"They're heading to London. They have several shows scheduled including Wembley Stadium tomorrow night."

"He used to talk about playing to a sold out crowd there one day. He's doing it. He's achieving his dreams."

"Wishes do come true."

"Sometimes," I say, "she's there with him. Maybe she's his good luck."

"Holli," she warns, treading carefully after. "I know how much he loves you. Everyone does. You're his world."

I set my sandwich down, my appetite suddenly gone. "I'm not

much of anything to him these days."

She continues as if she didn't hear me. "Rochelle told me his test results were clear. The doctors said his blackout was from stress, so they don't have a fear of epilepsy and there are no symptoms for other things. That's good news, right?"

She's not really asking me, but I answer anyway. "It's great news," I whisper.

"Still no word though—email, text, phone call?"

"Nope, not even a tweet." My monitor goes to sleep, so I wiggle the mouse to make it come to life again. "Is that all?"

"That's all."

I nod and get back to work reading resumes. "I think we need to start the Office Manager interviews next week. The sooner we bring someone on, the sooner you can move into CFO full time."

The sadness in her voice is heard, her empathy seeping out that I've changed back into the topic of work. "Okay. I'll start interviewing on Monday."

"Thank you." I don't mean to sound curt, but I can't help it today. I push away from the desk and leave. Ten minutes later, I'm standing on the boardwalk above the beach staring straight into the horizon and wondering if that water will ever touch his shores. Taking off my shoes, I go down the stairs and walk toward the ocean until it covers my ankles. I close my eyes and take a deep breath. This week has been the worst of my life.

"Hey you," Rochelle says, her boys in tow.

Smiling when I see her, I open my arms wide to hug Neil. We've become buds. Dalton and I are their Godparents. We see them quite a bit, but it's been a few weeks. "Missed you, little man," I say, hugging him.

"Missed you," he says sweetly. He runs past and Rochelle tells him not to get soaked.

I lift CJ into my arms, holding him on my hips. "You've

gotten so big, Sir."

"Yes, he has. He's a big boy."

In baby talk, I speak to him. "We like big healthy boys." I kiss him on the cheek, then set him in the sand. He seems content not to go into the water.

Hugging Rochelle now, I ask, "What are you doing here?"

"Just visiting and Tracy said you came down here."

"How'd she know?"

"I think she knows you well enough."

"Safe," I say remembering Danny's words from last week. Safe translates to predictable and boring. Maybe I'm both now.

She sits next to CJ, but looks up at me and says, "Tracy said she told you."

"She told me his tests came back clear."

"How does that make you feel?"

"Well, Dr. Floros," I start. I sit down next to her and watch Neil splash around the water's edge. "It makes me feel like shit that I have to hear about my husband either online, the gossip shows, or from my friend."

"I'm sorry."

"So am I." I ask, "I guess you know the full story?"

"Too many witnesses to the fight in New York. The story sold for 20K two days ago. Whoever sold it was on set, and has been sitting on it for the highest bidder."

Drawing a line in the sand, I swallow down the information. Humiliation creeps in and I remark, "Soon everyone will know that my husband thinks I sleep around and I'm carrying someone else's baby."

Rochelle absorbs that, then sighs. "I'm sorry."

"So am I."

20

Jack Dalton

"True love is what remains long after the person has gone." ~ Holliday Hughes

I've lost myself—my soul, my rhythm, every beat of my heart has vanished. It's gone to live with Holliday. I knew this life was too good to be true. I knew *she* was too good to be true. But I fell for her completely, disregarding my history with women. She was different... she was supposed to be different.

Fucked.

I've been fucked over again.

Tommy switches seats and settles in next to me on the private plane to London. I don't look up from the Rolling Stone on the tray table in front of me, and say, "Don't get comfortable."

"Don't worry, princess. I'm only here to talk."

"Make it quick."

"The label's worried."

"They should be."

"They're worried about your health."

I turn to him. "They don't have to worry about that."

"Between us. Are you okay to play these shows, Johnny?"

"I'm okay to play Johnny Outlaw like a monkey for money. Didn't they get the doctor's note? I'm okay to do my part to make the label happy. I'm okay to fucking lose who I am to be who everyone else fucking wants me to be."

Tommy stresses, but he's always held his shit together as well as the band. "Who do you want to be?"

Shaking my head, I turn the page of my magazine and reply, "Not this."

TR

A string of swear words is muttered under Tommy's breath. With my hand on the railing, I turn back. He taps Dex's back. "Go." Dex takes the steps by two while carrying his drumsticks in his right hand. Sixty seconds later, he's pounding his kit and Tommy says to the rest of us, "He nails it every time. Now get your asses up there and give 'em hell."

The spotlight remains on Dex as I walk up the steps and out onto the dark stage. I hit my mark, center stage in front of my microphone. My breath lumps in my throat momentarily staring out at the stadium crowd. I never thought we'd pull in a crowd this large. Our opening act was a popular English band that signed on for the European leg of our tour. They got the crowd pumped up. Now we have to deliver the best show of our lives.

Leaning forward my hands start playing as I begin singing and the light hits me. I focus into the space in the crowd where faces lose defined features and the lights don't reach. Sometimes it's easier than seeing the desperation and enjoyment of fans up close. The nerves I thought I might have aren't here as my fingers strum the rhythms that live inside me. The words come naturally, as they always have, but tonight they're twisted with Holliday, my emotions wrapped up in her as I sing—

Her lips are a rose, too soft to damage, but too pretty to overlook.

A light sparks in her eyes, a future of memories like a photo she took.

Her melody ran through my veins.

What became of the girl I used to know?

What becomes of us after the rain?

Two hours of singing, giving every ounce of myself over to the music. Two hours of bleeding my soul to a sold out crowd. Every minute worth it. Every memory of this will carry me. When I come off stage after the encore, Ashley hands me a towel, but she drops back behind the other guys. Tommy opens the dressing room and we file inside. I pull my sweat soaked shirt off and toss it next to my bag and towel off. When I put on a clean shirt... or semi-clean, I can't tell anymore, I say, "This was it, guys. This is what years of hard work and fucking torture for our art has led to. I hope you enjoyed it because it can't get better than that out there."

The air has changed, the band taking it in. We look at each other, quietly taking this high in. Dex comes over and offers a handshake. When I take it, he says, "That was for Cory."

I bring him in, patting him on the back and repeat, "That was for Cory."

Tommy adds, "That was for Cory."

We're left in a moment of reflection as we pack our gear. Kaz finally breaks the silence, and says, "I'm ready to do it again."

Fifteen minutes later, we're ready to leave. The guys walk out except for Dex, who says, "I meant what I said back in Seattle. You don't get to leave this world before I do."

"Race you to the finish," I joke, kind of.

"Nah," he says, chuckling. "I've found a new reason to stick around."

I grab his arm before he walks out. "About that." I stop when he looks back. "I see how you look at Rochelle. You know she's like a sister to me."

"I know." He turns to face me, crossing his arms.

"Don't fuck her around."

"I wouldn't."

There are so many memories of mine tied up in Rochelle and Cory being together. But something about the way Dex talks about her, I can see that he might genuinely care about her. I nod, but add, "If you fuck her over, I'll fuck you up."

Exasperated, he says, "You're such an asshole, Johnny."

Shrugging, I grin. "What can I say?" I walk past him and join the other guys.

The private club we go to is crowded as usual, but at least I can drink in peace, or so I thought. Tommy stands and shakes some guy's hand. I can tell he's American before he even speaks—converse, jacket, jeans. LA all the way. Tommy sits back down and introduces him, "This is Kiefer Keys."

"Have we met before?" I ask, shaking his hand.

"Once at a music video awards show."

"You're in a band?"

"Was. The Mattresses. We're taking an extended break."

"Why?"

He drinks his beer, seeming to think of what he wants to say. "Burn out and the grind gets old. We're getting old."

"You're what, thirty?"

The Reckoning

"Thirty-three, but the next level may not happen for us and we're tired, man. Don't you just get tired sometimes?"

"All the fucking time, but how do you walk away from music?"

"Maybe it's not in my blood anymore."

"I couldn't leave music," I say, refilling my glass of whiskey. "It's a part of me, like blood. It flows through me."

His tone changes and he says, "I got into music to meet chicks."

I laugh. "Did it work?"

"Like a charm."

"So what are you doing now?"

Tommy pipes in, "He's producing and he's good at it. He comes from the band's perspective instead of protecting the label's interest."

Looking him over, trying to figure out if working hard is as important to him as his looks seem to be, I ask, "You want to produce our next album? That's why you're here?"

"That's why I'm here."

I notice the calluses on his fingers that only years of playing the guitar create. He has drive by the way he looks me in the eyes when he speaks. Something about him is off; he's too confident, cocky even. He's hiding something. "Why should we hire you?"

"Because I'm good."

I eye him. "You're not the best?"

"I'm not the best, but I'm damn good. I'll work my ass off for this record, for you guys."

Ashley sits down across from us, the large coffee table dividing the group. She has her eyes on me, *always looking at me*. I never noticed until I left New York. But Derrick had his eyes on her, and like now, his hand is on her knee. When she sees me looking, she brushes it away. I can read women. They're always so damn obvious, except for Holliday. The only woman I ever truly wanted and... I down my drink.

Kiefer interrupts the storm brewing inside my head and says, "You and I have a friend in common."

Pouring another two shots into the glass, I ask, "Oh really. Who?"

"Holli Hughes."

Fuck me. "And how do you know my wife?" I eye him, waiting to hear how he feels so close to her that he drops her name so easily.

"We used to date."

Fuck me double. I swallow the entire drink, my throat numb to the burn. "Oh yeah?"

"I thought at one point we might get married. Not sure what happened there."

Using his words against him, I say, "She didn't want to settle for 'good.' She wanted the best." I stand just as the waitress warns us it's closing time. "I think we're done here."

"Because I dated Holli?"

"No, because you fucked my wife and act like that's gonna somehow bond us."

Tommy stands, "Whoa. Whoa. Whoa. Calm down, Johnny. Kiefer, I didn't know about your history. You should have probably mentioned that."

"I did to Holli when I saw her at Spago." He turns to me like I'll be his ally. "Everything's cool with her. I know you guys are going through a rough patch, but my relationship with her is copacetic, smooth sailing now."

I stare at him, wondering when he's going to stop spewing this hippie bullshit. When he does, I say, "You know nothing about me except what you've heard on TV. Yet, you come in here wanting a fair shot at a job that can make or break *my* album. Unlike you, the only two things that matter to me are music and my family. It seems you've already fucked with one and now you want to fuck the other, so tell me again why you think 'damn good' is good enough."

His arrogance rivals my own. I can almost respect him for it. But then he opens his mouth again. "I can make your record hit the charts."

"*I* can make my records hit the charts. I've done it three times and the current album is charting to the top."

"Look, if it's the Holli thing—"

"You look. We're done here. I don't need to drag more baggage into a situation that has become entertainment for the masses. You can't offer me anything that I can't do on my own. The Resistance is looking for a visionary, not just 'good.' So this," I wave between us, "isn't happening."

Ashley calls my name, "Johnny," she nods toward the door. "We're going back to the hotel. Come on."

I let my gaze follow the long line of her legs up to the curve of her tits highlighted by the low-cut shirt she's wearing. She's at least 5'9, her heels inching her higher. She looks different with her hair down. Her eyes are lined, making me take notice for the first time, especially since they're set on me.

She's nothing like Holliday. *Nothing.*

I bend over and light my cigarette and take a deep inhale, letting the smoke calm my insides. It's been a long time since I had this pleasure. I can't stop the smirk that follows. With the cigarette hanging out the side of my mouth, I tell Tommy, "Seems the party's moving to the hotel."

I'm not sure what the hour is, but I know England is sleeping, or should be. We drank until we were kicked out and came back to the suite to finish what was started at the pub. We have another show here tomorrow night and a talk show in the afternoon. Everybody left hours ago to get some rest, but I stayed in the living room with a bottle of whiskey. It's dark out. The street lamps highlight the fog and drizzle and the fucking fifteen by twenty foot billboard of Holliday and that asshole hanging on the side of the building across the street. The glass of my window is speckled with drops, but I can see the way he holds her, kissing her neck and her smile, the one only I was privy to before.

My gaze falls back from the outside to the phone on the table next to me. Holliday hasn't called. I'm not shocked considering the last two times we saw each other, but somehow I am surprised. What I thought were rumors have turned out to be true. She wouldn't fucking answer me because that baby is his. She hasn't called because she fucked me over. I grab the bottle and chug as I stare at the billboard.

Leaning forward, I rest my arms on my knees and drop my head. I still love her. I love her so fucking much.

But she's having that assholes baby. How did this happen? How'd I lose her? *When* did it happen? I start calculating time in my head, going backwards. But the numbers are fucked up and I can't concentrate.

Caressing fingers run through my hair and I look up. "Why are you still here?" I ask Ashley.

She kneels down in front of me, the robe she's wearing coming open, displaying the big tits I noticed earlier. "I must have fallen asleep," she says.

I look into her eyes trying to decipher if it's a lie, but she does look tired, like she just woke up. "Why'd you fall asleep here?" My gaze drifts down her body, my dick starting to harden. I shift to find more room in my jeans.

Her palms run over my legs and slide up my arms as she lifts up on her knees. She has great tits—full from the implants, but sitting natural on her chest. Her waist dips in at the sides, her hips giving something to hold onto when fucking.

The Reckoning

Moving between my legs, she takes my hands, running her fingers over the veins on top. "You have such strong hands." As if she's confessing her innermost secrets, she whispers, "I've touched myself watching you play guitar, wanting it to be me you play so hard." Standing up, she straddles me, her robe open, exposing her bare body.

"Fuck!" I mumble, my logic going fuzzy, relenting the courtesy of Mr. Daniels. "We shouldn—"

"We should." She takes my hands and moves them to her breasts. "Touch me here first..." Slowly taking my right one, she slides it down her stomach and between her legs. "Then here," she says with a weak breath. Her eyes are on me when she leans down to kiss me.

Pushing against her waist, holding her back, I look down, avoiding this, whatever she thinks is about to happen. Her disappointment is heard, but I don't care. I may want to fuck, but I want to fuck Holliday, not some groupie.

As if Ashley can read my mind, she leans forward whispers in my ear, "She's with Sebastian. She's having his baby." She lifts my face up to look at her. Even though my hard glare would deter most, she's more determined than that. "I'm here for you now." She grinds on me, holding my shoulders. "However you want me. However you like it. I'll make your fantasies come true, Johnny."

Johnny.

My ego is stroked, reminding me who I am. "I'm Johnny Fucking Outlaw."

"Yes, Baby. You're Johnny *Fucking* Outlaw."

I want to erase the memories that anchor me to Holliday. I close my eyes tight, wanting to drift away in the feeling of being free again, like I used to be.

My phone rings. Turning to look, 'Holliday' flashes on the screen before it goes black and silent again. Just when I was floating, getting high off the whiskey and easy sex, like a sign, I'm saved. "Get off!" I push Ashley away and grab the phone. Standing up, I stare at it as I move to the other side of the living room from her. "Come on. Come on. Come on," I say to the phone. "Ring again. Ring. Damn it! C'mon, Holliday."

"Johnny?" Ashley stands there naked, her hands on her hips. "She's fucking Sebastian Lassiter. You're really going to pass on me for a two-timing whore?"

My eyes glaze, the anger in me welling. "Get the fuck out!"

Coming closer she says, "I can make you forget all about her."

"I don't want to forget her, but I do want to forget you. The door is over there."

"You're an asshole."

I make a mental note that this might be the third time in twenty-four hours that I've been called an asshole. I laugh. Being an asshole doesn't bother me. Being without Holliday does. Grabbing the bottle of whiskey by the neck, I throw it against the mirror that hangs over the couch.

She screams and moves quickly, the message heard loud and clear. Staring ahead, I watch as the bottle shatters, the amber liquid splattering over the light blue sofa. I think about throwing my motherfucking phone for not ringing again, but I don't. I have to have this last connection to Holliday no matter how much she screwed up.

My breathing is harsh as I stand in the middle of this mess still staring at my damn phone. I hate myself for doing it, but I call her back anyway. I hold the phone to my ear and wait as the long distance call connects. But before it even rings my eyes land on the billboard again... and I hang up.

I remain there alone, unsure of anything anymore when someone knocks on the door. It better the hell not be Ashley again. When I peek through the peephole, Tommy stands with someone in

The Reckoning

a suit. I open the door and look at them.

"Sorry to disturb you at this late hour, Sir, but we've received a complaint about a loud noise and yelling coming from your room." The man, I'm guessing is the Night Manager, peers over my shoulder into the suite.

Tommy says, "What's going on?" He pushes past me and walks inside.

I step to the side and the Manager comes in. When he sees the mess, he asks, "What happened? Was there an accident?"

"Yes, I accidentally threw a bottle of whiskey against your mirror."

Tommy sighs heavily. "For fuck's sake, man. Can I get one night's sleep without having to babysit you guys?"

"Sure," I say, smirking. "I'm not keeping you."

"Actually, you are. What happened?"

He sees me glance to the Manager who is on his cell phone. "...Yes, suite 1090." When he hangs up, he says, "Our housekeeper will clean this mess. May I suggest you get some rest in the bedroom or we can move you to another room? This may take a while."

Heading toward the bedroom, I announce, "I'm going to bed."

"Yeah, I think that's best," Tommy says. I can tell he's pissed. I probably deserve it. "And maybe next time, you'll change rooms like I suggested when we saw that billboard out there."

Ignoring him, I yell, "I want Ashley gone from the tour," then I slam the bedroom door closed.

The next day, I open the door and walk into the living room. Tommy's on his laptop set up at the dining table. He doesn't acknowledge me, so the whole pissed off thing is confirmed.

I try anyway. "Morning."

"You have an hour until we're being picked up for the talk show. I ordered a full English breakfast. They made an exception for you since breakfast ended three hours ago."

217

"Okay."

I turn to go take a shower, but he adds, "Okay? That's it?"

When I turn back, I say, "Thanks?"

"Yes, a thank you would be nice."

"Did you start your period this morning, Tommy?"

"Fuck you. I'm tired of your shit. I'm tired of Dex's shit. And if I give Kaz and Derrick an inch, they'll fuck up too. I'm getting too old for this." He shuts his laptop and stands up.

"You're only thirty-three."

"You fuckers have aged me well into my fifties."

I've never seen him like this. I must admit, it's disconcerting. "I screwed up. Whatever. I'll pay for the cleaning and mirror. Okay?"

"You think that is what this is about? You think I give a shit about a mirror that I know you can more than afford?"

"Then what? What's it about?"

"It's about me trying to hold this band together while you guys are trying your damndest to pull it apart. I live and breathe this band. I don't have my own fucking life because I'm too busy babysitting you guys. I'm tired of the shit. I'm tired of hotel management contacting me at four in the morning because the Great Johnny Outlaw had another tantrum and I need to go clean up his fucking mess. I go well and beyond the description of my job and I don't think I can keep doing this anymore."

"What are you saying?" I ask.

"I'm saying I want a life. I want to work normal hours for a change and be home on the weekends. I don't want calls at two in the morning to collect Dex from the floor of a Paris bar or be the responsible one when we go out. I want to hang out with you guys and enjoy it. I want a woman to come home to. I want a woman in my life that's worth getting upset over."

I stand there staring at him, shocked by this revelation. "Well fuck, man, are you quitting?"

The Reckoning

He shakes his head. "Nope. Because as much as you guys drive me out of my fucking mind with your antics, I don't want to miss a thing. I've been with this band since it was in diapers. Playing Wembley just graduated you from college. I'm gonna finish this tour and when you guys go into the studio, I'm gonna try to get a life back." Opening the door, he says, "I'm not leaving, but I'm starting to look for reasons to stay."

It's just a phase. He's just pissy over last night. That's it. I smile. "You love us. Admit it, Tommy."

"That's the only reason I'm still here." The room service waiter arrives, and Tommy says, "Food's here. Be ready in forty-five." He leaves when the food is pushed into the room.

Sitting and eating, I think about what Tommy said. How much he's given up in his personal life to help us achieve our dreams. But the one thing that stands out the most is when he said he wants 'A woman that's worth getting upset over.'

What he doesn't realize is that sometimes what we want is not necessarily what we need. I go to the photos on my phone and start flipping through until I land on one of Holliday. She's fucking gorgeous, always was, always so damn beautiful. I remember the first time I saw her in Vegas...

Tommy is running down the shortened playlist after we wrap our sound check. The club at The Palatial Hotel is ready for tomorrow night's private gig. I cut the third song and replace it with 'Mortars,' a new song we've been working on. Dex starts talking about the tightening on his kit again, so I begin to tune out the conversation. Looking up, the area where we're standing has a few people wandering about. Not wanting any attention, I interrupt and say, "Let's go get a beer somewhere less public."

They get the drift because they get tired of the attention I get as much as I do, and Cory says, "I'm gonna go back to the room and call Rochelle. She's been sick. I'll catch up later."

"Brother," I say as we shake hands.

Tommy starts talking about a bar in the hotel when Cory walks away. I look out toward the hall, just past Cory and smile, seeing my next conquest. Sandy-blonde hair. Killer legs in a short skirt. Great body. She walks with confidence and purpose. When her eyes meet mine, I discover something else than a light brownish coloring them, something deeper, something mysterious that I want to uncover. I tilt my head and try to draw her in through a shared moment like the ladies love. But she looks away instead.

I cock an eyebrow in surprise. She's good. She's not a naïve little girl. She's a woman who knows herself. But I still laugh that she's actually trying to outplay me. Nice try. Real funny.

With her hand on the door, she stops and I take advantage by admiring the backside she was blessed with. Damn fine ass. Wonder what it looks like naked and bent over. If I see her again, I'll make sure to find out.

The little hottie disappears into the ballroom. She's stronger than I gave her credit for. I like that. Before we leave the corridor to find the nearest bar, I look back because I may be able to get pussy when I want, but I've also never had a woman get the better of me... until now.

After all we went through to be together, did she get the better of me in the end? I believed we would make it. I believed in us against the world. I believed all the lies and the miserable fucking truths that have come out since. I believed her... until now.

21

Holliday Hughes

"It's not about changing the course of your life. It's about accepting the course you've chosen."
~ Johnny Outlaw

It was the announcement none of us saw coming. One month to the day I last saw Dalton in the hospital, the band announced it will be taking a break at the end of the tour and pursuing solo projects. In LA, we all know a break means breakup.

The Resistance is no more...

My water falls from my hand and a pain shoots through my stomach. Gripping the counter with one hand and my stomach with the other, I start my meditation breathing to calm. Inhale. Exhale. Inhale. Exhale. *Please be okay, baby.* One. Two. Three. Four. Five.

The pain subsides, but my concern doesn't. Anger takes over, making me bitter that Dalton's not here to experience the good and bad with me. He's abandoned me when I needed him most.

I think about everything he said, his accusation running through my mind like a painful metronome. Minutes don't pass without thinking of him. Only seconds here and there give me amnesty from the heartbreak.

My phone sits on the counter in front of me, tempting me to call. But like I assume how he feels, I can't seem to get over the hurt to actually pick it up and dial after that one time weeks ago. I push the phone away and go to bed.

Lying there, I wonder what happened to the band, or if it's Johnny who made the final decision. He's spoken about going solo, but to do it now… Inhale. Exhale. I can't spend my time thinking like this. It's not good for me or the baby. He's chosen to believe the lies instead of his wife. I glance over at the framed photo of us from last summer. I thought he was getting better after Cory's death, but now from what I'm hearing, I don't think he's ever been healed. Add in the stress of the tabloids, and he put on a good show for as long as he could.

I wake up, my body bunched with my knees lifted as I lie on my side. An excruciating pain tightens, bringing tears to my eyes. I squeeze my eyes closed and reopen them. I try my meditation breathing, counting each one to relax my body but it doesn't work. Scooting to the nightstand, I reach for my phone, but it's not there. Mentally distressed when I remember it's downstairs in the kitchen, I grip my knees close to my body until I can't take it any longer.

Something's wrong.

Starting to panic, I stand up and make it to the door before the pain kicks in again, causing me to cringe and bend over. Wrapping my arms around my middle, the worst scenarios start running through my head. "Baby, be okay. Be okay, baby. I'm here for you." I push off the wall and despite the pain, I hurry to the kitchen and call Rochelle.

"Hello?"

I get on the floor with the phone in my hands. Curling over, I lie down. "Rochelle, help me."

The panic rises in her voice. "What's wrong, Holli?"

"I don't know. The baby."

"Holli, you have to get to the hospital. I won't get there fast enough. Call 9-1-1."

"I can't. Everyone will see it leaving the house. It will be everywhere within minutes." Tears blur my vision.

She knows I'm right, so she suggests, "Can you drive yourself?"

Holding my body tightly together, I cry, "I don't know."

"You have to. You have to get in that car and go. Don't think about it. Just go. I'll meet you there. For the baby. Do this. Okay? Do this for the baby."

Inhale. Exhale. Inhale. Exhale. I stand despite the pain. "Okay." I grab my keys and my purse. One. Two. Three. "I can do this," I say, psyching myself up. Four. Five. Six...

Twenty minutes later I walk into the ER. I get checked in quickly and Rochelle comes into my room just as the doctor does. She rushes over to my side. Taking my hands in hers, she says, "Everything will be all right."

The doctor introduces himself and explains that they're going to do an ultrasound. "I see here that you're eleven weeks along and you've had one ultrasound. We're going to give another and listen to the heartbeat."

I nod, wanting so desperately to hear that little heartbeat again. Rochelle moves to the other side of the bed and continues to hold one of my hands as he pulls the machine over and gets the goo out. I look up at her, knowing this should be Dalton. This should be the man who vowed to love me always. But he's not here. Inhale.

Exhale. I squeeze her hand tighter and pray my baby is okay.

A sob breaks free as soon as that heartbeat—strong and steady—is heard. The doctor smiles. "Seems the baby is good. The heartbeat sounds great. As for the pain you experienced. We should talk about that. Let me make a few notes first." He wipes my tummy with a wet wipe, then hands me a towel to finish. A nurse walks in to clean the equipment and take the towel. When she walks out again, he continues, "When it comes to growing babies, you need to be mentally healthy as well as physically healthy. I think this was your body reacting to stress, which is common among women who lead busy lives."

Staring at the ceiling, his words bounce around my head as I try to make sense that *this* is my life. *This* isn't. When I look at him, I say, "I'll try."

He pats my arm. "But you're doing a good job. You're maintaining a healthy weight. Keep up the positive work. That little baby benefits from all your good decisions."

"Thank you," I say, wanting him gone, wanting to be alone.

"We're gonna get some more fluids in you, but you'll be free to go in a few hours. Take care of yourself and that little baby."

"Thank you," I repeat.

When he leaves, I turn to Rochelle. "What a pair Dalton and I are. Both of us having stress related issues and still not able to talk to each other. How is this possible?"

"Stubbornness?"

I smile the best I can, but it falls flat in effort. "Some pride too, but how do I get past the pain, Ro?"

Shaking her head, she replies, "I'm not sure. I'm stuck in my own cycle I can't seem to break away from."

"I'm sorry." I hate being so insensitive. I lost my head in my own moment of despair.

Rubbing my arm, she says, "Don't be. You're allowed to be

upset. You're just not allowed to spend your life apart from the man you love."

"I want to call him, but how can I under these circumstances? How do we find our way back when he thinks I slept with someone else and that *our* baby is Sebastian's?"

"I'm not sure, but I do know he's suffering too, suffering to the point of self-imploding. Unfortunately, you can't worry about him right now. You need to focus on this baby and let Johnny figure his own shit out. He's not in a place to be good for you right now."

"That makes me want to cry hearing that, but I might finally be all dried up."

"I've been there. Trust me, more will come and they may come in waves, but ride them the best you can."

"Thank you for being here."

"I'm always here for you." She smiles. "Can I get you something to eat?"

"I'd love a breakfast taco."

"You got it. I'll go find one for you and then help you check out of this place."

"Thanks."

When she leaves, she closes the door. My gaze darts to my purse on the table next to me. I reach in and grab my phone out of it. Checking first to see if I have any missed calls or text messages. I haven't and disappointment, the feeling I've come to expect, sets in again. I find his name and number in my contacts and stare at it. My thumb hovers over the call button and before I can overanalyze, I press the button.

My phone doesn't make it to my ear before I end the call. Remembering her at his bedside shoots through my heart, crushing it again. I drop the phone back in my purse and focus on the beach to erase the negativity.

As much as my heart has packed its bag and flown away to set up house next to his heart, I can't think about him right now. He hurt me and he needs to clean this mess up. I have to concentrate on growing a healthy baby. I rub my stomach. "We can do this, baby. We can do this even if it's just the two of us."

TR

Over the next few months I discover just how strong I can be. I rediscover me—the me from before Dalton. It hasn't been easy or pretty if judging by the dark circles that reside under my eyes, but I'm managing. Sometimes the idea that I'm getting by saddens me. I never thought I'd have to get by without him. But that's what I have to do for the baby. Fortunately, my mother arrived earlier in the week. "Sweetie, where do you keep the cleaning supplies?" I hear her in the kitchen rummaging around.

It's weird having someone else around, someone who isn't him, someone who wants to tell me how to live my life and shows infinite interest in the operation of my household. "Mom, we... I have a cleaning service that comes weekly. You don't have to clean."

She walks into the living room where I have my feet propped up on the arm of the couch while I lie there trying to read a book. "I don't know why you insist on helping. I find cleaning therapeutic. You might also."

"Most weeks, I work fifty hour—"

"About that. You need to slow down. Your health should come first. It's not just about you anymore."

I roll to my side, away from her and keep reading. We've had this conversation more times in the last five days to last more than a lifetime. "Mmmhmmm."

She takes the book from my hands and sits on the coffee table in front of me. "Stop moping. If you're not working, you're moping. Your baby is gonna be born with that disease."

"What disease?"

"Resting bitch face. No one deserves to have that burden put on them in the womb."

I burst out laughing. "That is hysterical. Did you actually just talk to me about resting bitch face?"

"I did. Apparently all the hottest celebrities have it these days. Don't be one of them and don't put that on your baby."

Still laughing that I'm having this conversation, I say, "I did not see this coming. I think you've got Hollywood all figured out."

She touches my arm and smiles. "Maybe you should come home for a few days. Get a new perspective on things."

"This is my home, Mom."

"It's too big for you and a baby."

"I know, but it won't be just us."

Her eyes turn downward. I've brought up the unspeakable—Dalton. "Have you talked to him? The tour ended weeks ago."

Squeezing my eyes shut to avoid the tempting tears, I adjust the blanket over my body, wanting to hide from this conversation.

"Holli, he's not here, so where is he?"

Aggression shoots through, stirred from the reality that I might have to live my life without him. "I don't know, but I know we're not over. My heart knows, Mom."

"What if your heart is wrong?"

"He just needs time, like after Cory died. That's all it is. I know it." I move to my back, not wanting to face her anymore. "If we choose to go our separate ways, then I'll deal with it then."

"It's been over three months, Holli. You need to start thinking of a future without him."

Sitting up, I shout. "No! Not yet." I toss the blanket off of me and get to my feet.

"Then when? When you're giving birth?"

"I'm tired. I'm going upstairs to take a nap."

"It's called depression, Sweetie."

"It's called pregnancy."

She turns away and lets me go in peace, as peaceful as she can, considering how sad I am. I shut my bedroom door and sit on the loveseat by the window. Staring out with my phone in hand, I do what I do at least five or ten times a day. I think about calling him. Sometimes I wonder if I'm being stubborn or if the pain is ruling my thoughts. Other times, I feel strong in the sense that he has to fix himself before he can fix us. I just don't know how to feel today, so I set the phone down like I do every other time and silently call to him, my heart's song a version that speaks through aches, longing for its soul mate.

I rest my chin on the cushion back and stare out the window. All the doubts about my own part in this come back as a reflection in the glass. Sitting up, I take a deep breath and pick up the phone again. Like that one other time, I press the call button, but this time I hold it to my ear and wait. My heart thunders loudly in my chest and I slide my hand over my tummy. My breath stops cold when it doesn't ring or go to voicemail. There's no sound at all but the sound of silence. I bring the phone back down and look at the screen making sure I dialed the right number.

Dalton.

Yep. It's there, right there on the screen. I immediately dial again. The same thing happens. Alarmed, I call Rochelle, but I don't give her a chance to speak when she answers, "What happened to Dalton's phone?" She sighs into the phone and my body tenses, bracing myself. "Please tell me."

"I'll tell you, but I just want you to know I didn't want to worry you anymore than you have been."

"I appreciate that, I do, but he's my husband." The phone goes quiet for too long, so I ask, "Rochelle?"

"I'm still here." She pauses again and the silence is deafening, the blood rushing in my ears louder than my breath. "We lost contact with him a week ago, Holli."

The phone wobbles against my ear and I tighten my hold on it. "What do you mean you lost contact?"

"Tommy, Dex, everyone. We haven't heard from him. His phone isn't working and we have no idea where he is."

"Rochelle," I say, the name having a painful pitch to it. I squeeze the arm of the couch, the words staggering in an exhale. "Is he alive? Did you search for him?"

"We called his parents and everyone we knew who might have a clue, but no one knows."

"Did you call the police?"

"He's alive, Holli. He just doesn't want to be found."

Her words sink in, but make no sense to me. "I don't understand," I say, confused. "How do you know?"

"I got a letter from him."

Hesitant to ask, but needing to know, I plead, "Please tell me what it said."

"He's taking time to figure out what he wants and what's right. He loves you, but he doesn't know how to fix this."

Anger, frustration, and hurt burrow in and I snap, "He fixes it by coming home and talking to me."

"You know it's not that easy."

"I know it's not that hard either. I'm carrying his baby, going through this by myself and for what, his ego? He needs to get over himself and come deal with life like the rest of us."

"Hol—"

I hang up I'm so mad. I throw my phone on the bed and go downstairs. "I'm going out," I snap in my mother's direction as I storm toward the front door. I grab my purse and go to my car. Inside the car, the stale air surrounds me, deafening my crazed mind. I pull away from the house and drive. I have no idea where I'm going, but if he can lose himself for awhile, I can too.

22

Jack Dalton

"What happens when living your dream isn't enough?" ~ Holliday Hughes

I walk out of the coffeehouse and tighten my coat around me. Seattle is too damn cold. It seemed like a good idea to return here, to maybe start over here... to hopefully find the point where my life veered off in the wrong direction. I wanted to retrace my steps and follow the right path back home, but I lost my way. The only breadcrumbs I've found are the ones left behind from my wife walking out on me.

The one bonus of this city is that I've been able to blend in here. I grew a beard, put on a flannel shirt and a beanie, and walk around unnoticed. It's been good, grounding in ways, despairing in others.

I sit at the end of the bed on top of the scratchy brown cover that if blue-lighted would make me want to get STD tested. Staring at the yellowing wallpaper behind the TV rabbit ears, I know it's time to leave. I shouldn't be here and the music scene doesn't fit my mood any longer. I was angrier when I arrived. Now, I'm not so sure what I am anymore.

My laptop is open on the bed next to me and I pull up a car rental website.

Texas, here I come.

TR

Driving cross-country seemed like a good idea at the time. Fourteen hours of being stuck in the car with shitty radio stations and not enough good music on my phone to keep me interested, I turn off the highway and park in front of a diner. I hoped getting in touch with what was happening on the radio these days would take my mind off the rest of my life, but bad music makes me miss my life more than I already do.

A bell dings when I walk inside. Finding a seat in a booth by the window, I slide in. The place isn't crowded, which I like. Avoiding people has moved up my priority list recently. It's the kind of joint where the waitress pours the coffee in your cup without asking. I'm given a menu and Flo waits while I read over it. Since there are only a handful of customers, she has nothing better to do anyway. "Do you have an egg white omelet?" I ask.

"This is Wyoming, not California." She shoves the pen behind her ear, preparing to be standing here awhile.

"I'll have a cheeseburger and fries."

"Good choice."

When she walks away, I pull out the phone and set it in front of me. It's a cheap model that I've never had to use. It's not ever rung.

Not once. Nobody has the number. The decision to untie myself from my old life wasn't easy. Everyone else made the choice for me:

The media

Tommy

Rochelle

Dex

My parents

The lawyers

Rory

The record label

My other phone is in the front pocket of my bag in the car. I left the charging cable, lost it along the way to the hell I was headed to. I eye the cable behind the counter and for a brief moment debate whether I should charge it. I wonder what I'll find. I wonder if I've been missed. I wonder if anyone cared to notice my absence when I stopped answering.

Holliday called a few times, but she stopped trying. She always was a smart woman... everybody wanted something from me and I didn't want anything but her.

My mind has been fucked up over Cory's death, the pressures of the band without him, and not wanting to tour when the label said we had to. I've been doing what everyone else wanted me to do. The wheels are in motion, leading me right to the hell where I sit now, alone.

Car after car after truck and 18-wheeler cruises along the highway. I stare out the dirt covered window, wondering when I decided my pride was more important than my family. I've had too much time to think about everything that's happened, too much time to think about Holliday. I might have hated her for screwing me over back then. But time, like my anger has transformed into something else. What I used to not have enough of, I now have too much on my hands. My hand moves closer to the phone, but I don't touch it. Not yet.

Time has given me perspective. Maybe I grew up a little too. Holliday was never the problem. She's always been the solution. It just pisses me off that perspective has come at the cost of my wife, and expense of my baby. I screwed up. She hates me. She'll never take me back. Not after what I've done, not after losing faith in her, not after being gone while she carries our child.

I've let her down like I let my parents down. Maybe it was always inevitable, but why? Why does it have to be this way? Why can't I swallow down my demons and be the man she needs me to be? How did I even get here? How did I end up choosing to drive away from her instead of toward her?

Rash decisions with unseen consequences.

Dropping my head into my hands, I can see her when I close my eyes. Her smile. Her eyes, the damn sexy tattoo just above her hip. The way she tilts her head back when she laughs. The curve of her neck. The indention at the base of her throat that I like to lick. I can feel her in my bones. I mistakenly thought she was the blood that flowed through my veins. She's not. She's the marrow that gives me strength. She's so much a part of me that I can't believe how stupid I've been for letting it get this far. The first step is always the hardest, but it's time I take it. Looking up, I pick up the phone and call her.

"Hello?" The voice is desperate, but it's not the one I expect.

"Hello?" I reply, not recognizing her.

"Hello, who is this?"

"Johnny. Who's this?"

"Jack? Is that you?"

"Yes."

Her words are quick, desperation heard. "This is Marilyn, Holli's mom."

"Oh hi, sorry I didn't recognize you. Is Holliday there?"

"No. I was actually hoping this was her calling."

I sit upright. "Why would she be calling her own phone?"

Marilyn goes quiet, but finally says, "She left hours ago, leaving her phone behind and I'm worried."

"Why are you worried?"

"Jack, she's not doing well. She's had health issues—"

My stomach drops and my hand tightens around the phone. Afraid of what she's going to say next, I whisper, "Is the baby okay?" I pray she says what I want to hear.

"The baby is fine." I exhale as she continues, "As for my daughter, I'm not sure. That's why I'm worried. She went for a nap and shortly after, came downstairs and walked out."

I run my hand over my face. I'm such a selfish fucking prick. I abandoned her when she needed me most. "Did she say anything before she left?"

"She just said she was going out for awhile, but that was three hours ago. I don't know, call it mother's intuition, but I feel like something's wrong."

My mind frantically flips through a mental Rolodex of Holliday's friends. My food is set down in front of me, but I've lost my appetite. Without looking up at the waitress, I ask, "Did you call Tracy?"

"Yes. She hasn't heard from her today at all."

I eye the phone charger behind the counter again. *What if she's called me? What if she tried to get a hold of me and couldn't? Fuck!* Pushing the plate away, I slam my fist down. *Where is she?* I say, "My other phone is dead. Keep this number, Marilyn. If you hear from her you call me immediately or have her call me."

"I will. But Jack, please don't hurt her again."

"I won't. I promise." My voice drops as my guilt sets in. "I'm sorry." And I realize this is gonna be the first of many apologies I give.

"She deserves better than you've given her." She's right, so I let her finish. "Either be here or let her go, but don't let her live in this purgatory any longer."

I'm getting off way too easy. Holliday deserves so much more. But I'm gonna find her. I'm going to tell her what she means to me. And I'm going to love her with all that I can like I should have done all along. "Call me as soon as you hear from her."

"I will," she says, "And Jack, take care of yourself." She hangs up and I'm left there sick to my stomach.

The woman who has consumed my days for months has disappeared and I'm sitting in Wyoming eating a fucking cheeseburger. I stand and toss some money down. When I head for the door, Flo calls after me, "What about your food, Handsome?"

"I've got to go." I jump into the car and start the engine. Dirt flies up behind the car, leaving the diner in a cloud of dust as I feed onto the highway. I call Rochelle.

"Hello?"

"Rochelle, it's me."

"Johnny?"

"Yes."

Her questioning turns angry. "Where the hell have you been? I've been worried sick."

"Have you heard from Holliday?"

"No. Her mom called earlier, but I don't think we need to worry just yet. She's only been gone a few hours."

I have trouble controlling my emotions when I snap, "I need to find her!"

"Calm down, Johnny. She might be in yoga. She could have gone to a movie."

"In the middle of the day? She left her phone, Rochelle. That's not like her. She *always* has her phone on her."

She sighs. "There are plenty of things to be upset over. Holli needing a little time off isn't one of them. I'm sure she'll be home any minute. She probably just went to the beach to clear her head."

Fuck. The beach. *Why didn't I think of that?* "That's probably it." I feel my heart slow to a regular beat, and ask, "I know I've lost a lot of rights when it comes to her, but if I ask you how she's been, will you tell me?"

"Honestly?" Rochelle asks. "She's not good. How do you think she would be?"

"I love her, so fucking much, but I've screwed up."

"Royally, Johnny."

"How can I fix it?"

"You already know the answer." Her exasperation is heard.

I nod though she can't see me and confess, "I thought I could hide out and play music in some dive. But I can't go on like this anymore."

"Why not?"

My voice cracks as I swallow hard and say, "Because I need her. I love her, Rochelle."

"She needs you. But even more, she still loves you, too. I know this. I can see it in her eyes when she talks about you or you are mentioned."

"I've become a mere mention in her life."

"That's your doing. But you can fix this by coming back."

"I'm already on my way." I pass a sign that indicates I have another hour until I'm in the nearest city with an airport. "Her mom said the baby's okay. Is that true?"

"I'm not going to lie to you, Johnny. Things have changed with her. Holli's not the same woman you were with. She has wounds that aren't visible, but they're there. I just hope you find her before they scar her permanently."

"So you don't think it's too late?"

"It's never too late to make amends. You're better than your actions have shown. This isn't you, Johnny. You're not a careless person, so stop pretending you have no responsibilities. You have a wife and a child on the way. Be the man I know. Be the man Cory respected. Be *you* again. We're all here waiting for you to return to us."

From anyone else, this would be a knife to the heart. But Rochelle's different. She always was. She took a punk kid and helped to make me into a man. Not by insulting me, but by expectation. "You don't hate me?"

"You piss me off sometimes," she says lightheartedly. "But I could never hate you. I love you, Johnny."

"I love you too. Thank you."

"I didn't do anything."

"You've done more than I can thank you for."

She laughs. "You're making me all teary. Stop it," she jokes. "So hey, this is your number now?"

"It's temporary until I can charge my other one. You can use it if you need me."

"Thanks. If I hear from Holli, I'll pass it on."

"Thanks. You doing all right?"

"Better now that I've heard from you."

"Yeah, it's good to hear your voice." A small smile slips into place. "Take care. Okay?"

"You too and don't be a stranger."

"I won't. Not anymore."

TR

I drive to the closest city and hop on a flight a few hours later. I just hope I'm not too late. Rochelle's right. I've fucked up royally and I may pay the price and lose Holliday for good. I hope that's not that case, but I deserve it if it is.

The Reckoning

Maybe she can find it in her heart to forgive an unforgivable soul.

The air at LAX is thick with notoriety. Paparazzi are swarming the airport. I'm glad I shaved on the plane, but I wonder if I would have gone unnoticed if I'd kept the beard.

Security surrounds me, but it won't be enough. I've played this game too long to know that four guards won't stand a chance against them. We're pushed. One guard is called a name. I turn my music up, hoping to block the sounds of 'adultery', 'love child', and 'Sebastian' that are shouted at me. A cab is waiting for me, the door wide open. One of the perks of fame.

I call Holliday's mom as soon as we leave the airport. She answers after the first ring, "Jack?"

"I'm in LA. Where is Holliday?"

"I heard from her an hour ago, but your phone doesn't have voicemail so I couldn't leave a message."

My determination to get to her kicked in before we hung up back in Wyoming. I'm indomitable now. "Where is she?"

"I'll tell you where she is, but I'm only telling you because she needs you right now. If you go out there to hurt her—"

"I won't, Marilyn. Now where's 'out there?'"

"Ojai. She's at the property."

Letting out a huge sigh of relief, I say, "I should've known. I'm going straight there. Don't tell her. I think it's best if I see her first. How is she?"

"Okay health wise, but other than that, I'm not sure." She huffs as if she can't stop this, so she gives in. "I trust you to make this right, whatever is right *for her*."

There's no wavering on my part. "I only want what's best for Holliday." She's the only thing that matters anymore.

"Be careful, Jack, and safe travels."

"Thanks."

My phone rings as soon as I hang up with Marilyn. "Hello?"

"So you're back in LA, I see," Rochelle says, all knowing.

"News travels fast."

"The press works that way. You're all over the online gossip sites."

"I'm going to see Holliday, Rochelle."

She sounds anxious. "You know where she is?"

"Yes," I reply. "Would you have told me?"

"I would have if I believed you were ready *and* she was ready to see you."

"Do you believe we are?"

The silence indicates she's thinking. "Yes." There's another pause, then she says, "You don't have to figure out life apart. You can do it together. Life is fucking hard. I know that more than anyone, but it's so worth it when you have someone by your side going through it with you."

"I don't know if she'll take me back."

"And you won't until you try. I want you to know that I'm proud of you."

"Thanks. But I'm just the fool who let her get away in the first place."

"Holli's a great girl. She's level-headed, but her heart sure is weak to you. I think you two will be fine. Just be kind to one another and leave your ego behind."

"I will. I'll talk to you soon."

"Bye."

I tip the cabbie well. He's earned it for driving me out here. When he drives off, I walk up to the gate and punch in the code. After shutting it behind me, I stop, standing there looking at the house up

The Reckoning

on the hill. I've been away from her for too long and don't want to wait any longer. I jog up the rest of the way. The house is dark from the front, so I head for the back, choosing to go in that way instead. My heart rate picks up with each step as I approach. My palms are sweating by the time I round the corner, nervous what the night holds for me. I'm anxious to finally see Holliday after all of these months and I hope she doesn't kick me out. The fire in the pit on the patio grabs my attention and then I spot her. I stop, holding my breath, and stand there.

The top of her head is seen just above the back of the Adirondack chair she's sitting in. The wind is blowing lightly and strands of her hair float above her head highlighted by the soft light on the back of the house. Her feet are propped up on the stone surrounding the fire, her gaze focused up at the sky. I follow and look up. The stars are out, millions to be seen. Something I've always loved about this property is how you can see them so clearly at night without the distractions of the city.

I take a harsh breath. I want to go to her, to touch her, to be near her, but I hold myself back, which feels a lot like I'm stabbing my own heart. I set my bag down and move closer, but keep a distance so I don't scare her. I say, "Our bodies are stardust to bare. I left you when you should have been the one to part. Your beauty haunts me for the stars can't compare. The morning light gives us a new start."

For a few intolerable seconds, she doesn't move, but then she sits forward and turns around. Her eyes are shining, the stars little reflections in her tears. When she looks down, she wipes them, seeming to be embarrassed to feel this much. When she looks up again, she asks, "Do you think morning can still bring a new start?"

"I hope so."

"What are you doing here?"

"I'm here for you and the baby." I know I'm leaving myself open for a harsh comeback, but I'll take whatever she throws at me and let her get it out. I deserve worse.

But she doesn't throw sarcasm or hate or even anger. Her hand covers her stomach and she stands. My eyes go to her middle. Her shirt is loose, so I can't see any changes, but I can see it in her face. It's thinner. She's more beautiful than any other woman could even try to be, but tired. Then she uses something much more dangerous on me—kindness. "We've waited a long time for you."

We're standing just ten feet apart, but it feels like I have an ocean to trudge through to get to her. "If I..." I look down, ashamed. "If I could take it all back, I would. I lost faith in the one person that would never betray me."

Her head drops and she starts crying.

I take a step closer, not wanting to invade the space I forfeited months earlier. "Hollida—"

Looking up, tears streak down her face, she says, "After all you did, all you did to hurt me and this baby, you show up here after months of being gone, months of not calling and all I want to do is hug you. What is wrong with me? You're the last person I should want to hug right now. But here you are and my heart is beating again and just seeing that you're safe and healthy, and so damn annoyingly handsome that I want to run to you, but how do I push all the pain you put me through away?"

"You don't. I don't deserve you and you'd be smart not to ever talk to me again, but despite wanting to protect you and your personal space all I want to do is wrap my arms around you and kiss you."

She takes a step closer and I take another. Then I take a chance and close the distance. I can't resist her anymore. I hold her as tight as I can in my arms for as long as she'll let me. It's not nearly long enough. She pushes off gently and walks to the other side of the fire pit. With her arms crossed, her weight shifts to her right and she stares at me. "I'm really mad at you, Dalton."

"You should be."

With the back of her wrist, she swipes it across her face collecting the last of the reflective tears from her skin. Raising her chin, she says, "Why are you here now?"

"I'm sorry."

"For what?"

"For everything."

"Be specific."

"I know the baby's mine."

"Oh wow," she snarks, rolling her eyes, "you got all that without a paternity test? I thought for sure I'd receive a court order to prove who the father is."

Shot one to the heart. I'll take each and every one though because she hasn't kicked me out yet. "I know you didn't sleep with that model."

"How do you know?"

"Because I know you."

She shakes her head, getting annoyed. "You didn't know me when you came charging onto the film set, insulted me, humiliated me, then left me?"

"I have no excuses. I can't explain where my head was at, Holliday. I saw those photos and—"

"I could have explained those photos if you would have given me a chance." She looks me in the eyes, and says, "I shouldn't have taken the ride. I said no, but felt pressured into it. To me it was harmless, but out of respect for you, I will apologize for accepting. The rest was bullshit gossip that you believed."

"All I knew was my world was spinning out of control and I couldn't control it—"

"So you decided to destroy it the rest of the way, help it along?"

"You have every right to be mad. I'll give that to you."

"You don't have to give it to me. It's here, full blown. Oh wait, or is it Johnny to me as well these days?"

"You can hit me with your words or your fists if that will help, but I want you to know that I'm sorry. All of me. All..." I struggle to say the rest, my love for this woman clumped in my throat, wanting to come out, but stuck, just like we are. "I'm nothing without you."

"You figured that out now? You figured that out by leaving me to go through this pregnancy alone? My friends have stepped in where you left me. I went to appointments by myself. I heard our baby's heartbeat the first time and every time after without you by my side. I was puking every meal I ate while you were off fucking someone else and 'finding yourself', so when you say you are nothing without me, it makes me realize I didn't have that luxury because I had to be everything for this baby—mother and father. I was preparing to raise this child without you because you ran off to wherever you were this whole damn time." She turns her back to me and the action hurts just as much as the words. "I don't need you back, Johnny. We have learned to live our lives without you in it. That's your doing. That's your legacy to your family." Stunned in place, she leaves me, goes inside the house, and slams the door closed.

23

Holliday Hughes

"No one ever said it would be easy."
~ *Johnny Outlaw*

I'm not sure what he's thinking, but I don't want to fight, so I let it slide when I hear the alert that someone has entered the house. I stay in my room with the door locked, but I can hear him rummaging around the kitchen and watching TV. My attitude is bad right now, my sarcasm at a high. I'm so glad he's so okay with everything because I'm sure not. Rolling my eyes, I roll over and close them, hoping to sleep.

In the middle of the night, I open the door and sneak out. I tiptoe into the living room and find him asleep on the couch. I click off the TV and take the blanket from the chair to drape over him.

Sitting down on the coffee table in front of him, I lean down and tilt my head to the side to look at him, really look at him. It's been too long.

He's better looking than any photo or memory can serve. Like me, he has dark circles under his eyes as well and I find comfort in that, like he might have actually lost some sleep too while we were apart. Leaning in even closer, I tuck the blanket over his shoulder and slowly, ever so lightly kiss him on the cheek. I can't resist. He shifts suddenly and his lips are against mine, his hand on my neck. My eyes close and I stay there, needing this as much as he does. But I come to my senses and stand up quickly, trying to leave. He grabs my hand before I escape and says, "Stay, Baby. I want you to stay."

I can't say anything, unsure of the emotions that might come out, so I slip my hand from his and go back to the bedroom. I'm too tired to fight and it's too soon to make up. I get back into bed and go to sleep instead.

TR

I smell bacon.

Dalton doesn't cook, so I'm curious as to who is. I slip on my robe and open the door, peeking into the hallway and looking in all directions before I step out. The coast is clear so I continue down the hall and across the living room to the kitchen. Holding onto the corner of the wall, I spy Dalton standing at the stove with his back to me. There's a plate of bacon next to him and a stack of pancakes plated next to that. I watch as he goes to the fridge and pulls the orange juice out.

Even though I'm starved and the food smells amazing, I'm dumbstruck by the fact that he's here... and shirtless... and cooking for me. Or maybe he's cooking for himself. Who knows? I turn around to head back to the bedroom when I realize that many wrongs can be righted by crispy bacon, but our troubles run deeper than an incredible smelling plate of pancakes with extra syrup.

My stomach growls and I rub it, whispering, "I'll feed you soon, baby."

"You can feed the baby now, if you like. I cooked breakfast for you, for you both." I turn around to find him standing there with cooking tongs in one hand and a glass of orange juice in the other. He holds it out to me. "I didn't squeeze it, but I bought it for you."

A reply comes in the form of another growl from my tummy. His eyes lower to my hand. I remove it and loosen my robe just enough to hide the shape of my body, feeling a little uncomfortable. My body has changed in ways that he might not find attractive anymore. I've changed in ways he might not find attractive anymore. All my self-doubts about where we stand after all these lonely months hit me. "I should get dressed."

"You should eat, Holliday." He references behind him. "I made it for you. I know it doesn't make up for anything, but please... eat."

I lick my lips and my bottom one ends up tugged under my teeth in debate. "It smells really good. You've never cooked before."

"I've helped you cook before and I can read directions," he says with a smallish smile that hits my heart full force by its charm.

My head knows better than to fall for his lines this time around. "I'll eat, but only because I don't want it to go to waste."

I straighten my shoulders and take the orange juice from him as I walk by with the intention of getting stuffed. He makes me a plate and then makes one for himself and sits down across from me at the table. I inhale half the pancakes before I feel his eyes on me, drawing mine up to his. With a piece of bacon in hand, I point at him. "Don't think this makes it all go away. I'm serious."

"I know you are. But I am too. I'm back and I'm going to put us back together."

"What if I don't want to be put back together with you?" I take a big bite of the bacon, but keep my eyes trained on him.

He sets his fork down and rests his arms on the table. "Do you not love me anymore? Has it been that easy to forget me?"

Gulping, I look down not sure if I want to answer that because he'll see through my strong front, right into my weak heart. But my feistier side has every intention of doing just that. "Easy? The last four and a half months have been the hardest of my life. Everything we said we'd never be, never do to each other, we did. And then when I fly across the country to be by your side, I find another woman has already replaced me. So easy is not the word I would ever choose or ever think of when I'll think back on this time." I stand up and add, "Thank you for breakfast." Wanting to leave before the anger grips me again, I grab one more piece of bacon off my plate and the glass of orange juice and go.

"I hope we'll be able to talk about this soon. When you're ready, I'll be here."

Turning back, I say, "Who said I will be?"

His expression falls, taking any hope he held with it. And now I feel bad. I turn back around knowing now is not the time for this discussion. I can't carry around this much armor if I ever want to find peace.

After a long shower, I get dressed and settle down on the couch for a few hours to recover from eating too much. I've been using the paperback in my hands as a cover to sneak peeks at Dalton. He's been sitting in the chair by the window messing with his phone for the last twenty minutes. I can't seem to take my eyes off of him. I can see the difference in him this morning. Beyond his sweetness toward me, I don't quite remember his eyes being that green, that vibrant. I'm guessing as time passed without him, they had dulled in my memories. I shift on the couch so he's not framed so perfectly by the large windows. Trying to get back into my book, I turn the page with irritation, the corner catching my finger, tearing into my skin.

"Ouch!" I mumble to myself.

The blood pools at the tip and I hold it up when I decide I need a Band-aid. But Dalton's there taking hold of my hand. "It's not too bad," he says, analyzing it, then leans forward wrapping his lips around it.

Holy... the feel of his tongue wrapped around my finger shoots sensations through my body like a current being awakened. I wiggle as nonchalantly as I can as I pull my finger back. The blood is all gone. Gulping, I take my finger back from his gentle grip and look into his eyes. He asks, "Too soon?"

"I'm not sure," I reply, standing up and maneuvering around him to escape to the bedroom. As soon as I enter the hallway, I lean against the wall, needing to catch my breath. My heart is racing and my mind is a whirlwind challenging my best interest.

"You okay?"

I jump, startled, and so busted by him. He smiles as he stands there, watching me. All flustered, I wave my hands in the air erratically. "I'm fine. Okay. Just fine." I raise my chin into the air and hurry to the bedroom. As soon as the door closes, I fall against it and instantly lock it behind my back. Putting my hand to my head, I check my temperature because I feel so heated. "Damn him."

Running to the nightstand, I grab my phone and call Tracy. When she answers, I whisper, "He's here."

"Holli? Is that you?"

"Dalton's here."

She starts whispering. "Why are we whispering? And oh my God, he's there? Where's there? Where are you? At home?"

"He's here in Ojai. He showed up a few hours after me."

"When did you get there?" she asks back in normal volume.

"Yesterday. Long story, but Tracy, he's here and he looks really good and I missed him, but I'm still so mad at him and hurt."

"Take it slow."

"I am, but all I want to do is jump him." Damn him and his tempting tongue. "How am I this horny when I'm pregnant?"

"You're asking the wrong person. Ask Rochelle about that. All I know is you have to be strong—emotionally and physically. He can't just waltz back into your life like nothing happened. He owes you an apology or thirty."

"First of all, Dalton doesn't waltz, but even if he did, I wouldn't just let him back in that easily—emotionally or physically. But I can't keep him out of the house and I kind of don't want to. I need to hear what he has to say, but I can only do that when I'm feeling good and strong. Maybe after dinner or at least after another meal when I'm not so stuffed. Oh and he cooked me breakfast and he doesn't cook, ever. But he did for me and the baby."

"That sounds very thoughtful, Holli."

"I know. That's the problem. He came back and he's like a different person, but somehow is still him. You know I'm weak to him. Remember Vegas?"

"I do remember Vegas." She starts laughing. "Maybe different is good. I mean maybe he's realized his mistake and he wants to make up for it."

Sighing, I peek out the window. "He's been teasing me all day, dilly-dallying around the property, checking on things like the sprinkler heads and gutters. Just super normal things that he doesn't usually do. Oh," I say, completely offended, "And he's shirtless." Damn those abs and biceps. I lift up on my knees. *Did his shoulders get broader?*

"Well, well, well, Mrs. Dalton." Another loud laugh is heard. "It's hot out there today."

I snap, "It's not that hot. He's teasing me on purpose."

"Or tempting you. *Tsk. Tsk. Tsk.* You sound pretty damn weak right now. I think his evil plan is working."

Dropping my head against the cushion, I reply, "I know. I told you. I'm so weak. Send some backbone my way."

"I don't have any to spare, but I do have the final contracts for the card line."

"That's a positive. I'm behind on those by the way."

"I know. I also got you an extension."

"Thank you."

"Hey Hols?"

Dalton drops down into the grass and starts doing pushups. I roll my eyes, but return my gaze even faster. "Good God, that man!"

"Holli?"

Her screeching tone brings me back to the call. "Huh?"

"You don't have to prove anything to anyone. This isn't about the rest of the world. You and Johnny, what happens between you is only between you two. Don't let the media run your relationship anymore. Talk to him or let him talk to you, but talk."

She makes me smile. "I'll try to remember that."

"Do. For you and that baby. Now go enjoy your weekend and see what happens next."

"I'm on pins and needles myself, wondering exactly that."

"Love you."

"Love you too, Trace. Thanks and we'll talk soon."

"Bye."

After hiding out in the room for an hour, I decide to spend time reading in the backyard. When I walk into the living room I catch a glimpse of him through the window and stop to watch. With a measuring tape and spray paint in his hands, I can't tell what he's doing, but it's intriguing, so I stand off to the side so he can't see me and stare.

My gaze slips down like a sweat bead caressing each of his muscles. I gulp and then bite my lip. He sure didn't let himself go when he lost himself. From head to toe and back again, I enjoy the view and even linger a few moments on his strong jaw. He's always had that sexy, cut jaw line. Articles have been written about it. I've licked it, sucked it, and kissed it too many times to count. I take a long shuddering breath, my whole body remembering what it's like to be with him.

I drop down to his tattoos, admiring the tiger one on his chest that I've enjoyed in very dirty ways. But something else catches my eyes. I do a quick checklist of his tattoos. Hula girl. Forty-four for Hank Aaron. Texas Flag. Three .45 Colt guns over his ribs. The tiger covering his heart and an unrecognizable one in the center of his chest. Mother of Zeus... Ugh! He got another tattoo while we were apart. Furious, I grab his shirt on the way out the door.

Stomping toward him, I say, "What have you done, Dalt... I mean Johnny." *Damn it!* I've been trying to call him by the name he seems to prefer these days. *My slip. My bad.* I take a deep breath and try to pull myself together.

"What?" he asks, looking up, so freaking innocently.

I point at his body. "What's that on your chest?" Then I gasp, covering my mouth with my free hand. "Did you... You got—"

Looking down, he points to his new tattoo. "I got your name right over my heart. Some think the heart is on the left side of the body, but it's actually right in the middl—"

"I know where the heart is, but why'd you get my name tattooed? That's permanent, you know," I say stupidly, still dumbfounded.

"You were always with me Holliday. I could feel you. I just couldn't touch you."

My lips part and I suck in a breath since he stole mine away seconds earlier. It's hard to stay mad at someone when they say such amazing things, but I must. I throw the tee at him and say, "Put on a shirt!" I walk back inside and huff as I lean against the counter. He's playing hardball with this shirtless, tattoo business. If he keeps going like this, I'm gonna have to cause some trouble of my own.

Before I have time to put any retaliation plans into action, four men show up with boxes and lay them on the lawn. I toss the push-up bra and extremely low-cut shirt I was going to put on for Operation Counter-Tease Attack, and instead run to the kitchen window to spy on them. *What is he up to?* I have no idea what they're building, but I'm getting mad that they're messing up the lawn.

I stay seated with a bowl of soup in front of me and watch them like I'm watching TV. An hour after they start, I stand up when I realize what's happening. "For fuck's sake!" I storm back outside. Dalton waves at me, a huge smile on his face, an electric screwdriver in his hand. His shirt is off again and thoughts of romance novels come to mind as I imagine the dirty things I want to do to him right now. "Come here please."

He walks over, wiping the sweat from his hairline with his forearm. Gah! He's too sexy for his own good and mine. "Hi," he says so innocently.

"You're building a play-thingy?" My heart melts just a little saying it out loud.

"A playscape."

"I figured, but why?"

"For the baby. We don't have a park or anything nearby, so I thought I'd create one here for him... or her?" His voice goes up at the end as if I'll actually answer that. "And because I wanted to do something for it."

Rubbing my stomach, I snap, "It's not an 'It.' "

"I don't know what we're having. I'm sorry. I'm new at this."

"That's because you've missed it all." But even though I feel that way, I suddenly remember to leave some of the armor behind and say, "I don't know what we're having either, but I know it's not an it!"

I turn to leave, frustrated I even bothered to come out here, but he grabs my hand and says, "No matter if the baby is a boy or girl, the baby will be loved."

"Will it?" My anger slips out so easily and I hate that, but I can't help wanting to hear more of his declarations. His touch feels too good and I selfishly stay.

"I'm sorry, Angel. More sorry than I'll ever be able to express through words. I want to ask you for forgiveness, but I can tell you're not in a place to give that to me, so I'll try to earn it, even if it takes forever. I screwed up. It was a hard lesson to learn, but when I heard you had disappeared, all of that, all my problems seemed trivial in comparison. I was driving cross country and suddenly realized that everything I thought I was looking for was here all along. I haven't shown you how much I love you and this baby, but I promise I will."

The grin that greeted me in Vegas in that corridor shows up and I soften, just a little to the notion of our being together again.

He says, "Everything I need is standing before me wearing a Foo Fighters shirt that looks like the one Dave Grohl gave me three years ago at my party down on Sunset. And even though it makes me fucking insane seeing you wear another bands shirt, I understand that everything I own, you own, so I'll let you take the jab at me because I deserve it."

Heat rises in my cheeks and I take my hand back from him. Looking down at the shirt which has a large photo of Dave Grohl smiling on it, I feel that maybe I do want to have our talk sooner than later. The guys call him over to inspect something. When he turns back, I say, "Guess you need to go."

He sounds disappointed. "Yeah, guess so." He revs the electric screwdriver and that makes me smile uncontrollably.

As he walks backward away from me, I say, "Just so you know, the shirt wasn't a jab. It was just the top one on the pile. I'm still partial to The Resistance."

With an arrogant grin shining across his face, he takes a chance, "What about me? Are you still partial to me?"

"Don't push your luck, buddy," I say, laughing.

His screwdriver rests against his chest as he feigns a hurt heart. He revs it again and I roll my eyes because that man is utterly ridiculous. I walk back into the house with a huge grin on my own face. Even if I tried to wipe it off, I couldn't, so I let it stay just a little while longer, enjoying its return.

24

"One domino falling leads to a million more following in its path. The effect is more damaging than the initial action."
~ *Johnny Outlaw*

While the men wrap up the job of building the best playscape to ever be built, I decide to make dinner. When he bought the stuff for breakfast, he also bought other food that filled our fridge. I wanted something healthy after the big breakfast and the snacking I'd done all day, so I bake chicken and roast asparagus. When I look out at one point, Dalton is paying the men. I finish making the salad, then walk outside with a glass of water.

"Looks good," I say, holding out the glass... maybe it's a peace offering. My emotions are all over the place these days.

"Is that for me?" he asks, a devious smile wanting to escape.

Pushing it forward, I tease, "Yeah, yeah. Just take it."

He comes over and takes the water. Standing closer than he has since that first embrace the night before, he whispers, "Thank you."

"You're welcome." I walk to the swings and sit down. "Is this safe?"

"The safest. I made sure of it myself."

And I know he did. That is the Dalton I love and married. I push off, my feet catching in the warm grass. I've not allowed myself to get sentimental with him in fear of what I'll find out, but as I start to lower my guard, I need some answers before I'm left vulnerable by a surprise. "Tell me about Ashley."

He empties the glass, obviously thirsty, and sets it down on the table before joining me by the swings. "So is this it?"

"Maybe we'll take turns confessing our sins."

"Where do you want to start with her?"

"The hospital."

Coming up behind me, he takes my swing by the chains, pulls back, and releases me. "Tommy found out she signed in using your name. He had told them you were coming. She used that to get into the room."

I squeeze the chains tighter. The anger building inside that my name, my married name was used in such a way. "She sounds like a stalker."

He keeps me flying in the air, just enough that my feet are off the ground, but not enough to make me sick. It's quite nice actually regardless of the topic of conversation. But my swing stops, surprising me. His hands hold the chains as he settles me. Moving so he's standing in front of me, he kneels down, touching my knees. "I'm about to tell you something, Holliday, and I need you to hear me out."

My defenses go up, but the wall I've been trying to build to protect my heart is full of cracks. I strike back though all I want to

The Reckoning

do is hide from the truth that's about to be told. "I don't owe you anything."

"I'm asking you to hear me out."

I stare at him, not wanting to be hurt again, but not wanting to go on like this either. This is it. This is the moment when I decide which fork in the road to take. There was never a real decision to make. I've always known we'd end up right here one day. "I'm here, Dalton," I whisper, crossing my arms, protecting what's left of me. "Say what you need to say."

"I didn't sleep with her."

I start breathing again.

He adds, "She tried to kiss me."

"And?" My hands start sweating.

His eyes dart away and back to me, making me question his honesty. "I touched her."

My blood boils from the images racing through my head, my hatred for her at an all time high. But when I look at him, my heart starts to break from the betrayal. "How did you touch her?"

"How I shouldn't have."

I push back on my toes and untangle myself from the swing. I walk to the end of the structure, holding it for support and stare out over the vast property.

He adds, "Nothing happened."

Whipping around, I yell, "You just said something happened!"

"It didn't happen like it sounds." Standing, he steps toward me.

I move quickly around the pole, keeping it safely between us. Tears don't come, not this time. "Tell me what happened then. Tell me the truth and let's get this out now."

"I was drunk—"

Raising my arms in the air, I look up. "Ohhh, you were drunk. That just explains it all then, right?" Turning my back to him, I say, "Tell me everything, Dalton. I want to know."

As much as I wish I had more time to prepare for what I think I might hear, he's so open and starts talking too soon for that to happen. "She was wearing this robe, but it was open. It was right after New York and the hospital."

I stand there staring at the man I love, loved... still love with all my soul as he confesses his sins to me. I'm left speechless, my mind awash in a misery of images of the two of them together. I grip the wood behind me even tighter waiting for him to tell me the dirty details.

He sounds disconnected even from himself when he says, "I thought I had lost you. I thought—"

"I know what you thought. You told me all about it in an apartment full of people. You accused me of sleeping with someone else. You thought our baby was his. I get what you thought, but you were still wrong and I still paid the price for your misconception. This baby has paid the price and now you're telling me what I feared. You acted out of spite. You acted recklessly. So when you were 'touching' her, you took a risk even though you knew what you were doing was wrong." Closing my eyes, I rub my face with the palms of my hands, knowing I shouldn't ask for more, but I do anyway. "Tell me everything that happened between you."

"I'm not sure this will do either of us any good, Holliday."

"Now you're giving up? There's suddenly no talk needed?"

"I will tell you everything, but I don't want to hurt you more than I have."

"You've already done the damage. You made a choice when she was throwing herself at you and you chose wrong. So just tell me, damn it!"

Reluctantly, he just lays it out there for me, "She straddled me and tried to kiss me. I didn't and then she tried again... she took my hands and placed them on her body where she wanted me to touch her."

Wrapping my arms around myself, I say, "You said you didn't have sex."

"I didn't. I wouldn't have."

"Why stop there? Your hands were already all over her body."

"My vows."

"Our vows ran through your head when your skin was touching hers?" I spit, "Not likely."

"Yes, what I promised you when we got married. I said I would love and cherish you and I never stopped. How could I be with someone else when I said I would honor you?"

"So touching is all right per our vows, but going further is your hard limit? Apparently I've been doing this whole married thing wrong if those are the rules. So you were touching her and then our vows came to mind?"

"You called. I heard it ring. I saw your name. I kicked her out, but you hung up. That's the full story."

My breath is heavy in my chest. I'm unable to speak to him reasonably. I try to calm the storm inside and try to remember when I called him. "I called you when you were in London. So what you're saying is you only kicked her out because I had a moment of weakness." Arching my eyebrow, I say, "Well don't expect that to happen again." I start for the house. "I'm leaving. Don't bother coming back to the house in LA. I'm sure Ashley will be more than happy to take you in."

He takes this argument up a whole other notch when he roars, "I'm not letting you leave!"

I stop, taken aback by the harsh threat. How dare he! With my hands on my hips, I turn back, not willing to take his shit like everyone else does. "What do you mean you're not *letting* me leave? You have no say in where I go or what I do anymore."

"Yes I fucking do. I'm your husband—"

"Not for long." I regret it as soon as it leaves my mouth.

In slow motion, he drops to his knees, all life draining from his expression as he stares back at me.

I can't breathe. I can't move. I can't take my eyes off of him. It starts with the minutest shake of my head and goes from there. I run to him. My mind is a chaotic mess. My thoughts are only of him and fixing the damage I just did. By the time I reach him, he's bent over, sucker punched by my disregard for the words coming out of my mouth a moment earlier. Whispering, I begin to cry, "I'm sorry. I'm sorry. I didn't mean it." My apology loops, my words just as chaotic as my thoughts. I try to touch him, but he moves away from me. "Dalton... please..."

"Please what?" he asks with his head still down. When he looks up, I see the disappointment, the pain, and his spirit is broken.

"I didn't mean it. I promise I didn't." My eyes are flooded with tears, regret, and a love for him I don't know if I can salvage.

A sickness washes through me and I get lightheaded. With my arms over my stomach, I look down, blinking hard. My mouth dries and I close my eyes as I try to swallow just as a sharp pain shoots through my body, forcing me over in anguish. "Ow!"

"Holliday?" He's there in a flash, standing next to me with his arm wrapped over my back. "What's wrong?"

Turning, I press my head against his middle, and grab hold of his shirt. I plead, "Dalton." Before I can say more, I'm in his arms as he heads for the house, scooped up and protectively held against him. The pain continues and I try to mentally go to my happy place. I'm transported back to the present, being held by him. I missed his smell. I missed his arms. I missed his breath and seeing his stuff all over the house. I only remember the things I always loved about this man—all the bad that has happened between us is not worth a life without him. I look up at him and realize—*he* is my happy place.

"How are you doing?" he asks, setting me on the couch.

Holding my body tightly together, another razor-sharp pain

hits, so I curl onto my side, and cry, "Something's wrong."

"Hang on, Baby."

My mind goes fuzzy, the pain excruciating. His voice is further away, a vague understanding of what he's saying as he calls for help.

The ambulance arrives faster than we could have gotten to the nearest hospital. The paramedics are gentle as they help me into a position to check me. Lifting my shirt, they look for outward signs of distress. When I look up at Dalton, he takes my hand and says, "It's gonna be okay. The baby and you, you'll be okay."

"Promise me."

"I promise."

He keeps his word.

The pain ceases. My heart rate and the baby's are slightly elevated, but in a range they feel is safe. After they give advice to get some rest and see my doctor in the morning, they leave.

When he comes back to the couch, he says, "Let's get you to bed." Bending down, he lifts me into his arms. He lays me on the bed and I grab his pillow to snuggle with, hoping it will have his scent again one day.

The stress of our situation burdens his body. His shoulders are slumped, his emotions withdrawn to the depths of his eyes. The bed dips as he sits down. Resting his head in his hands, he hunches forward, away from me.

I reach out to touch him, not able to stop myself any longer. I don't know if I want to laugh from happiness that we're healthy and together or cry that we've fallen apart. I whisper, "We weren't on a break."

"I thought we were already broken."

"Like I said, you thought wrong."

"I know," he says. Angling toward me, he rubs my waist like old times and I let him because I miss our old times. "I know you're hurt. I know I'm the one who hurt you. You have every right to be mad and kick me out, but I hope you don't. I hope you can see that I made a mistake and I'm willing to pay for it, but I need you in my life and I want to be in our baby's life." Leaning down, he rests his ear lightly against my stomach.

I roll to my back, overcome with emotion. This is Dalton. This is the man I fell in love with. He's here and bonding with our baby for the first time. He lifts up enough to move my shirt above my belly. I swallow hard, feeling vulnerable and fighting all my instincts to cover back up. He places three kisses in a line over the small bulge and says, "I love you, baby."

Hearing him use 'baby' not for me, but for our growing child brings tears to my eyes. My hand goes to his head and holds him where he is, a dream I'd had many times now coming true. When he looks up, the scruff on his chin tickles my skin. He says, "You're so beautiful, Angel."

We still have so much more to talk about and even more to reconcile, but tonight, right now, I feel at peace with him here, loving that our little family is finally together.

TR

Sometime before sunrise, my mind becomes lucid and a warming sensation wrapped around my body causes me to open my eyes. Dalton's hand is on my baby bump, the weight of his arm balanced on my hip. Rolling over slowly so he doesn't wake, I look at him. His handsome features are still visible through the darkness of the early hour. I gently touch his cheek running my fingers down and over his hard jaw line.

Admiring him could easily become my full time dream job. Moving closer, I kiss him on the lips, savoring the feel of them again and how soft they are when pressed. In the softest of voices, I whisper, "No matter how far away you were, you were always inside my heart."

I kiss him gentler than before, but this time his hand moves into my hair and he kisses me back. He feels so good. This feels too good to stop myself after all this time. Our legs slowly entangle as our arms cover each other under the sheet. His shoulder dips over me, bearing some of his weight on me. Our tongues mingle and his hand glides over my chest with an assurance.

Maybe we should stop. We still have so much to talk about. He makes it difficult to resist when he kisses his way across my cheek until his lips reach my ear and he whispers, "You are my soul. I will always love you."

His hand goes between my legs and his mouth starts covering my neck. I missed sex with him, but I've missed him more. I push all my doubts away and enjoy this moment, this time that has us coming back together. "I will always love you," I say, not bothering to whisper.

He stills above me. Lifting up, he looks down at me. "Do you mean that?"

I nod. "I do."

While his thumb grazes over my cheek, he says, "I'm sorry." This time I just don't hear his apology, I feel it deep inside.

Sighing content in his words, I cover his hand with mine and say, "No more sorries."

Slipping further down, he kisses my chest and then a nipple before working over to the other making me squirm beneath him. His hands keep me warm as his mouth lowers to my stomach. I start to move my arms down to cover, but he slides his hands down my arms and takes my wrists, holding them to the mattress. Returning to my stomach, he kisses, but freezes as do I when I feel the baby move.

He eyes my stomach, and then looks up at me. "The baby moved."

I burst into tears while freeing my hands so I can lay my palms over my bare stomach.

"What's wrong?" His hands cover mine this time. "The baby moved," he repeats. "That was amazing."

"Nothing's wrong. Everything's right, Babe. The baby moved. That was the first time."

"What?"

Nodding, I smile between sniffles. "I felt fluttering before, but that was the first time the baby actually moved like that." In awe, I say, "The baby moved for you."

"The baby moved for me." He presses his lips against my belly and says, "Hi baby inside there. Daddy's here." He jerks up when the baby kicks. "He kicked for me. You felt that, right?"

"I did," I reply between laughs and sobs, my emotions once again all over the place. "She must have been waiting for you to come home."

He leans his head against me. I'm thinking his own emotions are getting away from him. I run my fingers through his hair and hold him because this is exactly where he belongs—with us.

"I love you," he says. "You hear that in there?" He taps lightly. "I love you and your mommy so much." Glancing back up at me, he adds, "I'll never forgive myself for not being here for you. I'm sorry."

"You're here now. That's all that matters."

25

"Forgiveness is when someone gives you the peace to forgive yourself." ~ *Johnny Outlaw*

Sitting in the exam room of my OBGYN, I think of Dalton out in the waiting room. I miss him and it's only been a few minutes since we parted. But deep down, I know it's more. It's that I missed him being a part of my life, part of this experience.

Lying here on the table in this room all alone, his absence is felt all around me. All these misunderstandings and pain, none of it matters when something more important is at risk. I lie back on the exam table and call him on the phone.

He answers right away. "Hey, what's going on?"

"I changed my mind." Starting to feel overwhelmed by how much I need him with me, I sniffle. "I want you here with me."

"I'll be right there."

Not even two minutes later, there's a light wrap on the door. The nurse opens it and says, "Someone's here to see you."

Dalton walks in and straight over to me. He places a kiss on my forehead and asks, "How are you doing?"

I don't hold my smiles back anymore. "Better now."

The doctor enters soon after. "Mrs. Dalton, what brings you in today?" he asks, but then sees Dalton standing there. "Umm, wow, you're Johnny Outlaw."

Dalton smiles. "You can call me Johnny." When they shake hands, the doctor seems embarrassed. "I apologize. I didn't expect to see you when I walked in. I'm a big fan."

"It's okay, but I'm here for my wife and baby."

When the doctor turns to me, he smiles. "I never put two and two together." Sitting down on a chair at the end of the table, he asks, "What brings you in today, Mrs. Dalton?"

"I had shooting pain last night. We called an ambulance and when the paramedics arrived, they checked mine and the baby's vitals. Elevated heart rates, but they said they didn't think I needed to go to the hospital last night and to check in with you today."

He's reading over the file as I speak, nodding, but then looks up and says, "I'd like to go ahead and do an ultrasound. I know we're ahead of next week's appointment, but it's always good for us to err on the side of caution. Are you okay with that?"

"Yes." Glancing to Dalton, I say, "You'll get to hear the heartbeat."

The doctor asks a few questions as the nurse prepares the gel and machine. "It's a good report from the paramedics. I'm thinking they did the right thing. You haven't experienced any bleeding and the pain described seems to be short-lived, but let's take a listen."

Dalton stands by my side, holding my hand. As he stares at the monitor I can't stop myself from staring at him in anticipation. When the first heartbeat is heard, his chest fills and releases slowly,

The Reckoning

the relief obvious. Pulling my hand to his mouth, he kisses it. His eyes have filled with tears, overcome by the reality. With my hand still pressed to his lips, he says, "That's our baby."

I peek at the monitor and see the baby on the screen. The heartbeat fills the room and I tear up like I do every time. "That's our baby."

The doctor says, "The baby sounds healthy and from what we can see on the monitor, growing just right. You're doing a great job. Just keep that stress down and stay active. Most expectant moms find it helps to take walks." Pictures are printed and he hands them to Dalton. "Here are some photos to take with you."

The doctor continues talking, but Dalton doesn't seem to hear a word he says. His mouth closes and his eyes flash to mine. "We have photos... of our baby." His hand covers my belly just as my shirt is lowered."

Smiling from his reaction, I reply, "Yes, I have more at home I can show you too. Pretty amazing, huh?"

"Yeah," he says with a grin that feels personal, just for us.

The doctor clears his throat and repeats himself, "If you'd like to find out the sex, I was told we have an opening. It's only a few days before your appointment, so if you'd like to find out, we'll send you over there now."

My eyes meet Dalton's, questioning without words.

"I'm happy the baby's healthy. I'd like to know the sex, but it's up to Holliday."

"I want to know for purely superficial reasons like décor and clothes, but also for the name."

"I'll let them know. They're just across the hall. You can gather your stuff and go when you're ready." He walks to the door, and says, "Make sure she takes care of herself and keep the stress to a minimum."

Dalton responds, "I will." The door closes and as if it hadn't occurred to him previously, he asks, "Have you chosen names already?"

"I've started paying more attention to names, but I couldn't bring myself to pick one without you."

"You had faith in me when I had none." He leans over and hugs me though the positioning is perfectly awkward. But like our mistakes, perfectly awkward doesn't matter.

We're together and that's what does. "I had faith that you'd find your way home. Now that you have, I hope you'll stay."

He looks me in the eyes with a new conviction. "I'm never leaving again."

Offering me a hand up, I lift up on the table and swing my feet over the side. Pulling him close, I say, "I won't go through this again, Dalton. If you leave again, I won't be there when you come back."

He kisses the top of my head. "I'll never leave you." Everything about the way he said it, the way he looks with this confidence in his eyes, and the way he's treating me reassures me in ways that words might not. So as I watch him gather my jacket and bag, I realize this is it. The war is over. We've both surrendered, choosing to love each other instead of fight. We win. It's then that I decide to move forward and let the past stay where it belongs, in the past.

Across the hall I lie there in tears when they tell us the sex of our baby. But even through my watery vision, I can see the heavy, life-changing emotion as it plays out across Dalton's face. There's no doubt on his face. None at all. He loves this baby wholeheartedly. His hand tightens around mine and his eyes are fixed on the screen. "Wow," he says. And I feel the same exact way.

The technician leaves the room quietly and when I stand up, Dalton takes me in his arms. Resting his forehead against mine, he closes his eyes and I close mine.

With my arms around him, I say, "How am I going to handle

two Outlaws?" A low chuckle is heard before he cups my face, and says, "No one could handle two of us better than you. But let's just hope his disposition takes after his mother's."

"For all of our sakes." I giggle. "So we need to come up with a boy's name."

"We can do that, but first I'm gonna kiss you."

The touch is sweet, but the kiss intimate—one that has forever laced all over it.

TR

The baby's room was painted a few days ago and dried since, but I open the window to let fresh air in anyway. New Daddy syndrome has struck. Dalton has gone overboard buying stuff for the baby—a Fender Stratocaster guitar, stuffed animals... basically a zoo's worth, and he wants to have the lyrics of a song he's working on painted onto the wall. I can't deny his excitement makes me happy.

The room overlooks the grounds, a garden of roses that was planted last year. They're thriving, much like me and Dalton over the last week.

"You're more beautiful than ever. Have I told you that?" Dalton says.

I turn and glance over my shoulder. "A few times," I reply, loving it every time he says it.

Leaning against the doorframe, he's relaxed, at peace with the world. Finally. "Rochelle's here to see you."

Rochelle walks in and Dalton excuses himself, closing the door to give us privacy. She embraces me like we haven't seen each other in ages or might never see each other again. I understand why, and I appreciate how easily she shows affection. The death of a loved one will make you appreciate the everyday a little more.

"This is the room?"

"Yep. I like the view."

She looks out. "It's very pretty. Happy." Taking my hand, she gives me a tug. We climb onto the bed that hasn't been moved out of here and lie next to each other. All giddy, she rolls to face me, and says, "Tell me everything."

Adjusting onto my side to get comfortable, I'm grinning stupidly, enjoying the fun girl talk. "He's back for good," I whisper with all the confidence in my soul.

"How do you know?"

I understand her questioning, glad she cares enough to ask. "Because when he showed up the other night, something was missing. I could see the vacancy in his eyes. And now it's gone. Filled. It's hard to explain, but I can see the difference."

"You were always the difference, Holli. What about all the yucky stuff with New York and Seattle?"

"We may have skipped a few steps in the healing process, but priorities change and this baby has become number one to both of us."

"Babies have a magical way of healing parts of us that no one else can." Taking her hand, I squeeze it. But the heaviness never suited her, so she says, "You're having a boy. I'm a little partial to them myself."

"I'm so excited. If I can be half the mother you are, my son will be very lucky."

"You'll be better. You have this great family. Just appreciate each day and each other. It all kind of flows from there."

We sit up, a thoughtfulness working its way through the air. Leaning against the headboard, I ask, "Am I weak for taking him back?"

"Taking him back shows your strength. Have you forgiven him?"

"My priorities have changed." I rub my stomach

absentmindedly. "It's not about who's right or wrong anymore. It's about the baby and a future that deserves a chance. And honestly, I don't want to lose any more time with him. I don't want to be upset anymore. I don't want chaos filling my days or my head. I just want to love him, love the calm. I knew what I was getting when we got married. I'm not going to make him apologize for being hurt by life and discount his suffering. So if that's what forgiving him results in, I forgave him before he walked in that door."

She laughs to herself and I see her eyes beginning to water. Looking down at her lap, she says, "That's what love is—chaos and calm, all rolled into one." Her eyes meet mine just as a tear slips down. I lean my head on her shoulder. "You've got so much strength. You're an amazing woman, Holli."

"I'm lucky to have amazing friends."

She leans her head against mine and says, "I feel the same way." Releasing a breath, she says, "I was just stopping by to check on you, so I better get going." As we walk to the door, she says, "I know Johnny can be an asshole, but..." She stops, choosing her words carefully before continuing, "I believe you have always been destined to be together. And I also believe you're the only woman who could bring him back from the hell he was living in."

Shrugging lightly, I say, "I don't know. What I do know is that I don't want to live this life without him, even if he needs time to figure himself out now and again. We all have burdens to bear."

"You give him the strength he needs, but if you ever need strength, please know you have me to lean on."

"Thank you."

Shifting in my seat, I sit across from Dalton at dinner, thinking. It's been fairly quiet so maybe he's thinking about things too. Finally, I look up and say, "Why did it take you so long to realize?"

His gaze rises from the steak in front of him and I know he understands that I'm talking about if Sebastian was the father. It's a topic we've steered clear of since his return. He sets his fork down and leans back in his chair. His fingers tap along the wet water glass, the condensation dripping down the sides. "I forgot who you were for a time, who *we* were. The tabloids altered who I knew you to be, messing with my perception."

It hurts to hear he was that far gone from me emotionally. Now I wonder where he was when he figured it out. "When did you realize this?"

"I think I was in Australia."

"What happened in Australia?"

"I was living another day without you in it." Putting my elbow on the table, I lean my head on my hand and listen as he continues, "I was playing a show and it was going great, then I just looked out and didn't see you. I couldn't feel you like I usually can. I sound crazy, but you were always with me even when we were apart. A piece of my soul was absent." He grins as if he's embarrassed to say it, but I love that he did.

"If you were missing me so much, why'd you stay away?"

"I didn't know how to face you, how to fix the mess I'd made. You hated me for what happened in New York. Then Seattle made things worse. Throw in there that I was fucking pissed that you were still spending time with him...have you ever been able to see the mess you're making of your life, but can't seem to stop the destruction?"

I wish I could relate, but I can't. "I've never had the luxury."

He nods, understanding most people never will. "I usually take time away to figure shit out—"

"You don't get to do that alone anymore. You're married. You're going to be a father to this baby. We are a family, a unit now. We

The Reckoning

stick together no matter what. Can you make that commitment to me?"

"I already have."

"No. I need more than a piece of paper and a Justice of the Peace witnessing you committing to me. I need to know deep down that you'll be here no matter what, Dalton."

There's sincerity in his voice that can't escape, a conviction that's seen in his body. "I will. I'll show you every day for the rest of my life."

"I'll do the same for you." For him, I will.

"You already do."

Feeling like today is the day to get it all out, we lie in bed later that night and I ask what I've been reluctant to ask since he came back. "Why did you quit the band?"

He doesn't rush to answer, but when he does, he doesn't hold back either. "I could say my heart wasn't in it, but really it was my head. I was standing center stage playing a song and all I could focus on were the mistakes Kaz and Derrick were making. The fans wouldn't be able to tell, but I could and I couldn't enjoy what I was doing. And if I'm not enjoying it, why do it anymore?"

I snuggle into his side, rubbing my hand over his abs. I almost feel guilty taking advantage of him like this when he's sharing his feelings with me... almost. "When it becomes a job, bail?"

"I did my job. I finished the tour. After that I needed a break, distance from the band, from Cory's death, from life. I needed to figure out what really mattered to me the most and find my way back to it."

"Those men have been loyal to you, to this band. You know without you, the band doesn't exist."

"I know. That's why it was a hard decision, but it's for the best."

"Whose best?" I whisper.

"No one's in the end."

"What do you want to do now?"

Sitting up, he angles toward me. "I want to be a good husband and a great father."

His words and commitment make me happy. "Are you leaving music forever or for now?"

"For now. One day I might record a solo album. I'm not sure." He confesses, "If you can believe it, I miss those assholes."

"I know they miss you too." Sitting up next to him with my back to the headboard, I wring my hands together and ask what I need to know to prepare myself for what he has planned. "If you went solo, would you tour to back the album?"

He's so relaxed, not holding back at all. "I don't think so. I'd prefer to play clubs, bars, small venues. Surprise performances to crowds that aren't there to see The Resistance."

I snort. "That's next to impossible to pull off in LA. You can't even walk down the street or get gas without being stalked."

"Very true." He looks at me and I can tell by the line between his eyebrows that whatever he's about to say is important. "I was on my way to Austin when I called you and your mom answered, telling me you were gone."

Shocked by his statement, I sit forward and angle toward him. Resting my arms on my belly, I ask, "You were going to Texas?"

"I was going to write or play or both. I needed to get away."

"You were away already." Touching his hand, I turn it over and say, "Too far and too long, so why did you need to go?"

A small smile appears and he shifts to get comfortable before it falls away. "I'd had a rough day. A rough few weeks... pretty much every day without you was rough. And then you disappeared."

I shrug. "I didn't drop off entirely... obviously, since you found me. How'd you know where I was?"

It occurs to me at the same time he says it, "Rochelle." Our fingers touch, heat exchanged. "She's a good friend."

Looking down, I say, "She was there for me when you weren't."

His face contorts, the reality a punch to his chest. "I'm sorry," he says, the words coming as fast as my apology. "I'm sorry."

Dalton lifts my chin until I'm looking him in the eyes. "It's true. Don't apologize. I should have been the one here for you and I wasn't, so the blame lies squarely on my shoulders. Not yours."

Mindlessly dragging my finger up and down his thigh, I say, "You're here now." Not wanting to dwell, I poke his leg twice and I touch back on something else he said. "You want to go back to Texas?"

"No. I want *us* to go to Texas." My mouth must be hanging open because he touches it and lifts.

"Still?"

"Still. I think it could be good for us to get out of here for awhile. Not forever."

"What about the baby? What about my company?"

"I don't know. I haven't thought it through, but it's something I'd still like to do.

"I didn't expect this." I lay my head on his chest and say, "Let me think about it."

"That's all I'm asking. Whatever you decide will be what we do." His hand strokes my back and he asks, "Are you tired?"

My smile is instant. "A little. A little not."

"Wanna?"

"Is this how pregnant women get sex?" Sitting up, I mimic his tone and say, "Wanna?"

That makes him chuckle, but his tone turns concerned. "I don't want to hurt you... or think about a baby being inside you when I am."

"Oh my God, did you actually just say that?" I burst out laughing.

"Go ahead and laugh it up. But I can't just bend you over, rip your panties, and fuck you."

"Why not?"

"Because you're pregnant. We have to be careful."

"Dalton," I start, resting my hand on his leg. "Because I'm pregnant doesn't mean I'm suddenly fragile or more breakable. Why don't we start slow and go from there, see where the night takes us."

"What about you on top?"

"I can totally be on top." His lips are covered by mine and slow goes out the window.

26

"Sometimes friends become our greatest enemies and sometimes they turn into our greatest allies." ~ Johnny Outlaw

"How's Katie working out? She's due for her three month evaluation, correct?" I turn in my chair and ask Tracy.

"Yes. We have it set up for tomorrow. How do you feel about her managerial skills?"

"I think she's doing a good job. She's not you, but you're rare like that."

"Ha ha."

"No joke. You are irreplaceable."

She stares, squinting her eyes at me. "What are you up to?"

I laugh. "Nothing. Just want you to know how valuable you are to the company. We have three full-time employees and a lot of contractors and nobody cares as much as you and I do about this company."

"True. We have a vested interest. I have stock shares I hope to cash in one day."

"First we have to become a stock holding company. You know, it might not be bad staying a privately owned company."

"I'm gonna need a big pay raise in that case," she jokes.

I laugh again, but realize she's not joking. "Don't worry about that. You're stuck with me and I'm willing to pay you what you deserve to keep you around."

"I do think we should bring on another employee. The interns are working out, but they rotate out too fast. I was thinking an entry-level clerk."

"Do what you think is best." I broach the topic I've been nervous to bring up. I start off casual. "So what do you think about the time off with the baby?"

"I think you need it. I've done a lot research and it shows that taking maternity leave actually improves work efforts when you return. Besides that, you should take the time to heal and take care of that baby."

"What about after?"

"I've been thinking about that and doing a little research. Why don't you bring the baby here during the day? We can set up a crib and other necessities in the bedroom and we have a full kitchen downstairs since it is a townhome. You can bring whatever you need here to make it easier. But I have to warn you, the owner can be a real bitch sometimes. If you give her a chance though, she has a heart of gold," she playfully teases, followed by a laugh.

"You're ridiculous. By the way, I need a month off or at least to be out of pocket from meetings and such."

Her jaw drops. When she recovers from the shock, she exclaims, "Holli!"

"I know," I reply with my hands up. "Please don't freak out. I'll be working. I'll just be working from Texas."

"Texas? What the hell's in Texas?"

"Dalton."

"Oh good lord, woman. Your life gives me whiplash." Grabbing a notepad and pen, she huffs, "Lay it on me. Give me the deets."

"Dalton wants to get away from LA and we both want to stay together, especially after all that has happened."

"Why Texas?"

"He wants to go to Austin. It's a music city and, well, we're not telling many people, but he's gonna do some solo shows, get a feel for the stage again, start fresh."

"This sounds serious. You're not moving on me, are you? Cuz I'm just gonna be perfectly honest here, I need you. You're one of my best friends."

"Charmer," I say, smiling ear-to-ear. "You're one of mine too, but it's not forever. It's just for now. Our new motto."

"When?"

Scared to tell her, I whisper because I figure that will ease the blow. "Five days."

Her jaw drops again, but this time, she doesn't seem to recover as quickly... or at all. I watch her stand and walk right out of the office. Her footsteps are heavy as she descends the stairs where Katie works in the living room. Then the front door opens and closes again.

I take off after her. As I run past Katie, I ask to verify, "She left?"

"Yes."

Running out the front door, I call to Tracy. She's walking quickly down the sidewalk toward the beach. I only have to jog to catch up with her, but when I do, she stops and glares at me. "You keep doing this and I'm left here to pick up the pieces."

"I work my ass off, Tracy."

"Yes, you do. You work more hours than I do and I work an insane amount of hours, but sometimes you need to be here."

"I can't work without him."

"You have to. You started and grew this business before you even met him. I'm not trying to be mean, but if you're taking time off then we need to hire more people—designers, artists, and the people who come up with those catchy slogans. Whatever they're called."

"I do all of that and I rarely miss deadlines, so this is kind of bullshit."

"What's bullshit is me feeling like I'm doing this alone. Once the baby comes, you'll never be here."

Shocked by this side of Tracy, I ask, "We just talked about that. So what's this really about? This isn't like you. We talk. Communicate all the time about everything, so where is this coming from?"

I see her glance down to my stomach and then turn around, putting her back to me. "Adam and I have been trying for months..."

Guilt fills my veins in an instant and my heart hurts. Not sure what to say, I say what I feel, "I'm sorry."

"I'm stressed. I read online to relax and that means working less, not more. Everything is so much easier when you're here."

I walk around and hug her. "We'll hire more people to help. Please don't worry about that. We've needed to for awhile now, but I need you to tell me when you need help. You don't have to do everything by yourself."

When her arms release me, she says, "It was just the two of us for so long. It's hard to let go."

Smiling in reassurance, I say, "We don't have to let go, Trace. We just have to loosen the grip a bit. Limelight is growing. It's time we grow the staff *and* our families."

"I just miss you and I miss the old days when we were like renegades in the business world."

"I miss you too. The old days were great. We were doing something that felt revolutionary. We are still those visionaries. We make a great team, Trace. I couldn't do this without you. Anything. Tell me anything I can do to help you."

"You can go to Texas for one month and work satellite, but only one month and then no more time off until your maternity leave. Capeche?"

Smiling, I nudge her as we walk to the beach. "Capeche."

27

Jack Dalton

"Sometimes the big picture is someone else's painting." ~ *Holliday Hughes*

The days fade into one another. Most of the time, I sit with my guitar trying to flesh out a song that has been rattling around in my head for months. The melody is elusive though I get parts of it at the most inconvenient times—like when I'm having sex with Holliday or driving—times I can't or don't want to stop to record the notes.

Other times, a melancholy hangs over our heads and I'm not sure if it's this place or the city. I need to get out of here. I just hope she agrees to leave.

Tommy shows up after five. "You're a mess," he says, walking past me like he lives here.

"Thanks. Good to see you too."

Chuckling, he goes to a chair and spreads out as he gets comfortable. "Admit it, you missed me."

"I can admit it. Your abrasive personality and shit attitude has been severely lacking in my life. That's why I called. Sometimes you're actually not an asshole."

"It's five o'clock. You saving your beers for a special occasion?"

"Others times you are. You know where the kitchen is and get me one while you're at it."

He gets up with a huff of protest. When he comes back out, he asks, "So why was I summoned to his majesty's?"

"Fuck man. You just here to bust my balls?"

I see him shaking his head, but he's smiling. "Nah, I might have missed you a wee bit too." I stand and we go outside and sit in some chairs close to the pool. Lowering his head, he says, "Sorry."

"For what?"

"Being a jerk."

"What's going on?"

"I've got bad news. Ashley filed a lawsuit against you and the band. You're gonna have to give a statement about what happened in London. The band is being included for sexual harassment."

The beer I'm swallowing catches in my throat and for a brief second I don't know if I should force it down or spit it out. I gulp. "What the fuck? When did this happen?"

"I got the call an hour before I came over. I thought you should hear it from me. The lawyers will be contacting you, but I wanted you to get it straight."

"But nothing happened in London." He's still looking down and picking at the label on the bottle. "There's more, isn't there?"

"Yeah."

I set the bottle down next to me and stare at him, not liking the way he's stalling. "Just tell me."

"She's pregnant."

"'Kay, but what does that have to do with me?"

"She says it's yours."

What the fuck? I shake my head knowing I just heard that wrong. "What?"

"She says the baby is yours."

"No," I say, "That's not right. It's not mine."

"I'm just telling you what she's claiming, Johnny."

Panic sets in. *Holliday. Holliday. Holliday. I'm* gonna lose her if... Fuck! "We didn't have sex. It's not mine." Covering my face with my hands, I drop my head. "She can't do this. Not now. I just got Holliday back."

"Hold up. You didn't have sex with her?"

"Fuck no, I didn't," I spew disgusted by the insinuation.

"Not once?"

I glare at him like he's the big fucking idiot he's acting like. "No, not once. We haven't fucking kissed or anything. Nothing happened."

"Huh?" He takes another pull of his beer, and then says, "It's not public. We can silence her and settle."

"If I settle, that's like me admitting I'm guilty, like I've done something wrong."

"No. It doesn't have to mean that. Just means she can't make this public. It will go away."

Standing up, I pace, my thoughts a mess as all the damage this will cause comes to light. "Holliday will leave me. She'll think I lied to her. She can't find out about this, Tommy. We've got to make this go away."

"There's no easy way to make it go away. The lawyers need to meet with you to discuss the options, but you're gonna have to deal with it."

I rub my eyes, hoping to see some light when I reopen them.

None is found and I realize this is what people mean when you witness your own world crashing down around you. Picking up my beer, I want to throw it. I want to see it shatter against the rocks that line the waterfall. But I want to drink it more. I down it and go inside for another. With the fridge door open, I finish the next, then pull out another and pop the metal cap off, tossing it into the sink across the room.

"I think you should tell Holli," Tommy says coming into the kitchen.

"Our relationship is balanced on a tight rope right now. This news will destroy her and she'll fucking leave me."

"You didn't sleep with Ashley, so it's her word against yours, but Holli should know and you should be the one to tell her. You know secrets don't stay buried forever."

Crazy thoughts are rampant as I come to grips that this is happening. This is how things are going to go down. In the midst of the insanity, I find clarity. "It's a trap. Ashley wins either way. If I deny it and fight her, the media finds out and will persecute me in the press. If I settle, she wins however fucking much she's asking for. Rubbing my temple, I say, "Either way, I'm fucked with Holliday."

"She'll understand."

"What woman would understand this? She's pregnant with my baby and I accused her of fucking some other guy and getting knocked up. I'm damn lucky to even be standing here. She can't take another blow like this. The stress alone is bad for her." Punching the air, I say, "I need to fucking hit something."

"Let's talk in the gym then."

"That's too sensible."

"At least you haven't lost your sense of humor."

I send him a hard glare. Once we're in the room, I head straight for the punching bag. Tommy holds the other side and I swing as hard as I can. With my eyes trained on the bag, I ask, "How do we end this quickly and quietly?"

"As I said, you need to talk to the lawyers, but it seems settling will be the fastest and quietest."

"Fuck her! I'm not settling. If this goes public, it will go public that she's a lying bitch by taking a paternity test."

"This isn't gonna be a one shot thing. It will be dragged out for months in the media if you go that way. Do you want that hanging over your head? Do you want to have your kid with Holli while the world thinks you're disowning another? There are repercussions either way you choose. I think you need to tell Holli and the two of you decide."

Five rapid hits and my knuckles crack. As blood speckles my skin, I crouch down, trying to catch my breath and forget about the pain. *Holliday. Baby. Hospital. Stress.* "She's gonna leave me, Tommy. I've put her through hell. I'm not good for her or the baby. She needs to be safe, feel protected. I love her more than life, but I'm the one causing her the most pain."

Coming around the bag, he shoves his hands in his pockets just as I stand up. "Don't underestimate her. She's gonna be pissed and probably hurt. But she's strong and she loves you despite your bullshit. Give her time after you tell her. Let her process it on her own and go from there."

"Times like these I wish I still did drugs."

"Times like these are when a man's true character comes out. What kind of man do you want to be?"

I'll sound like a pussy for saying this, but I don't care anymore. "I want to be the man who deserves her and a father the baby looks up to."

"Then be that man."

"I'll tell her soon."

That night I watch her. She notices, but doesn't say anything until she's drying dishes. "Why are you staring at me?"

Sitting at the bar, I say, "It's hard to take my eyes off you."

Her innocent smile shoots daggers straight into my heart. I gulp heavily and look away, the sight of her beauty crippling my logic. I should tell her, but I don't want to lose this moment. I have to protect her. I have to protect the baby. *At all costs.*

Protecting her means being honest with her these days. I need to tell her.

"Dalton?"

When she calls, I turn back. "Huh?"

"I was talking. Did you hear anything I said?"

"No, I'm sorry. What was it?"

"What's going on? You okay?"

"Fine." There's an edge to my answer I wish I could dull. "I'm fine."

After hanging the towel on the rack, she moves to the other side of the bar from me and asks, "Want to talk about it?"

"I want to enjoy our night."

"Is it something we should talk about?"

I slide my hand over hers. Honesty. "Yes."

Her eyes fasten on mine. I see the tentativeness in them, the trust disengaging. "You know that makes me worry, right?"

"Yes. I told you knowing that."

"Then why don't you want to talk about it?"

"I want tonight to be like today."

Her expression softens and she smiles. "It's been a good day."

"It's been a great day." She looks away and back, then says, "So you'll talk to me soon?"

"I will," I reply, covering and squeezing her hand.

"Okay." She seems to leave it at that, her trust back in place. "Well," she starts, her cheeks harboring a slight pink to them. "I was thinking maybe we could be together in *that* way."

My mouth quirks up on the sides, fucking bowled over by her cuteness. "And what way would that be?"

She giggles and I almost don't know what's come over her, but the lightheartedness is good to see. "In the sexy kind of way."

"So what you're saying is you want me."

She rolls her eyes though a big smile is still present. "Do you want me to beg for it?"

"As much as I like you begging, I don't want that."

Coming to stand next to me, she touches my arm and slides the other around me. She kisses my head and then my temple. "What do you want?"

I cup her face, holding her there just so I can selfishly see this face without the pain I know will replace the peace in her eyes. I have to protect this moment, save it from being destroyed like I am on the inside. "All of you. Forever." Leaning in, I kiss her.

Standing between my legs, her body molds to mine as our mouths become one. She moves away with my hands in hers, tugging me forth. "Come on," she beckons.

Within minutes she's above me like a goddess, her hair flowing down over her shoulders. I trace my hands along her curves as she rocks. Whispering, she says, "Why are you staring at me?"

"I'm taking you in, wanting to remember this."

Resting her palms on my chest, she asks, "What's *'this?'*"

"Heaven." Taking her by the hips, I help navigate her closer to release. Seconds. That's all it takes as I gaze up at her. Her eyes close, her nails scraping my skin as her body tightens around me. Her orgasm is strong, hitting her fast while I hold her hips, moving her. My own eyes close hoping to find that same pleasure, but my mind is attached to the devastation to come. Even the negative can't fight this. She feels too good and my body relents to her.

An hour later, she's asleep and I sneak out of bed. It's only ten, so I'm wide awake. I grab a bottle of Jack and a glass. I don't bother with a shot. A lowball works better for my mood.

I go outside, not wanting to disturb her sleep. Sitting on the patio table, I pour my first drink. The moon is out though it's competing with the heavy cloud coverage tonight. Swirling the liquid around, I watch as it coats the sides. Bringing it to my lips, I down it all at once and pour another.

Damn Ashley to Hell. I finish this glass and pour the third. The whiskey kicks in, making my anger rise. I throw my glass against the side of the house and yell, "Fuck you!" I flip off the world, then take the bottle and drink straight from it. I'd throw the bottle, but I learned in London that doesn't solve anything. Another swig is taken as I stand at the edge of the pool, staring at my reflection.

"Babe?" The softest of voices fills my ears like a melody that taunts my psyche. Just out of reach, but playing on repeat. "What are you doing, Dalton?"

When I turn around, she's there in my shirt. The moonlight hits her and I see her bump. Not wanting to worry her, I say, "Getting some fresh air."

Her eyes are sleepy. Beauty lives there, shining through. "Do you want me to get a glass for you?"

Innocence. "No. Thanks," I reply, rubbing the back of my neck.

"Do you think you'll be out here long?" She wraps her arms around herself. "It's getting chilly."

"Go back to bed. I'll be in soon."

"Promise?" Her expression lifts with hope.

"Promise."

The door shuts and I turn back to the pool. I've got to do whatever it takes to protect her, to protect my family.

The next day, I call Tommy. Desperate to get out of LA, I need to get him in on my plan. This time I'm ready with the beers. Figured it was only right since I'm asking him a favor and all.

"What did you decide with Holli?" he asks.

"I have a call into the lawyers. I should know how we're moving forward in the next few days. I'm gonna tell her when there's a plan in place. She's going to have questions and I want to have the answers."

He nods. "Understandable."

"How's that retirement working out for you?" I ask as he sits on the couch.

Tommy clinks the neck of his beer bottle against mine and says, "Fine and dandy."

"If you're able to retire at thirty-three we paid you too much."

"Eh, I'll have to get another gig eventually, but the time off has been good for the most part."

"You're gonna work for the competition?"

"I guess I'll have to unless some asshole musicians I know get off their asses and start making music again, like they should."

"Subtle."

"I wasn't going for subtle, ya asshole."

I turn away from him and look out over the backyard. "Hypothetically, what would you think about working for me?"

"Hypothetically, doing what?"

"Doing what you do, but on a smaller scale."

He rubs his chin, thoughtfully. "What kind of smaller scale are we talking about, hypothetically speaking, that is?"

So there's no misunderstanding, I look him in the eyes. "Small venues—bars, clubs. Places that hold hundreds, not thousands."

His eyes go wide. "Touring solo?"

"Yep. Hypothetically speaking."

"Fuck the hypothetical. You're going solo with an actual tour?"

he asks in disbelief.

"Not a tour. A few clubs. Unannounced. I want real music lovers, not Resistance fans flooding the place."

"Multi-city?"

"Texas. Maybe LA."

"All of Texas or certain cities?"

"Austin."

"So you want to play clubs in and around Austin, but not advertise? Just surprise performances?"

"Yep."

His excitement grows and he sits straight up. "How many?"

"Four or five."

Scoffing, he shakes his head and says, "You don't need me for this."

"You're right, but I want you there."

He starts laughing. "Aww man, you're such a pussy. You scared to play shows without me?"

"Ha! Nah, I've just gotten used to your ass being around." When I look over at him again, I roll my eyes. "Okay, what the fuck ever. I want you there. Happy?"

"I'll be happier once we negotiate the pay."

"Same pay as before."

"Wow, you really do want me there."

"Shut it before I change my mind."

His bottle taps against mine and he says, "Looks like we're back in business."

28

"What is it about fresh air that makes us cough so much." *~ Johnny Outlaw*

Dalton and I leave LA under the scrutiny of the paparazzi. Arriving in Austin is more peaceful. The media was tipped off, but this city has fewer soldiers on the ground so we only have to deal with a handful when we land. Dalton holds my hand as if I'll slip away from him if he doesn't. His head is lowered and his body becomes a barrier between them and us.

The usual rude comments fly from their mouths, saying the baby is Sebastian's and asking Dalton why he stays with me. From how tight he holds my hand, I can feel how tense Dalton is. I feel guilty he has to listen to this garbage.

A loud exhale releases from him as soon as the taxi pulls away. A minute later, he says, "I hope you like the place we rented."

"I'm excited to see what you picked out."

Forty-five minutes later, we arrive. The gate opens and there are two cars waiting in the driveway. The house is ranch style and rustic, and nothing like I was expecting. The cab leaves and when the gate closes, he says, "I know it doesn't look great from the outside—"

It's so quiet here. I can hear nature surrounding us. "It's perfect."

"This is nothing. Let's go in." He carries the luggage inside as I walk to the panoramic window at the back of the house.

The view is stunning and private and I can't see another house no matter how hard I try. "This is amazing."

"I'm glad the view lives up to the photos."

Turning around, I say, "I'm surprised you didn't rent a condo downtown so you could be in the heart of the action."

"I don't want to be in the chaos. I want to be with you and this," he says, turning back to the view. "I want to write music and perform the songs I've written without worrying about neighbors." I go to him and lean my back against his chest. His arms come around me and we look out together. "The doctor's right. You've popped out a lot more in the last few weeks."

While he rubs his hands over my stomach lovingly, I say, "I know. Even my yoga pants don't fit anymore."

His breath tickles my ear when he whispers, "You're so beautiful. You amaze me every day."

He beats the view any day. I turn in his arms and wrap mine around his neck. Lifting up, I kiss his chin. "Show me the bedroom."

I'm taken by the hand and we explore the house until we come to the master bedroom. Spun around, my back is pressed to the wall and he bends down to kiss my neck. His eyes are the shade of desire, a craving that only I can satisfy. I weaken under his touch, giving into the yearning that's built, and igniting it on fire.

His kisses—dedicated and hungry—become frenzied as do our bodies. I tug his shirt and he lifts it up, then tosses it. My shirt is pulled gently over my head and my skirt lowered. I remove my undergarments as I move to the bed. He stands there, watching me with an intensity, and I say, "C'mere."

His jeans and boxers come off before he joins me on the bed. "Take your hair down."

I pull the elastic out and throw it onto the nightstand. "Me on top?" I ask.

"Yeah." He lies back.

I climb over him. Bending down, I kiss his chest while running my hands over his shoulders. I kiss the tattoos and then run my tongue over the tiger. He reacts by pressing himself between my legs. My heavy breath comes out like a moan and I say, "I want to christen this home."

"I want to christen you several times over."

And he does—in the bedroom, the kitchen, and one last time just before dawn in the shower.

Life is beautiful.

TR

He's beautiful.

Just a few days in the Texas hill country and I can feel the change in him, and see it. His shoulders have lost the tension he was carrying around. His face even looks more relaxed, defying his age and appearing younger. He's been sleeping better and longer.

"Holliday, come out here," he calls from the balcony that seems to overlook forever.

Walking out, I drag my fingers across his sexy butt and get comfortable on a bench against the railing, propping my arm up.

He says, "I want to play a song for you."

Surprised by the offer, I sit up and ask, "Really?"

"Yeah."

"I'd love to hear it." It's been a while since he's completed a song and most of them he wants me to wait to hear live at the show.

My excitement must show because he's prefaces it with, "It's not perfect, but it's getting there."

His fingers strum twice across the acoustic guitar before he kicks into the song.

Four minutes.

For four minutes I sit across from him in complete awe. Not the beauty of the blue skies, nor the grace of the rolling hills capture the emotion I feel while he sings. My hands grip the railing, holding me in place, grounding me when his music makes me want to soar. The affection he sings of, the care of the melody as he plays, all of it speaks to the love he feels.

With the last note still lingering in the air, he asks, "What do you think?"

"Dalton," I start, knowing words will fail the emotions I feel. "That was amazing, just wow. I didn't expect that. I mean, I know how talented you are, but that's so different from your other stuff."

"I know. That's what worries me."

"Don't be worried. It's beautiful." With my hand over my heart, I say, "I'm blown away—the words, the melody, your voice—it's perfect. I wouldn't change anything."

"Really?" he asks, skeptically.

"I mean it. It's perfect. The line about a bird waiting for its song to return... so beautiful."

His eyes seem to light under the compliment as I walk to him. His guitar gets propped beside him, making room for me. I sit on his lap and look deeply into his eyes. "I think it may be your best song yet."

"I wrote it for you."

He's written other songs for me, but this one is different. This one was his heart singing to mine, a gospel of dedication and promises of an uninterrupted ever after. "Thank you."

His forehead touches down on my shoulder and he says, "Thank you." It's softly spoken, but I hear it how it's intended, personal and sweet, and full of meaning.

"What?" I ask, turning toward him, confused.

"I know you worry about me. But you don't have to anymore. I'm okay."

I study his features, the assurance of his words found by the serenity in his expression.

He says, "Cory was too good for this world." I try to hide my surprise, his statement knocking me off guard. I wait for him to say more, hoping he will. He does. "He's found peace. I think I have too." His blink lengthens and he takes a deep breath.

"How?"

"I finally realized that he didn't make the music. The music made us. It can recreate too, turning us into something new." He kicks the deck lightly, and he says, "I think he'd like the new songs."

I smile. "I think he would too." I bump up against him, leaving my body pressed to his and watch the sunset. My mind wanders back to what started this conversation. "If he was too good for this world, what does that make us, the ones who are still here?"

"Necessary."

Pondering his response, I start to understand what he means. "I need you."

His gaze meets mine and he says, "I need you too."

Necessary.

Nerves fill the car as we drive into downtown Austin. Dalton's usually really good about putting on fronts. He's had many years of practice, but tonight is different, new. At a stoplight, I peek over at him in the passenger seat. "Hi," I say, hoping to evoke a smile.

It works and I'm rewarded with one that's genuine. "Hi."

"You doing okay over there?"

"Just running through my set list."

"You're gonna be great." He nods, turning his attention back out the window in front of him. I learned years ago that musicians need their space before a performance, so I let him have his thoughts and focus on getting us there.

Tommy greets us in the alley. "Do you want your mic out of the trunk?" he asks.

"Yeah, my mic, guitar, and amp. That's all."

"Got it." The trunk door is slammed closed

I say, "I'll park around the corner and be back."

Dalton nods but doesn't say anything, his nerves showing more than I've ever seen before.

When I pull up to the end of the alley, I look in the rearview mirror. The guys haven't gone in yet. The conversation between Dalton and Tommy is tense by the body language. It makes me curious what they're talking about before the show. I want to know, but I need to park so I don't miss the opening.

I pull around the corner, but can't find any spots nearby. Three streets down and two over, I park. Hurrying back to the bar as quickly as I can, I get impatient. I don't want to miss his opening. I walk in the front door to a fairly empty bar. There are a few locals at the long wood top and a few small groups at the tail end of a happy hour. The place is small enough for him to be recognized, but deep down, for him, I hope he's not.

The bartender jumps the bar and hops up on the small stage. "We've got some live music for you this evening. A singer-songwriter some of you may know. Let's give it up for Jack Dalton."

The Reckoning

The crowd could care less. They're here for the drink specials, not the music. It's perfect, just the way Dalton wanted. He's wearing a baseball cap that I know has been through years of touring. He called it lucky when he tossed it in the car. And for him, I hope it is.

He starts playing and I order a Sprite before looking over and seeing Tommy sitting at a table in the back. When I sit, he leans in and whispers, "He sounds good."

"I'm nervous."

"Me too."

Tommy goes through a beer, his own nerves showing as he watches one of his best friends expose himself to the world in a whole new way. I keep wondering if I'm partial. Maybe I am, but I think he sounds strong, steady, and so good.

As soon as the first half of the set ends, we both meet him in the hallway that leads out back to the alley. There is no dressing room, so I follow them outside. His brow is cinched and Dalton says, "What the fuck was I thinking?"

Tommy says, "You sounded good. Stop stressing."

"I should have brought my electric guitar. They want Johnny Outlaw. They want The Resistance, not me."

"No," I say, "they haven't connected you to the band yet. That's what you wanted. This is your chance to win them over in a whole new way."

Tommy says, "Outlaw is who you fall back on. He's not real. Jack Dalton is right here and ready. You can do this."

Dalton looks distressed as he scans the alley.

Tommy adds, "They didn't know you were coming. Most of them are tanked. When doing something like this, wipe away your expectations and be open to what's happening now."

Dalton's expression changes, confidence seeping into his psyche and softening the hard lines. "You're right. I've got thirty minutes left to make a difference, to change their minds."

Holding him by the shirt and making him listen to me, I whisper, "Don't worry about them. Play for you."

He says, "I don't think anyone's even noticed me up there."

"Fuck 'em," I say. "If it helps, then play for me, babe."

Tommy looks at his watch, then says, "Stick to the set list and make them regret they missed the first half of the show." He steps up to open the door. "Time to make shit happen."

Dalton repeats, "Make them regret it."

"Break a leg," Tommy says, patting him on the back as Dalton goes back inside.

Our table is free, but I choose to sit in the center of the room. I want him to see me if he needs me, to know I'm here for him, and to give him the support he deserves. There's a moment of hesitation as he sits on the stool in front of the microphone. He says, "I've been playing music a long time, but I'm trying something new tonight." He adjusts his guitar strap, leans in and says, "This is for my angel."

Keeping his eyes on me, he sings, looking more youthful than his years. The vulnerability is stripping him of his onstage ego. This is the man I married. Sure, he was all bravado too, but this, this is Jack Dalton unplugged and he's just as magnetic as Johnny Outlaw ever was, if not more so.

When he finishes the first song, he laughs, the nerves seem to have gone. The rest of the show he's relaxed, such a natural talent. Thirty minutes fly by as I get to hear the results of all his hard work for the first time.

After his set, Tommy and I stand, clapping and the others who have wandered in join in. I hear some giggles from what appears to be college-aged girls, letting us know he's been 'found out.' Tommy's quick to the stage, grabbing the amp and mic while Dalton packs up his guitar. Dalton and I make it to the alley before the girls catch up with us. "You're Johnny Outlaw, right?"

He smiles, the weight of the anticipation gone from

The Reckoning

his shoulders. "Yes."

"Can we get a picture?"

"Sure," he replies breezily. "I'll be happy to take one of you."

They laugh, his charm working on them. "With you, if you don't mind," one girl says.

"Yeah, okay," he chuckles. He sets his guitar down next to me and they ask if I'll take the photo.

"Sure." They flank his sides and hold him tight around the waist. As soon as the camera on the phone focuses, I take the pic. "I think that looks good."

"Thanks," they say in unison.

Dalton says, "Thanks for coming to the show."

"Are you going to be playing more?"

"Maybe," he replies. Picking up the guitar he asks me, "Ready?"

"Ready."

Tommy runs after us and talks as we walk. "You just earned a hundred bucks." He laughs. "I bought the bar a round of drinks with it."

"Damn," Dalton jokes, "I had big plans for that money."

Tommy says, "So the new stuff. Let's talk about it."

"Wanna come out to the house?" I ask.

"Or we can grab a bite to eat while we're downtown," Dalton suggests, surprising me. He almost never wants to go out in public. Maybe Austin really will be the reprieve he needs.

We end up at an Austin tradition, Hut's Hamburgers. It's kind of dark and there's not much to look at, but the food is really good and the company even better. I lean on my hand, suddenly feeling depressed that I'm so big. "A year ago, I couldn't have finished half that burger. Now I finished the burger and a basket of onion rings. By the way, your son likes chili and jalapenos."

"My son's a badass. That's why."

"You're having a boy?" Tommy asks, sitting across from

us in the booth.

"Yeah, we found out, but we don't have a name yet."

"Congrats. That's great news. Oh and Tommy or Thomas is good," he adds, straight faced.

I let Dalton handle this one. "I think we're gonna go in a different direction."

"Whatever," Tommy feigns offense. "Let's talk about the music. It's different, not as raw as the band's stuff. It's more polished. How long have you been working on it?"

"Before the tour until now."

"I know you're taking a break from the band, but this could really be something interesting for the band to put out. What do you want to do with it? Go into the studio and record?"

"Maybe." Glancing at me, Dalton shrugs and says, "Probably."

"I think it could be a hit for you," Tommy says, "It shows your range. Would you tour?"

Suddenly playing a few gigs has turned into something much bigger, so I listen intently when he answers, "I don't know. I've not thought about it. I would have to tell the band. I'm not sure how to even tour without them." His hand rubs my leg under the table. "And the baby's coming."

Tommy sits back, settling in for the hard talk. "They know this is a possibility. They know you're down here playing your own songs. It's crossed their minds."

"Why does everything have to be so big?" I ask.

Tommy answers, "It doesn't, but this is how the industry works. You put out an album and you tour to support it."

"I understand that, but can't the tour be smaller, less cities. Maybe just the U.S. You know the last tour was rough on all of us." This is a subject we'll have to discuss soon, but not now. "Let's just celebrate tonight. I'm glad you did it."

"I'm glad it's fucking over and I'm ready to do it again."

Holding up my glass, I say, "To fresh starts and new adventures."

Dalton glances to Tommy before lifting his glass and tapping mine. "To fresh starts and new adventures."

29

"Anger is a solid emotion. It's coarse and rough around the edges, scarring on the inside. Much like life." ~ Johnny Outlaw

While Dalton stays home reworking his set before his next gig, I decide to go shopping downtown. There were a few boutiques I saw when driving in the week before that I wanted to check out. Not worrying about money in the last few years has been nice, but I still find myself being a bit frugal when it comes to purchasing on a whim. But as soon as I set my eyes on a pink diamond ring, I lose all focus on anything else. I try on the one of a kind design, holding my hand in the air and admiring it. I can't take my eyes off of it. I would have never guessed that a pink stone would wow me so much, but it has. Unfortunately, the price does not. I walk out of the store empty-handed.

After the disappointment of leaving the ring behind, I'm not in the mood to shop anymore and drive home. "Hello?" I call out when I walk in the front door.

Dalton peeks out from the kitchen. "Hi. You're home sooner than I expected."

"Did I walk in on you doing something scandalous?" I tease.

"Yes, this Nutella and Fluff sandwich is very scandalous." He holds it up just as I walk into the kitchen.

Stealing a bite, I moan in pleasure as I chew. "That's amazing."

"It's all yours," he says, handing it to me. "But only if you keep moaning like that." He rearranges his dick.

Apparently it does things to him so I moan again just for kicks. "Thanks and if you keep making me these sandwiches, I promise to do things to you with my mouth."

Reaching around me, he grabs my ass. "I fucking love your dirty mind and this great ass."

I try to laugh while keeping my mouth closed since it's full of food, but it's a struggle.

He asks, "Why are you home so early? Bored?"

"Shut your mouth! You don't ever say words like 'bored' when it comes to shopping."

"Why? Will shopping be offended?"

"No, but it kind of jinxes me and I may not find anything cute."

"Ahhh. Gotcha! That makes sense," he says, shaking his head, "not at all."

Making me laugh, I say, "Maybe it's a girl thing. Anyway, I didn't find anything cute today, but I did find something gorgeous."

He pulls out the bread to make another sandwich. "What?"

"This ring. It's to die for, Dalton. You don't even understand how amazing it was."

"Did you buy it?"

"No, I didn't buy it," I say, my pitch going up two octaves. "It was almost thirty-thousand dollars."

"And?"

Is he insane? "And nothing. I can't spend that kind of money on myself."

"Why?"

"Because," I say, trying to find a solid reason when money is no object. With my hands up, I huff. "I don't know why. Just feels weird."

"Okay, then I'll buy it," he says so easily as if money grows on trees.

Even though for us, money is no object, I try a rational approach. "You can't just go buy it."

He looks at me completely confused. "Why not?"

"Because it's expensive and so beautiful."

"That's why you should buy it."

I'm shaking my head at the ridiculousness of buying something so frivolous just because my heart has totally fallen in love with it. "I can't."

"I don't know why, and honestly I'm too tired to figure it out right now. I'm gonna nap." He heads upstairs while I finish eating and go into the living room with a glass of water.

I get more horizontal on the couch, a nap sounding way too good to not take one. My laptop is open on the coffee table in front of me. I search for the store's name and find the ring online. I admire it for a few minutes before my lids get heavy. I close my laptop and fall asleep.

TR

The following day, we head back downtown for Dalton's second gig. I know he's hoping for low key again to work out the kinks in the songs, but I'd be surprised if he gets it.

Word's gotten out that he's staying in town and the crowd tonight is great—enthusiastic and supportive, though I have no idea how they found out where he was playing.

I can tell the difference in Dalton too. On stage, he's charismatic and confident, sexy and completely captivating.

In the middle of the first half of the show, I feel the baby kick. Obviously he loves listening to his Daddy play as much as I do.

Life is better than ever.

After the show, I wait in the car as Tommy and Dalton load the gear. Tommy comes over and says, "I need to talk to Johnny for a few minutes."

"Okay," I say, wondering why he can't talk in front of me. But business is business so I start the car, turn on some music to pass the time, and check email on my phone.

"No!" I hear Dalton say, catching my attention. I turn back over my shoulder to see what's going on. They stand at the back of the car and like the last time I saw them like this, their body language is tense. Dalton turns his back to the car and paces away and back again. Both hands are planted loudly on the trunk and he looks down. "Fuck that!" he says harshly. Looking up, our eyes briefly connect, but something in his eyes hits me hard. I turn back, scared to what would upset him so much. I can't hear anything once I face forward, but I dare to peek into the rearview mirror. Tommy is using his hand to make a point. Tommy nods and says something that makes him shake his hand. I look away again when my stomach tightens, a bad feeling taking over my gut. The passenger door opens and Dalton gets in. "Let's go."

"Everything okay?" I ask wearily.

As if he's flipped a switch, he reassures, "Fine. You ready?"

"Yeah." I drive forward. Something's going on. I want to ask, but after the wonderful time we've had here, I'm afraid of the answer I might get. But I hate secrets more, especially his. Glancing from the road to him and back again, I say, "We never talked about whatever it was back in LA. Do you remember?"

I think I hear him gulp, but I'm not sure. When I stop at a red light, I turn to him. He says, "I should have told you by now, but things aren't how they should be, yet."

"So you're wanting to wait to talk about it?"

He sighs and cracks his window, the air in here feeling stifling to me too. "Is that an option?"

The light turns green and my gaze goes forward as the car moves. "When it comes to you, I must have the patience of a saint."

His fingers weave into my hair and he scratches lightly. It feels, reassuring in an odd way. "Thank you."

"Soon?"

"Ish."

"Okay. I'll give you soon-ish."

The following day I have an appointment up in North Austin. I find the shopping center easily and spend two hours with the owner of a store who I convince to carry the Limelight line of tees. Afterwards, I wander around the shopping center enjoying the nice day. When I turn a corner to go back to my car, I'm met with two men carrying long lens cameras. I immediately lower my head, avoiding them as much as I can. But I don't recognize where I am, so I head back the way I came. The paps take turns calling my name, approaching me, coming too close to feel safe.

Like in Los Angeles, the harassment begins. *"Mrs. Outlaw?"*

"Holli?"

"How's the baby? Will Sebastian be there for the birth?"

I pull my sweater tighter over my body, protecting my baby from their prying eyes and walk faster. *Ignore. Ignore. Ignore.*

One of them bumps my arm and the sound of the camera going off is just behind my head. They're too close and I grip my purse tighter.

"How does Johnny Outlaw feel about raising Sebastian's baby?"

My anger rises in reaction to their disgusting behavior. *Fuck them!* I pick up my pace and finally reach another parking lot, but I don't recognize it either. *Shit!* I turn around, not sure where I parked. While I look for a directory of the high-end shopping center, they continue tormenting me.

"Are you going to stay in Texas after the birth?"

"Guess you and Johnny are even now. You have the Lassiter love child and Johnny will soon have a baby with Ashley Dellacord."

My feet stop moving as his words trickle into my mind and I process what he just said. *And soon Johnny will have a baby with Ashley.*

"Have you decided to stay by his side like he did for you?"

Ashley Dellacord.

"What?" I ask, dumbly. My eyes fill with tears as I stand there, glued to the spot, their words slicing into me and tearing my heart apart.

"Ashley is suing for child support and the band for sexual harassment. Her lawyers say they have a solid case. Will you stand by Johnny through the trial?"

Ashley's pregnant.

Johnny's baby.

My knees go weak and I rush to the nearest space to get away from them before I collapse.

I hear the flicker of their cameras and I look around, unsure in which direction to go. I run to a corner on the side of a store that houses a back door for deliveries. My head starts to spin as the reality of their words hit me. I grip the wall with one hand and the baby with the other. "Leave me alone!" I shout. I try to stop the tears that are threatening, but they fall, streaming down uncontrollably.

Like a gun, their lenses rapid fire in my direction, the flashes become strobe lights temporarily blinding me. "Please stop!" I beg. "Please."

"Just one photo with a smile that we can sell?"

The other guy says, "The sobbing pics always pull in the bigger paychecks, man. Keep shooting."

A hand touches my shoulder and I scream. When I turn, his hands go up in surrender. "Miss, can I help you?"

I scan his uniform—property security. Grabbing hold of his arm, I plead, "Yes. Please help me get out of here. I can't find my car."

"I can help you find it. Come with me." Releasing his arm, the tears stop, though the burning in my eyes remains. I follow him, but before I turn the corner, I look back at the paps. Another guard is escorting them off the premises. Taking a deep breath to calm the commotion inside, I feel safer though my heart is shattered over the news.

The guard helps me find my car and as soon as I get in, I lock the doors, rest my head against the steering wheel, and cry again. I cry this time not from fear for me or my baby, but over the devastation that our life is about to be destroyed again. But if they found me once, they'll be on the hunt again. So I search the glove box and the console for a tissue, but when I don't find one, I lift my shirt and wipe my eyes before starting the car and making the long drive home.

The words those scumbags shouted at me, that they taunted me with, play on a loop. I turn on the radio to block out the noise in my head, but when The Resistance comes on, I click it off immediately. The last thing I need to hear is Dalton singing of his love for a hazel-eyed girl. I wipe away the wetness on my cheek and sniffle. Peeking into the rearview mirror I see my mascara is under my eyes. When I turn back to the road, I gasp, swerving, my nerves taking over as my car veers.

As soon as my car is righted, I pull over on the first street I come to, needing a moment to collect myself. But I can't fight it. I burst into tears again, leaning my head against the steering wheel. When I look up, I slam my hands down, banging on the steering wheel. "Damn it!" I just can't believe this is happening just when I thought we were back on track. *Does he know? Is this what he needed to talk to me about, but couldn't?* This is what he and Tommy were talking about. I just know it!

My wedding ring catches the light, sending little reflections of rainbow lights around the car. Leaning my head back against the rest, I close my eyes and take a deep breath in and exhale slowly. When I feel calm enough to drive again, I pull out and head home.

An hour later I'm sitting in the driveway, scared to face Dalton, scared to lose what we had just gotten back. But I have to face reality, so after about ten minutes, I get out. The walk to the front door, though only twenty feet or so, is torturous.

He lied.

I realize that now. He lied to me to get me back. I know myself well enough to know that I won't be able to get past this. I'm not strong enough to fight for us alone. There's no getting past the lie Dalton told me. Those guys knew before me. The entire world knew before me. The rage inside ceases any other emotion from taking over and when I look down at the ring on my finger, I feel sick to my stomach.

The door flies open when I walk through. It bounces off the doorstop and slams closed behind me. When Dalton appears from the bedroom, he says, "Hey there, how'd it go?"

I believed him.

I'm a fucking fool.

I glare at him, my breath crushing my chest then filling uncomfortably. "Tell me the truth, Dalton."

His expression changes, his body stilling as the realization that I know comes over him. The panic in his eyes insults my intelligence as if he could control this, as if he could hide this from me forever. "The truth about what?" His tone is cautious as he remains distanced from me.

One word. "Ashley."

The color drains from his face. "It's not what you think."

"What do I think?" Raising my voice, I yell, "Tell me what I think."

"I swear I didn't sleep with her. I swear to God, I didn't."

"You stand here before me swearing to God? You have some nerve. Her case is solid. She wins and I lose. I lose everything."

"Baby, please. Just listen to me—"

"Listen to you? What, now that you've been caught? Would you have ever told me?" He comes closer, but I back up, throwing my arms defensively in front of my body. "Don't come near me."

"It's not my baby, Holliday." His tone falters between stern and despair, his eyes wild. "You have to believe me."

"No, I don't have to believe you. She has evidence or she wouldn't be suing you. You can't run from this. You lied to me and now you can't run from that. I am done with you, Jack Dalton."

"Holliday," his tone is strong and forceful. "You need to calm down. For the baby. Don't put your health at risk over this crazy bitch's allegation. I'm telling you the fucking truth."

"The truth?" I ask, laughing. "I don't know what to believe anymore, but guess who told me your secret?"

"Tommy?" he asks, hurting my heart even more.

"Tommy knows? That's what all the talk after the show was?"

"Fuck," he mumbles when he realizes he just blew it.

Anger surges and I rush him, hitting him on the chest, so mad he would do this to me. "The fucking paparazzi! I found out how you fucked that whore and now she's having your baby from lowlife scum who trapped me in a corner while taking my picture."

His gaze hardens. His worst nightmare is now his reality. "Are you okay?"

Although I know what he means—physically, I reply, "No, I'm not fucking okay."

He looks away and the vein in his forehead becomes prominent. "I'll fucking kill them."

"I don't care about them." The tears strike again and I begin crying. "How could you keep this from me? I trusted you, again!"

"Please believe me. What I told you was the truth. We didn't have sex. I'm fighting the case, but because I'm fighting, I can't silence her. I tried. Trust me, I tried for us."

"Not hard enough. I'm done." I push past him and head for the bedroom.

"No. We need to talk this through."

Exhausted, and with my back to him, I reply, "I'm done, Dalton. Secrets always come out. I can't live like this, wondering what's going to happen next."

He follows me in and says, "Don't go. Please."

I grab the suitcase out of the closet and toss it on the bed. As I unzip it, I say, "If you aren't guilty, then why hide the truth? Why hide this lawsuit from me? Why risk everything over something that would eventually come out?"

"I was going to tell you, but I didn't know how. I just had legal send the letter yesterday. I wanted to tell you when I knew how we were moving forward. We were hoping to scare her into ending this. I didn't know she'd go public that fast."

"I don't want to hear anymore. I don't want you near me. I don't want to be with you in the same house. Do you understand what you've done to me... to your baby?" I scream, "You're having kids with two different women at the same time. I don't even want to look at you. You've humiliated me, Dalton!"

The Reckoning

"Don't forget, I've been humiliated too. Everyone thinks that baby in there," he says, pointing to my belly, "is that pricks."

Protecting my baby from the viciousness of this argument, I wrap my arms around my stomach. "But you know it's not and Sebastian isn't suing me to prove it's his. He makes no claims. That's all tabloid fodder."

"I believed in you because I know what kind of person you are and know you wouldn't do that to me." He seethes, "But you don't give me the same courtesy."

"You're turning it around on me like I did something wrong? How dare you!" I open the suitcase and grab a stack of shirts from the closet.

"I'm not turning it on you. I just want you to hear my side."

I throw my clothes into it in one fast swoop. Then realize I won't be able to fit my shoes and toiletries in this case and as he stands there watching me, I don't care about any of this. This is superficial. This *stuff* doesn't matter.

Staring down at the case, I lean forward and give into the tears. When I look up, my mascara blurs my vision and my tears turn black. "Your side? You had plenty of time to tell me your side and you chose not to, so why would I listen to you now? Why would I trust you? I found out from someone else when you didn't trust me enough to tell? What's next, Dalton? What other secrets are lurking, waiting to be revealed? I need to know."

Standing there, he keeps a slight distance though I see him wanting to come closer. "I was going to tell you. I just wanted to have things settled so I wouldn't worry you."

"Keeping something that will damage our lives, that can hurt our children..." I close my eyes. When I open them, I cool my temper and say, "You have hurt me so much. Could this have been avoided? Maybe. Maybe not, but I can't live like this anymore." I leave the suitcase and walk to the door.

He catches me by the arm as I pass and says, "We're not done."

Yanking out of his hands, I snap, "We are through. The fairy tale is over! I'm leaving."

I'm so distressed that I set my wedding ring down as I pass the table on the way to the front door. I'm spun around, caught, before I can open it. My arms are held at my sides as Dalton heaves, his rage directed through his eyes at me. "No."

"Don't tell me no. I'll do whatever I damn well please. Now let go of me or you're gonna regret it."

"What are you gonna do?"

I try to raise my arms to push him away, but he holds on tight. I push harder and when my wrist slips out from his grip, I fall forward, accidentally kneeing him. He barrels over in agony. "Son of a bitch!"

Taking advantage of the opportunity, I run outside. I get in the car and lock the doors. I quickly start the engine, but when I look up, Dalton's standing in front of the car. His palms go flat on the hood and he says, "You're not leaving."

Cracking the window, I say, "Move, Dalton. I mean it."

"No. We're not ending with you having half the story. If you hear my side and still want to go, fine, I'll let you. I won't like it. It'll fucking destroy me, but I'll move and let you go."

Gripping the steering wheel so hard my knuckles lose color, I close my eyes and lean against it. My breathing is worn and heavy, the anguish killing me. But when I look up, something changes inside of me. I don't see the man who betrayed me. I see the man I love more than I thought possible. And no matter how I feel or what I've heard, he's right. I haven't listened, really listened to his side. Even though I'm not wearing it now, I know when I put that wedding ring on my finger at the altar, I promised to do just that. "Fine." I roll the window down further and turn off the car. "Tell me your side."

He seems surprised and takes a deep breath. With his hands still firmly in place on the hood of the car, he says, "What I told you about that night is true. I told you everything that happened. Nothing more. She's lying. I would know if I had sex with her, Holliday. I didn't. I wouldn't. I wouldn't have, even if we hadn't gotten back together."

"You touched her."

He comes around to the side of the car and speaks to me through the window. "Yeah, I did and I regret it so fucking much. You don't even know how sorry I am. But you need to know that I didn't want to. I didn't instigate it, but I was the fucker who did it and I will have to live with that. I've said it before, but I'll say it again and as much as you need to hear it. I'm sorry."

From inside the car, I wipe my tears away on the hem of my shirt. Calming under the sincere tone of his voice, I say, "But she wouldn't go after you if it wasn't true. She says she has proof."

"There's no proof. I can take a paternity test and it will get us right back here, proving what I'm telling you. She's using the media to score a payday. She has nothing on me."

"Then why didn't you just tell me?"

"I wanted to have answers before stressing you out. I wanted you to know it was handled. But you found out from someone else and I'm also sorry for that."

"They took my photo while I was crying. They touched me. They harassed me, Dalton. I feared for the baby."

"Fuckers! I'll make them pay, Baby. I promise you."

"Security had to help me. This could have been avoided if I had known."

"No, it couldn't have been avoided. They would have found something to torture you with either way. But you're right," he says. "I should have told you. I kept it from you because I was worried about the baby and what this might do to you both." Looking at me through the open window, he adds, "The only way to keep this quiet would have been to settle the suit and I couldn't settle because that would feel like I was admitting guilt."

The car door is opened and when his hand touches my shoulder, I don't move away. I look down at my lap and then up to him. "You're fighting it?"

"I have to. I have to for you and our baby, and for me. She's going to use my public persona to get the result she wants, which is money."

"Dalton..." I cover his hand with mine. "You swear you're telling the truth?"

"I swear on my life that I'm telling you the truth. I have nothing to offer, but my words, my heart, and my soul. From here you're going to have to have faith in what I'm telling you and trust me." He briefly looks away. When his eyes meet mine again, he says, "It's your call, Angel. You either believe me or I stand here until you believe me. Your choice. What's it gonna be?"

He makes me smile, but I try to contain it while my fingers tap nervously on the steering wheel. My answer has been there all along. I just had to trust my heart to guide me back to find it. I open the door, leaving it to remain the barrier between us and hear a whispered, "I'm not going to let you leave me," no louder than a breath.

This man. This handsome, broken man. He's magnetic beyond his stage character and I'm too caught up in him to walk away now. "I'll stay."

A small smile filled with disbelief covers his mouth. "You will?"

"I will." Lifting up, I take his face between my hands and kiss him. Sliding around with our lips still embraced, we shut the door and he presses me against it. When his lips find my neck, I whisper, "I'm sorry."

The Reckoning

"No sorries," he whispers. "Just stay."
"I'll stay."

30

"There's a power that comes when you're completely honest with yourself." ~ *Johnny Outlaw*

Forgiveness comes in many forms. With Dalton, it was his green eyes that gave him away. Maybe it was just with me, and in a way I hoped it was, but he couldn't hide who he really was. I believed him. Not because I was naïve and just wanted to believe, but because my heart and my head knew he was telling me the truth.

He kisses me hard against that car and with his lips still pressed against mine, he says, "Inside."

I knew the meaning behind his demand and I wanted to be with him just as much. Something about fighting, getting out all that anger made us want to get it out in other ways too. We didn't walk. We moved with quickness to our steps. The bedroom door is slammed shut though we are the only ones here. The sun set minutes before, leaving the room with enough light to see what I was in for, to see his body tense against the only true exit. And I can tell tonight will be different. Careful and tentative has turned to desperation and need. I know the man I waited a lifetime for wants me the same, just like old times.

Standing there in silence, I briefly question if he still found me as attractive with my belly sticking out. Sucking in a jagged breath, I take off my shirt and slowly lower my skirt. "Is this okay? Am I okay?" I put my hands out and then drop them again, not sure what to do.

"What you're thinking, that's you, not me, Baby. You're fucking gorgeous. Now show me the woman inside, the woman who knows that." He says something that reminds me of the Holliday he sees, the wife he loves, the woman he desires. "Get your tits out, get on the bed, and turn around."

I see the spark in his eye, the flame that burns for me deep in his soul. Then he smirks and I'm done for. My bra is off in seconds. I turn around and climb onto the bed and wait. It's become a game that never loses my interest and only builds the anticipation.

His movements send me on alert as he comes closer, I hear his steps, the shuffle of his jeans rustling as he walks. Staring ahead, I close my eyes as I wait on my knees. His warmth spreads as his hand goes flat against my back. A gentle pressure has me bending forward on my hands. His fingertips tap to a silent rhythm down my spine, sending shivers through my body.

When he reaches my hips, they slip under the sides of my panties. The strings are ripped before they even had a chance to resist. I release a harsh breath as he rubs the skin on my hips, easing the fabric burn. His tongue touches the right side followed by a cool breath, giving me goosebumps. "How do you want me?" he asks and places a string of kisses on my backside.

I know what I want and am not shy about telling him. "I want

The Reckoning

your mouth on me first. Then I want you below me as I make you come."

"Motherfuc—" The rest of the curse word becomes inexplicable sounds. The sound of his belt clangs and I move up the bed, rolling onto my back. I settle against the pillows, propped up against the headboard. Dalton's jeans hang open and his head is tilted as he watches me. "Spread your legs," he says, leaving me no option. I do as he says and his eyes lower from mine to my center. He climbs onto the bed and comes toward me, licking his bottom lip once and making my body squirm. "I'm gonna make you feel so good."

He kisses my pussy twice, involving his tongue and going deeper. I grip the sheets on either side of me, preparing for the delicious torture. Within minutes, an urgent swirling is evoked deep in my belly and my breath expands when my mouth falls opens. The pressure overwhelms as the sensation takes control of my mind, freeing my body.

I hold him there, never wanting this to end while equally eager for my release. "So close, Dalton. More. Please." My nails scrape his scalp, gentle but enough for me to have a solid grasp of his hair between my fingers.

My back arches and I exhale on the verge of finding my haven, but he stops. Jerking up, my face surely reflects my confusion and irritation as my orgasm is ripped away from me. "What are you doing? Don't stop. Keep going," I say, the words come rushing.

He grins, wry and frustratingly handsome. Coming up, his body glides lightly over mine with care until he's over me, face to face. He dips his head down to kiss my neck, and says, "Not until you put this back on." When he lifts back up, my wedding ring is between his teeth.

When I reach for it, with his tongue he flips it inside his mouth before I can take it from him. "Dalton," I complain, ready to get back to the sexing. Taking his damn sweet time, he leaves me there impatient and horny as he gets off the bed. He walks to the end of it and grabs my ankles to pull me to the edge. Laughing, I slide, taking the blanket with me. "You're crazy. What are you doing?"

"What I've been meaning to do forever." He drops to one knee in front of me and with an innocence owning his smile, he holds the ring out, and says, "Holliday, *my Angel,* I dare you to marry me."

"Again?"

"Yes," he nods, "again."

Completely surprised by his sweet proposal, I touch his cheek and reply, "Don't you know? I always choose the dare." Moving to my knees in front of him, we kiss. After I catch my breath, I say, "Yes, I'll marry you, again and again."

"I don't want to live life without you in it, ever."

"You won't."

"I promise never to believe anything or anyone but you. I'm sorry."

Nuzzling into his neck, I whisper, "I'm sorry too, but no more looking back. We're together now. That's all that matters."

He holds me tight, my whole being safe in his arms. There is nothing better than this... except that orgasm he denied me. With wide puppy eyes, I say, "How about we pick up where you left off?"

Chuckling, he says, "Get your sweet ass back on that bed."

Two orgasms later, I lie there, sleepy and tired. His gaze lays heavy, his eyelids starting to close, giving into sleep. I kiss him on the lips and roll onto my side. Dalton's arm comes over me and I scoot back until I'm tucked safely against him.

TR

The next morning, I set a glass of orange juice in front of Dalton and say, "We're going to fight her together."

The Reckoning

His eyes lift from the laptop and he sighs. "I don't want you involved."

I sit down across the table from him. "I'm involved whether you want me to be or not. When she dragged you into this, she dragged me into it. I'm going to be there for you. We're husband and wife, parents together, and we'll stand as a united front."

"It's not going to be easy."

"The worthy battles never are." Reaching across and touching his arm, I say, "We have to do this together. We can't let her lies win and the only way to beat her, the media, and all the doubters is by sticking together."

His expression is light, almost weary, the line between his eyebrows tightening. Rubbing his eyes with his palms, he sighs. His eyes are reddish when he rests forward. "Promise me you'll tell me if it becomes too much."

"There's nothing you can do if it does, so let's just play her game and nail her for starting this war."

His head jerks back in surprise. "Wow, you're feisty."

I stand up. "I'm not feisty. I'm protecting what's mine and you, my fuckhot husband, are all mine."

"Did you just territorial piss on me?"

I flash my ring. "I sure did." I walk away to take a shower and get ready for the day.

His laughter trails behind me. "Shake that ass for me."

I send a little wiggle his way before the hall blocks me.

Five minutes later, I'm in the shower when he storms in, the door hitting the wall. "Holliday!"

Jumping, I reply, "What?"

"I'm going to fucking kill those paps."

"You scared the shit out of me. What happened?"

He opens the shower door and holds his phone up so I can see. I gulp hard. The feeling of being trapped by them yesterday comes back hitting me like a tidal wave. My eyes well staring at the photos of me cornered and crying. The heartbreak I felt then lumps in my throat again.

"You didn't tell me it was this bad?"

"I told you what happened."

His fist hits the wall and he grits through his teeth. "They have you caged like a fucking zoo animal."

"Just let it go," I say, letting the water rain down over my eyes to conceal any tears that might want to flow.

"I'm not letting it go. This is fucking war. I swear they're going to pay for this."

Cautious, I move to the opening and touch his arm, making him lower the phone so I don't have to see the pictures anymore. Swallowing down the fears they created and the sickness I feel over yesterday, I say, "They don't matter. I know what I got into when I chose to be with you. And their interest has only grown since the baby started showing. But we can't dwell on them. We have more important ways to spend our time."

As the lines of his forehead begin to relax, he sets his phone on the counter and says, "You're right." Stepping inside the shower fully clothed, he kisses me, and we let the world and all of our problems wash away.

Warm kisses become heated and Dalton presses my back to the wall, his hands wandering over my slick body. The drenched shirt is stuck to his body, but I push it up, wanting it off. While it's dropped to the ground, I work on his jeans. He playfully lifts, struggling to get the drenched fabric off. I bend down and yank and he kicks them off. I'm instantly pinned against the wall after that, but I want the control, so I push him against the other wall. I start to sink to my knees before him, but he takes me by the elbows and says, "Stay."

"I am," I reply, smiling.

"I mean, let's not do that right now. Let's just be together, like this."

Like an arrow, his sweetness strikes me straight in the heart. His arms slide around me and he holds me close. His voice lowers and although the sound of the water showering down tries to drown him out, I hear him say, "Thank you for staying, for standing by me, for believing me."

Running my hands over his shoulders and up his neck, I say, "Always."

"Infinity."

"Infinity." I repeat and kiss him again, and whisper, "We both have clean slates."

"I like that. Clean slates." Kneeling down, he kisses my belly. "I love you, baby." Looking up, he asks, "What's his name going to be?"

"You're trusting me with that?"

"Absolutely."

TR

With a sparkling water for me and an iced tea for him, I sit outside next to Dalton and ask, "How do you feel about Jack Dalton the third?"

"No. That's a tradition that needs to end with me. I'm not going to torture my kid like that."

"Johnny Junior?"

He bellows with laughter. "He'll most definitely be a little Outlaw, but not a Johnny."

We settle onto the bench that overlooks miles and miles of trees and undeveloped land. It's really breathtaking. "*Wellllll*, I've been thinking about a name that means something to us and yet, makes him his own little person too."

Dalton reclines back and says, "All right."

"So I was thinking of honoring Cory."

He sits forward, his brow furrowing as he looks out into the distance. "Cory Junior is his youngest."

"I know. I was thinking about his last name of Dean as our baby's middle name."

When he turns to me, there's a small smile in place. "You'd do that?"

"I love the name and he was important to our family, so it only seems right."

"You're an amazing woman, Holliday. What about the first name?"

Taking a deep breath, I prepare myself before trying to prepare him. "So I was thinking that I don't want a weird name. I know it's not the cool thing to do when celebrities have kids, but this is our child's name and I want it to be something I love, not just something to stand out."

"*Okaaay*. Makes sense. What did you come up with?"

"James." I start talking faster before he can put it together. "I just love the name James. It's old-fashioned but never goes out of style. Everyone knows how to spell it and the baby can go by Jimmy or Jamie, or Jim, or Jame—"

"James Dean?"

"He's named after someone we love because you know I wouldn't name our kid after an icon, but I have no control over the Dean part and I've tried a million names with Dean and read three books."

"Wait a minute. Slow down. You want to name our kid James Dean?"

"Well, technically, James Dalton would be his name. His full name would be James Dean Dalton. But if you prefer, I'm down with Hughes too."

"For his last name?" Dalton looks shocked and then a little hurt.

"For his middle name like James Dean Hughes Dalton or James Hughes Dean Dalton or," I speak even quicker because of my nerves.

As the same thought hits us at the same time, in unison, we say, "James Hughes Dean Dalton."

"Yes!" I exclaim. "James Hughes Dean Dalton." But then I waver wanting him to love the names. "Or James Dean Hughes Dalton. Whatever. I'm open. What do you think?"

"I think you're super cute."

Laughing, I reply, "Other than that."

His arm comes around me and he pulls me close. "I think it's a great name no matter what the order... Other than the Dalton. I fucking love that on the end of your name and our kids' names."

Patting his chest, I say, "I thought you might. So the rest is up to me?"

"You got it."

"I've got this," I reply, rubbing my belly. "Right baby?"

I get a few kicks as the baby responds to the attention. Here in the countryside of Austin, I find my solace with my growing family. Deciding right then that nothing and no one will come between us ever again.

31

"I've always heard good things come to those who wait, but I was gifted with good looks, not patience." ~ Johnny Outlaw

Austinites had gotten wind of Johnny Outlaw's surprise performances and somehow the dedicated fans had managed to figure out his next location before he stepped up on stage. So as Dalton stood up on stage at the Lonestar Bar in front of a packed crowd, I couldn't help but be proud. The entire audience swayed to the slow songs, danced to the faster songs, and sang along by the second chorus. He shined. His stardom is evident as he sings his songs from the heart. There's just something so mesmerizing about that man.

Tommy nudged me several times. Even without words I could tell how proud he was as well. During a break, we stood in the

Manager's office listening to Dalton's excitement. He was in the zone and knew he had connected with the audience. But what he was most excited about was that he did it on his own—just him and a guitar.

"This could be big." Tommy asks, "Are we gonna make this album?"

Dalton looks at me as if I can give him the answer he needs. I say, "What does your heart tell you?"

He finishes a drink and sets the glass down before sitting in a ripped up swivel chair. "I've been thinking about everything. My head's clear and I know what I want to do now."

Tommy and I wait. Pins and needles have become knives and swords in anticipation of his answer. A big part of our future seems to lie in his answer.

He says, "My heart's with the band. I hate those guys, but I fucking love them more."

I smile. He's so strong and yet so vulnerable. His heart is as big as his fame.

An enthusiasm is heard when Tommy says, "Dex has three new songs he's written. You have fourteen. We have the other twelve that you guys were about to go into the studio with. We've got more than we need for an album. We can release a double CD or we have the next two albums in the bag and you can take a break from the studio. How are you feeling about Kaz and Derrick?"

"I think they're better than they think they are and they think really fucking highly of themselves. It takes time, but they're gelling."

"What about a tour?"

"I can't commit to anything before the baby's born," Dalton says, "but we wouldn't tour before then anyway. What do you think Holliday?"

Leaning against a bulletin board, I say, "I'm hiring three new

The Reckoning

employees at Limelight with room for five more if the new lines take off. I don't want to work fifty, sixty hours a week when the baby comes. I don't want you gone all the time either, but we're both doing what we love so how can I ever ask you to not pursue your dreams?" Walking over to him, I settle on his lap. "I'll support you. With a family, we'll just have to work things out, but you do what you need to do. You'll be happier for it and that makes me happy."

He kisses me and then stands up, setting me down on my feet again. "Love you."

"Love you too."

Tommy stands and looks at his watch. I almost see the cogs turning as his focus expands to the possibilities Dalton's just offered up. "I'll call Dex tonight, but you need to get back out there and wrap this up."

We walk out and the crowd screams as Dalton takes the stage again. Tommy and I work our way toward the back of the bar. He stands next to me, a barrier to protect me I think. I lean my head on Tommy and say, "You're a big softie, you know that?"

When I lift back up, he wraps his arm around my shoulders and gives me a side hug. "Only for you." His arm falls away and he points up at the stage and says, "Know any single hot women who don't mind dating guys on the road all the time?"

Laughing, I think about all my friends. "I know a few single hot women, but I'm not sure this life is for everyone. But I'll definitely think about it and keep you posted."

Dalton hits a hard note, his voice holding steady. We both smile and Tommy says, "I've watched that man grow from an angry, punk-ass kid to a superstar. But he hasn't peaked. If he went solo he could own the music industry, but that he's chosen to support the band says what kind of man he is."

Dalton has his eyes closed. He's leaning into the microphone singing while his hands strum a melody that comes second nature to him. The first five feet of the audience is all women vying for his attention, hoping to get a look, a touch, an offer from him. When he opens his eyes again, he searches for me. I can tell by the way he's focused. It's a look in his eyes that's centered, all confidence and pride.

Tommy looks down at his phone, checking emails. He laughs, drawing my attention. "Holy shit! They got four Grammy nominations."

"What?"

He angles the phone so I can see. I read on the screen the official email that shows four nominations and in which categories. "This is huge." They've won three, but I know this album was rough since it was the first they made after Cory's death. Giddy, I say, "He's gonna flip. This is just what he needs right now."

"You know what's funny, Holli?" He shakes his head in disbelief. "I don't know if he even cares about awards or gold records. He gets to do what he loves. He lives his dream every day, but what I do know is at the end of the day, this baby boy will be his greatest achievement."

Feeling the love, I smile at him. "Thanks, Tommy. That means a lot to me."

A guy turns around and asks, "Johnny Outlaw's having a boy?" Then he snaps my picture.

Tommy shoves him away from me, and then grabs my arm, tucking me behind him. "Go Holli."

Coming back and madder than ever, the guy keeps snapping photos as I duck to get out of there. He shouts loudly, above the crowd, above Dalton singing, "Or is it Sebastian Lassiter's ki—"

Tommy punches him. I gasp, but hurry toward the door for safety. When I look back, he's gone down from the hit. The crowd encircles him as the bouncers rush past me. Tommy's right behind me, his hands on my back guiding me. Holding my arms around my stomach, I say, "I think that was one of the paps from the other day."

The music comes to an abrupt halt. Before I walk out the front door, I look back over my shoulder and see Dalton hopping off the stage. *Shit*. As soon as we're free from the crowd, I tell Tommy, "Stop him. He'll kill them."

When we get outside, he directs me behind two bouncers. "Stay here. Right here, Holli. Don't leave this guy's side." He taps the doorman, shoves a fifty in his hands, and says, "Don't take your eyes off her and don't let anyone near her."

"Sure, pal."

I push Tommy toward the door. "I'll be fine. Go!"

Holding my belly, I peek up at the very large doorman. "Hi."

He nods slowly, and replies, "Hi. So you're with Johnny Outlaw?"

Nodding, I answer silently.

"Cool."

And it is. It's pretty damn cool, though times like these I worry about Dalton's temper and the trouble it can get him into. Peeking inside the open door, I see Tommy pushing Dalton backwards by the chest. Dalton is shouting at the paparazzo, "I will beat the fuck out of you if you ever come near my wife again."

Tommy is yelling at him, the crowd is moving out of the way as he passes. Their phones are in the air. I'm sure capturing it all. The doorman says, "Guess the show is over."

"Looks that way." Standing there a few more minutes, I start to feel awkward, so I shift around to his other side. That's when I see him. Dalton is standing on the corner looking around. When he sees me, he jogs over. No words. Just kisses. With his arms enveloping me, he asks, "You okay?"

"I'm fine." I touch his cheek, relieved to see he isn't hurt. "How are you?"

He laughs humorlessly. "I don't even know. I just know I'm glad you're okay. Let's get the fuck out of here."

I tap the doorman. "Thanks."

"No problem. You guys have a safe night."

I can tell he's a little awestruck seeing Dalton. I understand the feeling. I still get awestruck by him too, but for different reasons entirely.

Stopping Dalton before we leave, I say, "This guy was nice to me. Maybe you want to take a photo or something."

He nods, turning to the guy. "Hey, thanks for helping her out."

He gets his wallet out, but the guy stops him and says, "The other guy already took care of me."

Dalton seems impressed. "You want an autograph or photo or anything?"

"A photo would be cool." He pulls his phone out of his pocket and holds it out in front of them. After he takes the pic, he shakes Dalton's hand, and says, "Thanks."

"Thank you."

The bar manager comes out with Tommy and they both escort us to the car. Tommy's in the driver's seat, the equipment already loaded in the trunk. When he pulls away, he says, "Always an adventure."

"That's for sure," I add.

Dalton laughs, nothing seeming to bother him. With his arm over my shoulder as we sit in the backseat together, he looks out the window. "It's good to be back."

TR

Tommy thought it best to cut the impromptu tour short for several safety reasons. Dalton agreed, saying it was getting out of hand. That means we're heading back to LA and going home. I'm ready to be home. I miss our house. I miss my friends. I miss working in my office and seeing Tracy almost every day. I want to finish the baby's room and have a mountain of things to do before the baby arrives including my next doctor's appointment.

Once we're back in LA, everything looks good and the baby sounds healthy. We are blessed in so many ways that I hate thinking about the bad, but we've had a major obstacle trying to block our happiness and I have every intention of ridding the negative from our lives once and for all.

Four days later, we walk hand in hand into the lawyer's office. "Keep your eyes down," Dalton says, gripping my hand tighter. "Don't give them anything."

I exhale, remembering this is part of our lives and probably always will be, especially since we fired back at Ashley, using the media the same way she has. The lawsuit has blown up, all the outlets carrying every crumb of information they can get their hands on. They're salivating from the salacious story.

Ashley and her lawyer are due in the office today, to hear the results of the paternity test we got court ordered. I'm still shocked she went through with it considering they didn't have sex. That she took the test, knowing it would be false, troubles me. I'm not sure what kind of crazy I'm dealing with anymore.

We're seated in the conference room, her lawyer is already there. Our lawyers sit across from him and we sit further down. We're there to listen, not participate. Surprisingly, Ashley does not show. Our lawyer, Ron Jacoby, says, "We received the envelope. We have, per our agreement, not read the results."

"There's no need," her lawyer says. "Ms. Dellacord has withdrawn her suit."

I huff in annoyance and roll my eyes. Everyone looks my way. "Oops," I whisper, "Sorry."

Dalton whispers, "It's good she's withdrawn."

Ron asks, "Did she give a reason?"

"She feels," he says, stacking the papers in front of him, "that the heavy involvement of public opinion has tainted her pregnancy and caused concerns. She does not want to further jeopardize the health of her baby."

"Bullshit," Dalton spews. "She sold the story for thirty grand and now she's about to be busted in her lie."

Ron puts his hand out, telling us to hold on. My fingers entwine with Dalton's, hoping to calm us both. We've been on edge all morning. Ron adds, "We'll be opening the results whether she's withdrawn the suit or not." He pulls the envelope from a file and starts to rip it open. The other lawyer looks uncomfortable as he watches, shifting in his chair. I think my heart stops altogether waiting for these results.

Ron announces, "No test was taken, so there are no results."

Dalton and I collectively release a breath. "She lied for money and the fifteen minutes of fame she thinks she's owed," Dalton says. He looks at Ron and says, "We're moving forward with our suit."

Ron turns to Ashley's lawyer and says, "On behalf of Mr. and Mrs. Dalton, we will be suing Ms. Dellacord for full legal fees of her withdrawn suit as well as $3.2 million for damages and distress. In addition, they are requesting a public admittance that she lied to not only extort money from my clients, but to deliberately damage the reputation of Mr. Dalton and the band, The Resistance."

The other lawyer tries to hide his shock, but the dismay is read loud and clear across his crinkled forehead. "As a representative of Ms. Dellacord, she has granted me the right to settle for a reasonable fee for this not to play out any longer. She's requested 1.2 million to end this today."

"Us pay her?" Dalton scoffs. "She can fuck herself."

Ron asks us to remain quiet as he handles the rest. "We will not be paying her anything and as I just mentioned, we will be moving forward with our suit against her. She brought the media into this, but we will use them to end it. Just in case I wasn't clear about what my clients feel is fair to settle, if she does not comply with the terms I've spoken of, we'll turn this case over to the FBI to further investigate the possibility of Ms. Dellacord using tactics of extortion." He stands. "Good day."

We follow Ron out of the room, leaving the other lawyer gobsmacked. Back in Ron's office, he calls in his assistant and asks, "Stacy, is there a way to verify Ms. Dellacord is actually pregnant?"

"We can pull records though not her medical file without a court order."

"Can we get one?" he asks.

"I'll start working on that now."

When Stacy leaves the room, I say, "We don't even know if she's pregnant?"

Ron shakes his head. "Unfortunately not. We've had a PI on her tail, but she's not been seen in public at all since the lawsuit broke."

"That's what it is," I say, everything so crystal clear. "She's not pregnant. That's why she didn't take the test."

Dalton stands at the window looking out. His arms are crossed and his shoulders tense. "She's disturbed, but she started this war. I almost lost everything because of her. I have to see this through or this could happen again with the next psychopath."

Ron says, "It's setting a precedence not to fuck with you in the future. I think it's wise to follow through with the suit even if she's not pregnant."

Five days later, we get a call from Ron. We're sitting at our kitchen table with a stack of baby clothes to fold in front of us, when he confirms my suspicion. "She's not pregnant. She's claiming she lost the baby, but she has not sought any medical attention in the last year related to a pregnancy. It was a con."

Relief washes over me, though when I decided to trust Dalton, I had decided then it wasn't his baby she was carrying. Now to find out she wasn't carrying a baby at all mystifies me to how she thought she would get away with this. I rub over my stomach, finding it easier to breathe knowing there won't be a question in the public's eye now. Dalton remains silent, ingesting the news. I suggest, "What if we lower the money to one million and demand the apology within ten days?"

Ron replies, "That sounds reasonable. Generous actually, but you know you can win more."

"I don't want to destroy anyone, but she does need to pay where it hurts and since she's a gold digger, her wallet is where it hurts. Her pride second. I want the public apology."

With one raised eyebrow, and a shit-eating grin on his face, he says, "No one messes with my family."

On the advice of her lawyer, three days later, a formal apology is published and shared all over the gossip shows, the tabloids, and radio. Payments started to the children's hospital where we decided any money from this would be donated.

We're finally vindicated, but more so, we're happy that no one will question Dalton's fidelity anymore. As for my pregnancy, Sebastian constantly denies having relations with me in interviews, but the media likes the juicy tales, so we have to just move on from it. We know the truth and once this baby is born, everyone else will too.

32

"Life continues and if we're fortunate enough, so do we." ~ *Johnny Outlaw*

On May 15th, James Dean Hughes Dalton is born, weighing in at seven pounds, seven ounces. He has blue eyes and a little tuft of blond hair right on top. He is the most handsome man I've ever seen. "He looks just like you," I tell Dalton.

Dalton is speechless as he holds our baby. "How can the world shift on its axis in the blink of an eye?"

I know exactly what he means. That happened the first time I ever laid eyes on my future husband. "It happens," I reply with a tired smile. "It happened with us."

"Yes, it did." He kisses the baby on the head and says, "We're parents, Holliday."

"We are." My eyelids dip closed. "I'm gonna rest. Will

you lie here with me?"

He nods, kicking off his shoes and gently climbing into bed with me. The baby is tucked safely in his arms and I rest my head on his shoulder.

Watching this little guy in his arms gives me peace like I've never felt before. My body is exhausted, but my heart beats strong, security encompassing us. The baby yawns and I watch in awe. "We made him," I whisper.

"We did good," he chuckles lightly, not disturbing the baby. "*You* did very good. Are you okay?"

"Better than ever." I turn and kiss his cheek and then kiss my baby's nose before closing my eyes and falling asleep.

When I wake up two hours later, Dalton is asleep. The baby is not, and I smile, touching his cheek.

Our first visitors come into the room after a soft knock on the door. Rochelle walks in with CJ and Neil. They stay for awhile until the boys start going stir crazy after being told not to be loud around the baby. They bring us gifts—homemade pictures the boys drew and Rochelle made us a baby blanket. She hands us an extra gift. "It's from Dex. He's dealing with some family stuff and couldn't come today, but said he'll stop by the house soon."

"That was very nice of him to send this," I say, taking the box. When I open it, I start laughing. "Guess what it is, Dalton."

He looks up from the chair by the window, baby in his arms, and says, "He's not gonna be a fuc—" he stops, and clears his throat, correcting himself. "Drummer if that's what he sent over."

Rochelle and I giggle as the boys stare at James, touching his tiny toes. I say, "He did send over drumsticks, but look." I hold up a tiny leather jacket. "It's a must-have for a future rock star."

I see Dalton's smile, but he forces it down. "Maybe my son will be a doctor."

Rochelle and I stare at him, surprised by this announcement.

The Reckoning

Then Dalton says, "Just kidding. He's gonna be the greatest guitarist that ever lived. He'll be a legend in my lifetime."

Snickering, I add, "I have no doubt."

Rochelle says, "Dex gave Neil and CJ their first set of drumsticks. He's given them a few lessons too."

"Really?" I ask, amazed.

She nods and admires the jacket. "This is the cutest thing ever."

The visitors continue with Tommy and my mom. Dalton's parents arrive late, but in good spirits and with tears in their eyes. Tracy and Adam come the next day, wanting to give us a break from all the early visitors and sneak some food in for us.

After we've eaten, Tracy continues to hold the baby, rocking him in her arms. "The media is swarming the place. Everyone wants to meet the offspring of the beautiful Holliday Hughes, successful entrepreneur, and the infamous Johnny Outlaw," Tracy says with a laugh. "I can't take my eyes off him. He's so cute, Hols."

"He takes after his dad."

Dalton smiles. "Again, for all of our sakes, let's hope he takes after his mother."

Rubbing his back, I say, "Awww, Babe, you're a great man. You'll be an even better father."

Leaning back, he kisses me, but then turns serious. "Be honest. How bad is it outside?"

Adam says, "Bad. No lie. There are at least fifty or more photographers. The hospital has roped the area off and hired security."

Tracy hands the baby back to me and asks, "Are you going to do a formal introduction and let them get the pic or maybe a magazine spread? We've gotten a ton of calls at Limelight."

Dalton speaks before I do, "I won't sell my son to them. No way." He looks at me. "What do you think?"

"I agree."

Tracy says, "Rory called me. He's worried what the first photo will go for if you don't do a spread."

"I'm worried," I add, admiring my son. "I'm worried about safety too. Will this ever end? If it's not one thing, it's another. I just want to go home and cuddle with my family."

"Don't worry. I'll get us out of here and get you both home safely," Dalton says, and kisses James' head.

Avoiding the paps outside the hospital has become a game that makes us laugh while we plot. But when it comes time to actually leave, the fun is sucked out of the room. Situations such as these can be dangerous, even more so with a baby on board. This is LA though, so we use the secret exit in the garage. We trust Tommy in his Expedition to get us out. Dalton has his arm over the baby's car seat that he spent twenty minutes securing. After he helps me into the backseat, he pulls my seatbelt over and buckles me in as well. "This is a whole new side to you, Mr. Safety," I tease.

"Not taking any chances."

I kiss him on the cheek. "You're so sweet."

He angles toward me and kisses me on the lips. I missed these kisses that felt like they could turn into more. Tommy threatens, "No making out in the car. I'll pull it right over if you start that up."

Dalton jokes by grabbing me quickly and kissing me harder, making a scene in the backseat.

"Stop it, Outlaw, or I'll dump your asses off at the closest hotel."

"Don't swear," Dalton and I say in unison, then burst out laughing.

I add, "The baby can hear." In the rearview mirror, I see Tommy roll his eyes.

Dalton is smiling and I laugh again. It feels good to be silly together.

Later that afternoon, after my shower, I walk to the kitchen, but stop in my tracks in the living room when I find Dalton asleep on the couch with James cradled in his arms. James wiggles as he wakes. Dalton didn't get much rest at the hospital, so I'm glad to see him getting some now. But to see him with James, so protective and caring... makes me want to make another baby with him right now.

James closes his eyes again and falls asleep. I run for the camera wanting to capture every moment of this kids' life.

Between our parents visiting and friends coming over to meet our son, a month goes by before we are alone, just the three of us. I cherish every second of it.

The band has started meeting over at Dex's studio and laying tracks for the new album. Dalton is gone about five or six hours a day and is home in time to have dinner with me and spend time with James. Sitting on the couch late one night while holding James after a feeding, I say, "He's a night owl."

"He just doesn't want to miss any of the fun."

"It's that nighttime fun that I'm missing."

Fingers find me, slipping into my hair. "Tell me about it. I'm counting down."

"I have an appointment tomorrow. Trust me, I'm counting down too. I'll talk to the doctor about it." A yawn escapes and I lean my head back and close my eyes. "I'm so tired tonight."

"Get some rest. I'll hold him and put him down."

"Now that's an offer I can't refuse." Dalton bends over and takes the baby. And there's just something about seeing him hold this tiny little person we created that melts my heart every time. "Are you staying up late?"

"No," he replies, tapping James on the nose. When he looks up, he smiles. "We'll be up soon."

I kiss them both and start up the stairs. I stop at the top just out of sight when I hear him say, "Your mommy is gonna love what I have planned."

My heart grows from all the love I feel. On top of the world, I go to bed.

TR

"I was given the go ahead," I blurt out.

Dalton looks at me completely clueless as to what I'm talking about... until he knows exactly what I'm talking about. He sets his soda can down and hops off the kitchen counter where we're preparing dinner. "You were?" He grabs me by the waist and sways my hips. "What are we waiting for then?"

"Nothing. No waiting."

He takes my hand and starts leading me upstairs, but I stop on a lower step than him. When he feels my hesitation, he stops and turns back. "What?"

"I'm nervous. Why am I nervous?"

No less than the most charming expression crosses his face, an excitement seen in his eyes. With his hands on either side of the railings, he asks, "Why are you nervous, Baby?"

"It's been a while. A few weeks before we had James and now just over a month has gone by after. I'm just nervous."

Coming back down the steps, he passes me until he's two below and eye-level. Touching my cheeks, he says, "We'll go slow. I don't want to hurt you."

"I know you won't."

He kisses me, takes my hand again, and we walk up side-by-side. He shuts the door behind him and I make sure the monitor is on. James is down for a nap, so we don't have long.

Music comes over the speakers on our nightstands. It's soft and romantic, making me giggle. "I love it that you're setting the scene, but is it really us?"

"It can be," he replies so easily. Holding his hand out for me, he stands in the middle of the bedroom. "May I have this dance?"

Slowly, I go to him and take his hand. He pulls me in quickly, our chests suddenly together. With one hand on my hip and the other holding my hand, he begins dancing and I follow his lead. I rest my head on his chest, loving being this close to him.

His mouth finds my neck and the sweet seduction begins. I give in wholeheartedly wanting him, wanting to feel him again. As he hardens against my middle, we continue an unhurried dance that leads me to the bed. Removing his clothes, he stands before me exposed and confident, sexy, and utterly beautiful.

I lie on the bed, getting comfortable when he leans forward and takes my shirt up. My yoga pants are quickly drawn down, leaving me bare before him. Dalton kisses my belly, and looks up. "I love you infinity."

"I love you infinity."

Our love is steadfast and kind, our bodies move with a familiarity that only home provides. As we lie there afterwards, I say, "You'll always be my home."

"You were always mine."

We hear a tiny cry come over the monitor and look at each other. "Best sound ever."

"Holliday, before you go, I want you to know how grateful I am to you."

"We did this together."

"I'm not just talking about the baby. Though I'm in awe of you when it comes to him. I'm talking about this life you've given me, everything you've given me. You've given me a purpose."

Rolling toward him, I say, "You've given me more than you realize. You gave me a life worth fighting for. You gave me your heart. You gave me your child. You make me feel a love I didn't know was possible." I kiss him on the lips. "I love you infinity, Dalton."

When the monitor lights up again, I whisper, "Meet you downstairs?"

"I'll be down in a few. I need to make some phone calls."

"Okay."

Though I'm curious to the phone calls he needs to make, I give him the privacy he seems to want.

When he comes downstairs, he comes into the kitchen and says, "Want to go out to Ojai this weekend?"

Standing in front of the stove, my eyes light up as I stir the noodles. "I've been wanting to go out there. It will be nice to take James out there too. It's so quiet and peaceful."

Taking notice of Dalton's silence, I look over my shoulder at him. He asks, "Do you want to have a dinner party?"

Surprised by this, I ask, "A dinner party? Wow, you're jumping into this settling down thing both feet first."

That makes him laugh. Leaning on the counter he says, "I'll handle it all. I know you're busy with the baby and trying to squeeze in work."

"You don't have to do that. You're busy too."

"I want to. I want to for you."

Bending down, I pick James up out of his bouncy seat and walk around the counter to Dalton. He takes him from me and snuggles him. "What's going on?"

"I just want to do something special for you and thought this might be a good thing."

"You're very sweet. If you're sure?"

"I'm positive."

Remembering his phones calls and what I overheard him say, I drop it realizing this is what he was planning. "So is it more dressy or you want to keep it casual?"

"Let's do dressy. We have a lot to celebrate."

"Yes, we do." I finish cooking dinner while he holds James. "Maybe I'll see if Rochelle wants to go shopping."

"That's a good idea," he replies while rubbing his nose against the baby's.

"Can you stop being so stinkin' adorable? You're very distracting."

He sends a smirk my way before continuing to love on James.

TR

The next day Rochelle meets me at a boutique down on Melrose. I run my fingers over a rack of clothes and moan, "I'm not feeling my best with this flabby belly."

She wraps her arm around me and says, "You look fantastic. You're active and eat healthy, so don't worry. It will melt away." Leaning down, she smiles as she coos. "Baby James, he's just gorgeous. So handsome. I see both of you in his features, but I don't see Sebastian at all."

"You're so bad." I nudge her in the side. "Did Dalton talk to you about the dinner party?"

"He did. He said he wants you in a dress."

My eyebrows shoot up. "He did? He just told me it's a fancy dinner and he's talking to you about what he wants me to wear?"

"I think he wants to make it special for you."

Glancing down at James who is asleep, I say, "I'm very fortunate. My life is a dream come true."

"That you appreciate it is what's important."

"I do. I wake up every day with a grateful heart. So about this dress..."

"Well, I got here early and scoped the place out. I saw this incredible dress over here. I think it will look so beautiful on you."

She leads me over and shows me a dress that comes in two colors—emerald green or blue.

"He always loved me in this color," I remark, holding the green dress out.

"Try it on. It's perfect for a dinner party."

She takes the stroller and I walk toward the dressing rooms, but I see a dress that grabs my attention on the way. The salesperson assists me in finding my size and I go into the dressing room. I slip on the green dress. It's lovely and hides all the parts I'm not comfortable showing just yet.

I walk out and show Rochelle. She says, "You look great. That's a definite."

"I have one more." I run back into the dressing room and try on the red dress. It fits my new curves and highlights the positives. I kind of love it, but I need a second opinion. "What do you think of this one? Honestly."

"Oh Holli, you look incredible. It's perfect for the Grammys and for the dinner party. You have to get that one."

"Well it's kismet that the first two dresses are winners. That almost never happens."

"Yes, kismet indeed."

TR

What I didn't know was that kismet was coming into play in a much bigger way. We arrive at our property in Ojai around four in the afternoon. There are trucks and cars on our property filling the road leading to the house. "What's going on," I ask, looking for hints that will clue me in.

Dalton parks the car and starts, "I have to confess something to you."

I usually get a sinking feeling when a confession is involved, but it's been so good between us for so long now that I have faith that whatever he needs to confess, we'll be able to take it in stride together.

"It's not a dinner party." He gets out and comes around to open my door, leaving me to guess why he lied about a dinner. After helping me out, he reaches into the back and pulls James' car seat out, being careful not to wake him.

"What is it then?"

He acts coy. "Remember when I dared you to marry me again?"

I know what he's going to say before he says it. "Dalton, what did you do?"

"You said you always choose the dare. I'm daring you to marry me tonight." He starts for the house. "Our parents are here already. They're going to take care of James for us. Tonight is about you. Me. James. Our friends. Our family. And infinity."

Standing next to the car, I put my hands on my hips. "You're really daring me to marry you again?"

"Double dog daring you. At sunset." He bites his bottom lip as he walks away from me.

I'm weak to him. Always. "I'll take that dare."

"I was hoping you'd say that. See you at the altar, Sexy."

"See you at the altar." I fall back against the car and enjoy the view as he walks away. *Kismet indeed.*

33

"A little hazel-eyed blonde is my Achilles' heel. Without a doubt that woman owns every breath I take." ~ Johnny Outlaw

Every detail is handled. I had no idea how he pulled this wedding off, but Dalton did and it is amazing. The sun is setting up ahead when I walk out of the house. It's as if it's waiting at the end of the aisle like Dalton is. Everyone we care about stands from their chairs on either side of an aisle created from petals. Dalton stands at the other end of the aisle with a huge smile on his face, holding James in his arms.

When I begin walking, music starts playing. I recognize it instantly. The melody makes me swoon every time just like my husband. When I look to the left, I stop and laugh from pure delight when I see the actual band playing live, just for me as I walk down the aisle. I turn back to the men I want to see them most. As the band plays "One Day Like This" I walk, not worried about all the eyes on me or that I'm wearing a red dress at a wedding. None of that matters. All that matters is the two waiting for me at the other side.

Dalton's clean shaven, his hair styled, but not overly so. He's wearing a black suit that was made to fit, showing off his broad shoulders and lean body. The white shirt is crisp and the black tie, not too wide or thin, perfect in fitting the man wearing it. I thought he was the most handsome man I'd ever laid eyes on when I saw him in that corridor back in Vegas years earlier, but today, he surpasses that because I know the man behind the captivating features. When I reach Dalton and James, I lean down and kiss my sweet boy on the head, then I lift up and kiss my sweet man on the lips.

My baby is dressed in a onesie with a tuxedo design. His eyes are still blue, but I see hints of green starting to take over. One day, he's going to have his Daddy's eyes and drive the ladies wild, just like Dalton does. I laugh lightly to myself imagining the trouble he's going to get into. That's a worry for another day.

Dalton's mother joins us and takes James from him before returning to the front row. Dalton reaches forward, taking my hands in his, and says, "You're breathtaking."

"You don't look too shabby yourself, handsome."

The minister clears his throat and I remark, "Nice touch by the way. I didn't take you for the religious type."

"I'm covering my bases," he says with a wink. "We have a date with infinity, remember."

Nodding, I become emotional all of a sudden. The man before me is standing so sure, so confident in spending his eternity with me. I'm not nervous to make the same commitment. I can easily tell him the same, but I want to spend my infinity showing him how much I love him.

The minister starts and as we repeat the vows to each other, our eyes don't drift, our hearts bond strengthens, our love deepens. He pulls a ring from his pocket and I realize he got me the pink diamond ring I saw in Austin. My eyes begin to water from the overwhelming emotion when I take in all that he has done to make this day happen, all he has done for me. Inhaling, I look up hoping to rid the tears I don't want falling. When I look back at him though, I know that's going to be impossible. One slips down my cheek as he slips the ring onto my finger. Before our lips touch, he whispers, "I'll always be yours. You'll always be mine."

"I'll always be yours. You'll always be mine." Our lips come together cementing our promise.

The small gathering cheers for us and when we part, I reach for James. He's set in my arms and together, we kiss his cheeks. The band begins playing again and with his hand wrapped around mine we walk back down the aisle as petals rain down over us. James starts crying from all the excitement so we detour quickly into the house.

Standing in our living room, we look at each other, words not seeming necessary. When I lean my head against him, his warmth surrounds me as his arm comes around me. As a family, we stand there watching the guests move across the lawn to the reception area set up beyond the new playscape. There's a dance floor, a stage, plenty of tables and chairs, and a buffet setup next to a bar. When I see a cake, I say, "You thought of everything."

"I had a lot of help from Tracy and Rochelle. They're good friends. They love you."

"They're good friends."

"I owe them."

"For what? The wedding?"

"No," he says, holding me a little tighter. "For being there for you when I wasn't, when I should have been."

Turning in his arms, I hug him gently, trying not to upset James who seems content with us alone in here. "When bad things happen, we have to remember them so we don't repeat the same mistakes. But our hearts have to let them go to find happiness."

He kisses my lips, then whispers, "I've found my happiness."

"And you've given me mine."

James starts squirming. "You ready to go party, little man?" I ask, cradling him closer.

My Mom knocks lightly on the back door before coming in. "Hey there," she says, holding her arms out for James. "I'm ready to snuggle with my grandson." I hand him to her and she continues, "Congratulations on renewing your vows. Now go enjoy your celebration."

"I already made a few bottles for when he gets hungry."

"Okay. We'll be fine. You two have fun and I'll call you if we need anything." We start for the door, but she adds, "Holli?" With the door open, we both stop and look back. "You're a wonderful mother. I always knew you would be. Jack, I'm proud to have you as my son-in-law. I can see how much you love my daughter and your son and I know how much they love you. We all do."

"Thanks," he replies, appearing sheepish from her words. Maybe it's the day. It's making us all a little more emotional than usual.

As soon as we close the door, the DJ starts playing "Push It" by Salt n' Pepa. I burst out laughing. "Is there meaning behind this?" I ask Dalton.

When he stops laughing, he says, "I have no idea. I didn't request it."

In the excitement, we hurry across the lawn to the dance floor. "May I have this dance?"

"Yes, you may," I say performing a slight curtsy and take his offered hand.

Dalton spins me around and dips me. "For the rest of my life?"

"For as long as we both should live."

"Deal."

He lifts me up. We're cheek-to-cheek as "These Foolish Things" starts playing. Smiling, I close my eyes and say, "I love this song."

"I know."

He makes me giggle under my breath. "Are you always so cocky?"

"Yes."

Leaning back to see his eyes, I ask, "Oh really? You're that sure of yourself?"

"Sure am."

"I bet I can still surprise you."

"Try me."

"Later. Let's enjoy the party."

He spins me out, twirling me back in. Trapped in his arms, I say, "We've never really danced before. Where'd you learn these moves?"

"Don't laugh. Okay?"

Laughing already, I say, "I can't make you that promise."

He turns me around once, then whispers, "Dex."

"Dex? For real?"

"For real. But it's not like we danced together or anything. His mom had a DVD and I don't know," he says, shrugging. "He just knows this kind of stuff."

I want to laugh so hard at the awkwardness, but I don't want him to be embarrassed. Unfortunately the laughter wins.

Dalton rolls his eyes. "Whatever."

"I love it. I really do. All of it. Thank you, Babe, for going to so much effort." My new ring sparkles on my finger. "How'd you know about the ring?"

"Oh Baby, I just know these things," he replies more Johnny than Dalton.

I eye him. "No really?"

He wavers, but finally confesses, "I searched online for pink diamonds in Austin. There are only two stores that carry them. I looked them up and put in my price limit and two popped up. One was ugly. The other is very you. Pretty. I took a chance this was it."

"You did so much," I say. "It's stunning, but you shouldn't have spent that much on me."

Surprised by my response, his eyes squint. "You do realize how much money we have, right?" I gulp, then nod. He continues, "So you might get the occasional extravagant gift. Next time, just enjoy it okay. There's no guilt attached. I wanted you to have something that you really wanted."

"Thank you," I reply quietly. "I love it." Tilting my head up toward the colorful sky, I say, "Tonight is magical."

"Our love exists beyond the stars. Magic is just a small part of it. I love you, Holliday."

"I love you, too."

The party carries on into the late night. Near the bar, I spy a familiar face. I walk over and order a Perrier with a twist of lime. "Hey," I say, resting my elbow on the high counter and turning toward Danny. "Thank you for coming. I'm glad you're here."

"How could I say no? Your boy came by with a personal invite."

Glancing at Dalton sitting by the fire pit playing his guitar, I smile. "This was a total surprise."

"I think it's time to admit defeat. The better man won."

"Eh, you're not so bad," I muse.

"No, I'm not so bad, but I'm not the man for you. He is."

"You've changed your mind about him."

"I told you way back then that he loved you."

"You did." Changing the topic, I ask, "Did you bring a date?"

"Nah. I was hoping to meet someone here, but other than your mother, no one else is single."

My eyes go wide. "Back off my mother, buddy!"

Chuckling, he says, "I see where you get your looks, but she's safe." Taking his keys out of his pocket, he leans in and kisses me on the cheek. "Congratulations, Holli, on tonight and on the baby. I'm still trying to figure out how Danny didn't make it into his moniker, but I'll forgive you in time."

"I don't know what we were thinking. James Danny Dean Hughes Dalton just rolls off the tongue."

With a chuckle, he says, "That's what I was thinking." We stand there in silence a few seconds before he spins his key ring around his finger. "I'm gonna go. Long drive home. Take care of yourself and I'll see you around."

I reach up and hug him. "Thank you for being here and thank you for being my friend." Stepping back, I say, "See you around."

Later when everybody's left except for Tommy, Dex, Rochelle, Tracy, and Adam, I sit snacking on sliders and tell Rochelle, "Look at them," referring to Dex and Dalton. "There's a mutual respect between them, a friendship that's a lot deeper than either of them admits."

"It's good to see," she says. "We have to remember our roots. They've made history together as a band, but they're part of each other's personal history too. Hey." She turns to me, placing her arm on mine. "It was crazy at the hospital, so I wanted to make sure you knew how thoughtful it was of you to use Dean in James' name. I'm so touched by the gesture. I know Cory is too." She glances up to the star filled night sky.

"He was an amazing man."

A kind grin surfaces. Taking her champagne glass between her fingers, she sips. "He was. I miss him all the time."

"Dalton misses him so much. I just think there are parts of us that are left open as reminders to appreciate what we have now." I follow her gaze back to Dex and Dalton. "It's okay to miss him."

Dex and Dalton are getting louder and drunker. The ties came off hours ago. The more animated they get, the more attention from the few of us that remain they get as well. Standing, they strip off their suit jackets and shirts, leaving them in undershirts and pants. They do another shot of whiskey, then run and jump in the pool.

"That's hysterical," I say, jumping from my chair. "Should we go get 'em?"

She nods. "I can borrow some clothes, right?"

"Yep." After taking off our shoes, we take each other's hand. "So much for a Grammy dress." Together we plunge into the pool. When I come up for air, Dalton's leaning against the far wall in front of me. Hot as all get out with his eyes trained on me. He licks his lips, beckoning me to him. All wet, I swim, maneuvering my dress higher as I go. When I reach him I wrap my legs around his waist and my arms around his neck.

With me in his arms, freedom is felt. He spins us around and I drop my head back in the water, letting the water soak my hair. When I lift back up, I ask, "This whole night is amazing. Thank you, but you know you didn't have to do this to prove anything."

"I wasn't proving anything. I wanted to give you the wedding you deserved the first time. Selfishly, all I wanted back then was to tie you to me as fast as I could."

"I was already tied to you hook, line, and sinker, Mr. Dalton. A piece of paper doesn't change what's imprinted on our hearts, but it does mean the world that you would do this for me." Squeezing him even closer, I kiss him hard. "You know what I just realized?"

"What's that?" he asks.

The Reckoning

"That you've planned both of our weddings."

"Yeah, that's weird. How about the next one, I let you plan?"

"Sounds good, but yours will be hard to top."

"Not talking about weddings at all, I know something I want you to top."

He grows hard between my legs. Rubbing my cheek against his, I whisper, "I feel like topping you soon. Should we go to bed?"

"I'm ready." He swims to the edge of the pool and sets me on the side. His arms go straight as he lifts himself, pushing himself up. Every muscle defined by shadows and ridges. The white shirt clings to him, showing all the definition of countless sit-ups and pushups. Standing over me, he reaches down and helps me up. Without delay, I'm scooped up as if I weigh nothing, causing me to giggle as we head for the house. At the edge of the patio, he gives a two finger salute and says, "Thank you for coming. I'm gonna go fu— *make love* to my wife. Goodnight."

I'm whisked around and we're inside before I can even say my own thanks. Setting me down gently, we start to tiptoe once we reach the hallway. James is sleeping in the guestroom with my mom tonight. I fed him twice during the party and rocked him to sleep, so we should have a good four hours before the next feeding. My mom said she'll use one of the bottles in the fridge to give us extra time tonight.

Dalton pauses just outside her bedroom, and asks, "Should we check on him?"

My heart beats faster, wanting to hold him again, but I shouldn't wake him. "No, let them sleep."

We hurry down the hall and straight into the bathroom. Turning around, he has the door locked within seconds. I start tugging at my dress to remove the soaked fabric, but it's stuck to my body like a glove.

After starting the bath, he says, "Turn around." A light pressure is felt and the zipper slides down. He kisses my bare shoulder. "I like this dress on you. You look pretty."

"I have a feeling it's ruined."

"You can buy another."

"I'll save this one. It's my wedding dress after all. By the way, you looked very sexy in that suit. We should find more occasions to dress up or maybe do a little role playing."

He works on removing his pants as I tug the dress down. "Like CEO and secretary? I could get into that."

"I didn't know you had fantasies of being a secretary," I tease.

"Ha. Ha!"

I'm stunned when I look up, all laughter stopping. Dalton's in front me, a man I've seen countless times in my life, but something about him tonight is different. The band earned another gold record, so he has a new gun tattoo on his ribs next to the others, but it's healed. Besides that, it's something in his eyes, something I've only caught rare glances of before—contentment.

He's with me, present in the moment and in our lives.

I see it all through the mixture of happy and satisfaction blending together in the depths of his dark greens. I kiss him. When our lips part, I say, "What an incredible day."

He's eyes crinkle at the sides and a light seems to spark from inside him. "Let's finish it with a bang."

"Literally?"

"No, figuratively," he replies sarcastically. "Get your ass in that tub. I want to take advantage of my wife."

"It's not taking advantage if I give in willingly."

He dips down into the water and looks up at me. "Come on in. The water feels great."

I slip my feet into the tub on either side of him, facing him and sit down. He shifts until he's centered exactly where I want him.

"You ready for your surprise?" I ask.

Grinning, he says, "Yeah, I'm ready."

Turning ever so slightly and with my hands on my hips, I angle my left side toward him. His hand goes to my tattoo and runs over it. "You had my name added."

In the swirls of colors that blend together in a figure eight on my skin, I added his name flowing on the inside, giving it the life it needed. 'Choose the Dare' and 'Dare to Dream' still encircle the freeform colors and his fingertip runs smoothly over the design. "I wanted to do it for awhile, but not while I was pregnant. So a week ago, I figured there was no time like the present."

"I'm part of your infinity."

"You *are* my infinity, Dalton."

Holding me by my waist, he pulls me forward until our mouths come together. As our kisses deepen, I lift up. Positioned, when I slide down his length I suck in a harsh breath. His hands push back my wet hair, away from my face, and he whispers, "Let's have more babies."

I stop moving, staring him in the eyes. "We just had James."

"I want a whole band."

Relief escapes me. "Thank God you didn't say team. So you want three or four kids?"

"I want as many as you'll have. I just want more with you."

Rubbing his cheek, I say, "I'm not going anywhere. We don't have to rush."

"You make me want it all. You make me want more than I dreamed possible."

"You do that to me too. But tonight, let's just be together. Be happy. Enjoy this moment."

He nods as I start to move on top of him, loving the feeling of him deep inside. Pushing off of his chest, I lift and drop back down slowly, torturously blissful. Fingertips dig into my skin as his head drops back on the tub, his mouth wide open. Leaning forward I take his lower lip between my teeth and run my tongue over it. When his hand slides over my hips and between my legs, he searches for the spot that he knows will tip me over the edge.

I rock hard until I fall apart under his touch. The water begins to slosh around us as he thrusts up. Holding the side of the bathtub, I anchor myself as he begins to lose control. Making love becomes needy, and impulsive, deriving from a carnal desire.

Minutes later, I lie with my back on his chest. The water is cooling around us, but neither of us is quite ready to move just yet. It's late and been a busy day. I open my eyes and look around the bathroom. That's when I spot them. "What are those?"

"Hand towels," he says, flat.

I slowly get out, wrapping a towel around me and go in for a closer inspection. I try to hold back my laughter, but yeah, that's not gonna happen when I see the silhouette of Princess Leia and Han Solo on the towels. Embroidered on one is, 'I love you.' The other reads, 'I know.'

"Do you like your present?"

Still laughing, I reply, "I love them and will treasure them always." I swat at him with my towel, but miss when he jumps out of the way.

"Be careful. I don't show mercy when I pop back."

A towel comes whipping through the air, but I move just in time. The harsh snap showing he means business. "Eek!" I run for the bed and dive in, quickly ducking under the covers.

Dalton runs fast. I know he could've caught me if he tried. But he comes in slow, almost teasingly, making it clear that I got away only because he let me. With his swagger engaged, he makes his way to the bed—naked, proud, and smirking.

Good lord, that man drives me crazy in the best of ways. Talk about God's gift to women. I sigh, swooning.

"Liking what you see, Angel?"

"Loving what I see. Now get under the covers with me." I hold the sheet and blanket up and he slips into bed next to me.

I can tell he's tired like me, worn out from the day and the nightcap of activity in the tub. Lying on his back, he puts his hand under his head and looks straight up at the ceiling. "I want to have a girl."

Making me smile, I roll onto my side and ask, "Why?"

"Because we need more Hollidays in the world."

I should be able to say so much, but the waterfall of emotions that tumbles through me causes me to choke up.

Glancing over at me, he adds, "I'm not just saying that to win brownie points either."

"You're not? Cuz I'd totally give you all the brownie points for saying that. Now kiss me, you big charmer."

He does and I do, willing to do it anytime and every day. My eyes drop closed and his hand finds my hip. Just a whisper between us, "Sleep, pretty girl."

TR

The red dress shrunk from being in the pool and there was no saving it. But I found the best sparkly black dress for the Grammy's. I wasn't back to my pre-baby size, but somehow it didn't matter. I felt good about the progress I had made getting back in shape and I kind of enjoyed having a little more curve for the time being.

The reporter standing in front of me asks, "Your husband has four nominations tonight. How do you feel about his continued success?"

"I'm so proud of him and the band. They've worked hard."

"It takes a strong woman to find her own success in life, be married to one of the biggest stars in the world, and juggle being a new mother, but you seem to handle it so well."

"Thank you. I'm here to support his dreams however big or small they may be. He makes it easy for me to succeed as well."

"How's the baby? Are you ready to share the name with the world?"

"No, we're gonna hold onto that a little longer, but the baby's doing amazing. Our lives have changed for the better. Our love has grown in ways that we didn't know it could. It's incredible how your heart just opens up bigger than the universe for our children."

She catches me off guard when she asks, "Did you send well wishes to Sebastian Lassiter?"

Having no idea what she's talking about, I shake my head confused and ask, "What happened?"

Leaning in as if to tell me a secret, she says, "He was caught sleeping with a married woman. Apparently the heir to the Caslo Department stores walked in on him and broke his nose."

I look down, wanting to laugh because this news does not surprise me at all. "I didn't know. I haven't seen him since we shot the last campaign."

Dalton is next to me, his fingers touching my lower back as he wraps up an interview next to me. He turns to the reporter talking to me, fortunately not hearing the news that I know would make him a little too happy. "My wife looks amazing, right? How lucky am I?"

She smiles, blushing under his attention. "Very lucky. What are you most excited about tonight?"

"Celebrating the album with the band and all of the musicians I respect so much. It's mind-blowing that we're nominated with such legends and popular bands."

When he's tapped on the shoulder, he thanks the interviewer before turning. To me, he asks, "They just said we need to go in. You ready?"

"Yes," I reply, still uncomfortable with all of this attention.

The band wins two Grammy's before their performance. Dalton takes to the mic with the guys behind him when they w in Album of the Year. "This is dedicated to the fans. You've stuck by us when we struggled to find our place in this world. And you made us believe that we could carry on after the death of one of our own." He looks down in contemplation. When he looks back up his gaze lands on me. "For me, I owe this and more to my amazing wife who has given me a beautiful life. I owe her everything. Thank you, Holliday." He steps back and the guys all hug while Dex steps up.

Dex says, "Thank you to our label, our producer, our tour manager, our roadies, our families, every radio station that plays us, and I want take a quick moment to thank Rochelle Floros. When Cory Dean died, she stepped in and played guitar on the album despite her grief. She's always been an unsung hero in The Resistance and without her, we wouldn't be here at all. So here's to you, Rochelle."

The guys walk off the stage and I start searching for anything to wipe away the tears both of them have evoked.

By the time I pull myself together, the lights go down and the spotlight lands on Dex behind his drum kit. I wait like everybody else, my anticipation building with every second that passes, to see the great Johnny Outlaw himself. When the song kicks in and the spotlight hits Dalton, I'm drawn to the man center stage, my pride for him and love making my heart swell with pride as I sing along to the hit song.

Captivating.

Magnetic.

Charismatic.

He's all of those things whether he's Dalton or Johnny. I watch the man who came into my life unexpectedly and shifted my world on its axis. Things have changed so much over the years since we've been together. *We've* changed so much. The biggest difference being that I used to think Johnny Outlaw was for everyone else. He's not. Just like Jack Dalton, Johnny Outlaw is all mine.

The End

Surprise
Jack Dalton

"It's hard to stop the stars from shining."
~ Holliday Hughes

Sitting in the chair, this is easy. I barely feel a thing. The blood is wiped away as the needle digs into my skin, leaving a black trail of ink behind. When I look up, Holliday is watching with rapt attention. She didn't say no, but she didn't want to go first either.

"Does it hurt?" she asks as if she's never gotten a tattoo before.

"No."

With her fingers almost touching, she says, "Not even a little?"

"Not even a little. It hurts on the ribs."

"I bet." Her gaze goes back to my wrist. "Don't hurt him," she warns the tattoo artist.

Javi, my tattoo guy's eyes look up at her, but he doesn't say anything.

I keep my wrist still as he finishes up. "There's a lot of blood."

This time he says, "Hands, wrists, underside of the arm tends to bleed more." He wipes the blood away and adds, "All done. What do you think?"

I hold my wrist up to Holliday and ask, "What do you think?"

Her smile speaks volumes, but she also says, "I love it. It's perfect. Simple and clean. Perfect. Now can you make mine match?"

"Sure can," Javi says. "Infinity symbols are popular, but I like the meaning behind your idea."

"He came up with it. I thought it was sweet."

Javi finishes with me and then asks Holliday to hop into the chair. "Hold still," he says.

She doesn't move, not even blinking for longs periods.

I take her hand and say, "Relax. I can see how tense you are. You'll bleed more."

"I'm nervous."

"You've gotten tattoos before."

"It's been a while."

She scrunches her face, closing her eyes when the needle touches her skin. "Relax," I whisper again.

Her face goes back to normal and she looks at me. "Thanks."

It's quick, the design simple like Javi said, but what we wanted. After he wraps her wrist, we're done. When we walk out, I take her hand, our fingers entwining, our wrists and new tattoos are touching like we planned. I see a smile spread across her face and she says, "Infinity."

For the rest of my life and beyond, I repeat, meaning it, "Infinity."

*The End.
For real... or maybe for now.*

About the Author

New York Times and USA Bestselling Author, S. L. Scott, was always interested in the arts. She grew up painting, writing poetry and short stories, and wiling her days away lost in a good book and the movies.

With a degree in Journalism, she continued her love of the written word by reading American authors like Salinger and Fitzgerald. She was intrigued by their flawed characters living in picture perfect worlds, but could still debate that the worlds those characters lived in were actually the flawed ones. This dynamic of leaving the reader invested in the words, inspired Scott to start writing with emotion while interjecting an underlying passion into her own stories.

Living in the capital of Texas with her family, Scott loves traveling and avocados, beaches, and cooking with her kids. She's obsessed with epic romances and loves a good plot twist. She dreams of seeing one of her own books made into a movie one day as well as returning to Europe. Her favorite color is blue, but she likens it more toward the sky than the emotion. Her home is filled with the welcoming symbol of the pineapple and finds surfing a challenge though she likes to think she's a pro.

Find S. L. Scott on social media:

Facebook: https://www.facebook.com/slscottpage

Instagram: https://instagram.com/s.l.scott/

Twitter: @slscottauthor

Blog: www.slscottauthor.com

Other books in the series

The Resistance

The Redemption

Made in the USA
Las Vegas, NV
03 February 2025